A PERFECT PLACE

When they returned to the rented cottage, Quinn lit a fire because the evening was cool, then turned to Jasmine. To her surprise, he reached out and took her hands in his.

"Jasmine, that old man made me realize that I've been selfish. What we're doing could be dangerous."

She stared down at their clasped hands. It seemed as though his great strength and his equally great gentleness was flowing from his fingertips to hers, his body to hers.

"You don't have to come. I'll give you the gold I offered you," he added.

"I don't need it now," she said, knowing that she still wasn't answering his unspoken question.

"It was a promise—and I keep my promises."

She looked up at him. "What will you do when you find the valley?"

He dropped her hands and shrugged. "I don't know yet, but I think I'll know when I need to."

She stared at him. She wrapped her arms around herself and shivered. "I'm frightened, Quinn."

He reached out to her, tentatively at first, and then, when she didn't resist, he drew her slowly into his arms. It felt as though she were being embraced by a great tree, tall and hard. He bent his head and she felt his breath against her hair.

Something very strange began to happen inside her. It was as though her very bones were softening, starting to melt. Heat spread through her, tiny curling tendrils of warmth that made her tingle all over.

"I want you to come with me," he murmured. "I need you."

THE MAGIC OF TWO

SARANNE DAWSON

LOVE SPELL BOOKS   NEW YORK CITY

LOVE SPELL®

May 1999

Published by

Dorchester Publishing Co., Inc.
276 Fifth Avenue
New York, NY 10001

ISBN 0-505-52308-6

Printed in the United States of America.

Prologue

Steep, dark mountains rose to jagged peaks capped year-round with glistening snow. In the dark
glens at their base, ancient trees formed a thick
canopy over a clear, swift-running stream that
sparkled with rainbow-scaled fish. Delicate-
looking deer came down to the mossy banks to
drink, as did the huge, lumbering brown bears and
the haughty gray wolves. The glens were fragrant
with a profusion of flowers.

At one end of the valley that was totally encircled
by the mountains, a waterfall sprang from the
highest peak to feed the stream. Rare and wondrous flowers clung to life along the edges of the
waterfall, peeking out from the safety of rocky outcroppings.

In the valley itself, the land was gentler: rolling,
forested hills and open meadows where thick
grasses vied with wildflowers. Herds of animals
grazed here: sheep and cattle that had never
known humans. And there was also a herd of white

horses that ran free, with no memory of ever having been tamed or ridden.

Through the valley ran a road, so overgrown as to be nearly invisible in places, and across the very center of the valley, stretching from mountain to mountain, there were tall stone pillars that had once anchored a fence whose logs had rotted away.

At each end of the valley was a town. Both were strange, silent places filled with empty stone houses whose thatched roofs had long since decayed and whose once carefully tended gardens had become overgrown.

The valley was a very ancient place, but a visitor—if there had been one—would have said that it must once have been a happy place.

But the valley changed when night fell. That was when strange, misshapen forms emerged from a cave above one of the empty villages and came into the valley to dance their evil, triumphant dances through the empty villages—as they had been doing for nearly two centuries.

The valley belonged to them—but it had not always been that way.

Chapter One

Jasmine struggled up the narrow, winding back stairs with two large buckets of steaming water. Her arms were threatening to tear from their sockets before she reached the landing midway up. She allowed herself a moment to rest, then struggled on, pausing only to brush away a few wisps of pale hair that had escaped from her net cap.

The mistress was waiting impatiently in her boudoir, wrapped in an elegant velvet robe. Her eyes flashed annoyance at Jasmine as she hurried to dump the water into the high bathtub.

"Where is Tabby?" she demanded. "She would have had my bath drawn long ago."

"She is ill, milady."

"Again? This will not do. If she cannot do her work, then she must be replaced."

"I'm sure she'll be well again soon, milady," Jasmine said, though she knew that wasn't true.

"And in the meantime, I suppose you intend to do the work of two—you, who can barely manage to do your own work?"

"I will manage, milady," Jasmine said in a quiet, firm voice.

The mistress stared at her, and Jasmine took a small but important satisfaction from the fear that shone briefly in her protruding black eyes. She'd never understood that fear, but she knew it was there.

"Begone, then," the mistress said with a wave of her bejeweled hand.

Jasmine hurried from the room as the mistress shrieked for her maid. A few moments later, she was back in her own domain: the kitchen. Cook had set out for her a steaming mug of broth, and she grabbed it and drank greedily, burning her tongue in the process. Cook handed her a crust of bread and she devoured that as well.

"Get on with it, then, girl," Cook said gruffly. "There's potatoes to be peeled and herbs to be gathered and dried. And milady would like angel cake for dessert, so you'll need to fetch me some eggs."

Eggs, thought Jasmine excitedly. Perhaps she could hide a few in the henhouse and then return to pick them up later. She'd done it before, though she knew it was dangerous. But the boy who tended the chickens was less watchful than Cook.

A day that had begun before dawn ended, finally, as dusk crept over the great estate. Jasmine hurried home, cradling her precious eggs in the small sack she carried to collect dropped fruit from the orchards—when there was any to be found, that was. Most days, others got to it before she did.

The hunger that was an ever-present companion had abated for the moment. Cook had been kind today because by the time the angel cake was ready for icing, she was too drunk to make the rosettes, and Jasmine had been told to do it. As a reward, she'd been given a few scraps of meat and had then begged a meaty bone to take home.

The Magic of Two

She hurried past the stables, her eyes darting about in case any of the stablehands might be lurking about to waylay her. Most of the time they contented themselves with lewd comments, but several times they'd chased her to the very edge of the estate. Only her fleetness and their drunkenness had saved her.

This night, she passed the stables without incident and made her way into the orchards. A nearly full moon had risen, and she moved along the rows of trees, her eyes searching the ground for any dropped fruit. Once or twice she'd dared to pick fruit. They all did when food was especially scarce. But they were careful not to take more than one piece from a tree because the orchardmen had sharp eyes. Jasmine was certain that they never actually counted the fruit—how could they?—but too many missing would surely not escape their notice.

She saw something pale on the ground beneath a heavily laden pear tree and quickly scooped it up. A wonderful find! It was barely bruised. And then she found another. She smiled. She was fond of pears, though she liked peaches best. But the peach grove was too near the long, low housing where the fruit pickers stayed, and it was too risky to go there—especially alone.

She was halfway through the orchard when suddenly two figures materialized out of the darkness: the guard and his dog! A chill ran down her spine. She wasn't worried about the fruit; he could see that it was bruised. But what if he found the eggs? She was tempted to drop them into the thick grass and straw, but her mother needed them.

"So it's Jasmine," the burly guard said with a leer. "I hope you haven't been picking, lass."

"They're leavings," she said, taking out the two pears and holding them up for his inspection. At the same time, she half-hid the sack among the

11

folds of her skirt, hoping he wouldn't demand that she turn it over.

He stared at the pears, then nodded. The big dog at his side regarded her with a malevolent grin. The guard raised his torch and peered into her face.

"You're a comely lass, for all that you're but skin and bones. You could make some gold, girl. A few tumbles in the hay and you'd have enough to feed yourself properly."

"No, thank you," she replied, thinking that starvation was definitely preferable to that. But she couldn't help but think that this guard wasn't so bad. At least he asked, rather than tried to simply take.

"Be off with you, then. It's past curfew."

Jasmine thanked him again, though she wasn't certain for what. Then she hurried home to the tiny stone cottage at the far edge of the orchard.

Four cottages were clustered tightly together just inside the high outer wall of the estate. Lights gleamed in three of them. The fourth was presently unoccupied, its tenant having died two weeks ago of fatigue.

Jasmine rapped three times in quick succession on the door of the middle cottage. Then she pressed her ear to the wooden boards and held her breath, listening for sounds inside. After what seemed to be a very long time, she heard noises, and then her mother's raspy voice, saying she was coming.

Although she'd seen her mother only this morning, Jasmine was struck again by the rapid deterioration of this once healthy woman. Her mother's skin hung loosely on her wrinkled face, and her breathing was labored. She walked in a strange, hunched-over posture, as though she'd been struck in the stomach.

But when Jasmine produced the eggs and fruit,

her mother's still-bright blue eyes gleamed with pleasure.

"You take such chances, child," she whispered.

"Not so much. Eggs are easy." Then she reached into the bottom of the sack and drew out her big surprise. "Cook gave me a bone. I can make soup for you."

Her mother smiled, but the smile died away quickly. "Did the mistress ask after me?"

"No," Jasmine lied. "I think she is preoccupied with the guests who will be arriving in two days."

"Two days? I should be well by then."

Jasmine said nothing as she put the bone into the big pot steaming upon the hearth, then added some carrots and potatoes plucked from their small garden. Unshed tears stung her eyes. She understood why they kept up this pretense that her mother would be returning to work—but it was so hard.

Her mother came over to peer hungrily into the pot, and Jasmine stared at her in the firelight. She was still a relatively young woman, only the age of the mistress—but she looked old enough to be not her mother, but her grandmother. Hard work and a poor diet had caused the deterioration—and now her illness had accelerated the process.

Jasmine hugged her mother's bony shoulders and led her to a chair. "Shall I play for you while dinner cooks?"

"No, dear. You must be tired, doing the work for both of us."

"I'm never too tired to play, Mamman. You know that," she replied, switching to their native tongue.

It was true. No matter how tired she was, playing the ancient lute soothed away the aches and pains. She took it out of its worn leather case and tuned it quickly, then seated herself at her mother's feet and began to play.

Jasmine had learned to play the lute when she was barely old enough to talk. Her grandmother had taught her on the instrument that had been passed down for generations. And as she played, she thought about that strong, wonderful woman— her father's mother—and about the stories.

At that time, they'd lived miles from here, farming a small plot of land too infertile to interest the large landholders. But then they'd gotten caught in a battle between two of the great families whose lands bordered their tiny place. Her entire family had been killed, save for her mother and herself, then only a child of five. And as her mother had lamented many times, it might have been better if they too had died. Instead, they were taken captive and set to work at the estate of the victorious lord: work for which there was no pay, except for the right to live in a squalid little cottage.

Jasmine marveled that she still remembered those stories, considering how far away that time now seemed. Her grandmother had told them while Jasmine practiced on the lute. For some reason, her mother had never approved of the story-telling, though she'd also never forbidden it.

They were stories of a magical place of swift-running streams and thundering waterfalls and placid lakes with lily pads and secret, flowery bowers in fragrant woods—and tall mountains whose white peaks reached into the heavens. Gramman said they were capped with snow, but Jasmine didn't understand that. If they reached into the heavens, to the place where the sun was, then why didn't the snow melt? Gramman had said that must be magic as well.

But best of all, it was a peaceful place, where food was abundant, no one had to work hard, and everyone was free.

Although she could picture this magical place vividly, it was the notion of freedom that had stayed with Jasmine through the twenty-five years since she'd come to this hated place.

Her fingers flew over the strings while she whispered that wonderful word in her mind. When she pictured freedom, she always thought of it as a bird, soaring through the heavens, far above this ugly place and its cruel people.

Quinn paused in his labors to stare up at a large bird—probably an eagle. It soared high above the noisy, dusty quarry, drifting on the wind, its great wings moving slowly. He wondered what the world looked like from up there. Certainly it must be better than the view from the huge quarry where he stood.

He could feel the supervisor's malignant stare, but he ignored it. The man might hate him, but he wouldn't give him any trouble. No one gave Quinn any trouble. Even when he was a child, growing up on the dirty, squalid streets of the city, where fights to the death were commonplace, no one had ever challenged him.

Quinn stood nearly six and a half feet tall, with impossibly wide shoulders and a trim waist and hips. His curly black hair was worn longer than was the fashion, swept back from a face that couldn't be called handsome, but nonetheless attracted women. It was a harshly masculine face, the nose slightly crooked as the result of a childhood accident, with a narrow, jagged scar that ran from his hairline down to his prominent cheekbone. The scar, too, was the result of an accident, though a more recent one.

But for all that, it was his eyes that captured and held one's attention. They were gray: light gray under most circumstances, but dark when anger took hold. And they were deep-set under a slightly jutting brow. But most of all, they were eyes that gazed steadily and unafraid at a world whose rigid caste system had placed him near the bottom.

Unlike many of the men who labored in the quarry six days a week, twelve hours a day, Quinn was not a slave. The others had been captured in war, while Quinn had been born in this land. Their lives had been spared only because their new masters needed strong men. Quinn had risen to his present position for that reason as well.

The rulers of this land were a small race. Even the tallest of them came barely to Quinn's shoulders. Furthermore, they had a long history of disdaining physical labor in favor of the arts and other cerebral interests. Their military, in which Quinn had served with considerable distinction, was comprised mostly of mercenaries. After the most recent war, Quinn had actually been offered a commission—an unheard-of occurrence. But he'd chosen instead to come here and labor in the quarry for the simple reason that the pay was better. The Estavians didn't trust their slaves, and with good reason, so they paid extremely well for native labor.

Quinn was already a crew leader, and if he stayed he would surely become a supervisor in time. But he had no intention of staying. His carefully hidden cache of gold was growing. In a few weeks—a month at the most—he would slip away.

If anyone had known about his plans, they would have been shocked that such foolishness could be found in him. But Quinn had a dream, and he was determined to follow it.

Jasmine lifted her face to the warm sun as the wagon bumped along the road into town. This was her day off, and she was determined to enjoy it as best she could. Every two weeks she was given one day off—a whole day to do as she pleased, with no shrieking mistress and no drunken Cook to harass her.

She hadn't intended to go into town. Her mother's condition was deteriorating. She'd gone back to work for a few days, but then had collapsed and had to be carried home. If the mistress hadn't been preoccupied with her guests, she would surely have fired her.

Jasmine had intended to stay at home with her today, but her mother had insisted that she get away, and a neighbor had kindly offered to stay with her.

The wagon, which was full of servants like her, entered the town. Jasmine stared at the well-dressed people who milled about, making their way to the large market. She herself had no money, of course, but she did have a sackful of carefully dried herbs. She'd never been able to raise the fee required to set up a stall, but one of the stallkeepers had long ago made an arrangement with her to sell her herbs.

The herbs were rare and much in demand. Jasmine and her mother grew them in their small garden plot from seeds that had been passed down in her family for generations. Some were medicinal, while others were prized for their scents alone. Jasmine knew that if the mistress were aware of her little business, she would demand the profit. It always made her smile with grim satisfaction to see them in the estate kitchens, or in small crystal bowls in the mistress's boudoir.

The wagon came to a halt at the edge of the market square and everyone tumbled out. No one asked her to join them—but then, no one ever did. She and her mother were outcasts, even among the lowliest of servants. The men, especially when they were drunk, would have welcomed her into their beds, but otherwise they had no interest in her.

So she strolled alone, a painfully thin, tall figure, with hair of the palest gold, nearly white. Her hair and her height always attracted attention. The people among whom she was forced to live were mostly dark haired, and she was nearly as tall as most of the men.

Then there was her skin, as pale as her hair and possessed of a porcelain quality that was partly heredity and partly the result of the herbal potions she mixed from ancient family recipes. Her mother had once possessed such skin, but she'd stopped tending to herself long ago, claiming it was useless to be concerned with her appearance.

It was useless for Jasmine as well, if the purpose was to attract a husband, because she had no intention of marrying. Marriage meant children, and while she loved them dearly, she had no interest in bringing them into this world, to live as she was forced to live. Besides, the only men with whom she came into contact were crude, harsh villains she would never marry.

Although she'd been only five when her father and her other male relatives were killed, she remembered them well: gentle, kind men who never drank to excess or used that as an excuse for inexcusable behavior. They were good men, and she knew that she couldn't hope to find such a man in this terrible place.

She made her way to a particular stall, ignoring the other wares on display. She couldn't afford them, so why should she even look? The woman saw her approaching and broke into a smile. Jasmine returned the grin, even though she didn't trust the woman. She was quite certain that the stallkeeper was selling her herbs for many times what she paid Jasmine for them. But still, a welcoming smile was so rare in her life that it could not be ignored.

She opened her sack and spread out the neatly packaged herbs, noting the greedy gleam in the woman's eyes. The woman named a price, and this time Jasmine balked.

"I think I should get more—especially for the scented herbs. After all, they are bought only by rich people, who can afford to pay more."

The woman stared at her, and Jasmine thought she saw a begrudging respect in her small, beady eyes. She wished she had thought of this before.

"Well now, that's as might be, but without me, you can't sell them at all. And if you was to go elsewhere, the word might get back to your mistress."

"Then I would tear up the garden and have nothing else to sell," Jasmine said firmly. "And without my herbs, you would be just one of many selling fruits and vegetables."

The woman's lower lip jutted out as she thought, her gaze going from Jasmine to the herbs. Then, finally, she nodded and named a price. Jasmine was tempted to try to get it increased still more, but she decided to accept it—for now.

She left the stall feeling positively giddy. The extra money would allow her to purchase a few small sweets for herself and her mother—and for the kindly lady next door, she decided. Only now, with her mother so very sick, was the woman showing any kindness to them, but Jasmine was still grateful.

Then she frowned. If she bought sweets for the neighbor, wasn't that likely to make the woman suspicious? And might she not tell her suspicions to others, who would then carry the tale to the manor?

Jasmine felt a terrible sadness. What kind of world was it when she could not do a kindness for someone without risking retribution?

She bought a pear—a wonderful, juicy pear of the kind she dared not pick from the estate orchards. Then, slicing it neatly with her small knife, she began to eat it slowly, instead of devouring it like other servants would do. "We might be little better than slaves," her mother had told her, "but we will not stoop to their level." Mamman had always stressed the importance of fastidious habits, even when others had sniggered at her family's "uppity" ways.

Jasmine was even careful to speak the language properly, never lapsing into the vulgarities used by the other servants. While Estavian was not her native tongue, she had carefully studied both it and the language her grandmother spoke, and had even learned to read and write, thanks to a quick mind and the kindness of a tutor now long gone from the estate.

She left the market square and headed toward her favorite place in the busy town: the harbor. The great ships and the babble of many languages never failed to exhilarate her in a strange sort of way. She could sit for hours on a crate and watch the activity of the busy port, imagining herself embarking on some wondrous journey.

Often, she thought about the magical place her grandmother had spoken of, and imagined that it was out there, somewhere beyond the edge of the gray-green sea.

Once, a friendly lad of twelve or thirteen had struck up a conversation with her. He was fairly bursting with pride because this was his first sea voyage as an apprentice. He'd come, he told her in his strange accent, from a place far up the coast. She asked what it was like, hoping that he might describe the land her grandmother had told her about. But he said that it was much like here.

She'd asked if he'd ever heard of a beautiful place surrounded by very high, dark mountains with snow on their tops. He'd frowned and scratched his head, then said that he *had* heard about the tall mountains somewhere. He thought they might be far to the north of his homeland. But no one ever went there, he said, because there were no towns—no people at all.

She'd also inquired about the cost of booking passage on a ship like his. He had no idea what it cost, but he knew it must be quite a lot, because only rich people traveled that way. Her much-mended dress had told him clearly that she had no hope of doing such a thing.

Jasmine strolled along the docks now, thinking that if only she were a man, she could hire on as the boy had done. Certainly she was as strong as he was. But then, she couldn't leave in any event—not as long as her mother was alive.

That thought struck her with the force of a blow. It was the first time that she'd consciously considered her mother's death, even though she knew deep down that the day could not be far off.

What will I do then? she wondered. She was certain that the mistress would not permit her to remain in the cottage alone. They would find someone to replace her mother and then force that person to move in with her.

Or she might be fired and turned out onto the street. Cook had hinted a few times that the mistress kept her on only out of pity for her mother's ill health. Jasmine was hard-pressed to believe the mistress capable of anything approaching compassion, but perhaps it was so. She did know that the mistress didn't like her; she didn't need Cook to tell her that.

For once, Jasmine drew no pleasure from watching the ships. She was far too wrapped up in her bleak thoughts.

Quinn counted his money a second time, then grunted with satisfaction. He had more than enough now to finance his dream. He'd prefer to leave the very next day to make his way to the port, but he decided to wait and give notice. It was a bit risky, but he didn't think anyone would try to stop him, and giving notice might keep him in the good graces of his employer should he ever need to return.

But perhaps his decision to wait a week or two more was actually the result of his facing up to this quest he'd set for himself. It was one thing to dream, as he had for many years now—but it was quite a different matter to take that first step.

Quinn had been born in Estavia, but he'd always known that this was not his home. Possessed of a keen, inquiring mind, he'd quickly noted the differences between his small family and their neighbors and asked why that was so.

"We come from another place," his father had told him before ending the conversation. His mother had said the same, though in a more wistful tone. Neither of them would tell him where that place was and why they had left it.

Surely, young Quinn had thought, it must be a better place—but if so, why had they left it to come to this ugly city with its foul-smelling streets?

It was, finally, his grandfather who'd told him. He was near death at the time, which perhaps accounted for his recklessness. Quinn's parents, Granda said, had made him promise not to talk about it. Such stories would only turn a boy's head—and it was likely that they weren't true in any event.

But just as his parents had feared, his grandfather's tale had changed Quinn forever. It had given him a dream. And he believed in that dream, even though his grandfather had said, in a final note of warning, that it was almost certainly nothing more than a fool's tale.

According to Granda, his people had come from a place far, far away—somewhere on the other side of the great sea. Their homeland, which had never had a name that he knew of, lay in a beautiful valley, protected by a ring of tall mountains crowned by gleaming white snow.

They had lived there from the beginning of time, Granda said, sharing their valley with another race. The old gods had blessed them two races, giving them not only their beautiful land, but also the ability to make magic.

The purpose of that magic—Granda was a bit vague about what it actually consisted of—was to enable them to hold at bay the demons that tried incessantly to capture their valley. According to Granda, however, the magic was tied to the peaceful coexistence of the two races. Once, in the very beginning, they had fought with each other to gain control of the land. It was then that the gods had intervened, offended by their pettiness. It was then that things had changed.

From that time on, the magic both races needed to protect themselves from the demons could be wielded only jointly by a man and a woman of opposite races.

The gods' dictum worked, and the two races lived in peace for many centuries, successfully beating back the demons' many invasions.

But something had happened. Granda didn't know what it was. All he knew was that somehow the demons had finally succeeded in driving them out. Not only that, but they had driven the two races apart, destroying forever the union that had made their defeat possible.

For generations his people had wandered, seeking out the Latawi. That was the name in their language for the other race. It meant "light," and his people were the Dartuli, the "dark." Together, they made a whole. Apart, they were nothing.

But they never found the Latawi, and over the years the survivors, the remains of a once-cohesive people, had gone their separate ways. Their spirits broken, his Granda claimed, they had apparently decided it would be better to try to fit in as best they could in a world that was not their home. They had begun to settle, mingling with the people who had never known of the Latawi, Dartuli, or the beautiful valley they'd been forced to flee. To many, their heritage was lost.

Quinn stared at his cache of precious gold coins. There was enough for him to purchase the small cottage he called home, with perhaps enough left over to build an addition so he wouldn't feel so confined.

He wasn't a foolish man. He'd always accepted the world as it was. So why was he willing to take the fruits of years of work to roam the world, seeking something that probably didn't exist, that had probably never existed? Aside from his own small family, he'd never even encountered anything to substantiate his Granda's wild tales. Even if they'd ever existed, it was likely that long ago they all had intermarried with some other race and ceased to exist as a distinct people.

It was possible, he supposed, that someone of mixed ancestry might be able to work the magic— but how would he find such a person? He knew what the Latawi looked like; Granda had told him. They were tall, though not generally as tall as his own people, and they were very fair, often with hair that was nearly white.

And then, even if he somehow succeeded in finding such a person and persuaded her to join him, how were they to find their lost land? It wasn't likely that she would know any more than he did— and perhaps she would know nothing at all of their unique heritage.

Then there was the matter of the demons. That was where Quinn's doubts really began to set in. He didn't believe in such nonsense. But then, if he didn't believe in demons, why was he willing to believe the rest of Granda's tale?

Quinn put his gold back into the box, then placed the box back into the small space he'd excavated beneath the hearthstone. Finally he lifted the stone and put it back into place. It weighed nearly two hundred pounds, which made the space a relatively safe hiding place.

He thought about going to the tavern, then decided against it. He was accepted there, although with the same degree of wariness with which most people treated him. But he had no taste for company this night. Instead, he turned up the oil lamp on the table beside his big, comfortable chair and sat down to reread his favorite book of poetry.

The book was very old, so old that the pages were crumbling and the print had faded badly. It was impossible in this land to buy books unless you were a member of the upper classes, but that only made his small collection all the more precious. He'd come upon them in the ruins of a house that was being cleared away for a new construction. He was well aware of the fact that possessing them was a crime, but he reasoned that no one would ever suspect him of having them in the first place.

Quinn hated those who ruled this land. He despised the Estavians for their cruel disregard of the widespread poverty and their arrogant assumption that the poor existed because of their own sloth, and not because of the opportunities that were denied them to better themselves. But he admired their literature and their art. He'd even gone to the great museum once, where he'd ignored the astounded looks of his "betters" as he'd studied the paintings and sculptures. And many times he'd lingered along the edges of crowds listening to musical performances, unwelcome but unnoticed.

He began to read. Within a short time, he had temporarily set aside his misgivings and lost himself in the beauty of the words.

Once again, it was well after dark when Jasmine dragged herself home, too tired this night to look for fallen fruit despite the fact that she'd had only two crusts of bread all day. The mistress's guests had departed, and the woman had demanded to know about her mother's condition. Lying with what she hoped was an earnest look, Jasmine had promised that her mother would return to work the next day.

Now, as she headed home, she was trying to believe that—and not succeeding. Regardless of what her mother said, she was getting steadily weaker. The potions Jasmine brewed from ancient recipes had soothed her cough, but they did not take away the wasting illness. Jasmine had seen it before, and she knew that nothing could cure it.

Her heart leaped into her throat, then fell to the pit of her stomach in a cold mass when she first glimpsed the darkened cottage. Her mother must be too weak even to have lit the lamp. Despite her fatigue, she ran the remaining yards to the tumbledown cottage that was really only a hovel.

"Mamman!" she cried as she flung open the door that should have been bolted at dusk.

It took a few seconds for her eyes to adjust to the darkness, but then she saw that her mother's bed was empty, as was the single chair near the cold hearth. Terrified Jasmine had to will her feet to move, to carry her across the tiny room to the lamp. But before she could reach it, her foot struck something soft.

She recoiled in horror, knowing instinctively what it must be even before her brain could make sense of it. She knelt in the darkness and touched cold, rigid flesh.

Knowing she was being foolish, Jasmine still tried to bring the woman back to life. She wrapped her in their one warm blanket, then rubbed her stiff wrists and listened again and again to her silent chest. And finally she sat back and cried: for her mother, who had lived a life so undeservedly harsh, and for herself, because she was now alone and would probably soon have no home.

After a while, she got up and went to the neighbor's house. She didn't know what to do with her mother's body. She was hoping that she could find some help carrying her out into the woods, to a pretty spot where they'd often gone together, just beyond the borders of the estate.

"They bury 'em out in back o' the stable," the neighbor told her in as kind a voice as she could apparently muster. "One big grave. They just dig it up again ever' time someone dies."

Jasmine stared at her in dismay. "But that's *wrong*."

"Not wrong for the likes of us, m'girl. We don't mean nothin' in life, so why should we mean somethin' in death?"

"I want to bury her in the woods—in a place she liked."

The woman regarded her sadly and sighed. "You two was always different. I'd help you if I could, girl, because your mama was good t' me. Tried her best to save my little boy, she did."

"Then could you help me carry here there—to the woods?"

For a moment, Jasmine's hope rose as the woman seemed about to say yes. But then she shook her head. "Canna do that. If we was to get caught, we'd both get beaten."

"But why should anyone care where she's buried?"

"Who knows, but they use any excuse to beat us—or worse."

27

Jasmine had no response to that, since it was true. She thanked the woman and returned to her cottage—and her mother's body. Her pain had transformed itself into anger that swelled still more as she stared at the shroud she'd made of their one warm blanket. Her mother had had so little in life, and Jasmine could not allow this final indignity.

It took her more than two hours to reach the spot in the woods, which she wouldn't have been able to find if it hadn't been for the good fortune of a full moon. And before carrying her mother into the woods, she'd gone across through the orchard to the rear of the stables, where she'd found a shovel. It stank of manure and she had no way of cleaning it, but she managed to tie it to the shroud and carry it with her.

It surprised her that her mother was so light, even though she'd seen her flesh falling away for months now. But even so, her arms ached badly by the time she found the spot. After all, she'd just finished working a fourteen-hour day.

Digging the grave took a long time. The ground was soft, but the moisture only made it heavier to lift. And she knew she had to dig the hole deep, so that no wild creature would dig it up again.

When the hole was nearly as deep as she was tall, Jasmine climbed out and then dropped her mother's body into the hole as gently as she could. After that, she immediately set about refilling the grave and then replacing the thick matt of moss and the dried leaves and twigs. The moon had set by then, so she couldn't see if she'd done a good job of concealing the grave, but she thought she had.

She dropped exhaustedly to the ground and began to recite the only prayer she knew in her own language—the language that her grandmother had taught her—a prayer for protection from the demons and a plea for the favor of the gods. Jasmine didn't believe in demons, but neither did she believe in gods who granted favors. If they existed at all, those gods had certainly never listened to her mother.

The sky was lightening by the time she trudged home. She was beyond exhaustion now, but she still managed to pick up her pace. She didn't want anyone to see her out where she had no business being. And she had only an hour to bathe away the grime and try to clean up her stockings and shoes as best she could. Fortunately, her one other dress was clean. She knew better than to ask for a day off. She didn't dare do anything to call herself to her mistress's attention now.

Chapter Two

Somehow Jasmine got through her long workday. Even she did not know how she managed it, or where she found the reserves of strength. At any moment she expected to be summoned before the mistress to explain her mother's continued absence. And failing that, she expected to be hauled before the estate manager or some other official to explain what she'd done with her mother's body.

But the day ended with the overwhelming sense of relief one has when one's worst fears have failed to materialize. For once, her stomach was even full. Cook had been kind to her. Jasmine didn't think Cook knew about her mother's death, however. It was in the woman's nature to be occasionally generous, and Jasmine suspected that it had more to do with events in her own life than with anything she might or might not have done to merit such generosity.

She dragged herself home to her dark, silent cottage, too tired even to cry. Instead, she drew a thin blanket around herself and curled up in her mother's chair and thought about her situation.

Sooner or later, the mistress would learn of her mother's death. What would be better: for Jasmine to tell her and hope she might be allowed to stay on, or to wait and plead her case when the mistress found out?

The truth was that she couldn't begin to guess. The mistress was volatile; everyone knew that. Cook said it was because she was going through "the change," but Jasmine doubted that. Jasmine had been working in the manor since she was ten—twenty years now—and the mistress had always been this way. It was said that the master, who was rarely home, was a good man, or at least better than most—but he left the running of the large household to his wife and the rest of the estate to a manager who was thoroughly detested and feared.

Jasmine didn't believe the stories about the master, either. If he were truly a good man, he would never have put such people in charge of this place.

She knew that she had to plan for the worst—but how could she, when there seemed to be no other path to take? Despite the fact that her work was good, she could not hope to land a position in another household if she was discharged from the manor. Any prospective employer would certainly listen to the ill reports from her mistress.

There were, of course, other avenues open to her, but she cringed at the mere thought of them. She hadn't led such a sheltered life that she didn't know about women who sold themselves, or worked in the taverns where they were pawed by customers—or worse.

She laughed bitterly. Even if she could bring herself to do such a thing, it wouldn't work. She wasn't pretty enough. She'd seen some of those women. They had soft, curvy bodies with full breasts that all but spilled out of their low-topped dresses. No one would want a tall, skinny woman like her—at least not when they were sober enough to see straight.

Finally she fell into a troubled sleep from which she awakened only when the rooster crowed from his perch near the henhouse. Then she got up and started another day, pushing her fears down into the permanently cold place deep inside her.

Quinn stood at the rail, breathing deeply of the salt-scented air. Ahead of him the sea stretched to the horizon, while behind him the land that had been his home but not his home faded into the mist.

He smiled the kind of smile that made men cross the street to avoid him. He was pleased with himself for having come up with his little scheme to avoid paying passage on the ship.

He could have afforded the passage with ease, but since he didn't know how long his quest would take, or how far he would have to go, he wanted to hang on to his gold. He'd gone down to the docks in the hope of working his way across the sea. Unfortunately, there were no ships in port at present that were taking on new crew members and he was eager to be gone before someone in authority should decide that he belonged back at the quarry. The supervisor had been greatly displeased with his announcement that he was leaving and had hinted darkly that he might act to prevent it. Quinn knew that he was far too distinct to hide even in the teeming port city.

So he'd gone to a tavern frequented by sailors and struck up conversations with various men until he found one from the ship that was sailing at dawn for his destination. Then he'd plied the man with drink—not a difficult thing to do with sailors. And when the tavern closed and the man staggered

out onto the street, Quinn maneuvered him into
an alleyway with the promise of women, knocked
him out with a single well-placed blow, and then
trussed him up and left him in a bawdy house. A
small amount of gold to the women there guar-
anteed that they would keep him well occupied
when he woke up. They'd offered their favors to
him as well, for no extra charge, but Quinn had
politely declined. He wasn't above frequenting
such places, but his mind was on other things.

When dawn came, he was down on the docks
again, standing with a small group of men who
came each day, hoping to be paid to load or unload
ships. He wasn't worried about the competition,
however, because he towered over them all.

He knew by appearance the captain of the vessel
he wanted, so when the man appeared on the
docks and started in his direction, Quinn knew
that his scheme had worked. He didn't feel too
badly about what he'd done to the sailor because
an experienced man like him would have another
ship quickly. Quinn was never unnecessarily cruel,
but when such behavior did become necessary, he
wasn't inclined to let his conscience trouble him.
He'd grown up on mean streets and he understood
the ways of the world.

So now he was bound for Borneas, the land
across the sea where he would begin his search.
His grandfather had been vague about their ancient homeland's location, but he'd thought it was
across the sea, so Quinn had decided to begin
there.

In the four days he'd been at sea, he'd learned a
bit about the place—enough to suspect that it was
just as bad as the place he'd left, and perhaps even
worse. Was the entire world this way? He was beginning to think so, which lent even more urgency
to his quest.

He'd also asked his shipmates about a valley en-

33

circled by tall mountains capped with snow, but no one had ever heard of such a place. The ship's navigator had shown him all their maps. Quinn had never seen a map before and was fascinated, which pleased the man. Together they pored over the large maps, but nowhere did they find mention of mountains like those he sought. Of course, as the navigator pointed out, there were very large uncharted regions, mostly in the vast interiors of the landmasses.

The work required of him on the ship was minimal compared to his customary work, so he had a lot of leisure time—perhaps too much, since he spent much of it questioning his decision to chase after his dream—especially since it might not be as easy as he'd thought to return to his old position.

On the other hand, Quinn was resourceful, and he'd never yet been anywhere where there wasn't demand for someone with his great strength and remarkable agility.

So, as he stood at the rail staring out at the as-yet-unseen land of Borneas, Quinn had no regrets at leaving behind the land of his birth. He was a man who liked challenges, and the challenge of finding the one woman who could help him with his quest appealed to him.

Jasmine worked harder than she had ever worked before, even though her normal routine would have taxed most people beyond endurance. Each day she went to the manor certain that it would be her last, then returned to the cottage at night to pray for another day.

Two days after her mother's death, she had a rare day off. But instead of going into town, she set out to visit her mother's grave. She was in the tiny garden behind the cottage picking flowers to take with her when the woman from next door approached her.

"Ye laid her to rest in the woods after all, didn't ye, lass?" the woman said as she stared at the flowers. "They were your ma's favorites."

"Yes, I'm taking them to her grave now," Jasmine replied, uncertain as to whether she should admit her transgression.

"I could come with ye," the woman said somewhat hesitantly. "Your ma was a good woman— and you're a good daughter."

Touched by the woman's words, when she heard so few kind ones, Jasmine told her that would be very nice. But it was a measure of the kind of life she led that she worried the woman might be making the offer so that she could report the location of the grave.

It is wrong to have to live this way, she thought as they set out. *It's wrong to have to look for cruelty behind kindness.*

But then, as they walked along, Jasmine learned that the woman wouldn't reveal her secret—because she had one of her own. It turned out that she had buried her child in her own little garden, where she grew flowers from seeds given to her by Jasmine's mother. Her mother had known about this, the woman told her.

Jasmine thought about this woman who'd been their neighbor for more than ten years now. She had two grown sons, both of them drunken louts who had caused problems for Jasmine more than once. They worked in the mines at the far edge of the estate, and paid for their mother to stay in the cottage because the woman's crippled arm made her unsuited for work at the manor. Jasmine despised them, but she had to acknowledge that they at least took care of their mother. How she wished that she had someone to take care of her.

No, she thought. *I can take care of myself—if only*

I'm given that chance. Being dependent upon someone else struck her as being very dangerous, given the fact that so many men she'd known had met sudden and violent ends. But it would still be wonderful to have someone, just the same.

When they found the spot, she was greatly relieved to see that her mother's grave was undisturbed and virtually indistinguishable from the surrounding area. She put the flowers on the grave, then knelt and recited the prayer she remembered. When she had finished, the woman looked at her curiously.

"Where d'yer people hail from, lass? I always wanted to ask yer ma, but I never did."

"I don't really know," Jasmine answered truthfully. "When I was little—before we came here— my Gramman used to talk of a magical place, but I don't know if she meant that we came from there. My mother never wanted to talk about it."

She described the place and the woman looked at her doubtfully. "Sounds t' me like a dream—not a real place at'all."

"Yes," Jasmine said. "I think you're right."

"But we all need our dreams, then, don't we?" the woman said with a sigh.

Jasmine thought that was the most profound statement she was likely to hear from this woman. She nodded.

Another week passed—pleasantly enough, since the mistress had gone to visit her married daughter. Jasmine had noted before that on those rare occasions when she was gone from the manor, the household ran very smoothly and the staff even wore smiles some of the time.

But the best thing that happened was the food. When the mistress was gone, they all ate much better. Jasmine asked Cook at one point if she didn't fear the mistress's finding out about it, but the big woman shook her head.

"Nah, no worry about that. She don't pay much attention to the stores after she's been gone. Her mind don't always work too well, and she forgets what was to hand when she left. So eat up, lass. Ye can use it. Sorry about your ma, by the way."

"When did you find out?" Jasmine asked nervously.

"Just t'day. Old Saul told me."

Jasmine cringed. The plate of chicken she'd been enjoying suddenly lost its taste. Saul was the majordomo, the man in charge of the household. He was a terrible gossip, and it was known that he was the chief source of information for the mistress.

"I hope she'll keep ye on, girl," Cook said kindly, obviously seeing Jasmine's distress. "Ye're a good worker, and I told Saul to tell her that."

"Thank you," Jasmine murmured, forcing herself to finish the chicken. Who knew how many more meals she would get?

The mistress returned on a cool, rainy day. Jasmine was picking carrots in the kitchen garden when she saw the ornate carriage being driven toward the stables. Her fingers trembled as she pulled the carrots. One way or another, it would likely be settled today.

She was summoned before the mistress only an hour later by the woman's personal maid, a sharp-faced creature who had long ago taken a dislike to Jasmine.

"You lied to me!" Her mistress stated coldly without preamble, when Jasmine entered her boudoir.

"I didn't lie to you, milady. The last time you inquired after my mother's health, she was still alive and seemed to be on the mend."

37

"Don't sass me! It will be a pleasure to see the last of you. You will leave here, and leave the cottage immediately!"

With the recklessness that comes when all hope is gone, Jasmine drew herself up straight. "That suits me just fine. I don't want to stay here any longer. This is a bad place—and you're a cruel woman!"

She enjoyed—at least for a moment—the outraged expression on the mistress's face as she turned on her heel and left without bothering to curtsy. But by the time she had reached the kitchen again, her legs were trembling and her stomach was threatening to disgorge the tea and bread she'd had a short time ago.

"Has she sent ye packing, lass?" Cook said uncertainly.

Jasmine blinked back tears and nodded. Cook peered around the empty kitchen, then withdrew a sack from beneath the counter.

"I feared that would happen. I don't know why, but she's disliked you for ages. Here. This should help a bit."

Jasmine took the sack and started to open it, but Cook took her arm and ushered her toward the door. "Be off quickly. If she finds out I've given you anythin', she'll likely fire me, too."

Murmuring her thanks, Jasmine left the manor. As she walked through the orchard, where fruit pickers were at work, she hid the sack as best she could in the folds of her skirt and ignored the lewd remarks of the men.

When she reached the cottage, a new horror awaited her. All her meager possessions had been tossed in a heap outside the door. She fell to her knees and began to sort through them, hoping that everything was there. Not that she had anything worth stealing. And then she cried out in protest when she saw that the one thing she treasured most was gone: her lute. Why would they take it? The men who would have been sent to do this certainly could have no use for it. Perhaps they intended to sell it. She had even thought about that herself, though it would have been very painful to part with it.

Half-blinded by tears, Jasmine continued to sort aimlessly through the things, trying to decide what she could carry with her. The rain was turning everything into a sodden mess.

She would take her mother's woolen shawl, she decided. She didn't need it now, but it would come in handy when the weather turned cooler. And she could use it to wrap everything else in. It would work better than the thin blanket.

She had gathered her few things into a heap upon the center of the shawl and was trying to tie it together when she felt something hard along the hem. Curious, she paused to examine it, and discovered an extra row of stitching along one border. Whatever it was that she'd felt was sewn inside. She began to pick loose the stitches, then stared in amazement at what was revealed.

The thin gold chain was finer than anything she'd seen the mistress wear. Suspended from the chain was a small pendant: a circlet of thin gold threaded with fine gold wire that held two stones: a diamond and a flat black stone the likes of which she'd never seen before.

Jasmine stared at it as the rain poured over her. She simply couldn't believe what she was seeing. She knew that the shawl had originally belonged to her grandmother. It was woven of the fine dark wool from the sheep she barely remembered from their farm. But surely her mother must have known it was there.

She heard voices and quickly slipped the necklace into her pocket. Then she turned to see two of the men who worked for the estate manager—

probably the two who had thrown her things out here and had stolen her lute as well.

"Ye're to git out o' here now, girl," one man said with a sneer.

She stood up to face them. "Where's my lute? It isn't here."

"All yer things're there," the other man said. "Now git!"

Jasmine gathered up the shawl and left. As she reached the edge of the orchard, she turned and saw them pawing through the things she'd left behind.

By the time she reached town, she was shivering beneath her wet clothing, even though the day wasn't that cool. She still had no idea where to go.

Quinn walked down the gangplank and onto the busy dock, his quick gaze taking it all in. The sailors were right; this place didn't look any different from home. The land was somewhat flatter, but otherwise it was much the same.

Shouldering the bag that held all his posessions, he made his way from the harbor into the town. One of the sailors aboard his ship spoke a bit of the Borneash tongue, and Quinn had learned it as best he could. At least, he thought he had the essentials. The rest he could pick up along the way.

On a side street not far from the harbor he found the small inn recommended by his shipmates. They'd said it had decent accommodations at a reasonable price, and it was attached to a tavern that sold good food.

He went in and paid for a room for three nights, then paid the innkeeper to hold his bag, as his shipmates had suggested. His gold he kept with him, of course, most of it hidden in his clothing. Quinn was handy with a needle and thread, and it had served him well.

It turned out that the innkeeper spoke a bit of

Estavian, since many of his guests hailed from Quinn's homeland. Quinn asked him where he could find a mapmaker. He'd become fascinated by maps, and thought that he just might find one here that showed more detail.

The innkeeper gave him the information, and Quinn set out again, heading toward the shopping district. A market was in progress, so he stopped at a few stalls and purchased some food, some bits of which were familiar to him, while other items were strange. He particularly liked the little meat pasties and went back for more.

People stared at him, as they always did, but he ignored them and continued his leisurely stroll through the marketplace, his eyes always scanning the crowd. He knew better, though, than to think his search could end this quickly.

He'd decided that he would search for her himself for a day or two before he began to ask questions. People might loosen their tongues a bit if he began to seem familiar. Besides, he could use that time to improve his knowledge of their language.

He was deep in thought about the impossibility of his search when a familiar scent caught his attention. What was it? He glanced at a fruit and vegetable stall where a sizable crowd had gathered to be served. Then he shrugged and walked on. He'd just spotted the mapmaker across the street.

The wizened old man got up from his stool behind a table that displayed a huge map. Quinn nodded in his direction, then bent to examine the map. It was almost the opposite of the one he'd seen on the ship—showing his native land in very little detail, while giving much greater attention to Borneas and the surrounding land. But he could see that there was a vast area to the north that was filled with fantastical illustrations, but was obviously unexplored.

Doing his best with the language, Quinn explained to the mapmaker what he was looking for. The old man scratched his stubbly chin in thought, then pointed a bony finger at the uncharted area.

"Never heard of such a place, but if it exists, it must be here," the man said. "The land is hillier there," he added.

Quinn had already seen the little triangles clustered together that indicated hilly land. He asked the man if anyone had ever explored that region.

"Mayhap a few have, but I've never seen maps."

Quinn bought the map anyway. It would at least guide him toward that empty spot. Then, with the map rolled up under his arm, he set out to see the rest of the town.

It wasn't until much later, after he'd filled his stomach with an excellent meal and was about to fall asleep, that he remembered that scent from the marketplace—and why it had seemed familiar.

Quinn barely slept all night, unable to believe he could be right, and he was eager to return to the market the next morning.

Jasmine woke up with a start as something touched her skirt. She had barely gotten her eyes open when a large orange cat leapt over her and disappeared through the narrow opening in the wall behind her. She drew the shawl tighter, not wanting to think about what the cat might be chasing.

She rubbed her eyes and stared up at the narrow strip of sky visible above her hiding place. It was milky white, but beginning to give way to blue. Now that she lived beneath the sky, the weather had become very important to her. She was sniffling and her chest hurt.

She'd spent her first day in town sodden and searching for a safe place to sleep. And in the last of the daylight, she'd come upon this spot. It was a narrow alleyway between two shops on the street that bordered the harbor. The noisy taverns were all some distance away, which meant that drunken men were unlikely to stumble upon her. And at the rear of the alleyway there was a small alcove of sorts, a place where one of the building's walls were set back a bit. It was perfect—more than she'd dared to hope for. The alcove meant that she couldn't be seen from the street even in daylight.

When she'd awakened yesterday morning, following her first night there, she'd belatedly realized that there was a rather strong smell of horses emanating from somewhere. Following her nose, she slipped through the narrow opening the cat had just used and discovered a small stable that probably belonged to the inn that backed up against the two shops.

Before she'd quite decided how to use that to her advantage, she heard male voices and realized that the stable help must have arrived already. Or else they slept there.

So she returned the next evening and did some cautious exploring. No one was about, and she could see no evidence that anyone had slept there. Using her shawl as a sort of basket, she gathered up some fresh straw and carried it back to her hiding place to use as a bed. Using the stable itself was too risky because people might come and go from the inn at all hours.

She also took advantage of the big watering trough to wash herself as best she could after taking a drink. She was learning.

But the fact that she'd survived thus far did not reassure her. The small supply of food that Cook had given her was nearly gone, even though she'd eaten very sparingly. And before she'd even reached town, she'd realized that she hadn't brought with her the herbs she'd prepared for the next market. They hadn't been with her things in front of the cottage, so she could only assume that the men had left them inside, thinking them useless.

She sat huddled in her tiny corner and stared up at the clearing sky. Several gulls wheeled about. She could hear their distant cries. *Freedom,* she thought. *I am free now—but at what cost?*

Yesterday she had begun her study of the taverns in the town. It occurred to her that some of them must surely be better than others—and therefore safer for her to work in. The ones that were nearest the harbor all looked like dreadful places to her, filled even in the daytime with raucous men. But just before her energy had flagged, she'd happened upon one on a side street. It was attached to a very clean and respectable-looking inn, and the few customers she saw coming and going appeared to be of a better breed than the others she'd seen.

After casting a quick glance out into the alleyway to be sure no one was coming, Jasmine slipped out of her dress and into her other one, which she'd washed in the horse trough at dawn yesterday, then left to dry upon the straw. It was dark and plain, but it was the best thing she owned. Then she left the shadows of the alleyway to go sit at the dock and eat the crust of bread she had allotted to herself for this day. Later she would go to the tavern and see if there might be work, perhaps in the kitchen.

Quinn was up early and off to the marketplace without even stopping for breakfast. He still couldn't believe that his nose had been right, but that didn't stop him from hoping.

The reason that the scent had seemed familiar to him was that it smelled exactly like a fragrant herb his grandmother had grown in the tiny square of dirt behind their small house. Unlike the other herbs she grew for medicinal purposes, this one had been grown for its scent alone. The dried plants had then competed all winter with the more potent smells in their crowded little house.

Someone—either his mother or his grandmother—had told him that they'd carried the seeds for the herbs with them as they roamed the land, passing them along from one generation to the next. And Quinn was certain that he'd never smelled their like since.

Of course, what was unique to his family might well be commonplace here, but he preferred to think of it as being his first, tentative lead. And even if it didn't pan out, the trip to the market wouldn't be wasted. There were those meat pasties and the opportunity to study the crowds.

When he reached the market square, the stallkeepers were just setting up for the day. The space he remembered as being where he'd smelled that familiar scent was empty, but he went there and waited as he studied the people—most of them women—who were already arriving with their baskets and sacks.

The woman with the meat pasties arrived and Quinn made himself her first customer. She smiled in recognition and teased him about cleaning out her supply before the market had even begun. Quinn could be very charming when it suited him, so he flattered the woman and flirted a bit with her. He was thinking about asking if she'd ever seen any tall, very blond women, when the other stallkeeper arrived, leading a heavily laden donkey cart. He excused himself and hurried over there.

A mixture of scents met him—but not the one he remembered. And for sure, this woman couldn't be Latawi. She was dark haired and bronze skinned but far too short to be one of his own people. Still, he approached her.

When she saw him, the woman's face registered

a fear that Quinn was familiar with. It seemed that his size and his appearance either attracted women or made them afraid. He greeted her and gave her his best smile, one he thought made him appear relatively harmless.

"I passed by your stand yesterday," he said in his best Borneash. "There was a smell—some herb, I think. But I don't smell it today. Is there something you had then that you don't have now?"

It took a few repetitions before he made himself understood, but then the woman nodded. "My best herbs are gone. Mayhap it was the bluish one you mean."

Quinn nodded eagerly. He remembered that the herb was blue-gray in color.

The woman sighed and looked around her, as though searching for someone. "I buy them from someone, but she hasn't been here for a while."

Quinn felt his blood pounding in his ears. "Could you describe her? It may be that I know her."

"Aye. She's very tall—not like you, of course—but tall for a woman. And she has very pale hair, nearly white. Skinny as a rail, she is, too. Her name's Jasmine."

Jasmine. The name took his breath away. It was the name of a flower, one with a scent as lovely as the herb. His grandmother had grown them, too, and he'd never seen them elsewhere.

"Strange sorta name, ain't it? Never heard it before."

Quinn was having trouble focusing on the woman's words. He simply couldn't believe his luck, though luck had not been a stranger to him in the past.

"Where does she live?" he asked, having trouble containing his glee.

The woman shrugged her ample shoulders. "She never said, but I think she's a servant somewhere.

Someone said they seen her come into town with a wagonful from the manor."

Quinn asked where the manor was and learned that it was the largest of the great estates in the area, some ten miles from town. He was torn between waiting here to see if she would show up, as the woman hoped, or hiring a horse and riding out there to find her.

Jasmine drew herself up and smoothed her dress as best she could, then walked through the open doorway into the tavern. The wonderful cooking smells nearly made her swoon. Only a few people were there this early, and one of them, a stout man sitting alone at a table with a huge breakfast before him, got up and came toward her.

"I'm seeking a job," she told him. "I have some cooking skills, or I could learn to be a barmaid."

"Sorry, lass, I don't need anyone now. But you might try the inn next door. They might need some kitchen help."

Jasmine thanked him and left. At least he'd been civil to her. She started toward the inn, then decided to go around to the kitchen entrance. If she could persuade the cook of her skills, perhaps the innkeeper would hire her.

Once again, she was assaulted by mouthwatering aromas. Three people were working in the big kitchen: two young girls and a massive woman who must surely be the cook. Jasmine approached her with a smile and explained that she was looking for work and that she had some experience as a cook.

The cook cast a glance at one of the girls. "Ye're too late, dearie. I just hired someone." Then she lowered her voice to a whisper. "Come back around in a few days."

Jasmine thanked her and left, trying to feel optimistic. It sounded as though the new girl wasn't working out. She hated to wish anyone ill fortune, but she dearly hoped that was the case. It would be a good place to work, she thought. The kitchen was cleaner than the one at the manor, and the cook seemed quite pleasant.

She spent a few hours wandering aimlessly through the harbor area, trying to ignore her growling stomach, which had been awakened by the aroma of food, and trying as well not to think about the last remaining piece of fruit back at her hiding place. That and one small biscuit would have to be her meal tomorrow.

Finally, late in the afternoon, she wandered into the marketplace. She probably owed the stallkeeper who sold her herbs the courtesy of explaining that she wouldn't be bringing her anything anymore. And she was also hoping that the woman's conscience might prick her into at least giving her a few pieces of fruit or a wilted vegetable that hadn't sold. Jasmine was convinced that the woman had made a very nice profit off her.

She found the woman dozing on her stool. The bazaar was nearly empty and some of the merchants were packing up. She passed the one that sold those delicious-smelling meat pasties and wondered if she'd ever have the money to purchase one. At least she didn't have to smell them this day; the trays were empty.

"Hello," she said, waking the woman from her doze and at the same time noting that there were some bruised pears and plums left.

The woman blinked, then looked down at Jasmine's empty hands. "You didn't bring me any herbs."

"No, I came to tell you that I won't be able to bring them anymore."

"Have you gone into business fer yerself, then?" the woman asked suspiciously.

Jasmine shook her head. "No. I've lost my job

and been turned out of my house, so I can't grow them anymore."

For a long moment the woman said nothing. Jasmine wanted to think that her expression meant she was sad for her, but she suspected that the woman was only thinking of her lost business.

"Someone was here, lookin' for ye," she said, startling Jasmine.

"What? Who? Did he say why he was looking for me?" Cold fingers slid down her spine. Had the mistress sent someone to punish her for her parting words?

"He dinna say. A very big man—biggest I ever seen. Black curly hair and a scar right here." She drew a line from her forehead down across her cheek.

Who was he? Jasmine frowned. Several of the men who worked for the estate manager were big men, but she couldn't recall any with black curly hair and a scar.

"When was he here?" she asked, looking around the nearly deserted marketplace.

"First thing this mornin'. He was here before me. Come to think on it, he dinna ask for you straightaway. It was that herb that brought him—the bluish one that smells so nice. He said he'd smelled it the day afore. They was all gone by the time he came back. Then he asked where I got them, and I told him about you."

It made no sense—unless the mistress had discovered her herb business after she left. Maybe she was planning to charge her with stealing.

"He hung around a while. Ate a lot o' them pasties and bought some fruit. Then he left."

Jasmine stood there frowning in confusion while the woman watched her. Then she began to pack up her things, and thrust a pear and a plum at Jasmine. "Take these, dearie. And if you get set up again, be sure to come see me."

Jasmine had the presence of mind to thank her before she wandered away. When she slipped the fruit into her pocket, her fingers brushed against the chain of the pendant. Somehow she'd nearly forgotten it. Now she had two mysteries to consider.

She took a different route back to her hiding place, and she'd nearly passed the shop before she saw it. Then she stopped with a gasp of recognition. In the shop's grimy window hung her lute!

Jasmine knew what the building housed: a pawnshop, where people sold things or left them when they borrowed money, then retrieved them after payment. She went in.

The proprietor told her that he'd bought the lute outright. He was asking far more for it than she would have guessed it would fetch. She wanted to tell him that it belonged to her and had been stolen, but she knew that might draw unwelcome attention to her. The proprietor certainly wouldn't hand it over. She left the shop, thinking about the pendant in her pocket. It would fetch a nice price, but how could she bear to part with it, even though she hadn't known of its existence until a few days ago? Why hadn't her mother told her about it?

Quinn brought the big bay to a halt when he crested a small hill and saw the manor house. He'd been riding for some time past planted fields that he knew must belong to the manor. The crops were abundant, but the people working in the fields and the children scampering about near the tumbledown cottages were scrawny. It was obvious that they weren't reaping any benefits from the success of the farming.

He stared at the big house, wondering why it was that hard work wasn't rewarded, while the mere accident of birth was.

He surveyed the manor house and the outbuildings and decided to head for the kitchen door. Cooks and other kitchen help were notorious gossips and often generous with a mug of tea or a piece of pie as well. The ride had reawakened his appetite.

He turned into the road that led around the side of the house, then dismounted and tied his horse to a tree near the kitchen garden. But before proceeding, he studied the garden, wondering if this might be where the girl, Jasmine, was growing her herbs. That didn't appear to be the case. Everything he saw looked like ordinary herbs and vegetables.

The kitchen door was open, so he stepped inside, inhaling the delicious aromas. But his sensitive nose caught something beneath the odor of food, and when the cook turned to face him, he knew what it was. The woman regarded him through eyes that wouldn't quite focus. People—and especially women—who drank too much offended him, but he put on a smile.

"I was hoping that you might help me, missus. I'm looking for the girl, Jasmine. I was told that she might work here."

The woman steadied herself against the counter before speaking. "Used to do. She's gone. My mistress fired her."

"Why?" Quinn asked, even though what he should be asking was where she had gone.

"Never liked her—the mistress, I mean." She paused to hiccup. "I expect it was cuz she put on airs, but I dinna mind that."

"Do you know where she is? Did she go back to her family?"

"Ain't no family to go back to. Was only her and her ma, and her ma died a short time back."

Quinn digested that bit of information, then asked where she had lived when she worked there.

"Back yonder," the cook said, waving a spoon in

the general direction of the orchards he'd passed.

At that moment, an officious-looking older man pushed through the door that led into the front of the house. Quinn disliked him right away, so he gave him his most unpleasant smile. For a moment the man seemed about to flee, but then he turned his attention to the cook and began to bark orders. Quinn left.

He got back onto his horse and rode through the orchards, pausing beneath a heavily laden tree to pluck a juicy pear. Two men picking in the next row stopped and stared at him openmouthed, then turned quickly back to their work when he gave them his "go to hell" look.

At the far end of the orchard, he found a row of tiny cottages, barely more than hovels. Once more he tied up the horse and then walked around to the back of the row. All had small gardens, but it was the middle one that drew his attention.

With a smile of satisfaction, he stared down at the plants. This was it; no doubt about it. It was smaller, but otherwise it looked just like the garden his mother and grandmother had kept. He breathed in the fragrant scents happily.

Then, seeing that no one was around, he pushed open the back door to the cottage. It was empty, except for two sagging beds, two chairs, and a table with a battered oil lamp. But the scent was there, too, though he saw no dried plants.

He went back outside and, after looking around to ensure that no one was anywhere in sight, he took out his knife and cut off some of each of the herbs, then wrapped them in a piece of burlap he found lying near the garden.

A short time later he was on his way back to town, once more smiling as he thought about what the cook had told him. He didn't waste any time feeling sorry for the girl, Jasmine. Her bad luck was his good fortune. It sounded as though she must be pretty desperate, which meant that he could persuade her to come with him.

Quinn knew that he could be very persuasive, but he had begun to worry a bit that if he found the girl, she might not be amenable to accompanying him—or worse still, that she might be married. He was prepared to kidnap her if he must, but he would rather have her agree to come with him.

He rode along, humming to himself, then chuckling as he remembered what the drunken cook had said about her "putting on airs." He kind of liked the sound of that. Coarse women had never appealed to him—except, of course, when he was unable to find any other kind.

Chapter Three

Jasmine stayed close to her hiding place for the next two days, never venturing more than a few blocks from the alleyway. She had precious little energy in any event. Her coughing was waking her up regularly during the night, and the pain in her chest was worse. She was also certain that she had a fever. When she did sleep, she ran dreamed of the fragrant concoctions her mother had used in such situations when she was a child.

She had other dreams as well—dark dreams where she was being pursued down endless streets by a giant of a man. The worst part of those dreams was awakening to the knowledge that he was real. So ran when she did leave her hiding place, she was constantly on the lookout for him, grateful that at least he would be easy to spot.

On the third day, she did the best she could to make herself look presentable and returned to the inn. This time, when the cooking smells reached out to envelop her, she actually became weak-kneed. She had eaten the plum—her last bit of food—the day before, and then had tried to fill her protesting stomach with water from the horse trough this morning.

Her hopes of gaining employment were extinguished when she entered the kitchen and didn't see the cook to whom she'd spoken. She also saw that the new girl that the cook had indicated was still there. A frog-faced woman with a turned-down mouth informed her that the cook was off for the day.

As she turned to leave, Jasmine suddenly felt faint and braced herself against the counter. Her fingers touched a bowl of warm, crusty rolls, and she quickly slipped one into her pocket. Action had preceded thought. When she was outside, she was horrified at what she'd done. Taking fruit from the estate orchards was one thing: She'd justified that on the basis of their failure to pay her. But this was stealing, pure and simple. Furthermore, it was stealing from a place where she hoped to be employed.

She could feel the heat of the warm roll against her thigh the whole way back to her hiding place, and within a few minutes of Jasmine's reaching it, the roll was gone and she was picking the crumbs from her lap.

She stayed there until late afternoon, dozing fitfully and thinking about the pendant in her pocket. It was strange that she'd become so attached to it, but then she'd never had a piece of jewelry before, let alone something so obviously valuable. Besides, even if her mother hadn't told her about it, it must have some significance or she herself would have sold it.

But pawning it was not without its danger. It would be logical for the shopkeeper to assume that she'd stolen it. She'd think the same thing herself if someone like her brought in an expensive piece of jewelry.

On the other hand, wouldn't he have thought the same thing of the men who'd stolen her lute?

The loss of the lute brought tears to her eyes as she scrambled to her feet. There was nothing to do for it but to take that chance. If she recalled correctly, one could pawn an item for less cash than its actual worth, then redeem it by paying back that amount, plus interest. She'd heard some of the manor staff talk about such things. She would ask for only enough to buy herself some food and the ingredients to make a remedy.

She emerged from the alleyway and started to walk slowly toward the pawnshop. The curly-haired giant had slipped from her mind.

Quinn was becoming ever more frustrated. For two days he'd been searching the town for her without success. Now he began to wonder if she might have found employment elsewhere, perhaps at another estate or in one of the grand houses belonging to wealthy merchants.

He'd gone back to the stallkeeper the morning after his visit to the estate. The woman claimed that the girl hadn't been there, but Quinn had keen ears and eyes for untruths, and he was certain she was lying.

It was late afternoon and he was strolling slowly along the street, thinking that he might start checking the inns and taverns the next day. She might have found employment in one of them. It was then that he saw her.

There was no doubt that it was her. Quinn drew in a sharp breath. Until that moment, he hadn't been certain, despite the evidence, that she was Latawi. But there was no doubt in his mind now. He felt drawn to her as the moth is drawn to the flame—and for the first time, he wondered uneas-

ily if the tale about the magic and demons could
be true.

But with success now in his grasp, Quinn became cautious. Instead of continuing toward her,
he stepped into the space between two shops and
watched her. He couldn't see her face clearly, but
what he saw—along with an inner tingling—confirmed that she was his quarry. She was tall and
very thin, with pale skin and hair that was nearly
white as it flowed unencumbered across her shoulders.

She was standing staring into the window of a
shop he couldn't identify from where he hid. Twice
he saw her hand go to her side, as though she were
about to take something from her pocket. Once,
she even started toward the shop entrance. But
then suddenly she turned away and began to walk
down the street in the opposite direction.

Quinn followed her, prepared to jump into an
alleyway or shop entrance if she turned. He suspected that the stallkeeper had told her about him,
and who knew what she was thinking at this point?

When he came abreast of the shop where he'd
seen her, he paused long enough to look in the
window—and saw immediately what must have
attracted her attention. Prominently displayed on
a wooden stand was an ancient lute, ornately
carved and decorated with mother-of-pearl. It was
nearly identical to one that had once been in his
family, one his grandmother had described as being very, very old. The lute had been lost, along
with many other things, in a fire some years ago,
not long after his grandmother's death.

She'd obviously sold the lute in her desperation.
Quinn was tempted to go into the shop and buy it,
but that would take time, since he wasn't about to
pay the asking price. Then he saw her turn a corner and vanish, and he hurried past the shop.

He didn't run because he knew that his much

longer strides would close the distance between them quickly enough. But to his chagrin, when he turned the corner where she had vanished, she was nowhere in sight.

He stood there for a moment, studying the street. It was a short street of tiny homes, running at an oblique angle and ending at the street that bordered the harbor. Could she be staying in one of the houses, perhaps renting a room?

He thought about going door-to-door to ask for her, then decided against it. She might have warned her landlord about him. What made more sense was for him to return in the early evening, when he could be sure of finding residents out on their stoops and in the street. He'd lived on such a street himself, and he knew the habits of such people.

Jasmine collapsed onto her bed of straw and gave in to the tears that had been threatening ever since she'd gone to the pawnshop. *One more day,* she told herself. *Tomorrow the cook will be back and perhaps I'll find work. I can survive until then.*

She drifted into a light doze, then finally into a deep sleep, where the giant returned to torment her.

Quinn had an early dinner at the tavern, then returned to the street where the girl Jasmine had disappeared. He smiled at his earlier inspiration. It just might work. At the very least it would tempt her.

After losing her, he'd returned to the pawnshop. The shopkeeper had tried for a time to stay with his asking price. Quinn offered him half that amount. Then, when the man wavered, he mentioned that he was buying it back for its rightful owner, who he'd discovered was not the person who'd brought it into the shop. He told the pawnbroker that they could settle it quietly between themselves; he was prepared to be reasonable. But if that failed, he would tell the owner that it was here and they would contact the local constabulary.

The pawnbroker finally gave in, as Quinn had known he would. So now he had the lute in its cracked leather case—an offering to the girl. He thought it might work—especially since he knew now that she wasn't likely to have any money.

As he'd guessed, every stoop and the street itself was filled with people escaping from their stifling little houses into the pleasant evening air. Curious gazes were turned his way as he walked along the street, scanning the crowds for her. Then he began to ask after her.

A half hour later, he had established that she didn't live on the street, but two residents had seen her several times, which meant that she was staying somewhere nearby.

Quinn started toward the street that bordered the harbor. If she had turned in here, she must have been headed toward the harbor. Furthermore, her appearance and the fact that he now knew she hadn't sold the lute suggested that she was totally without funds—and homeless. Even better for him, though he did spare a moment's sympathy for her. He himself had never been in that situation, but he'd helped some who were, and he also knew that it must be much worse—and far more dangerous—for a woman.

So he started to walk along the street next to the harbor, seeking out a hiding place as though he himself were homeless. He passed a group of noisy taverns quickly. She wouldn't look for a spot here. Then he came upon a row of shops that catered to the shipping trade. The stores were closed and the area was quiet.

Most of the shops abutted each other, with only

the narrowest of spaces between them. She was skinny, but even she couldn't fit into one of those spaces. Finally, a block or so down, he came to an actual alleyway between two shops. It was dark back there, and he couldn't see any sign that it was inhabited. Still, he decided to check it out.

And that was where he found her, sound asleep on a bed of straw with an old shawl pulled around her thin body.

"Jasmine!"

She struggled up from sleep, her mind awake just enough to tell her that it wasn't a dream. She opened her eyes to darkness—then opened them wider when something moved in that darkness.

For one brief moment she thought—or hoped— that she was still asleep and this was just a new version of the nightmare. But then the giant spoke again, and she knew he was real.

"Don't be afraid. I won't hurt you. I've come to help you."

Jasmine drew the shawl more tightly around her. Her gaze slid to the narrow opening that led to the stable. She could slip through it easily enough—but could he?

"I'm here to help you," he repeated in a heavy accent. His voice was very deep, befitting his size, but she sensed that he was making an effort to speak gently. She stared at him, while at the same time making a slight move toward the opening.

He moved with an agility she would have thought impossible for a man his size, and now crouched between her and the opening.

"Will you let me help you?" he asked.

"Who are you?"

"My name is Quinn. I know you were fired from your job and have no place to stay. I can help you."

Then he reached out suddenly and she screamed, thinking that he was about to grab her.

But the scream died in a gasp when she saw her lute case in his hand.

"This is yours, isn't it? I got it back for you."

She stared at it, then tried to see him more clearly in the darkness. His features were shadowy, but what she saw didn't reassure her. It was a harsh face, even though he was smiling a very gentle smile.

"Why?" she asked.

"To prove that I want to help you," he said, laying the lute at her feet.

"Why do you want to help me?"

"Because there is something I want you to do. It's a very long story, and would be much better told over some supper. Will you come back to my inn with me? There's a nice tavern next door where we can eat, and then I'll get you a room."

Jasmine could not believe what she was hearing. Why would he want to help her? It made no sense. What could she possibly do for him—except the obvious?

"I'm not hungry."

"You're half-starved, and if I found you here, so could someone else—some drunks from the taverns, for example."

"I've always been thin," she said defensively, ignoring the rest of it.

"Because you've always been half-starved. I'll change that."

It was so tempting. A real meal. A comfortable bed. Now she understood why women came to sell themselves. But why would he want her? There were so many other women, women who weren't skinny and who dressed and smelled better than she did.

She shook her head, denying the temptation. He stared at her in the darkness for a moment, then straightened up. When he leaned down again, she started nervously, but he was only picking up the lute.

"I'll have a job tomorrow," she told him suddenly, as though that would explain her refusal of his offer.

He tucked the lute under his arm. "I'm taking this with me so that it can't be stolen from you again. I'm staying at the Wild Boar. It's only a few blocks from here. If you change your mind, you can find me there."

He started to walk away, then turned around and came back. She shrank back against the wall, moving again toward the opening. But he merely reached into his pocket and pulled out a coin, then dropped it onto the ground in front of her. A moment later, he had vanished into the night.

Jasmine would have been convinced that it had all been a dream if it weren't for that coin at her feet. She snatched it up, then held it tightly in her fist.

Who was this Quinn—and why should he think that she could help him? For that matter, how had he known about the lute? If she believed in the supernatural, as many people did, she'd have thought him to be a ghost of some sort—a very large one.

Early the next morning, Jasmine left her hiding place that wasn't a secret anymore. She emerged from the alleyway cautiously, checking the entire area for signs of him. Then, with the coin he'd given her clutched in her hand, she made her way to the market just as it was opening for the day.

The coin proved to be worth more than she'd thought. Jasmine didn't know much about money, never having had it. But it was enough to buy three of the wonderful meat pasties, a piece of fruit, and a mug of strong tea. She sat on a bench at the edge of the marketplace and devoured it all, remembering only halfway through her meal that she should eat more slowly because her stomach was unaccustomed to such bounty.

The pleasant fullness gave her confidence as she started toward the inn. Surely the cook would be there and would hire her. But she experienced a moment of uncertainty when she reached the inn and noticed for the first time the big painted sign out front. The Wild Boar. It was the inn where the man Quinn had said he was staying. She hesitated, then hurried around to the kitchen entrance.

The cook had returned, but when Jasmine inquired if there might be a job for her, the woman shook her head. "Sorry, miss. I was a bit hasty in my judgment t'other day."

Jasmine's spirits, which had soared to great heights, now crashed to the ground as she left the kitchen. Tears sprang to her eyes, and she reached up to brush them away. Then she looked up—and there he was.

In daylight the man was even more frightening. The jagged scar only added more harshness to a face that already had more than its measure. But he was smiling again.

"So you didn't get a job after all?"

She said nothing.

"Have you eaten yet?"

She nodded.

"That job wasn't meant to be, Jasmine," he said in that deep, gentle voice. "You were meant to come with me."

She stared up at him—so very far up. She wasn't accustomed to having to do that, but she came barely to his shoulders. He frightened her, but she also felt strangely drawn to him.

It's because I'm so desperate, she thought. *That's all it is.* And once more, she told herself that she would never again condemn women who sold their bodies. The only remaining question in her mind was why he should want *her* body.

"There are other places," she said. "I'll find a job."

His pale gray eyes darkened and his wide mouth firmed into a thin line. "And if you do, I'll get you fired," he said very matter-of-factly. "All it will take is a bit of gold slipped to the cook, and out you'll go."

She was too shocked to respond immediately. But she didn't doubt that he would do—or at least try to do—just what he said. Good worker or not, she would be fired. After her dismissal from the estate, she had no illusions left about hard work guaranteeing employment.

"So why don't you make it easier on both of us and just come with me?"

"Why?" she demanded, challenging him to say what she knew he was thinking.

"I told you before that it's a long story. I've come a long way to find you, Jasmine, and I won't let you go now."

Jasmine was horrified. Why hadn't it occurred to her before that he was mad? She'd seen madness a few times before, and she knew that such people could seem to be quite normal at times, then lapse into irrational behavior.

She ran. Her chest ached as she gulped the air, but the food in her stomach gave her energy. She wove her way through the crowds when she reached the marketplace, knowing that his size would be a disadvantage if he were following her. Then, when she reached the far edge of the market square, she paused, slipping between two stalls, and looked for him.

She saw him across the square, scanning the crowds easily with his height advantage. She shrank back quickly, then made her way along the rear of the last stalls and into a side street. There she slowed to a walk, casting regular glances back over her shoulder.

He was a madman, no doubt of it. Surely he would do something outrageous that would draw the attention of the authorities, who would then lock him up somewhere. She just had to stay out of his way until that happened.

But that meant she could not return to her hiding place. She would have to find another spot. She walked along, frowning in thought. There was the stable itself. She knew by now that no one slept there, and as long as she found some dark corner, it wasn't likely that she'd be caught.

Many of the streets near the harbor were crooked and winding, and it took her a while to find the stable without returning to her hiding place. Two young boys were there, mucking out the stable, but she ignored them and they ignored her. Then she slipped cautiously through the opening to her hiding place and grabbed her few belongings, bundling them into her shawl and tossing it over her shoulder.

She spent the remainder of the day visiting various inns and taverns in a search for employment, always on guard against the mad giant, Quinn. Once, when she turned a corner, she spotted him a block away, but he didn't see her.

There were no jobs at any of the places she visited, including several that appeared to be less than respectable. By late afternoon, she was tired and becoming feverish again—and she was hungry. She was surprised at how hungry she was, since her meal this morning had been more than she was accustomed to having for an entire day— especially since she'd left the manor. She wished that she'd been more careful with the money he'd given her.

She made her way down to the harbor again,

knowing that it was too early to return to the stable.

Quinn spent the day searching for the girl and cursing himself for having let her escape. But another part of him admired her courage. He doubted that many women in her circumstances would have refused his offer—whatever she thought that offer might have been. However, her courage was his bane. He longed to get out of this place and begin their real journey.

He dined at the inn this time, where the food was good, but not as good as the tavern's. And as he ate, he pondered where she might go now. He wasn't going to waste his time looking for her in the same place; she'd never go back there.

But she might stay close by. He guessed that she'd come to feel safe in her little spot, and that she probably had gotten to know the neighborhood well. It seemed likely that she would look for another place nearby.

After polishing off two pieces of fruit pie for dessert, Quinn strolled down to the nearly deserted harbor. The only signs of life were at the taverns. He checked all alleyways, but there were none that would offer her much protection. Then he turned in to the alley where he'd found her.

She wasn't there, of course, but his gaze fell thoughtfully on the narrow opening nearby, the one she'd been trying to reach after he found her. It wasn't wide enough for him to get through, but it had to open onto something. His nose picked up the smell of horses. A stable. He smiled to himself and left the alleyway, then made his way around through the maze of streets to the other side.

Jasmine returned to the stable just after dark. She knew she should have waited longer, but her fever was becoming worse and she feared that she wouldn't make it if she waited.

Fortunately, the building was devoid of people. In the darkness, she began to search for a place to sleep and finally found a spot behind some bales of hay. Her teeth were chattering and her body felt as though it had been set ablaze. For the first time, she feared that she might die. Instead, she fell asleep almost immediately.

She awoke to darkness, the sound of horses whickering, and men's voices. The dim light of a torch reached her. She pulled herself into a crouch, prepared to run if she was discovered. Her body was still on fire, and her chest ached badly.

She was still clutching the shawl around her, and when her nose became ticklish from the hay she was slow to realize what was going to happen. She tried to muffle the sneeze—but she was too late.

A man's voice responded in surprise. "Someone's here! Over there!"

She was trapped. She realized it too late. The men were between her and the door, and as she listened to them searching for her, she also realized that they were drunk. A moment later, they found her.

"Lookit this," one man said, his face thin behind the light of the torch.

Two other faces appeared beside him as Jasmine got to her feet and discovered to her horror that she could barely stand.

"Aye, drunk she is—and ready fer some fun," one of the others said.

She knew there would be no reasoning with them. She'd encountered their like before, and only her fleetness had saved her. Now she was trapped in a corner and barely able to stand, let alone run.

One of the men began to advance, making lewd

remarks about her body. Jasmine wondered if they would kill her when they were finished; such things happened. The mad giant's face swam into her fevered brain, and she found herself wishing that she'd gone with him. He couldn't be worse than these drunken farmers who smelled of manure and liquor.

A man grabbed her and she tried to wrench free. He wasn't much taller than she was—and for a moment she thought she might succeed because he was slow and clumsy in his inebriated state. She had just pulled free of him when the second man lunged at her.

Jasmine twisted and struggled and heard the fabric of her dress tear. She screamed, even though she was sure it was useless.

"Let her go!"

The deep voice was calm and familiar. Her first attacker turned, though the second man retained his bruising grip on her. The third man, who still held the torch, turned toward the voice as well.

All three men froze as the mad giant stepped into the torch's light. Jasmine thought that he looked truly mad now as the light flickered over the pale scar that stood out against his darker skin.

"We found 'er first," the man with the torch stated, trying for bravado, but not quite succeeding.

"Let her go!" Quinn repeated, his voice no louder than before.

Jasmine saw the men exchange glances. Then her first attacker lunged at Quinn, followed quickly by the one who held the torch, who was tossed into a watering trough.

In the darkness, Jasmine could barely see what was happening. There were blows and grunts and groans. The man who held her arm released her and joined the fray. She couldn't move because she was still trapped in the corner.

Suddenly all was silence, except for a low moan and some heavy breathing. The mad giant materialized beside her and took her arm, his fingers closing around bare flesh. The sleeve and part of the bodice had been ripped away.

"Where's your shawl?" he asked, then bent down, having apparently noticed it near her feet.

He put it around her shoulders, bundled her other things into her arms, and began to lead her from the stable. She stumbled because her legs weren't working very well.

"Come on! Whatever you think I am, I can't be as bad as them. And if we don't get out of here now, I'm going to be tempted to kill them."

Then he stopped trying to urge her on and instead put a hand on her brow. "Fever," he said, then cursed. "I should have guessed. You looked sickly before."

The words had barely left his mouth before he had picked her up. She made a sound of protest, which he ignored as he carried her out of the stable.

Jasmine had no idea where they were going as the mad giant carried her along deserted streets and through alleyways. Despite his burden, he moved in long, easy strides. Not so surprising, her fevered brain told her. After all, he'd just dispatched three men.

She could barely keep her eyes open, but even so she saw the sign for the inn. He carried her inside, where an old man dozed behind a high desk.

"The lady needs a room," Quinn said. "The one next to mine is empty."

The man stared at her disapprovingly, but before he could speak, Quinn had managed to extract some coins from his pocket. "For the room—and for you."

A few minutes later, Jasmine was lowered onto the softest, most wonderful bed she'd ever known.

It felt like a cloud. She barely heard the old man's response when Quinn asked about a doctor.

Then the man was gone and Quinn was pulling off her shoes, muttering to himself about her foolishness. She started to protest, then thought better of it.

She had nearly dozed off when she felt herself being lifted into a sitting position. A mug was pushed against her lips.

"It's water. Drink it. You need it, with that fever. The doctor will be here soon."

She drank, then repeated dumbly, "A doctor?" She knew they existed. One had come several times to the manor when her mistress had been feeling poorly. But they treated only rich people. She drank some more, wondering how it was that a madman could be rich.

Then he took away the mug and she fell back into the cloud. As she drifted somewhere between wakefulness and sleep, she could hear Quinn pacing restlessly around the room.

The doctor arrived and seemed about to leave after one look at her. But Jasmine saw Quinn produce some more gold, and then the doctor laid a hand on her brow and asked her questions she could barely answer. She began to drift again as the two men talked about her.

Jasmine awoke to sunlight peeking around the edges of lace curtains and her body clammy with sweat. A fragrant compress covered her chest. She was both hungry and thirsty, but as she tried to struggle up in the bed, a strange woman suddenly appeared.

"Now, dearie, you need to rest. I'll get ye some water—and a bite to eat if yer up t'it."

Jasmine smiled. She hadn't felt so pampered since she'd been very sick once as a child. But this was even better, because of the cloud-bed. She thought she might never want to leave it.

She drank some water, and then drank a mug of thick, rich broth. The rest of the day drifted by as she slept and then awoke to find the kindly woman fussing over her again. Once, she thought she heard the voice of the mad giant, but it could have been a dream.

Time had lost its meaning for Jasmine. It might have been the next day, or perhaps the one after that, when the woman suggested a bath. By this time she was nearly clearheaded, and the pain in her chest was almost gone. The fever seemed to have vanished as well.

She luxuriated in the fragrant bath, recalling all the times when she'd drawn a bath for the mistress and wished that she could have such a wondrous thing herself. She stayed until the water grew cool and the woman insisted that she get out. Then, when she was wrapped in thick towels, the woman gestured to the cupboard in one corner.

" 'E brought you some clothes, dearie. Put them on while I see to some food for ye. Or d'ye need help?"

Jasmine shook her head. She still felt a bit weak, but much better than she'd felt for days. And the mention of food appealed to her.

After the woman had gone, she opened the cupboard to find it full of clothing. Several fine cotton shifts were folded in the bottom, along with stockings and a new pair of shoes. And there were three dresses: wonderful, soft dresses in pretty colors, two of them with lace trim. She fingered them dazedly, unable to believe they could all be hers.

By the time the woman returned, bearing a heavily laden tray, Jasmine had dressed in the prettiest of the gowns, of a soft green that nearly matched her eyes.

"Ah, that looks lovely on ye, dearie. 'E will be pleased."

Jasmine frowned. Somehow she'd managed to keep the mad giant out of her mind, or at least consigned to its deeper recesses.

"Where is he?" she asked nervously.

"Out, I 'spect. He stopped by to ask about ye earlier. A fine man he is, too. Very much a gentleman."

Jasmine said nothing, instead turning to the dinner that the woman set up for her. A gentleman? Didn't this woman know that he was mad?

"D've think ye'll be all right now, dearie? I'd like t'get on home to my little ones now, but I'll stay on if ye need me."

Jasmine left off her thoughts about the man Quinn and smiled at the woman. "I'll be fine. Thank you for all you've done."

The woman wished her well and left. Jasmine attacked her dinner, even forgetting her manners in her sudden surge of hunger. The only times in her life when she'd had such a meal had been those rare times when the mistress was away and Cook was generous.

She had just finished off the fruit tart when there was a soft knock at her door. Without thinking, she called out for whoever it was to come in.

He opened the door and stopped in the doorway, frowning at her. Then, without saying a word, he stepped in. He turned as though to close the door behind him, then left it open and peered closely at her.

"Are you feeling better?" he inquired politely.

"Yes," she replied, then added, "thank you."

"It's a wonder you didn't manage to kill yourself before I took you in hand," he said, still frowning at her.

She said nothing, then gasped when he withdrew from his pocket something very familiar: her pendant. She'd forgotten all about it, and now realized that her old clothes were gone.

72

"I found this in your pocket as I was throwing out those rags you were wearing." He handed it to her. "Where did you get it?"

"I didn't steal it," she said defensively, assuming that was what he was implying. "I found it only a short time ago."

"Where?"

"It was sewn into the border of my mother's shawl. But she never told me about it. The shawl had belonged to my grandmother, but my mother must have known it was there."

He merely nodded, and she couldn't begin to guess whether he believed her. She put the necklace into her pocket.

"If you're feeling up to it, I thought some air might do you good. I've hired a carriage."

And so, a short time later, she found herself reclining in a comfortable leather seat, being driven slowly through the streets toward the dock, with the mad giant seated across from her, trying his best to keep his long legs out of her way.

He cocked his head to one side and stared at her consideringly. "You know, you just might be pretty once you get some meat on your bones."

The remark was matter-of-fact and not at all suggestive, but Jasmine didn't know what to say. Instead, she asked him where he came from.

"Over there—Estavia," he replied, gesturing toward the sea.

"I've never heard of it," she replied, wondering if that were true. Who knew with a madman?

"Have you ever heard of the Latawi and the Dartuli?" he asked, watching her closely.

She frowned. The names had a vaguely familiar sound to them. "I'm not sure."

"Where do you come from?"

"I was born on a farm not too far from here." Then she told him about the war and her family's

73

deaths and how she and her mother had been brought to the estate.

"And no one told you where you came from before that—where your people came from?"

She shook her head, but she was thinking for the first time in days about her grandmother's stories, about the beautiful valley and the tall, snow-capped mountains.

"Do you speak any language other than Borneash?"

She nodded. "The language my mother and grandmother taught me, but I don't know what it's called. They never gave it a name."

Then, to her utter amazement, he began speaking in that language, asking her if she understood him.

Chapter Four

Jasmine was struggling to make some sense of all this. The only thing she continued to be certain of was that this man who walked beside her was mad. She felt rather close to madness herself at the moment.

He had directed the carriage driver to stop at the edge of a large park, a pretty place Jasmine had seen before, but had avoided because the people who strolled there were so well dressed, and it was clear that the place wasn't intended for the likes of her.

She still felt uncomfortable and wished that they'd stayed in the carriage. People were staring at them. She cast a sidelong glance at Quinn. He was dressed as well as most of the men, if a bit less formally. Her dress was perhaps not quite as stylish as those worn by other women, but it was of undeniably good quality. She supposed that the stares they were receiving were the result of their being strangers to this place, and of his great size as well.

He found a bench beneath a tree and they sat down. If he'd even noticed the stares, he was certainly paying them no heed, which, to her mind, was simply another indication of his madness.

"How can you know this language?" she asked him again, since her initial question had drawn no response.

"Because we come from the same place, Jasmine. Do you know the source of your name?"

"My mother told me Jasmine is a kind of flower, but I've never seen one."

"I have. They're very pretty and have a wonderful scent. My mother grew them in our garden."

She wasn't interested in flowers at the moment. "Where is this place you say that we come from?"

He leaned forward, resting his elbows on his knees as he stared at the sea beyond a low wall. "That's the problem. I don't know exactly where it is—but we're going to find it."

Jasmine tried to edge away from him, but there was very little space. "If you don't know where it is, how can we find it?" she asked, deciding it would be best to humor him for now.

"I bought a map. There's an empty space on it—a big area northwest of here that has never been explored, according to the mapmaker. It could be there."

In spite of her fear, Jasmine felt a certain sympathy for this mad giant. If what he'd said about his home was true, he'd come a very long way in pursuit of his dream.

"How will you know it if you do find it?" she asked while she tried to think how she was going to get away from him—not to mention what she'd do after that. It would be hard to give up a soft bed and good food.

"I'll know. I grew up hearing descriptions of it all the time."

Jasmine glanced at him, then looked away

quickly. She was thinking about the place her grandmother had described. "Wh-what is it like?" she asked, holding her breath to await his response.

"A beautiful valley with wooded glens and fields of flowers. And it's surrounded by tall mountains with snow at their tops."

He had turned to her as he described the place, and this time Jasmine didn't look away. Instead, she simply stared at him in openmouthed amazement.

"You've heard about it, too, haven't you?" he asked triumphantly.

"Yes . . . no. I mean, my grandmother described such a place, but my parents said it was only a tale—a place from a dream."

"It's real, Jasmine—and we're going to find it."

"How do you know it's real?" she asked, trying to regain her senses with considerable difficulty. Of course it wasn't real.

"Because my parents admitted that it was—after my grandfather told me on his deathbed. The story was handed down in the family."

"But that doesn't make it real, Quinn," she said. "All sorts of tales are handed down like that."

"This one is real."

Jasmine lapsed into silence. There was no point in arguing with him. He clearly believed it. Arguing might make him become violent. She thought about the three men he'd left unconscious at the stable.

"Two tribes shared the valley," he went on. "The Dartuli—who are my people, and the Latawi—your people. They fought for a time, then made their peace with each other. And then, about two hundred years ago, I think, they were driven out of the valley."

"Who drove them out?"

"That's not important. What's important is that we're going back there to reclaim it."

Quinn had decided that he was going to tell her only what was necessary at this point. He didn't want to frighten her, and he didn't believe the nonsense about demons and magic anyway. Or so he told himself, though if he didn't believe it, he was hard-pressed to explain why he was trying to persuade her to go with him, instead of searching alone. But something had told him that he'd never find it without her.

He slanted a glance at her as she stared out to sea. What did she think of him? Her carefulness suggested that she thought he was mad. Or maybe she just feared his size and still distrusted his motives for helping her. He decided to clear the air about that, at least.

"I'm not going to force myself on you, Jasmine. You have my word on it."

She glanced at him, then looked quickly away, but not before he saw the faint flush creep through her pale skin.

"Look at it this way," he said, determined to press his case. "You have no home and no job and no money. I can afford to provide for us both. If you come with me and we don't find the valley, I will give you enough gold when we return to keep you comfortable until you can get yourself situated."

"Where did you get this gold, Quinn?" she asked without looking at him.

"I earned it, girl—working hard for fifteen years, mostly in a quarry."

"And you would spend it all to try to find this valley?" she asked doubtfully.

He nodded. "And I'm not mad, either, though I know that's what you're thinking."

Then she asked the question he least wanted to

answer. "Why do you want me to accompany you?"

"Well, it isn't *you* necessarily. But I was hoping to find a Latawi. It seemed right to me, since we both lived in the valley."

He watched her to see if she accepted his words. Seeing her in profile, Quinn was struck again by the possibility of beauty beneath that gaunt face. She pursed her full lips, and her smooth brow furrowed. He guessed that she didn't believe him, but was afraid to say so.

"How long will this take?" she asked.

"Uh, I don't know. What does it matter? You have nowhere else to go."

"Well, it seems to me that you should have some notion of how long this will take. Otherwise you might run out of gold."

Quinn thought she had beautiful eyes, too: light green, the shade of tender new shoots in the spring. "Don't worry about that. I have enough for both of us."

"But I have to worry about that, don't I?" she sisted. "If we run out of gold in some distant place—"

"It would be no worse for you than it is right now," he cut in. "Better, actually, since I can always find work."

"I must think about this, Quinn."

"Fine. We can't leave until you've regained your strength, in any event."

He smiled to himself. Now all he had to do was prove to her that he was trustworthy and not some raving lunatic.

Jasmine lay on her cloud-bed thinking about what she should do. The mad giant's story had unsettled her far more than she'd let him see. How was it that he shared her dream—or rather, that he'd actually dared to dream and then pursue that dream—while she had scarcely even let herself think about her grandmother's tales?

He dared because he was insane; that was the obvious answer. And yet that answer didn't satisfy her. If what he'd told her was true—and she had no way of knowing if it was—he'd worked hard for fifteen years to be able to chase this dream.

She would never have done that. Her feet were planted too firmly on the ground to have engaged in such foolishness—and yet she couldn't help admiring what he'd done. In fact, she admired it all the more because of who and what he was: a rough-hewn laborer not so different from her old neighbor's sons and other men she'd known who worked hard and then spent their earnings on drink and games.

On the other hand, she had only his word for it. For all she knew, he might have stolen the wealth. In fact, that could account for his flight from his native land. Of what value, after all, was the word of a madman?

She conjured up an image of his harsh face. Try as she might, she could not fault his behavior toward her thus far. He'd been unfailingly kind and generous. Furthermore, not once had she seen that gleam in his eye that signaled a desire to take advantage of her.

But Jasmine's experience with men did not give her cause for optimism. Men were by nature predators—and women were their chief prey. Unattractive women like herself were supposed to be grateful for their attentions. One of her old neighbor's sons had said as much to her one evening, when she'd come upon him as she was returning from the manor. And the three men in the stable had likely felt similarly as well.

Then she recalled his offhand remark that she might be pretty if she had some "meat on her bones."

What should she do? What *could* she do? If she ran away, he would probably find her again. And she would be back to the same desperate situation. She liked the soft bed and the wonderful feeling of not being hungry.

But if she went with him, she was trusting her very life to a crazy man.

She had a few days, she thought. He'd said that she needed to regain her strength before they could leave. Maybe some alternative would present itself to her.

She drifted off to sleep—this time to pleasant dreams about the valley—a paradise he said was real.

"Do you feel well enough to leave tomorrow?" Quinn asked as they dined at the tavern two evenings later.

His sudden question caught Jasmine by surprise. She'd thought—foolishly, she now realized—that she would have more time. But it must be as obvious to him as it was to her that she was herself again—better than herself, actually, since good food and a soft bed had left her more comfortable than she'd ever been.

Finally, knowing that he was waiting for an answer, she nodded. There seemed to be no choice, other than to flee and hope that she could stay away from him long enough that he would go on without her. During the past two days, she'd managed to get away from him long enough to seek work at various inns and taverns, and even a few of the grand houses belonging to merchants. But even though she looked far more presentable now, no one wanted to hire her. Maybe, she thought ironically, she now looked too presentable.

The woman who had huddled in an alleyway and made do with a piece of fruit for an entire day had been relegated to the past. Jasmine simply could not imagine living that life again.

Quinn's rugged face broke into a wide smile, and he briefly laid his hand over hers, withdrawing it quickly when she started in surprise. But her hand tingled from his touch.

"You won't regret it, Jasmine. I promise you that."

Once again she nodded mutely. She was still convinced that some madness lay buried in him, but she'd seen no evidence of it. He'd been the perfect gentleman. Last night he'd asked her to play her lute for him, and she'd done so—playing for an hour or more in his room, which was larger than hers. He'd kept the door open the entire time.

And yet she could not quite shake the feeling that he was holding something back from her, and that it most likely had something to do with his real reason for wanting her to accompany him. She didn't for one minute believe the story he'd told her.

It was a fine evening, and he suggested they stroll down to the harbor. They walked along the streets, where Jasmine now ignored the stares of passersby. She'd decided that it was Quinn's great size that drew attention to them, and nothing more.

By the time they reached the park, Jasmine had decided to confront him about his lie. In his response, she could surely see whether he was mad—a fact about which she had begun to have some doubts.

"Before we leave, I want to know the truth, Quinn," she told him, raising her face to stare directly into his gray eyes. "I know you've lied to me about why you want me to accompany you."

To her surprise, he actually looked chagrined—definitely a strange expression on such a face and such a man.

"Uh, well, I didn't exactly lie. I just didn't tell you *all* of it."

"Tell me now."

"It has to do with the reason our people were driven from the valley. According to the tales my parents and grandparents told, we were driven from the valley by demons."

"Demons?" she repeated in disbelief.

"Well, I don't believe it, either—but that's what I was told. The demons were supposed to have been there from the beginning, but our people used magic to hold them off. Then something went wrong."

Madness, she thought. *There it is.* An old woman who'd lived for a time in one of the cottages near hers had mumbled about demons and magic all the time. Some said she was a witch, but most just thought she was crazy.

"What does that have to do with your wanting me to accompany you?" she asked, once again humoring him while her mind raced with thoughts of how she could get out of this—away from him.

"Well, the story goes that our people could make magic and drive away the demons only by working together. So I decided to try to find a Latawi."

"But you just said that you didn't believe that nonsense," she pointed out.

"I don't," he said stubbornly.

"Quinn, listen to yourself! You're not making sense!" Jasmine knew she was taking a risk. At any moment he might turn on her. But there were people around, and surely they would help her if it was obvious that he'd become violent. Then she would be free of him because he'd be locked up.

But he didn't become violent. Instead he turned away from her and stared out at the sea. "That's why I didn't tell you about it. I figured you already thought I was mad, so I shouldn't say anything that would make you sure of it."

"But you *do* believe it, don't you?" she asked in a gentler tone.

"I don't know—and that's the truth."

His uncertainty touched something deep inside her, coming as it did from a man who seemed so very sure of himself in all ways.

"Quinn, even if it were true—and it isn't—how are we supposed to make magic? Do you know how? Because I don't."

He shook his head. "All I know is that my parents knew I intended to try to find the valley someday, and they made me promise not to go there unless I'd first found a Latawi woman."

"Why not a man?" she asked curiously.

"Because they said it had to be a man and woman together to make magic." He turned and peered at her. "You do believe that I'm mad, don't you?"

"I'm not sure," she replied, which happened to be the truth. What he said was crazy, but she still wasn't sure about him. And then he seemed to reach right into her thoughts.

"Maybe I'm wrong in what I believe—but I'm not mad. Maybe there is no valley, let alone demons and magic—but I've got to find out."

Jasmine nodded. "All right. We'll try to find this place."

"But you wouldn't go if you had a choice, would you?"

"No, I wouldn't," she replied honestly. "I don't believe in dreams any more than I believe in demons and magic."

"Why didn't you tell me this before?" Quinn asked in exasperation.

"I just didn't think about it, that's all."

"You didn't think about it because you never intended to come with me."

That was true, so she said nothing. They were

on their way back to the stables, and she'd just told him that she didn't know how to ride. She had vague memories of being on a pony as a very small child, held securely in her father's arms. But she hadn't been on one since.

"It isn't difficult," he said. "We won't be riding fast."

"Maybe we should just wait for a few more days—until I can learn."

"Or until you can change your mind about coming along. We'll ride slowly and you'll get used to it."

They entered the stables and Jasmine froze. Because they'd come the back way from the inn, she hadn't realized that it was the same stable where the drunken men had attacked her. A chill swept through her as she stared at the corner where she'd hidden behind bales of hay. Quinn was speaking to the owner, but she didn't hear their words. Instead she was hearing those men and reliving her terror.

"Jasmine," he said, coming toward her, his voice low. "You're safe now."

She shook off the memories as he took her arm carefully and led her over to the stalls. "Come see this mare."

"She's a good 'un," the man said in the overloud voice of one hoping to make a sale. "Sturdy as they come, but gentle. A good horse for a lady."

Jasmine looked at him to see if he was jesting. No one had ever called her a lady before. But he seemed to be serious. She turned her attention to the dappled mare in the stall. The animal had a wonderfully gentle face.

"Well," Quinn asked, "what do you think?"

"She'll be fine," Jasmine stated, hoping that would prove to be true.

Quinn moved off with the man to look at pack-horses, and Jasmine stood there, absently stroking

the mare's sleek neck as she stared at the corner.
If Quinn hadn't come along . . .

I owe him a lot, she thought, *perhaps my very life.
And he's asked nothing more than that I accompany
him on a quest to find his dream.*

She still thought of it as being Quinn's dream,
not her own. A part of her wanted very badly to
embrace that dream, but she couldn't let herself.
Long years of drudgery and hopelessness had
chased all of her own hopes away. She envied
Quinn. He too had worked long and hard, but he'd
held on to his dream.

Quinn returned and everything was settled.
They would go back to the inn and find someone
to help them get their things to the stable. He was
in high spirits, and his accent was much thicker.
They'd fallen into the habit of speaking in their
shared language when they were alone, but using
the Borneash tongue in the presence of others.

The stable owner promised to have the horses
ready when they returned, and they left, once
more making their way through the alleys to the
inn. When they reached it, Quinn found a young
boy to carry her belongings, which had multiplied
considerably in the past few days. Now, in addition to three dresses, she also owned two of the
split skirts for riding that fashionable women were
wearing. She also had a wonderful pair of boots,
as well as a warm jacket Quinn had insisted on
buying in the event they had to cross the snowcapped mountains.

Barely a half hour later they were riding out of
town, and Jasmine was already gaining confidence. The mare was as gentle as promised, re-
sponding immediately to her slightest command.
Quinn rode a very tall chestnut stallion with a
white blaze on its face. The animal clearly wanted
to run. But Quinn kept it under control easily,
while also keeping an eye on her and on the pack-

horse that trailed along behind them. Jasmine thought that the stallion mirrored its new owner's eagerness for this adventure.

Their journey would take them past her mistress's estate, and the closer they came to it, the more nervous Jasmine felt. She didn't really believe that anyone there would stop her, but she feared the feelings that would resurface after seeing the place that had been her home for most of her life.

"Would you like to visit your mother's grave?" Quinn asked suddenly, startling her. He'd been silent, and the question came just as she was thinking about her mother and how she'd had to bury her on an estate they had both hated.

She hesitated, torn between wanting to visit her mother's grave and her fear of setting foot on the estate. Once again, it seemed that Quinn had guessed her thoughts.

"Is there a way to reach her grave without going near the manor?"

She thought about it and nodded slowly. There was a road that led from the mines at the far edge of the estate to the main road on which they were traveling. They might encounter the carts coming from the mines, but that was all. She explained it to him.

They reached the road to the mines just as four heavily laden wagons of coal were turning onto the main road, heading toward town. They slowed down to wait, then turned onto the deeply rutted road as soon as the coal wagons had passed. The drivers cast curious looks their way, but said nothing. Jasmine didn't recognize any of them.

Coming from this direction, it took her a while to find the spot in the thick woods. They had to dismount and lead their animals through the forest, but Quinn didn't object. It wasn't until she stood before her mother's grave, where the flowers she'd placed had wilted and faded, that Jasmine thought about his kindness in making this detour when he was so eager to get on with their journey.

She began to recite her prayer softly, then faltered when Quinn's deep voice joined hers. It was a strange moment for Jasmine—the first time she'd consciously acknowledged that they shared something, even though they spoke regularly in their own language.

Tears sprang to her eyes as she wondered what her mother would think of this journey—and of this man. It struck her painfully that she couldn't answer her own question. Her mother had been a highly practical woman, concerned only with doing her best for her only child. If she'd had future hopes, she hadn't shared them.

And yet she'd kept that golden pendant. Jasmine reached into her pocket and withdrew it, staring down at it through her tears, barely aware of the big, silent man at her side.

Somehow, she thought, the necklace must have represented a dream to her mother. Otherwise, she would have long since sold it to improve their lives. But she'd never shared that dream—whatever it was—with her daughter.

Finally remembering Quinn was with her, she looked up at him to see him staring at the pendant, too.

"I've been thinking about that," he said, indicating the charm. "And I think maybe I understand it."

"What do you mean?" she asked. What was there to understand about a piece of jewelry?

"I think it's meant to represent our two tribes: the diamond for the Latawi, because it's full of light, and the onyx for the Dartuli, because it's dark."

The moment he spoke the words, she knew they must be true. It was almost as though she'd heard that explanation before, though she could not re-call having seen the pendant before she found it hidden in the hem of her grandmother's shawl.

"Onyx?" she asked. She'd not known what the black stone was called and yet now the word sounded familiar.

Quinn nodded. "I've seen it a few times. Why do you hide it in your pocket?"

"I've been afraid that someone would steal it," she replied, but even as she spoke, she realized that wasn't the only reason. Wearing it seemed to be some sort of acknowledgment of her past—of *their* past.

"You needn't worry about that. Wear it if it pleases you."

She compromised, slipping it around her neck, but hiding it beneath her shirt. It felt strangely warm against her skin, even though it was cool there in the forest. Long before they emerged once more into the sunlight, that warmth had spread pleasantly through her. But she said nothing of it to Quinn, for surely it was only her imagination.

They rode on beneath bright blue skies, passing fields where summer crops were ripening rapidly. She found herself, quite without conscious intent, asking Quinn about the magic their people were supposed to have wielded.

"According to the stories, they used magic as part of their lives, and not just to battle demons. They could control the weather in the valley, so the crops grew well. They could soothe a crying baby or a frightened child. And, along with herbs, they used their power to heal sickness."

She slanted him a glance. There was something new in his voice. "You do believe it, don't you—in spite of what you said before?"

He considered her for a moment. "As a child, I believed it, and that child is still within me. But the man I am doesn't believe any of it—except, perhaps, that the valley exists."

"But if the valley exists and it's as wonderful as that, then why did we leave?"

"I think our ancestors were driven out, though probably not by demons." He hesitated. "It's that truth that I seek to discover, as much as the valley itself."

"If you're right, then we aren't likely to be welcomed back," she pointed out.

He nodded. "But it all happened long ago, and those who drove us out are likely all dead. Unless some others have found their way back, anyone living there now isn't likely to recognize us."

They talked more about what might have happened to their people when they left the valley. Quinn thought that it was likely that most of their tribes had been killed in the battles against the "demons."

"Then why didn't those who survived stay together?" she asked. That certainly was what she would have done.

"I don't know. That question has always troubled me, too."

"What reason did your parents and grandparents give?"

"They said that the demons were responsible for scattering us, so that we could never retake the valley."

In spite of the sun's warmth, Jasmine shuddered, then was shocked to realize that she wasn't able to dismiss the idea of demons quite so easily anymore.

They stopped in midafternoon to rest the horses and themselves, choosing a pleasant place where a small stream ran close to the road. Jasmine dismounted—and winced with pain. Quinn, watching her, chuckled.

"It will get better," he promised.

She tested her aching muscles gingerly. "How can just sitting on a horse do this? I've worked much harder without pain."

"I think it's *not* working that causes the pain," he pronounced as he searched through their food supply, then produced some bread and fruit.

They settled themselves beneath the trees lining the stream and ate in silence. Jasmine studied Quinn covertly. Somewhere, somehow, she'd stopped thinking of him as a madman. She had even begun to feel a certain closeness to him, and for her that was a new feeling. She'd worked with mostly the same people for many years, and yet she'd never felt more than a vague sense of familiarity toward any of them.

It was different with Quinn, she realized. She'd never much cared what the others had thought—about her or about anything. But now she found herself growing ever more curious about Quinn.

She had noticed before how fastidious he was in his eating, and in other things as well. From what he'd told her, he'd spent his life working as a laborer, and in her experience such men were crude in their habits. Those who, like her, worked inside the homes of the wealthy often picked up better habits, but she found it curious that he displayed these manners as well.

He must have learned such things from his family, she thought, recalling all the times that her mother had insisted she comport herself with a dignity befitting a lady of the manor, even though they lived in a cottage that was little more than a hovel.

That thought made her feel even closer to Quinn, and when he glanced her way, she smiled at him. A smile spread across his face as well.

"I thought never to see you smile," he murmured. Then, as though fearing that he'd become too personal, he began to talk about their journey, unfolding his big map and indicating the village where he hoped they could find shelter for the night.

"But we might have to spend some nights in the open," he warned her. "Especially later on. The farther we go, the fewer people there will be."

"That won't bother me," she told him with another smile. "I've done that before."

He chuckled again. It was a sound she was beginning to like very much. "So you have. But now you'll be safe."

Jasmine nodded. She knew she was safe with Quinn. How was it that she'd gone from fearing this madman to trusting him in such a short time?

They reached the village shown on the map just before dusk. Quinn had begun to express doubts regarding the accuracy of the map, but when they reached the top of a small hill, the village lay in the valley beyond, seemingly ablaze in the last rays of the setting sun.

They rode into the village square, where Quinn dismounted and approached a group of old men who were gathered around the well. Jasmine watched as they regarded him somewhat fearfully. Soon, though, they began to speak animatedly, no doubt vastly relieved that this giant was no one to fear, after all.

At length, he returned to her. "There is a widow who has a room available in her house. I've made arrangements for you to stay there, and I'll sleep in the stable."

Jasmine shook her head. She had just begun to realize that she was far from anyone she knew. She hadn't encountered any hostile glares, but she felt unaccountably afraid of being separated from Quinn.

"I'll stay in the stable, too."

"It would be an insult to turn down the widow's

hospitality now," Quinn told her. "No doubt she depends upon travelers to earn her living."

She knew he was right, so she agreed, though very reluctantly. She could hardly tell him that she was afraid to be separated from him when she didn't understand the feeling herself.

The widow, a kindly woman, provided dinner for them, and then Quinn departed for the stable after telling her that he wanted to set out at dawn. Jasmine stood in the doorway of the widow's little house and watched him until he had vanished into the darkness. Then she went off to bed, where sleep overtook her quickly.

She was in the valley—the place from her grandmother's tales. Never had it seemed so vivid, so real, even though in the way of some dreams, she knew that it wasn't.

It was all as she'd pictured it: meandering little streams that sparkled in the sunlight, then darkened as they flowed between banks thick with fragrant firs and blanketed by moss. She seemed to be floating along, following the stream through woods that were so ancient it was impossible to imagine their origins. Trees taller than seemed possible towered over her. Around their mighty trunks, thick vines grew, dotted here and there with clusters of flowers of a shade of pink so pale as to be nearly white. As she passed near them, she caught their faint scent, reminiscent of the roses that bloomed in the old manor gardens.

Birds called out high in the trees, and when she squinted up into the branches, she caught sight of them as they darted about in a private world high above her head.

Then the birdsong was submerged beneath a low rumble that grew steadily louder as she floated through the forest. Finally she saw the source of the sound: a huge waterfall thundering down over dark, glistening rocks to a rock-lined pool she knew instinctively must be very deep.

Abruptly the scene shifted and she was floating through a huge meadow, where tall flowers of purple and yellow nodded gaily in the breeze, filling the sunlit air with mingled scents: a sharp, tangy aroma overlaying something darker, earthier.

The wild meadow gave way to green pastures with grass darker and thicker than any she'd ever seen. Herds of cattle and sheep grazed there, along with a smaller herd of goats. Off in the distance, she could see something white—horses, she thought, but she couldn't be sure.

There was something else in the distance as well: a village. No sooner did she see it than she was there, drifting among rows of neat cottages, stone with thatched roofs and brightly painted front doors and window boxes filled with a profusion of flowers. As she moved through the streets, she could see that the buildings were arranged concentrically, with the innermost circle of houses enclosing a large park where flowering trees unlike any she'd ever seen sheltered stone benches.

But there were no people. She knew that instinctively as well, even though she didn't stop to peer into the windows. The silence that hung over the scene told her that no one had been there for a very long time, and she felt a sadness so deep that it seemed to come from her very soul.

And yet she thought she could hear voices—soft whispers that seemed to surround her as she glided along. There was laughter, too, and the high-pitched shrieks of children at play.

Suddenly the light began to fade. She looked up at the sky, expecting to find clouds, but discovered instead that the sun, which had been overhead only moments ago, was gone, leaving only a faint trail of light. Time had sped up, and night was approaching.

The Magic of Two

Fear clutched at her with hard, cold fingers scrabbling along her spine. The light faded still more and it was dusk. Shadows lengthened and she shivered as a cold wind began to blow through the village.

They are coming. The words welled up from deep within her, accompanied by an even deeper chill. She stared into the shadows that grew ever darker—and then she thought she saw something move within their depths. Suddenly a strange ululating cry pierced the silence.

Demons!

*   *   *

Jasmine was jolted awake in the small, hard bed, disoriented. Quinn's name formed on her lips, but she stopped it as she realized where she was. In the next room she could hear the widow snoring.

She sat up, then quietly got out of bed and pushed aside the rough curtain, needing to prove to herself that nothing lurked in the shadows out there. The moon was bright and all was still, except for the distant barking of a dog.

The breeze that came in the window was warm, but Jasmine still felt chilled—except for a warm spot between her breasts. She reached up to touch the pendant, and once again found it to be unnaturally warm, almost hot.

She lifted it and stared at it in the moonlight. The tiny diamond winked brightly, contrasting with the flat black of the onyx. And even as she held it, she could feel it grow cooler.

Jasmine wandered back to bed, her sleepy brain still filled with images of the beautiful valley—and of the things that moved in the darkness.

Chapter Five

"I'm afraid we'll have to spend another night in the open."

"Why didn't you tell me that before?" Jasmine asked with an edge in her voice. Every muscle in her body ached, and the thought of spending a second night sleeping on hard ground definitely did not appeal to her.

"What difference would it have made?" Quinn asked reasonably. "Anyway, I didn't tell you because I'd hoped we might find a farm where we could at least sleep in the stable."

He turned to her with a gleam of amusement in his gray eyes. "It seems to me that you've turned into a lady very quickly."

"If I were a lady, I wouldn't be here," she snapped.

"Ah. Do I detect a sense of humor?"

In spite of herself, Jasmine grinned. It seemed that it was impossible for her to become angry with Quinn—or at least to stay angry with him. All things considered, he was an excellent traveling companion, always in good spirits and very considerate of her.

The gods help me, she said to herself. *I think I'm actually beginning to like him, even though a few days ago I was certain he was mad.* Or was it only that she was dependent upon him now, and frightened at being farther from home than she'd ever been in her life?

High above them, two large birds circled lazily in the blue sky. Jasmine watched them, thinking how she'd always associated them with freedom. Now she was free herself—except for her dependence upon Quinn, that was. Like everything else, she supposed, freedom had its price.

On the other hand, she could never have come this far on her own. That fact had been made abundantly clear to her on numerous occasions over the past three days on the road. Most of the people they'd encountered were respectable enough, but there'd been a few who would have made her very uneasy if it weren't for Quinn's presence.

Then, as if to prove her point, they came around a tree-lined bend in the road to see four men on horseback approaching. They were exactly the kind who made her uneasy: rough-looking men with darting eyes that missed nothing. Quinn nodded pleasantly at them as they passed, receiving only dull stares in return.

"I don't like the looks of them," she said when they were past.

"Me either," he agreed. "I'd heard that there's been a problem with brigands on this road lately, but they'll likely look for easier targets."

"But there are four of them, Quinn."

He shrugged his wide shoulders. "That makes it close to an even match. More than four and I might need your help."

*   *   *

An hour later they were riding into the setting sun through a thick pine forest, where the shadows were already deep. Quinn had slowed down and was studying the land, seeking a resting place for the night. Finally he brought them to a halt.

"I don't see a campsite," she said, peering into the woods. They'd passed other campsites earlier in the day, places used regularly by travelers through this region.

"There isn't one," he replied. "That's why we'll stay here."

"But we stayed at a campsite last night."

"We're alone now, and I think it's better if we stay here."

She urged her horse forward and they plunged into the forest. But for the first time, she was feeling truly scared. Last night, when they'd camped out, there had been a family at the site, itinerant peddlers with two small children in tow. Now they were entirely alone, and she realized that was likely to be the case every night when they reached the huge empty spot on his map.

Whereas only a short time ago she had been thinking kindly of Quinn, she now felt a twinge of distrust. How well did she really know him, after all? Just because she no longer believed him to be a madman didn't mean that he couldn't have the unpleasant traits she'd seen in most of the men she knew.

Furthermore, she'd already seen evidence of the charm he could turn on and off seemingly at will. Her body reacted as she imagined the coming evening, and she trembled.

The spot Quinn had chosen was down a gentle slope, next to a small stream. Moss grew thickly along the bank and would provide an extra cushion beneath their blankets. It was also well hidden from the road.

The Magic of Two

While Quinn tended to the horses, she sorted through their food supply. When they'd stopped earlier in the day, they'd eaten the roast chickens he'd bought in a village they had passed through. Now, since Quinn had said he didn't want to build a campfire that might attract attention, she fixed a cold meal for them, making certain to prepare enough food. She'd long since discovered that Quinn had the appetite of two normal men.

Overhead, the last of the day's light leaked from the sky, but the stars were bright, and a sliver of moon just above the horizon cast some illumination as well. Quinn returned carrying something—rope, she thought—and said he would return in a few minutes. He vanished into the darkness up the slope toward the road.

By the time he returned, she'd already eaten some cheese and two apples and was devouring a slice of crusty bread, wishing that they'd had some butter. Her appetite knew no bounds these days, it seemed. After a lifetime spent trying to ignore an empty stomach, she now imagined herself to be hungry even when she clearly shouldn't be.

Quinn dropped down beside her and began to eat. "If the map and my reckonings are correct, we should reach Halaban in another three days."

She nodded. Halaban was the last town they would pass through before entering the huge, unexplored region. It seemed strange to her now that they should run out of civilization so quickly, and she told him that.

"It's likely that there *are* some people there," Quinn replied. "The map is old, and the Borneash strike me as being a people lacking in curiosity—much like the Estavians. They spend all their time jealously guarding the territory they've claimed for themselves and have no interest in exploring."

"Yes, you're right. They've fought war after war over their small pieces of land when it seems

99

there's so much out there to be discovered."

"That's exactly what's happened in Estavia as well. I suppose that both peoples are seafaring and have no interest in places far from the water. In the past few years, though, there've been some people who've packed up everything they own and moved off to the eastern lands. Hundreds go at a time, in big caravans. Mostly they're poor farmers looking for a stake they can call their own.

"I nearly joined them a few times," he went on. "I probably would have gone if my parents hadn't been convinced that our homeland lay across the sea."

"Do you really believe that the valley's out there—where we're going, I mean? Couldn't it be in an entirely different direction?"

"It could be, but I don't think so. There were a lot of maps on the ship and some men who'd actually traveled the coast here. Their stories give me hope—and even more, I can almost sense that we're on the right track."

Jasmine found herself hoping he was right, even though she told herself that she truly wanted to return to the only home she knew. She'd be content, she thought, with his gift of gold to buy a small cottage and set up an herb business.

She wondered what would happen if they did find the valley, and then realized with a jolt that she hadn't actually considered that event. It had been Quinn's plan, not hers. It was his dream. He must surely intend to stay there. How would she get back?

They were questions she wanted to ask Quinn, but she remained silent. What could she say?

Quinn began to talk again about the valley. Jasmine barely listened as she struggled with her own thoughts about the future. But then something he said drew her attention.

"White horses? You never mentioned them before."

"I didn't?" He looked surprised. "Perhaps you weren't listening," he said with a meaningful look.

She chose to ignore that and focused instead on his previous words. "Tell me about the horses."

"What is there to tell? Our people bred them in the valley. They were supposed to be beautiful animals, all white, and they could be trained to dance and leap."

Jasmine said nothing, but she was thinking about the dream she'd had. It hadn't recurred, so she hadn't told Quinn about it. But she remembered that she'd seen white horses—or thought she had. She drew her jacket more closely around her, recalling the dream's terrifying finale.

Quinn got up to lead the horses down to the stream for another drink, then tethered them loosely to the trees nearby before returning to spread their blankets on the soft bed of moss. Jasmine's earlier nervousness about their isolation vanished as he settled down and drew a blanket over himself. Within minutes, she was fast asleep.

She awoke to darkness and voices, uncertain at first whether they had come from some unremembered dream or from the darkness around her. Then she heard shouts and grunts—and a scream. Quinn was no longer there, his blanket tossed aside.

She finally realized that the sounds were coming from the slope above her, between them and the road. They were being attacked! She thought immediately about the four men they'd passed earlier. Her hand went to the small knife she carried in her pocket, and she threw aside her own blanket.

As she began to scramble up the bank, she heard more shouts and screams of pain—and as she climbed she made out two dark shapes ahead. Picking out Quinn wasn't difficult, but even as she spotted him, she saw the shadow of a weapon in his hand as it darted forward. There came a terrible gurgling sound from his opponent, and then there was silence.

Four men lay scattered upon the uneven ground, and none of them was moving. Jasmine froze, staring in horror as Quinn came down the slope, still carrying a knife that was dark with blood. When he reached out with his free hand to grasp her arm, she drew away from him, horribly mesmerized by the still bodies.

"Are they dead?" she asked in a thin voice she barely recognized as her own.

"Yes. If they weren't, we would be."

He turned and started back down to their campsite, and after casting one last look at the fallen brigands, she followed. He washed his knife in the stream, then turned to her.

Jasmine stared at him with mounting terror. When he'd beaten the three men in the stable, she'd been so grateful for his intervention that she hadn't given it much thought. Besides, he hadn't killed those men. But this was different.

She knew at some level that what he said was true: the men would have killed them. But that didn't prevent her from being horrified by what he'd done. For the first time, she truly feared that Quinn might not be all that different from the other men she'd known.

She returned to her blanket without saying a word, but she slept little the rest of the night.

In the first pale light of morning, Jasmine rose from her bed on the bank of the stream and crept quietly away from her sleeping companion. From where she climbed, she could see nothing. The bodies of the men had been hidden behind thick berry bushes and the trees that grew on the slope, so she was nearly upon them before she actually saw them.

She quickly stuffed a fist into her mouth to stifle a scream. Jasmine was no stranger to violence; she'd seen drunken men fight on the estate. But those fights had resulted in little more than broken bones and teeth and ugly bruises.

She shivered and her legs trembled. She knew they had put up a fight; she'd heard them. But it was as though their efforts to save themselves hadn't meant anything. Quinn had killed them as easily as if he'd come upon them in their sleep.

She was about to turn away when she noticed something that had escaped her attention before. A long piece of rope snaked its way along the ground near the bodies. The ends had been tied to two trees on either side of the path that led down from the road.

Now she understood what had happened. She'd just assumed that Quinn slept more lightly than she did and had heard them approach. But, he had laid a trap for them. The ground was still soft from recent rain, and the highwaymen must have had a torch that allowed them to see where she and Quinn and the horses had left the road. Likely they would have extinguished the torch when they started down the slope. Either that or they'd simply failed to see the rope where it had been stretched across the path at about knee level.

Jasmine turned away and went back to the campsite, their bloody images still all too clear. Quinn remained asleep, and she stood, staring down at him. She knew that they both owed their lives to his cleverness and his fighting skills. There wasn't a shred of doubt in her mind that the men would have killed them both—she'd seen the glances they'd given her as they'd passed.

Even so, she was appalled at what Quinn had

done—and even more appalled at how easily he'd done it. It reminded her that he was a truly dangerous man. How could the good, decent man she was beginning to see in him be capable of such cold, efficient killing?

There wasn't a mark on him that she could see, even though the robbers had been armed. Still, Quinn slept peacefully, the harshness of his features relaxed, his big chest rising and falling slowly beneath the blanket.

Jasmine turned her back on him and went down to the stream, where she did her best to wash away the dust of the road and wished she could as easily wash away the images that kept tormenting her. She was sitting on the bank of the stream, lost in her chilling thoughts, when suddenly he joined her, lowering himself down on the mossy bank. Startled, she moved away and would not look at him, though she could feel his eyes on her.

"You went back up there, didn't you?"

She nodded without speaking.

"They would have killed us," he said in a low but firm tone.

"I know that."

"I'm not a murderer, Jasmine. I've never killed except in self-defense."

Now she did turn to him. "It seems to me that you're very good at it, Quinn."

"I was in the army. I was part of a small group that often made forays behind enemy lines to scout out their strengths and weaknesses. In such situations, killing quickly is important. If you don't, you'll soon be surrounded and outnumbered."

"Why would you kill for the Estavians?" she demanded. "You said that you hated them."

"I did and I do—but I lived in their country, and their fate was my fate. I was young."

She got up, and Quinn rose to his feet as well.

He started to put out a hand as though to take hers, then dropped it again. "We should be on our way. We can breakfast later."

"But what about them? You can't just . . ."

"What else can I do? I don't have a shovel, and even if I did, it would take too long to bury them all."

"It's wrong, Quinn." She was thinking about her mother and how she would have been tossed into a communal grave.

"I can't make everything in this world right," he stated coldly before turning on his heel and striding back to their camp.

The silences between them that had seemed so comfortable before were now fraught with tension. When they stopped to eat, Jasmine found that she could barely choke down half of what she'd grown accustomed to eating. Several times she almost spoke out to beg to return, even if it meant being homeless and penniless again.

They stopped in a village at midday and Quinn purchased food. A market was in progress, and there were many tasty treats to be had, but when Quinn bought her some sweets, she simply thanked him and put them into her pocket.

When they were back on the road again, he told her that one of the men in the village had said that there was an inn in the next town that should afford them decent accommodations.

"And we can both have a proper bath, followed by a good dinner," he added. When she failed to respond, his tone showed exasperation.

"Are you going to brood for the rest of the journey?"

"I want to go back. I could travel with one of the groups we pass all the time."

"Back to what—living in an alley and starving? I thought you were sensible, girl."

"I am sensible," she replied hotly, glaring at him. "You're the one who isn't."

"Oh? It isn't sensible to kill someone before they kill you? Maybe we have different ideas about being sensible."

"I hate violence, Quinn. It's all I've seen: violent, drunken men. Except for when I was very small, before my father and uncles were killed. They were gentle, good men—and I thought you were like them."

"Are you telling me that they wouldn't have done what I did—that they'd have let you be raped or killed? Didn't they try to protect you when the soldiers came?"

She said nothing. Her memories of that terrible time were mercifully vague, though she was sure he was right.

"What really bothers you isn't that I killed them—it's that I did it easily. I suppose if I had a few wounds, you'd feel better about it."

"That's not true," she replied defensively—but it was.

"Well, if this happens again, don't expect me to get myself cut up just to please you."

Jasmine remained silent as they rode on, but she was thinking about what he'd said. It might very well happen again, as they rode farther and farther into unknown territory. Shouldn't she be grateful for his ability to protect her? She supposed she was, but what she really wanted was to be far away from violence and cruelty, altogether.

What you want, she told herself disgustedly, *is to share his dream of a peaceful valley where we can live in comfort and happiness. But that is a dream—and nothing more.*

They rode into a bustling, prosperous-looking town just as the sun was setting. Neither of them had spoken for several hours, though she'd felt his eyes on her from time to time and she'd stolen quick glances at him as well.

Quinn broke the tense silence to tell her that this was a gold-mining region, which accounted for its prosperity. The gold, he said, was near the surface, unlike the mines in his homeland, and people often found it by sifting through the silt in streams that flowed down from the nearby hills.

"Maybe we need to rest here for a few days," he went on. "And we could try our hand at finding gold."

"Is that permitted?" She couldn't believe that anyone could simply pick up gold.

"According to what I was told, it is legal in certain places. If you're interested, I could find out more."

She nodded quickly, thinking about what it would mean if she actually had some wealth of her own. Then she wouldn't have to continue this journey with him. She could use it to pay for her journey home and then set up her herb business without his help.

Quinn found the inn suggested by the man in the other village, and after paying for separate rooms, he asked the innkeeper about panning for gold. The man chuckled and shook his head.

"It's out there, all right—but it isn't that easy to find. People come here thinking they can just dip their fingers into the streams and come away with gold nuggets. It was true years ago, but there isn't much to be had that way now."

"But there are places anyone can go?" Quinn persisted.

The man nodded. "There are maps for sale over at the Assayer's Office. They show what land is owned by the mining companies and what's there for any other fool who wants to try."

Quinn gave the man a grin. "Well, maybe we'll just turn into fools for a few days, then."

The man laughed. "That's the spirit. I do it myself from time to time. We can always dream, can't we? But be careful. There're always a few bad ones around who go after folks like you if you do find anything."

Then he looked Quinn up and down. "Of course, they'd have to be blind as well as thieving to go after *you*."

As they were led to their rooms, Jasmine tried to quell her disappointment at the man's words. She told herself that was what always happened when you let yourself hope—even a little bit.

By the next morning, after luxuriating in a bath and eating two good meals, Jasmine was ready to apologize to Quinn for her angry outburst. He had probably saved her life—again—and she knew she owed him much. But the words just wouldn't come. Every time she thought about saying something, she kept seeing those bloody, dead men.

They went to the assayer's office and bought a map, then listened to further admonitions about thieves and about the guards who protected the mining company's land. The assayer directed them to a store, where they bought two of the sieve pans that were used to sift through river silt for gold. Finally, Quinn said he had one more stop to make before they set out on their quest.

Jasmine waited on a bench outside while Quinn went into a shop. The day was warm and pleasant and the streets were filled with women bustling through the marketplace. She listened to their various conversations and realized that the farther they went from her home, the more difficulty she was having understanding the people. They spoke Borneash, but their accents made it sound like a foreign tongue.

Suddenly she was filled with a powerful longing to be home again, even though the place she called home had been anything but pleasant. She wondered why Quinn didn't feel that way, since he was much farther from anything familiar.

But she knew. He was living on dreams, and putting his happiness in a foolish fantasy. She shook her head sadly.

When Quinn returned, he was carrying a longbow. She stared at it in dismay.

"I should have bought one earlier," he said, ignoring her expression. "I prefer a knife, but this has its advantages."

What advantages? she thought. *The advantage of being able to kill more easily and from a greater distance?* But she kept her silence, determined not to provoke another argument.

They rode out of town into the low hills, passing other people who were also carrying the sieve pans and maps. Quinn paused at one point and studied the map some more. Then he set them on a course that took them away from the others.

"Why are we going this way?" she asked.

"Because most of the others aren't," he replied. "The ride will take longer and it'll bring us closer to the mining company's land, but it could be worth it. Whoever made these maps seems to be guiding everyone to the other streams. I think we should try the far side of the hill."

Jasmine could see the sense of that. Most people would want to spend their time panning, not riding—and they'd probably stay as far as possible from the company-owned land, where the guards were known to shoot first and ask questions later. She just hoped that Quinn was reading the map correctly—or that the mining company land was marked in some way.

They continued to pass people riding and panning in the stream until they reached the crest of the hill, where the forest grew thick and the path ended. Quinn paused to study the map again and frowned.

"The map is wrong. According to it, there should be a stream down there." He pointed ahead of them.

"Maybe you're reading it wrong," she stated, hoping that didn't mean they were encroaching on company land.

"No. I know how to read it well enough. I think maybe it's deliberately wrong."

They started down the other side of the hill, sometimes getting off and leading the horses through the dense woods. Then Quinn suddenly came to a halt.

"Listen! Do you hear water running?"

She nodded. The sound was faint, but there was definitely a stream around here somewhere. It was impossible to guess where it was, however. The forest was thick and the land was very uneven.

It took them another hour to find it, and most of that time was spent walking through over-growth and tangles of berry bushes that snagged their clothes. But then they saw it: a narrow but swift-running stream wending its way down the hillside.

Quinn squinted up at the sky. "We won't have much time if we want to get back to town before dark. But at least no one else is here."

And probably for good reason, Jasmine thought as they maneuvered themselves and their horses down the steep hill.

Still, when they reached the bank of the stream, she was as eager as he to begin their search. She knew that the chances of finding anything were very slim, but that didn't stop her from hoping.

For the next hour they filled and refilled the pans with mud from the river bottom, then washed it out carefully. There was no glitter of gold to be seen.

The Magic of Two

At one point, Jasmine straightened up from her labors to relieve her aching back. Her gaze fell on Quinn. He was squatting in the stream, his pant legs rolled up and his dark head bent to his task, totally oblivious to her stare.

She owed him so much, and they'd traveled so far together—and yet she still felt ambivalence. Whenever she considered him, she could not help thinking about the dark, violent side of his nature, though what she wanted to think about was his kindness to her.

On the other hand, that kindness sprang from need. He claimed to need her in order to work some magic, but she knew that was nonsense. Still, he believed it even if she didn't, so from his point of view, he needed her.

She was wondering uneasily what would happen if he came to his senses and realized that he didn't need her at all. And just at that moment, he turned her way.

Jasmine suppressed a shudder. In that half-second before he smiled at her, she saw again the man who was capable of ruthlessness and violence.

"Have you given up?" he asked.

She shook her head. "I'm going farther upstream." What she really wanted was to get away from him—and her thoughts.

"Don't go too far," he cautioned her. "We'll have to start back soon."

She ignored his warning. They hadn't seen anyone at all, and he'd said that they were well away from the mining company's land at this point. She walked along the bank of the stream, peering into its depths even though she was convinced that there was no gold to be found there.

After a short time she reached a point where the land began to slope upward. The stream remained shallow, but it ran faster there, flowing over mossy rocks in swirling eddies. Sunlight filtering through the overhanging branches dappled the water with light, making it impossible now for her to see the stream's bottom.

Then she came to a spot where the little stream curved around a huge boulder, creating a quiet pool between the boulder and the bank where she stood. She climbed onto the flat-topped rock and swung her legs over the side into the cool water. Even though they'd found no gold, it had been a pleasant enough day—a welcome break from their journey.

But the worst of that journey lay ahead of them. Soon there would be no villages or towns, no people at all. She had been trying not to think about that, but the thought intruded anyway, filling her with a dread she couldn't quite explain. She still didn't believe that Quinn would ever harm her, if only because he believed he needed her. But that did little to ease her mind.

It's my nightmare, she thought. *That's what frightens me.* But it hadn't returned, so she took some comfort in that.

She drew her feet out of the water, then peered down into the clear depths, seeing that there were a lot of pebbles down there. It occurred to her then that anything carried along by the water could easily have come to rest here, trapped by the boulder. Not allowing herself to get too excited at this thought, she nevertheless climbed from the rock back to the bank and picked up her sieve pan. In the distance she could hear Quinn calling her name. He sounded far away. She must have walked farther than she'd intended.

She ignored his call, knowing that her voice wouldn't carry that distance in any event, and slid the pan into the stream, digging it beneath the pebbles and other debris.

When she saw the glitter of gold in the pan, Jasmine at first simply didn't believe it. She thought it must be a trick of the sunlight on ordinary wet stones. Quinn's voice was becoming louder, but still she ignored it as she carefully lifted out one of the glittering pebbles.

"Gold! It *is* gold!" She spoke the words with awe, then carefully set aside the pebble and reached for another. By the time Quinn found her, she had gathered seven small nuggets into a pile and was back in the water, frantically searching for more.

Quinn squatted down on the bank and picked them up, then whooped with joy as he splashed into the pool beside her with his own pan. They both laughed as they plucked out still more tiny nuggets from each pan, adding to the pile on the bank.

"I think that's it," Quinn said finally, after they had sifted more pans than they could count.

They stood there grinning at each other, both of them dripping wet from the waist down. Their shared pleasure had a childlike quality to it, creating one of those moments for Jasmine that she knew she would cherish forever.

Quinn climbed out of the pool, then helped her out, and they both stood there, hands still clasped, staring down at their treasure.

"What do you think it's worth?" she asked.

"I don't know, but it's more than you started out with, girl."

"But half of it is yours," she pointed out.

"No, it's all yours. You found the spot."

"But you brought me here."

He gave her an exasperated look. "You found it, so it's yours. Now let's get back to town and see what you can get for it."

What she got for it turned out to be less than she'd hoped, but more than she'd expected. The assayer weighed it, then gave her a small bag of coins. Jasmine still had only a limited understanding of the value of things, so when they left the assayer's office, she asked Quinn what she could buy with the money.

"There's enough to set yourself up when you get back," he said, then added in a teasing tone, "so I guess I won't have to keep my promise."

She frowned at him—not because she was upset by his words, but because she was wondering if there was enough to pay for her journey back, too.

"I was only teasing you, Jasmine. I'll honor my word."

"I know you will," she said. But she was thinking that she wouldn't ask him to. Instead she was going to find someone with whom she could safely travel.

They returned to the inn, and after a pleasant dinner Jasmine pleaded fatigue and went to her room, hoping that Quinn would take himself off to one of the taverns for the evening. When she heard him leave his room a short time later, she knew that must be where he was headed.

She went downstairs to the desk, where the innkeeper was still keeping an eye on the traffic in and out of his establishment. She'd noticed that the inn was very busy, and was hoping that he could help her find a group traveling to her destination.

"I thought you were headed on to Halaban," he said with a frown when she explained her purpose.

"My friend is, but I've decided to return to Mavesta. Do you know if anyone here is going there?"

He nodded. "There's a party of six headed that way tomorrow morning. They're still in the dining room."

He pointed them out to Jasmine, who was pleased to see that there were two women among the group and that they all appeared to be decent people. Still, she approached them hesitantly, because she was unaccustomed to dealing with strangers.

She told them that she had traveled here with a friend who was going on to Halaban. She'd come to visit her grandmother, whom she hadn't seen in years. But unfortunately, the grandmother had died some months ago, and now she wished to return to Mavesta, her home. She explained that she was in the herb business, which wasn't as much of a lie as the rest of it, since she planned to go into that business as soon as she returned.

They seemed to accept her story without question and invited her to join their party, saying that she would be foolish to travel on her own. They were leaving at dawn.

Jasmine arranged to meet them at the stables, then thanked them and returned to her room. She felt confident that Quinn wouldn't be up that early after a night spent at the taverns. He'd said he hadn't planned to resume their own journey until the following day.

She undressed and fell asleep quickly, a smile on her face as she thought about her suddenly happy future.

Jasmine awoke in the predawn darkness. She'd had no fear of oversleeping. Her body had long since grown accustomed to waking at that hour.

She lay for a few minutes in the comfortable bed, thinking about the long journey home—and what lay ahead for her. Then she got out of bed and immediately took the bag of gold coins from its hiding place in one of her boots. She still could scarcely believe her good fortune, and she spent a few moments imagining a little cottage with a large herb garden in back and customers flocking to her stall in the market. Then she dressed hurriedly, bundled up her belongings and left the room.

She'd heard no sound from Quinn's chamber. No doubt he was exhausted from the night before and wouldn't be up for hours yet. Still, she crept quietly past his door, holding her breath, and only when she was out of the inn and on her way to the stables in the pale light did it occur to her that she should have left him a message of some sort. But she had no paper, and there had been no one at the inn's desk. Besides, she rationalized, he couldn't read Borneash, and neither of them could write in their shared language.

Still, Quinn's image stayed in her mind until she reached the stable and found her party already there, saddling their horses. She had never saddled her mare herself, but one of the men kindly did it for her—and then they were on their way.

As they rode along into the rising sun, Jasmine learned that one of the women, who was perhaps ten years older than her, made jewelry that she sold at the market in Mavesta. As she described the jewelry, Jasmine could recall having seen it once, though she had generally stayed away from such frivolities that she knew she could never buy. The woman, as it turned out, had been a regular customer at the stall where Jasmine's herbs were sold, and she was enthusiastic about being able to acquire them from Jasmine.

All of the group were pleasant to her, and Jasmine began to realize just how different her life would be now that she was no longer poor and a servant. Any doubts she'd had about returning home dissipated. Her old life was gone forever.

They were on the road about an hour when Quinn's image rose unbidden in her mind. She tried to put it out, but it lingered there. She would miss him, and she wished that there were some way she could repay his kindness to her. Perhaps when he gave up on his ridiculous dream, he would return to Mavesta and she would see him again.

Everyone was talking and laughing, and Jasmine did her best to join in, but with each passing minute her thoughts of Quinn became more overwhelming. His face loomed in her mind's eye. His deep laughter echoed through her mind.

Although the morning was as yet quite cool, Jasmine began to feel uncomfortably warm. The pendant nestled between her breasts felt almost hot against her skin. She tried to ignore it and attempted not to think about Quinn, but it was no good.

Finally she brought her mare to a halt. The woman with whom she'd been riding stopped too, a quizzical look on her face. Jasmine opened her mouth to say that she wanted to stop to remove her jacket, but what came out instead was something very different.

"I've made a mistake," she told the woman. "I must go back."

And then she turned the mare around, pausing only to thank the woman and the others before starting back to the inn.

Why am I doing this? she asked herself even as she urged the mare to greater speed. *Everything I want is back where I came from. Quinn's valley doesn't exist—and even if it does, what kind of life could I have there?*

But she kept the mare flying along the deserted road—until she crested a hill and saw a single rider moving in her direction. She reined in the mare and squinted, telling herself that she was wrong. But the rider was coming slowly toward her—and there was no doubt that it was Quinn.

Jasmine fought her panic. He was coming after her—and that meant he was angry. Images of those bloody bodies filled her brain. Then, just as she was about to wheel the mare around and ride back to the party she'd left, something struck her. If he was in fact in pursuit of her, why wasn't he riding harder? From the moment she'd first seen him, he'd been riding at barely more than a walk, and he hadn't picked up his pace yet, even though he must know it was her.

She urged the mare forward, still fearful, but less so than before. A few minutes later, they both came to a halt in the middle of the road. She waited for him to say something, but he merely sat upon his horse his gray eyes scrutinizing her.

"I wanted to leave you a message, but I couldn't," she told him. "I had decided to return to Mavesta with a group from the inn."

He nodded. "I saw you leaving."

"You did?" Why hadn't he come after her more quickly?

"Have you changed your mind?"

Jasmine took a deep breath and felt again the heat from the pendant. It seemed somewhat cooler now, she thought. "Yes. I don't know why, but I have."

He smiled. "Perhaps you believe, after all."

"No, I don't," she protested.

"Then why did you change your mind?"

"I don't know."

He was silent for a moment as he turned his horse and they started back to town. Then he turned to her. "I'm glad you did."

"It wouldn't have made any difference, would it? You were coming after me."

He shook his head. "No, I was just following you, hoping that you'd change your mind. If you did, I didn't want you to be riding back alone."

She stared at him. Try as she might, she could not detect a false note in his voice or see a lie in his eyes. "You would have let me go?"

"Yes. You're not my prisoner, Jasmine."

His words followed her back to the inn. She

knew that he'd spoken the truth, but there were different kinds of prisoners. Something had forced her to turn around. Was it Quinn and his dream— or something else entirely?

Chapter Six

The dream came back that night. Jasmine awoke in the darkness of her room at the inn, her body chilled by fear. It was the same: the beautiful valley, the silent village, the sudden onset of darkness—and the misshapen forms moving in the deep shadows.

Her fingers found the pendant. It was warm, but not hot as it had been the previous morning. And perhaps it only felt warm by contrast with her chilled body.

She lay there, thinking about the dream and the pendant and her sudden decision to return to Quinn. After a lifetime of being in thrall to someone else, she had just begun to taste freedom, and to like it very much. Now she sensed that her freedom was in danger, though she couldn't have said why. She wasn't Quinn's prisoner; she was free to go anywhere she chose, and now she had the means to do so.

Her fingers continued to clutch the pendant and

she felt a great urge to rip it from her throat. But that would be foolish. The pendant could hardly be responsible for her fears. It was a piece of jewelry and nothing more. She turned her thoughts to Quinn instead, and to the day they'd just spent in a fruitless search for more gold. She was disappointed, and Quinn had teased her about her newfound greed. He'd said that the gold they didn't find might be found by someone else in need someday.

She liked Quinn. She didn't want to like him, but she did. Everyone she'd ever cared for had been taken from her: her father and the others suddenly, and her mother more slowly. A boy who'd been her playmate and friend when she was growing up on the estate had gone off to war—and never returned. The kindly tutor hired to instruct the master and mistress's children had shown great interest in her—but then he, too had gone away.

So she refused to like Quinn because one day he too would be gone like all the others. Besides, there was that violent streak in him that frightened her, even if it had been used thus far only to protect them.

Three days passed on the road. There were few other travelers now, and only a sparse scattering of villages. The land had grown much hillier, so their progress was slowed considerably. Quinn was less concerned about brigands now, pointing out that if they had any sense at all, they would stay with the more heavily traveled roads. But still, he chose their campsites with care, then rigged his trap.

After a day spent climbing seemingly endless hills, where the downsides were always shorter, they came upon a string of small lakes, and Quinn suggested that they stop for the day. The horses were tired, and a lake would afford Quinn and Jasmine an opportunity to catch fish, as well as the chance to bathe away the trail dust that covered them both.

Jasmine readily agreed. She felt as tired as the horses, though for a different reason. The dream that had been plaguing her was coming every night now, always exactly the same. She hadn't told Quinn about it; she was certain that he would see it as being some sort of sign.

They made their camp on the shores of the lake nearest the road. While Quinn was tending to the horses, Jasmine stared at the lake, wondering how deep it was and how she could find privacy to bathe if it were shallow enough. She couldn't swim, though she'd always thought it must be wonderful.

When he had finished with the horses, Quinn announced that he was going to do a bit of exploring, but wouldn't be far off if she should need him. As soon as he was gone, she took out her dirty clothes and began to wash them in the water. The lake seemed shallow enough close to shore, but she felt too exposed to undress and bathe, so she contented herself with washing her face and hands.

Quinn returned just as she was spreading out her wet clothing on the grassy bank. "I found a spot where you can bathe," he told her, pointing off in the direction he'd taken.

"I can't swim," she admitted.

"You won't need to. It's shallow."

Touched by his thoughtfulness, which he'd displayed on more than one occasion, she followed him to the place he'd discovered. It was perfect: a tiny inlet that was surrounded by thick bushes and was completely invisible from the road.

He left her there, and after a few moments' hesitation, she stripped off her dusty clothes and waded into the sun-warmed water. It felt wonderful: cool enough to be invigorating, yet warm enough so that she wasn't chilled.

* * *

After leaving her to bathe, Quinn continued along the shore of the lake instead of returning to their campsite. He had his long bow with him and thought perhaps he might find some small game to add to their evening meal. After following the lake for a time, he angled off into the woods, hoping that he would still be able to hear her if she called to him.

Not that that was very likely, he thought with amusement. She was doing her very best *not* to need him. She'd done that all along, but it hadn't really bothered him because he'd known that she did need him. Now, however, she had her own gold.

He moved quietly through the forest, wondering if he would have gone after her and brought her back if she hadn't returned on her own. It was probably just as well that the question was moot.

Lost in his thoughts, he almost didn't see the doe and fawn standing motionless only a short distance away. The doe had certainly seen him, but she wouldn't leave her fawn even to save herself. Quinn stared at them for a long time, then circled past. Fish would make a fine dinner.

He started back toward the lake and found himself on a rocky promontory high above the water. And there was Jasmine below him, bathing in the shallow pool.

He should turn around and go back the way he had come. At least that was what the better side of his nature was telling him. He'd found her a private spot, and now he was invading that privacy.

But he didn't move. He'd noticed some time ago that she was no longer the skinny, shapeless

123

woman he'd met, but seeing her now, he was struck by just how beautiful she was.

He sensed trouble to come. That she had no interest in him as a man had been made clear long ago, but it hadn't troubled him because she wasn't to his taste either. He smiled at the irony. He was partly responsible for the transformation—and now the results threatened to bring him grief.

He tried to ignore the familiar stirring in his loins, though that might have been made much easier if he could have just brought himself to stop staring at her. Her long body had a grace and elegance that stirred him deeply, even though he'd always preferred plumper, more rounded women.

Finally he tore his gaze away—but only because he feared that she would turn and see him up here. Already his hold on her was tenuous, he suspected, based on gratitude and nothing more. He couldn't afford to do anything that might cause her to run away again.

Still, as he made his way back to the campsite, his male ego began to assert itself. Why wasn't she interested in him? He'd never had a problem before. Some women feared his size at first, but when he wanted to, he'd always been able to win them over with his practiced charm.

A week passed. Quinn and Jasmine rode ever deeper into the heart of the land, passing through small villages that were separated by many miles of increasingly hilly wilderness. When they stopped in the villages to buy food and seek shelter, it was Jasmine who had to deal with the people. Their thick accents were beyond Quinn's limited knowledge of the language—and very nearly beyond Jasmine's as well.

The narrow, winding road was empty, except for the occasional traveler. Quinn continued to be careful in selecting campsites, but neither of them feared any longer the brigands who plagued the more widely traveled portions of the road.

They journeyed in a companionable silence much of the time, two people lost in their separate thoughts. Quinn's thoughts were on that vast stretch of empty land on his map, an area they were fast approaching. And when he wasn't thinking about that, he was thinking about Jasmine, tormenting himself with images of her long, lithe, naked body.

Jasmine was thinking about her home and the life she would have there, when Quinn finally gave up his impossible guest. She, too, had seen the map, and knew that if the valley did indeed exist— which she continued to doubt despite the recurring dream—they would surely see the great mountains that encircled it soon. Surely such tall mountains would be visible from a great distance.

She also thought more than she wanted to about Quinn. Isolated as they were, forced to spend their days and nights together, she sometimes felt that she knew him better than she'd ever known anyone except for her mother.

She'd learned so many small things about him: his fondness for sweets that he satisfied every time they found a village where they could be purchased; his habit of humming to himself as they rode along, which he denied when she teased him about it. She'd discovered his love of poetry when he'd brought out a worn volume one day when they'd stopped to make camp before dark after a particularly tiring day.

The poems were in Estavian, which she of course couldn't read, but Quinn had attempted to translate them for her. Jasmine wasn't impressed; they sounded like nonsense to her. Besides, it was strangely disturbing that this man could be so attracted to the very things he'd claimed to dislike about the Estavians. She'd never known anyone so complex—or perhaps she'd just never gotten to know anyone well enough to see their complexities.

Slowly she began to realize that Quinn had become almost a part of her. At first she put him into the same category as her mare: something that was always there, a sort of temporary extension of herself. But there were times when she saw and felt a difference: times when their eyes would meet, times when they laughed together over small things, times when his touch would linger long after the fact when he'd helped her mount or dismount or had taken something from her hand.

At such times, she felt a strange disturbance deep inside, in a part of her that had never been touched before. But she didn't try to give that stirring a name. It was too startling, too unsettling. Before this, all her energies had been directed at simply getting through the day. Now there was something more.

By the end of a week, the villages they passed had once again grown more frequent and were separated not by stretches of wilderness but by farms. Jasmine had never seen their like, since she was accustomed to wide, flat fields. Here the farmers planted their crops up and down the steep mountainsides.

They reached the large town of Halaban late one afternoon. As they paused at the top of a hill and looked down into the valley, Jasmine thought it must be the biggest city she'd ever seen, though when she told Quinn this, he said that it probably wasn't any bigger than Mavesta. But there was no hilltop near her home from which she'd been able to view her entire hometown.

They rode through the streets, staring and being stared at. Jasmine was uncomfortably aware of her dirty, wrinkled appearance, though Quinn seemed unconcerned about his own. Still, they both agreed that a few days at an inn would be welcome.

Unfortunately, the town had only two inns—despite its size—and both were filled.

After failing to obtain a room at the second inn, Quinn inquired if there might be a small cottage they could rent for a short time, and was directed to a tavern on the next street. The owner there informed them that he did indeed have a cottage available at the moment. It had been occupied by his elderly parents, he said. Following his mother's recent death, his father had moved in with him, leaving it empty.

The building was located off a narrow alley only a short distance from the tavern and was still furnished with his parents' belongings. He planned to sell it, he told them, but he was glad to rent it out for their stay.

Quinn paid him his asking price, then remarked to Jasmine after he'd gone that he was clearly an honest man. Given their situation, the man could have demanded a much higher price.

The cottage was barely any larger than the one Jasmine had shared with her mother, but it was in far better condition and very comfortably furnished. She liked the idea of having an actual home, rather than a room at an inn, even if it was only temporary. In fact, she was so pleased that she failed to contemplate that there was only one bed in a tiny bedroom at the rear.

Quinn opened a cupboard that was piled high with thick quilts and said that he would use them as a bed in the small living room.

"We'll take turns," she insisted. "You must want a soft bed as much as I do."

They were in the bedroom at the time, and when their eyes met, Jasmine felt her skin grow warm. It was a very strange and frightening moment for her—and the first time she'd allowed herself to acknowledge that no matter how close they'd become in many ways, a very great barrier still existed between them.

For one very brief moment, she had been about to say that they could share the bed. It was large—much larger than the one she'd shared with her mother all her life.

When she looked back at Quinn, she had the impression that he'd been smiling. It was gone from his mouth, but it lingered in his gray eyes, and she felt herself flush again.

Fortunately, that discomfort vanished when they went out to the market to buy food and visit the numerous merchants. Quinn found a tiny shop that sold wonderful sweets, while she herself went to another and bought some scented soap. She'd been dreaming about the luxury of having a nice warm bath ever since her last experience.

The marketplace was larger even than the one in Mavesta, since Halaban served as the territory's trading center. And because the summers were much shorter here in the hills, many items that were sold at outdoor markets in Mavesta were on display here in tiny buildings clustered together and often connected to each other in what seemed to them to be mazes.

It was Quinn who first spotted the jewelry, because Jasmine was busy examining the herbs in another of the shops. He found her and took her arm.

"Come see this!" he said excitedly, all but dragging her along with him.

Jasmine stared in amazement at the jewelry on display. The workmanship wasn't as fine as that of her pendant, but she immediately saw what had captured his attention. Nearly every piece on display was set with diamonds or onyx—or both.

At first she didn't realize that the brownish gems

were also onyx, but the shop's owner, a young woman of about Jasmine's own age, explained that the stone came in a variety of colors, and that the brown was actually the most common. Black onyx was relatively rare, and rarest of all were the smooth black stones without striations, of which she had only two pieces.

"Where do you get them?" Quinn asked, barely containing his excitement.

"They come from the hills out there," the woman told them. "So do the diamonds, though they're far more difficult to find."

Quinn had some difficulty interpreting her response, so Jasmine repeated it to him. Then Jasmine withdrew her pendant and held it out for the woman to examine.

"Oh." The woman sighed. "This is beautiful. I've never seen workmanship like this. Where did you get it?"

Jasmine explained that it had been in her family for a long time, then slipped the pendant beneath her dress once again. The woman asked why she hid it, saying that thievery wasn't really a problem here.

Jasmine had no answer to that, but was saved from embarrassment by Quinn, who picked up another pendant with a boldly striped brown stone.

"Perhaps you'll wear this," he said to Jasmine.

Before she could protest, he was fastening it around her neck, his fingers pleasurably grazing the sensitive flesh. He then paid the woman and began to ask her questions about the area.

"Does anyone travel farther west?"

"Not often," the woman said. "And not very far. There aren't any roads in that direction. No one lives there."

"The road ends here?" Quinn asked. His map had indicated such, but he'd hoped it was wrong.

She nodded. "I think there is a trail of sorts,

maybe more like a path the deer use. But there are often landslides, especially in the spring when the snow melts. And anyway, there's no reason to go there. The men can find enough game in the hills around here."

"Is there a mapmaker in town?" Quinn asked. "I haven't seen one yet."

She said that there was, and directed them to a side street off the main shopping thoroughfare, where a man sold maps from his home. They thanked her and left hurriedly.

Jasmine saw Quinn's disappointment when the man's maps proved to be exactly like the ones he already had. She knew that the discovery of the jewelry had sent his hopes soaring.

"Has no one ever explored the land west of here?" Quinn asked with a trace of exasperation in his voice.

"Of course. People have gone out there from time to time, but no one's ever drawn a map that I know of," the man answered. "Are you planning to go there yourself?"

Quinn nodded and the man gave him a thoughtful look. "Well, you might want to talk to old Ezra Bartegan. He's close to eighty now, and he's not always in his right mind. But he used to tell stories about his grandfather, who once took it upon himself to go out there."

"Where can I find him?" Quinn asked eagerly.

"He lives with his grandson. They have a farm about a half-day's ride from town—the last place you come to before the road ends. I haven't seen him for a while, but I'd have heard if he'd died. He probably just can't make it to town anymore."

Quinn was up and ready before Jasmine the next morning, eager to be off to see the old man. He paced restlessly around the small cottage while she drank some tea and ate a thick piece of bread

130

spread with creamy butter and sweet jam.

"Quinn," she said when his pacing began to irritate her, "I don't think you should expect much. He warned you that the man isn't always in his right mind."

"That may be—but he could still remember his grandfather's tales. Old people are like that. They forget who they are or who their children are, but they remember things that happened in their own childhoods."

Jasmine had no way of knowing if that was true; she'd lost her own grandparents at such a young age. And now she had no one.

She looked up to find Quinn watching her and wondered if he cared for her at all, or if he merely tolerated her because he needed her. At times she thought maybe he did truly care, but at other times she was far less certain. Quinn talked freely, but he seemed to hold his feelings in check.

It seemed odd that someone she knew had grown up with loving grandparents and yet remained so reserved, but then, there were many things about Quinn that seemed unfathomable.

They found Ezra Bartegan sitting in a rocking chair in front of his tiny cabin. His grandson's wife had told them that he insisted on living there alone, even though he was no more than a few hundred yards from the Bartegan family's big farmhouse.

His mind, she told them, was sometimes clear and sometimes cloudy, like the weather here in the mountains. If he was having a bad day, she would tell them what she recalled of his tales, but she'd paid them scant attention. Her husband, she told them with a snort, didn't have time to listen to foolish old stories. He was too busy trying to coax corn and wheat and barley out of stubborn land.

Ezra was a tall man, though bent with age, but his big, gnarled hands spoke of a lifetime of hard labor, as did his weathered and creased face. He seemed glad to see them, however, and even apologized for remaining seated when Quinn introduced himself and then Jasmine. He stared hard at them both, studying their faces as though he might find something familiar there.

It took very little prodding to get him to repeat his grandfather's stories, though he was slowed down a bit by the fact of Jasmine's being forced to translate much of what he said.

When Ezra's great-grandfather was a young man, about a hundred and fifty years ago, he and a friend had gone off to explore the mountains despite the fact that his parents had urged him to stay away from there. They'd claimed that no one who ever went there came back to tell the story.

But his great-grandfather had come back alone after a month. His friend had been killed by wolves one evening at their campsite, while he'd been out gathering more firewood.

"Leastwise, he thought they was wolves," the old man said. "Even though they looked a bit strange to him. But it was nearly dark, and he said he didn't see 'em that good."

"Why did he think they were strange?" Quinn asked, repeating the question until Ezra Bartegan understood him.

"He only got a quick look at 'em as they was runnin' off into the woods, but he said that a couple of 'em was walkin' on their hind legs like bears— and he'd never seen wolves do that."

Jasmine felt a chill as her mind filled with the images of the shadowy creatures from her dream— the dream she still hadn't told Quinn about. She hadn't thought of them as resembling wolves, but now it seemed to her that perhaps they had.

When she glanced at Quinn, she saw a rapt expression on his face, but he didn't ask any other questions about the creatures. Instead, he asked

Ezra if his grandfather had described the land out there.

"He said there's big mountains—much bigger than anythin' here."

"Were they snowcapped?" Quinn asked, repeating that as well until the old man understood.

"Well, I don't rightly know how it coulda been snow. It was summer, after all. But he said it looked like there was somethin' white at their tops. He thought maybe it was chalk cliffs. We got some of those around here."

Then Quinn asked if he'd seen a valley—a very beautiful place completely surrounded by the tall mountains. But to Jasmine's considerable relief, he shook his head.

" 'Course, he didn't try to climb up the big mountains. He said they were going to see if there might be a pass—a way through—but that's when the wolves got his friend, and he came back."

Quinn sat there silently, obviously in no hurry to leave. Jasmine wanted to get away from the old man's stories. She felt increasingly nervous. If Ezra Bartegan's story was to be believed, then there were indeed snowcapped mountains out there—and that, combined with his tale of death, was enough to set her to thinking again about returning to Mavesta.

Quinn broke the silence to ask if there were other stories about the place. Ezra had mentioned that his grandfather's parents hadn't wanted him to go out there.

Ezra told them that others were supposed to have gone there from time to time—and never returned. "Why do you think there's no road?" the old man asked. "As far as Granddad knew, he was the only one who ever came back."

"Did others go after him?" Quinn asked.

"A few, from time to time. But they never returned, either. I 'spect the wolves got 'em. Or maybe they tried to climb them mountains and fell off."

The old man scratched his nearly bald head. "Seems like it's just not a good place to go, and folks around here have enough trouble just tryin' to make a livin'. But Granddad did say once that there was supposed to've been people livin' out there once upon a time—strange people who kept to themselves."

He paused for a moment, frowning. "I seem to recollect that old Miz Cossamen used to talk about them some—stories she'd heard from her folks."

"Where can we find her?" Quinn asked eagerly.

"You can't—leastwise not on this earth. She died mebbe twenty years ago. Most of the Cossamens are gone. They never was a big family. But her great-grandson owns the harness shop in town."

He looked at Quinn, then at Jasmine. "Are you two fixin' to go out there?"

Quinn nodded, and the old man shook his head. "Foolish thing to do—'specially to take a lady."

Quinn said nothing, and Jasmine noticed that he didn't look her way. They left Ezra Bartegan soon after that, and Quinn was silent until they were once more on the road, headed back to town.

"Maybe he's right," he said, still not looking at her.

"About what?" Jasmine asked, though she thought she knew.

"About my being foolish to take you out here."

Jasmine drew in a breath. Here, then, was her chance. Quinn was having his doubts, and he wouldn't blame her if she decided to go back.

"But you'd still go on, wouldn't you?" she asked.

"I have to," he replied simply.

Jasmine said nothing. She could feel the force of his thoughts, his for an answer. She didn't *want* to find whatever was out there. She didn't even want to find the valley, if it existed. But she didn't want to leave Quinn, either. It was that simple—and that complex.

They found Jed Cossamen still in his shop when they reached town late in the day. He was a robust, ruddy man in his thirties, and when Quinn explained to him, with Jasmine's reluctant assistance, why they wanted to talk to him, he shook his head and chuckled.

"Those old stories? Sure, I remember them. Granny Malva told them often enough. She claimed that there were people living out there in a valley somewhere. Mostly they kept to themselves, but every once in a while they came into town, mostly to buy gold and gems. They had their own language and didn't look like us, and she said they had these beautiful white horses that danced." He chuckled again, oblivious to the shocked look on their faces.

"Granny Malva was a great one for stories. Claimed she got them from *her* granny, who was one of the lucky ones who survived the plague."

Tall mountains with white tops. Wolves. And now people who spoke a different language and looked different—and white horses. It was all seeming so likely now. Jasmine was stunned. Quinn obviously was, too, though he was now asking about the plague.

"I guess it must have been about two hundred years ago," Jed Cossamen told him. "It wiped out nearly half the town—especially the old folks and young kids. Granny Malva claimed her granny said that it didn't hit anywhere else—just here. People died real fast."

"It's *real*, Jasmine! It has to be. The story is the same."

Jasmine slanted him a glance as they walked back to their cottage. He looked ready to burst with excitement. She tried to be glad for him, but all she could feel was a deep sense of foreboding.

He went on, oblivious to her silence as he repeated the stories they'd been told. It became clear to her that he would leave the next day—with or without her.

They ate dinner at a local tavern, where the food was as good as anything she'd ever had. But it was wasted on her. She ate because it was there and she was hungry, but her mind was turning over and over the question he had yet to put to her.

When they returned to their rented cottage, Quinn lit a fire because the evening was cool, then turned to her. To her surprise, he reached out and took her hands in his.

"I want you to come with me, Jasmine, but that old man made me realize that I've been selfish. It could be dangerous for you. If you want to go back home, I'll understand, and we'll find someone reliable for you to travel with."

She stared down at their clasped hands. It seemed as though his great strength and his equally great gentleness were flowing from his fingertips to hers, his body to hers.

"I'll give you the gold I promised you," he added.

"I don't need it now," she said, knowing that she still wasn't answering his unspoken question.

"It was a promise—and I keep my promises."

She looked up at him. "What will you do when you find the valley?"

He dropped her hands and shrugged. "I don't know yet, but I think I'll know when I need to."

She heard something in his voice: certainty. "You weren't telling me the truth when you said you didn't believe in the magic, were you?"

"I don't know what I believe. All I know is that this feels right. It's felt right to me all along—but especially after I met you."

She turned away from him, unable to bear the look in his eyes.

"I've had dreams," she said, her hand going of its own volition to the hidden pendant.

"What dreams?" he asked, and she could feel the tension in him even though she was still turned away from him.

"Dreams about the valley. It's the same—over and over. I see little stone houses with thatched roofs. But there aren't any people. Then it gets dark all of a sudden—and there are . . . creatures in the shadows."

"I've had them, too," he said quietly.

She whirled around to face him. "You didn't tell me! The same dream?"

He nodded. "It's like I am floating around through the valley, seeing everything. The houses, too."

"And the darkness and the . . . creatures?"

"Yes. I thought about them when Ezra Bartegan was talking about wolves that walk on their hind legs. But I don't think they're wolves."

"Demons," she whispered.

"Yes, I think so. If all the rest of it is true, then that must be, too."

"No!" she said fiercely, nearly shouting the word. "Even if the rest of it is true, that part doesn't have to be. Our ancestors could have been killed by the plague, just like the people here—and then the ones who survived fled."

"That's possible," he replied, but she could tell that he didn't believe it.

"The time is right," she insisted. "He said it was supposed to have happened about two hundred years ago—and that's when you said our people were driven out of the valley."

She stared at him, willing him to accept that explanation. Then she wrapped her arms around herself and shivered. "I'm frightened, Quinn."

He reached out to her, tentatively at first, and then, when she didn't resist, he drew her slowly into his arms. It felt as though she were being embraced by a great tree, tall and hard. He bent his head and she felt his breath against her hair.

Something very strange began to happen inside her. It was as though her very bones were softening, starting to melt. Heat spread through her, tiny curling tendrils of warmth that made her tingle all over.

"I want you to come with me," he murmured.

"Because you need me if there *are* demons." She couldn't believe what was happening to her. She'd heard about such feelings. The maids at the manor had talked about it—about the way a man could make a woman feel.

He released her, then cupped a hand beneath her chin and drew her face up until she was forced to look into his eyes. "It's more than that, Jasmine. I just want you with me. I need you to be with me."

And then his mouth was covering hers softly, and he was swallowing her small cry of surprise. His lips were gentle but very firm as they moved expertly over hers. Both hands slid around her neck, holding her prisoner as the kiss deepened and his tongue slid into her mouth, teasing hers.

Her eyes were closed and she was floating on pure sensation, not even aware of her feet touching the floor. Time had stopped. The world had suddenly ceased to exist. There was only Quinn: his strong hands, his gentle lips, the heat of his body—so close, but not quite touching hers.

Then, abruptly, he let her go. His eyes were dark with confusion, as though he wasn't quite sure what he'd done and why he'd done it.

Jasmine was confused, too, still half-caught in the touch and taste and feel of him, and paralyzed by the sensations that continued to ripple through her, trailing behind them a voluptuous heat.

"I'm sorry," he said, his voice thick and rough.

She wanted to know exactly what it was that he was sorry for, but the words wouldn't form themselves into speech. Instead she made a small gesture to indicate that it didn't matter—a wholly automatic response, and a dishonest one. It did matter. The very floor beneath her feet seemed to have shifted. The woman she'd been only moments ago was not the woman she was now, though she couldn't define the difference.

It had only been a kiss, she told herself desperately. It meant nothing. She'd seen her fellow servants on the estate stealing kisses—and more—and afterward the women had laughed them off. Quinn probably expected that she'd do the same. He couldn't know that she'd never kissed a man before, nor even wanted to.

Quinn had turned away from her and was crouched in front of the fire, poking at the logs, though it seemed to her that the fire didn't really require his attention. Perhaps the confusion she thought she'd seen in his face was real. She'd wondered if she might be reading her own emotions in his eyes.

She struggled to remember their conversation, pulling the scattered threads together as she tried to decide what to say. She hadn't been tongue-tied with Quinn for a long time now, but in the space of a few moments, he'd become a stranger again.

No, not a stranger, she thought. A different man entirely, even though he looked the same.

He got up slowly and faced her once again—warily, she thought.

"It won't happen again," he said.

"I'll go with you," she said at the same time.

Both of them stopped, and a charged silence hung in the air. She felt awkward and then embarrassed as she wondered if he thought that his kiss had changed her mind. Had it?

"It could be dangerous," he said, his gray eyes still searching her face carefully, as though he were trying to understand why she would be willing to put herself at risk.

"It won't be the first time I've faced danger," she reminded him.

He was silent for a long time, and she wondered if he'd now decided that he didn't want her to accompany him after all.

"What if the stories about demons are true, Jasmine?"

"They aren't," she insisted, her tone more certain than she felt. She forced herself to smile, and she shrugged.

"Anyway, if they are, then the stories about our being able to make magic will be true as well."

Chapter Seven

"Did you have the dream last night?" Quinn asked as they rode out of Halaban on what seemed the final leg of their long journey.

"No. Did you?"

He shook his head.

She wanted to ask what he thought that meant, but she kept her silence. Until now the dream had come to both of them each night. She *had* dreamed, though—but a very different one. Thinking about it now, she felt a rush of heat and embarrassment.

When she'd awakened a few hours ago to the sounds of Quinn moving about the small cottage, she'd still been half-caught in that sensual vision. For a few moments she'd even thought that perhaps it had actually happened. In her mind, they'd made love in a place that she knew somehow was in their valley. She'd been uncomfortable in his presence ever since, unable to meet his eyes lest somehow the dream make itself known to him.

Now she thought about the other dream: the one they'd shared. Had it ceased because they were finally close to the end of their journey? she wondered silently as they rode into the steep hills beyond the town. Had the dream meant to lure them there?

Jasmine was very uncomfortable with such flights of fancy. She just wasn't given to silly dreaming. But it seemed that she'd been drawn into Quinn's quest and now she knew she must see it to its conclusion.

"I think they stopped because they aren't needed any longer," he said, startling her out of her thoughts by seeming to reach right into them.

But as soon as he suggested it, she rejected it, deciding that they'd stopped because she now had something else to dream about. But that didn't explain why he hadn't had the dream again. She was certain that the kiss had meant little to him, despite his seeming confusion over it.

Around midday they passed by the farm where Ezra Bartegan lived. The old man was once again in his rocking chair in front of his little house. They waved, uncertain as to whether he could see them from this distance, or whether he would recognize them if he did. But he waved back, and Jasmine thought she saw a smile on his face.

The wide road ended abruptly only a few hundred yards beyond the farm and became a path just barely wide enough for the two of them to ride abreast, with the packhorses trailing behind. Quinn had acquired two more packhorses, since they were now carrying far more supplies.

The thick forest, mostly pine and fir and hemlock, seemed to be pressing against them. The path led them uphill and down, and then turned at sharp angles to avoid still steeper climbs. The silence was unnerving. There'd rarely been a time until now when there hadn't been a gurgling brook nearby or the sounds of other travelers.

Quinn kept turning in the saddle to scan the woods on both sides. She wondered if he could be looking for demons, but then he commented on the lack of game.

"He told me that was the reason no one ever came out here to hunt," Quinn said, referring to the man who'd provisioned them for the trip.

Jasmine realized that was another reason for the silence. There were no rustlings in the underbrush—and no birds, either. Before, every time she'd looked into the forest she'd seen squirrels or other small animals, and many times deer as well. The woods here were empty.

The path became steeper and steeper, with only brief downhill stretches. It was impossible for her to tell how high these hills were, or to see what lay ahead, because the forest was thick and it blocked their view on both sides.

Night came early, after only the briefest of dusks. They made camp in a small hollow, just below the path. There was no stream in sight, and she was glad that Quinn had brought water with them, although it wouldn't last long.

Quinn studied his map by the light of the fire. "There must be water around here somewhere," he told her. "The headwaters of the stream we followed on our way to Halaban must be up here."

Jasmine didn't like looking at the map now because it reminded her that they had moved into uncharted territory: that huge blank spot that so fascinated Quinn.

The night was colder than it had been before, and there was no moon. Even the stars seemed much more distant: tiny pinpricks of light that were lost in the all-engulfing blackness. The darkness seemed to Jasmine to be a living thing, a malevolent presence waiting to swallow her up. She recalled the sudden onset of darkness in her dream and shivered beneath the blanket she'd wrapped around herself. Then she wondered if Quinn felt it, too. They'd both been talking in near-whispers.

"Are you sorry that you decided to come?" Quinn asked.

"No," she said quickly, startled to realize that she wasn't, despite her fears.

"You feel the same way I do, don't you?" he asked, his eyes dark in the firelight as he watched her. "We have to go there."

"Maybe," she said, unwilling to admit the truth, even to him.

Quinn smiled, but it was a smile touched with a certain grimness. "Always the cautious one," he said with a chuckle.

"It seems to me that *one* of us should be cautious," she replied defensively.

"I'm not reckless," he ventured, "just determined. There's a difference."

"A very small difference. Besides, you can afford to be reckless. Who could challenge you?"

"There is that," he agreed.

They arranged their blankets—closer than in the past when they'd camped out, but still with some distance between them. That separation had become very important to Jasmine now. She lay awake long after she heard the slow, regular breathing that told her he had fallen asleep.

Jasmine's eyes flew open to darkness and a certainty that some sound had awakened her, even though she heard nothing now except Quinn's breathing. She had no idea how long she'd been sleeping, or even if she'd slept at all. Before lying down, Quinn had built up the fire, and it appeared to have burned down only a little bit.

Had she been awakened by a dream? She had no recollection of one. Moving carefully so as not to disturb Quinn, she sat up and turned slowly, staring into the impenetrable blackness. Nothing moved. The fire crackled and a log shifted, and she wondered if that had been the sound that had awakened her.

Then suddenly she felt something: a cold certainty that she was being watched, that somewhere out there in the darkness there were eyes up on her. She drew in her breath sharply, her own eyes wildly darting about, trying to see what couldn't be seen.

A surge of anger flowed through her—a rage she couldn't explain. She heard a voice whispering in her people's language—and realized it was her own, forming words she didn't even understand, words that made no sense. And then the sensation of being watched was gone. Quinn hadn't stirred. She lay down again and somehow managed to go back to sleep.

The path became gradually steeper, with many twists and turns. Their progress was slow, and Jasmine could feel Quinn's impatience even though he was careful not to tire the horses.

She had said nothing to him about the night before. When she'd awakened to sunlight, she'd at first been certain that the episode had been real, but with the clarity of daylight, she finally decided that it must have been a dream. She'd waited for him to say that he too had had such a dream, but when he'd said nothing, she'd kept her silence.

By midafternoon the sky had darkened and thunder was rumbling in the distance. As the storm drew closer, Quinn began to look for a sheltered spot to wait it out. When they found a place where the forest was thick with tall trees, they stopped and he rigged a shelter for them, using some saplings for poles and then spreading oiled skins over them. They crawled beneath it just as the first fat raindrops fell.

There wasn't much space, so they sat huddled together—too close for Jasmine's comfort. She could feel the tension in Quinn as well and wondered if he were worried about the storm—or about being too close to her. It troubled her that their easy camaraderie had vanished after that kiss, but she didn't know how to tell him that.

Then the storm was directly above them. Claps of thunder shook the ground and lightning flashed, turning the air blue-white around them. She shuddered and Quinn's arm came around her shoulders, drawing her close.

"We're safe here," he told her, his breath fanning against the top of her head as he settled her against him.

Jasmine felt safe from the storm, but she didn't feel safe from the feelings that engulfed her. She was reliving that kiss and the dream that had followed it. She was stunned to realize that she wanted that dream to come true. She wanted Quinn to make love to her. Never before in her life had she wanted a man, and it seemed that only days ago she had thought him a madman.

Panic rose up in her. She wasn't so innocent that she didn't know what happened between men and women. Once, returning to the cottage at dusk, she'd come upon two other servants in the orchard. They had neither seen her nor heard her, but the image was burned into her brain. It hadn't seemed at all to her like making love; rather, it had seemed like two animals. The only emotion she'd felt was disgust. How could she want such a thing to happen to her?

Quinn felt her tremble slightly as he held her, and he tried to settle her more comfortably against him. He regretted that kiss—not because he hadn't wanted to kiss her, but because he could see the difference in her. She no longer trusted him—if indeed she ever had.

After all this time spent with her, he still didn't understand her, and sometimes wasn't sure he knew her at all. He'd never met a woman like her: so self-contained and so silent much of the time. In his experience, women talked constantly and held nothing back.

He looked down at her, thinking about that body he'd glimpsed that one time. It seemed that with each passing day, she was becoming more desirable. And, of course, he hadn't had a woman for a very long time now: too long for someone with his appetites.

But he knew that he would have to restrain those appetites and win her trust once again. She'd become far too important to him to risk alienating her now. Besides, he had other things to think about. Without understanding how he knew, Quinn had become convinced that they would both be tested somehow. They would not reach the valley easily.

What would they do when they found it? he wondered. He'd worked for years to come to this place—and now the end seemed fraught with uncertainty. Quinn was anxious, and it was a wholly new feeling for him.

He rested his chin against Jasmine's silken hair and tried to ignore both the ache in his loins and the anxiety that filled his mind.

This time it was the heat from the pendant that awakened Jasmine. In that moment when she was struggling up from slumber, it seemed that it was actually pulsing as it nestled between her breasts. And then she heard Quinn stirring, too.

She was about to rip the pendant away when he reached out to take her hand. "Did you hear something?" he asked in a voice still thick with sleep.

"No," she replied, then added after a moment, "It was the pendant."

He stared at her, his eyes shadowed by the fire's light. "The pendant? What do you mean?"

"It . . . it gets warm, and it felt like it was moving."

His fingers touched the thin chain and he drew it toward him, then grasped the pendant. "It's hot," he exclaimed. "Are you feverish?"

She shook her head. "It's happened before."

"Why didn't you tell me?"

She had no answer to that, and Quinn's eyes left her to stare off into the woods. Then he dropped the pendant and reached for his bow.

"Something's out there," she said. She could feel eyes on her again.

"Probably wolves," he replied, cradling the longbow in his lap as he continued to peer into the darkness. "They won't come any closer because of the fire."

He got up and added more wood to the fire while she continued to stare into the trees, her fingers clutching the pendant. It was still warm, but not as hot as it had been. When he sat down again, she told him about her dream the night before.

"Are you sure it was a dream?" he asked.

She started to nod, then shook her head instead. "I . . . I don't think I can tell the difference anymore."

Quinn reached for her and drew her against him while keeping his bow close at hand. "You have to trust me, Jasmine, and tell me these things."

"But why am I the one who's dreaming? Maybe it's the pendant."

She made a move to take it off, but Quinn's hand stopped her. "No, don't take it off. I think it's protecting you somehow."

Suddenly they both heard the sounds: twigs snapping in the darkness beyond the fire's light.

They both turned in that direction but saw nothing.

"Wolves—or maybe deer," Quinn said after the sounds stopped.

But Jasmine had heard the doubt in his voice. "You don't believe that, do you? You're not being honest with me, either, Quinn."

"Do you want to go back?" he asked, catching her by surprise.

Jasmine turned within the circle of his arms and stared up at him. Their faces were scant inches apart, and she could feel him tense as he awaited her response. She knew that if she said yes, he would give up his quest and take her back. She shook her head and felt him relax. Moments later she fell asleep again, this time in his arms.

Jasmine awoke to sunshine and blue skies and the impatient whickering of the horses. But all of that barely registered because she was lying with Quinn, their bodies pressed together beneath the blankets. Her head rested against his shoulder, and she lifted it carefully, only to see his eyes flicker open.

A thrill rippled through her as she saw the look in his gray eyes. Only later would she realize that it was she who moved—she who brought her mouth to his. It was one of those times when something seemed so right that the questions were held in abeyance for a time.

He hadn't shaved since they'd left Halaban, and his beard felt pleasantly rough against her skin. For one brief moment, he tensed and seemed to hesitate, and then his expert lips were overwhelming her tentative kiss.

His hand curled around her head as his lips and tongue moved gently against hers. His other hand moved slowly down her spine, pressing her to him until she could feel his hardness. And then she lost

her awareness of his kisses and felt only his need
for her—a need that frightened her and made her
suddenly stiffen with resistance even as a part of
her wanted much more.

Quinn released her immediately, then sat up
and ran a hand through his hair. She could see his
hand tremble even as tremors ran through her as
well. But the moment had been shattered, and Jasmine knew she'd been saved from a decision she
wasn't ready to make. She wondered if he'd known
that—or if he'd stopped for some other reason.

She drew in a shaky breath. She felt so disoriented, so uncertain about everything. Unpleasant
as her past life had been, there was at least a reassuring certainty to it: the routine of her job, the
love of her mother, the small pleasure of her fortnightly day off and a trip into town. Although the
person she'd been then had become nearly unrecognizable to her, she found herself wanting that
life back again.

But that would mean a life without Quinn—and
she knew she didn't want that, either.

"Jasmine," he said, his voice still husky, "I didn't
intend for that to happen."

She said nothing because she was confused by
his words. Only after he'd spoken them did she
realize that it was she who had initiated the kiss—
not him. Or was she mistaken? The memory of
how it had happened was all but erased by the fact.

He apparently took her silence for anger because he hurried on. "I'm a man and you're a
woman and these things happen. But I never intended to force myself on you. I've never done that
to a woman."

"Many men do," she said neutrally, still struggling with her thoughts.

"I know that—but I don't. It's wrong." Then he
chuckled in that slow, deep way she'd come to like
very much.

"I haven't always done the right thing. I'm no better than any other man. But I'd never force myself on a woman." He paused, his expression becoming grim. And when he continued, Jasmine could hear the barely contained rage in him.

"I had a sister. She was three years younger than me. One night a group of drunken men attacked her, then left her for dead when they were finished. It might have been better if she *had* died, because the girl we knew was gone.

"I wasn't living at home when it happened, but when I found out, I hunted them down and killed them. It didn't help her, though."

He threw her a challenging look. "So I lied to you when I said that I'd never killed except in self-defense. But they deserved to die."

"You were defending her," Jasmine said quietly.

"That's what I told myself at the time."

"What happened to her—afterward, I mean?"

He shrugged. "She still lives with my father. My mother died a few years ago. But her spirit is gone. If we find the valley, I'd like to bring her there. My father, too, if he can make the journey. I think that if it's as beautiful a place as I believe, she might find peace there."

"What happened just now wasn't your fault, Quinn. I was the one who started it."

He smiled at her. "Maybe so, but I didn't resist the temptation."

She wondered why he felt that he had to resist, but before she could decide whether to ask that question, he got up and walked off into the woods.

She thought about his story. She was touched by his concern for his sister and his desire to help her. He'd never talked much about his family before, except to say that he had two brothers and a sister.

How wonderful it must be to have a family, she thought. Not only didn't she have one herself, but she'd never even known a family not broken apart by misery or death. All that had been taken from her before she could begin to appreciate it.

Quinn returned and they ate breakfast. She kept stealing glances at him, and could feel his eyes on her as well. Something was changing between them—at least from her point of view. She couldn't begin to guess how he truly felt. Quinn talked easily, but he said little that gave her a clue to his feelings.

She watched him as he stamped out the embers of their campfire. Was she falling in love with him? Was this how it happened: in small steps that could easily pass unnoticed? She didn't really know how people fell in love. She'd never had friends to talk to about it, and her mother had never discussed such things with her.

They packed up their things and began to walk the horses back to the road. Quinn was in the lead, and suddenly he stopped. She saw him staring at the ground and she led her horse up to the spot as well.

"What is it?" she asked when she saw the print in the muddy ground. She'd all but forgotten last night.

"A bear, I think," he said after a moment, but she thought that he sounded uncertain.

Jasmine stared at the prints. She'd never seen a bear, except in drawings once, in a book the tutor had shown her from the manor library. Certainly the prints looked large enough to be a bear's, but she thought they looked almost like human footprints.

"Well, that explains what we heard out here last night," Quinn said as he started once again toward the road.

"Are bears dangerous?" she asked.

"No. They're big and they look dangerous, but they usually don't attack people without provocation. He might have smelled our food, or he might just have been curious."

Quinn was even more silent than usual as they rode along the winding path. After two days of climbing higher and higher, the path was now almost level, and they made good time. On one of the few occasions when he did speak, Quinn expressed concern about finding a stream. They were nearly out of water.

They were almost upon the stream before they saw it or heard it. Between the sounds of the strong breeze in the trees and the clipclop of the horses, the small brook had been inaudible to them.

The horses needed no urging to plunge down the bank toward the stream. Quinn had already been forced to ration their water. Jasmine slid down from the saddle and set her mare free to drink as she pulled off her boots. Quinn removed his as well, and they both waded into the stream.

The stream was both swifter and deeper than she'd expected. Her foot slipped on a submerged rock and she fell, floundering helplessly in cold, waist-deep water. But before she could do more than utter a cry of surprise, Quinn was there and his arms were around her, hauling her to her feet. Then they both stood in the middle of the stream and laughed.

"Next time I suggest that you let me go first," he said with a grin. "Or is this your way of taking a bath and washing your clothes at the same time?"

She laughed. She was soaking wet from her head to her toes, and even though the water was quite cold, it felt very good. Quinn helped her back to shore, then turned and plunged into the deep part of the stream again, swimming a few strokes before standing up and shaking the water from his curly black hair.

"I should teach you to swim," he said when he joined her on the warm, sunny bank. "Then you'd be safer."

"Not here," she said, shaking her head. "The current is too strong."

"Then maybe we'll find a lake somewhere. Or even a waterfall with a pool at its base."

"In the valley," she murmured, thinking about the dream she'd had so many times.

He nodded. "I know we're going to find it. The only question is how we get over the mountains around it."

"But if the story we heard is true, our people must have found a way in and out. After all, they traveled to town from time to time, and surely they couldn't have been climbing mountains to do it."

"There's probably a pass, but it could take a while to find it."

He stretched out on the grassy bank. "I want to see those mountains. I keep thinking that maybe we should leave the road and ride up one of these hills to see if we can find them."

"But they could be days—or even weeks—away."

"I don't think so—not weeks, anyway."

"Why?"

"Just a feeling, that's all."

"Quinn," she said slowly, not at all certain that she wanted to say this, "do you really think those were bear tracks?"

She had her answer even before he spoke. Her own doubts had combined with his unusual silence all day to make her suspect that he hadn't been entirely honest.

"No, I don't," he said finally.

"You think it was a demon," she stated.

"Yes. It definitely wasn't a bear—or any other animal I know of."

Jasmine lifted her face to the sun, then looked

around at the peaceful forest and the sparkling stream. Demons. How could she possibly believe in such things? How could he?

"If it was a demon, then why didn't it attack us?" she asked, still hoping to prove him wrong, even though something deep within her believed him.

"I don't know." He sat up and ran his hand through his still-damp curls. "That's the problem. There's too much we don't know."

"Could they be waiting—to see if we find the valley?" And even as she spoke, she was wondering how they could be sitting here talking about the stuff of nightmares.

"They might be—or maybe we're protected somehow. Your pendant might be protecting us."

She withdrew the pendant from beneath her shirt and stared at it. Was it only a lovely piece of jewelry or something more? Once again her mind and that deeper part of her were in conflict.

"We're going to turn back," Quinn said. "I'm taking you back to Halaban."

Jasmine said nothing. She wanted very much to see the valley now, but not at the cost of her life—a life that that had suddenly gained some meaning, some hope.

"Then you'll come back alone, won't you?" she asked, realizing that with her question, she was agreeing to his decision.

He nodded. "But I think maybe I'll try to see if I can find out more before I do. There must be more information somewhere."

Jasmine followed him back to the horses, then kept silent as they climbed up to the road and turned toward Halaban. She was moving automatically, her thoughts in a state of turmoil. Her clothes were still slightly damp, and as they rode through the woods, where the sun's warmth didn't reach her, she felt chilled.

But in that chill came a spot of warmth: the pendant. She even thought that it might be pulsing again, though she couldn't be sure because her heart was beating rapidly. She reached for it, pulling it from its hiding place. And as she did, her horse suddenly came to a stop. She glanced up and saw that it had stopped because Quinn had—and then she saw why.

For long seconds, Jasmine simply stared, unable to believe what her eyes were seeing. They had stopped in the middle of a wide curve in the road. She remembered that there'd been a hill beyond the curve, and indeed the hill was still there. But the path was gone. It ended abruptly just a few yards up the hill, and beyond it lay nothing but forest.

We must have turned the wrong way, she thought, even though she knew they hadn't. There must have been another road and somehow they'd strayed onto it. But that, too, was impossible; they'd passed this way just a short time ago and there hadn't been any other trail. In fact, there'd been only this one since they left Halaban.

She even blinked a few times, thinking that perhaps she wasn't seeing properly, even though the scene was very clear.

Quinn turned to her and his expression told her that he, too, was having difficulty believing his eyes. He turned back to stare at the end of the road for a moment, then urged his horse forward until he was at the very end, where the forest closed in.

"How can . . ." she began, edging forward more cautiously herself.

"It's magic," he said, his voice surprisingly calm, considering his words. "We're meant to go forward."

He brought his horse around and started away from the now absent trail back to civilization. Jasmine started to follow him, then stopped, her mare half-turned in the road. Something in Quinn's calm voice and his almost dreamy expression troubled her. So did the fact that he'd just turned and simply ridden away from such a bizarre occurrence.

With one last glance at his broad back, Jasmine urged her horse toward the end of the road, then brought the mare up when she reached it. As she dismounted, she felt something: a sort of delicate shiver that ran through her from head to toe. She ignored it, determined to disprove Quinn's words.

She grasped the reins and led the horse past the end of the road, into the woods where the road should be. That strange feeling became even stronger, and then it seemed that something was wrong with her vision, because the forest ahead of her was fading, as though a thick fog were moving through it.

"Jasmine!"

She turned, drawn by the urgency in Quinn's voice. But she couldn't see him clearly, either. He was as blurred as the woods around her. Then suddenly she felt his hand touch hers, then grasp her wrist firmly. She didn't resist, but he still pulled her hard, and she fell against her mare's flanks, frightening the already nervous animal.

Quinn grabbed the mare's reins with one hand and wrapped his other arm around her waist, hauling them both back to the road—back to the sunlight and the sharp, clear outlines of a familiar world.

"Wh-what happened?"

He dropped the mare's reins and wrapped both his arms around her, holding her so tightly that she could barely breathe. "You started to disappear!"

"What?" She managed to turn in his arms and stare at the place she'd just been. It was as they'd first seen it: the road ended abruptly and the forest remained beyond. The mist was gone.

Then she listened in horror as he described it: how he'd felt what she herself had felt, how he'd also felt very certain that it was a sign they must go on—and then how he'd turned to see that instead of following him, she was vanishing into the forest.

"When I turned, I could barely see you, and then you were gone completely and all I could see was the horse."

Jasmine frowned, still staring at the forest. It wasn't thick enough to have swallowed her up so quickly. "It was that mist," she said, even though that didn't quite describe it.

"I didn't see any mist."

"Then how did I disappear?"

"You just vanished. I could see the trees clearly— but you weren't there. Except that I knew you were, because I could see the reins standing out in front of your mare as though you were still holding them."

"That's impossible, Quinn."

"I know it's impossible—but that's how it happened. It's magic, Jasmine. It must be."

Tears sprang to her eyes. "I don't want magic. I want to go back."

He ran a hand soothingly along her spine. "We have to go on. But we have magic on our side, whatever may be against us."

"You mean *that*?" she asked scornfully, waving an arm at the disappearing road. "How can you say that magic is on *our* side?"

"Because it's true. What I felt wasn't evil. It was good and peaceful."

"I didn't feel that."

"Maybe that's because you're not ready to believe."

Or maybe you're *too* willing to believe, she replied silently. There was no point in arguing with him over it. She was reminded of her thoughts when she'd first met him and had believed him to be mad.

"Did you really want to go back?" he asked softly, still holding her loosely.

"You're the one who said we were going back," she reminded him, not wanting to answer his question.

"Only because I thought you did. You haven't answered my question."

Unwilling to meet his eyes, Jasmine stared straight ahead, which at the moment meant his chest, where dark, curly hairs stood out against his open-necked white shirt.

"I don't know what I wanted," she said. "But I know what I don't want. I don't want magic and demons and nonsense like that. That's madness."

Quinn let her go, and she was barely able to restrain a cry of protest that sprang to her lips. "Anyway," she said angrily, "it doesn't matter what I wanted. We have no choice but to go on."

She stalked back to her mare and climbed into the saddle without waiting for him to assist her. She was frightened: frightened of things she couldn't explain and frightened of her attraction to a man who was willing to follow his dreams into a dark world where nothing made sense.

Quinn kept his distance from Jasmine for the remainder of the day and night. At times it seemed to him that he could actually feel her confusion and her resistance to allowing that magic was now a part of their lives. For him, that acceptance had come far more easily. He'd been raised with stories about his people's magical heritage, and even though he'd had his doubts about it, once he saw evidence of magic, he accepted it.

He wanted to make Jasmine understand what had happened to him back there at the end of the disappearing road. But he knew that even if he could find the words, she wasn't ready to hear them.

Something had touched Quinn back there—not physically, though he'd felt that, too. Rather it was a sense of something or someone speaking directly to his mind, telling him that this was meant to be, that they must go on and find the valley. The only way he could describe it to himself was to say that he'd been filled, for one brief second, with a bright, warm light that had reached into his very soul. He wished that Jasmine had felt that, too.

He lay on his earthen bed, staring at the tiny sparks from the campfire that vanished into the darkness, rising rapidly as though they aspired to reach the cold light of the stars. He'd made his bed this night farther from hers, as though distance alone were enough to keep him from wanting her.

He shifted to his side and watched her in the flickering light of the fire. She lay on her back with one slim, pale hand resting on top of the blankets. He thought she was asleep, though he couldn't be sure.

Quinn had had his share of women—more than his share, if the truth were known. But none of them had ever been more than a temporary diversion. So it was with consternation—and even some fear—that he suddenly realized that Jasmine had become central to his life.

Suddenly he saw with great clarity what he should have seen long ago, at the very beginning of their journey. He'd never been one to ignore the wants and needs of the women who'd passed through his life, but even so, he'd never before become so adept at reading their thoughts or guaging their moods. Now it seemed to him that he knew Jasmine as well as she knew herself—and perhaps better. Furthermore, he understood that this emotion was very important.

He thought about the tales he'd heard all his

Thrill to the most sensual, adventure-filled Romances on the market today...

FROM  LOVE SPELL BOOKS

As a home subscriber to the Love Spell Romance Book Club, you'll enjoy the best in today's BRAND-NEW Time Travel, Futuristic, Legendary Lovers, Perfect Heroes and other genre romance fiction. For five years, Love Spell has brought you the award-winning, high-quality authors you know and love to read. Each Love Spell romance will sweep you away to a world of high adventure...and intimate romance. Discover for yourself all the passion and excitement millions of readers thrill to each and every month.

Save $5.00 Each Time You Buy!

Every other month, the Love Spell Romance Book Club brings you four brand-new titles from Love Spell Books. EACH PACKAGE WILL SAVE YOU AT LEAST $5.00 FROM THE BOOK-STORE PRICE! And you'll never miss a new title with our convenient home delivery service.

Here's how we do it: Each package will carry a FREE 10-DAY EXAMINATION privilege. At the end of that time, if you decide to keep your books, simply pay the low invoice price of $17.96, no shipping or handling charges added. HOME DELIVERY IS ALWAYS FREE. With today's top romance novels selling for $5.99 and higher, our price SAVES YOU AT LEAST $5.00 with each shipment.

AND YOUR FIRST TWO-BOOK SHIP-MENT IS TOTALLY FREE!

IT'S A BARGAIN YOU CAN'T BEAT! A SUPER $11.48 Value!

Love Spell ✦ A Division of Dorchester Publishing Co., Inc.

Get Two Books Totally
FREE —
An $11.48 Value!

▼ Tear Here and Mail Your FREE Book Card Today! ▼

PLEASE RUSH
MY TWO FREE
BOOKS TO ME
RIGHT AWAY!

Love Spell Romance Book Club
P.O. Box 6613
Edison, NJ 08818-6613

AFFIX
STAMP
HERE

life—about the magic that could exist only when one of his people was teamed with one of hers: male and female. Why hadn't he considered the implications of that before? Probably it was because he'd already become so familiar with the stories before he'd learned what could occur between men and women.

He wanted to awaken her and explain to her that they were meant to be more than just partners in this quest, but he remained still, fearing that she was already close to believing once again that he was a madman.

* * *

The dream came to Jasmine again. This time it was a blend of both previous dreams. She was in the valley—but not alone this time. Quinn was with her and they were floating as before through woods and meadows and the silent village.

The air was warm and scented: the dusky aroma of the dark pine forest was mingling with the lighter fragrances of a thousand flowers. A pleasant breeze blew through her gauzy dress, its touch on her bare skin wonderfully sensuous.

They left the village, running, but without their feet touching the ground. And then they were back in the deep woods again, settling gently onto a bed of bright green moss, their bodies already entwined.

They made love in that perfect place, moving in slow motion from kisses to caresses to the final act of giving themselves to each other. And in that final, perfect moment, Jasmine lost her sense of herself and became truly one with Quinn.

Jasmine awoke the next morning with a clear memory of the dream. Her body still felt a part of his—so much so that when she opened her eyes and found herself alone, she at first believed she'd simply moved into another, less pleasant dream.

Could it really be like that? Could it be so different from the ugly sweating and grunting that she'd once witnessed?

She shook off the dream with considerable effort as she began to wonder where Quinn had gone. It seemed to her that she'd been awake for some time, still caught in the dream while being aware of her surroundings.

She sat up and saw that the horses were still there, together with all their gear. But Quinn was nowhere to be seen. She felt the first stirrings of fear. It wasn't like him to go off and leave her alone like this.

A voice inside her began to whisper faintly about demons, but she ignored it. Even if they did exist, they couldn't have carried him off without awakening her. Or could they have? If they could make a road disappear . . . ? But Quinn had been insistent that that occurrence hadn't been the work of demons.

She scrambled to her feet and began to call him, but the forest swallowed up her cry. Truly terrified, she shouted even louder, while at the same time turning in a circle to scan the woods. And then she heard his voice, calling her name.

She raised her head, shading her eyes against the bright morning sun, and saw him on the hillside above her, waving for her to join him. She needed no invitation. Seeing him wasn't enough. She had to touch him, smell him, know that he was real.

She made her way up the steep slope. He came partway back down and grasped her hand. It was all she could do not to cry out with relief at that solid touch. "What is it?" She gasped as he half-dragged her up the hillside.

"See for yourself," was his only response.

And she did. They'd reached the top of the hill, whose far side dropped away even more steeply. And there, etched against the blue sky, lit by a sun that had only just risen, were the mountains.

Chapter Eight

They seemed to fill the horizon: jagged, dark peaks that rose far above the lower green hills, thrusting into the very heavens. The tops of some of them were white, tinged now with a delicate pink from the sun.

Jasmine stared at them in silence, awed by their majesty and aware that she could no longer deny their existence—or the reality of what must lie beyond them.

"It'll be days yet before we reach them," Quinn said, breaking the silence in a low, husky voice. "But the road is headed there—see it?"

She'd paid scant attention to the land between themselves and the mountains, but now she saw what he meant. Here and there, in both the valleys and on the hills, she could see traces of the road.

She turned to Quinn and saw unshed tears glazing his eyes. He smiled at her, and a single tear threaded its way down his cheek. Her hand seemed to move of its own volition to brush it away.

"You've found your dream, Quinn."

"*Our* dream. We've found it together."

He caught her hand just as she was about to lower it, and pressed his lips against her palm, sending a trail of heat down through her arm. "Our dream," he repeated softly, his eyes still shining with tears and more.

Jasmine stared at him—and saw a stranger. Quinn had changed—but how and when? Was it so slow that she simply hadn't noticed, or had the change happened suddenly? She didn't know, but she did know that something in him had been transformed.

She turned away from him to gaze upon the mountains once again. He was still holding her hand, and it felt like a lifeline connecting her to reality, while the dreamworld shimmered in the distance.

"I dreamed of the valley again last night," she said softly, her eyes still on the distant horizon.

"So did I—but you were there with me this time."

She turned to him, feeling a flush creep through her skin as she wondered if he'd dreamed *every-thing* that she had. He smiled.

"Yes. I dreamed that, too."

Her lips felt his imprint even before he lowered his face to hers, even before she lifted her hands and twined her fingers through his thick, curly hair. He was so very gentle, but she could feel the fiery passion trembling just beneath that gentle-ness, and she knew that the same hunger was awakening within her own body.

Quinn's lips and tongue traced slow, hot lines down the taut cords of her neck, down, finally, to the deep vee of her shirt, where the pendant rested in the valley between her breasts. He brushed it aside, kissing the soft, exquisitely sensitive swells, following the curve upward to her rapidly beating heart, then back again to lips that parted eagerly.

"I want you, Jasmine, more than I've ever wanted any woman." His voice was low and rough edged.

"I want you, too, Quinn," she replied huskily, her voice scarcely more than a whisper that was snatched away by the breeze.

Quinn stared at her and she sensed a war being waged within him. He turned to stare at the mountains, then back at her. "We will wait—until we reach the valley."

For three days they traveled through the hills, sometimes not seeing the mountains at all in the impenetrable thickness of the forest. But they could feel their presence, feel themselves being drawn ever closer.

At night they lay side by side near the campfire—close but not touching. When they kissed, it was no more than a promise, and there was a promise, too, in his hand that would close around hers, in his arm curved about her shoulders as they sat before the fire, and in the gray eyes that seemed always to be watching her, peering into her very soul.

Jasmine began to experience something wholly unknown to her: a feeling of being cherished. She was living happily in the body of a stranger. When she bathed in the stream, she stared at herself and for the first time saw how her body had changed. Lush curves had replaced sharp angles.

She found a small, quiet pool formed by rocks that projected into the stream, and bent to peer at her own reflection. She barely recognized her own face. The gaunt, hungry look was gone, replaced by smooth, firm flesh. She thought with astonishment that she might actually be called beautiful.

There were no dreams and no sounds in the night—nor had their sense of being watched returned. It was strange, but they couldn't agree on the reason. Jasmine thought it was because there had never been any demons to begin with. Quinn was of the opinion that they were gathering their forces in the valley.

"If you're right, Quinn," she said in a voice that indicated she was sure he was wrong, "then how do we fight them? Is someone going to appear to teach us how to work magic?"

"Perhaps," he said with a shrug. "Or perhaps we'll learn when it becomes necessary."

Jasmine regarded him with loving but skeptical eyes. Since they were drawing ever closer to the valley and nothing more had happened, she was quite willing to forget about those footprints and about the disappearing road. The prints had undoubtedly been those of a bear, and she'd been checking the road behind them from time to time.

On the third day, they both noticed how the forest was changing. The trees were much taller and thicker and bespoke great age. Quinn remarked that they looked as though they'd been there since the beginning of time, and she thought that described it well.

They rode steadily uphill on the winding road—the longest stretch yet. And when they reached the top, they both gasped in astonishment. Before them, the great mountains stood in all their majesty, rising precipitously from a broad grassy plain where not a single tree grew.

It was Quinn who saw the problem, because she was still staring at the mountains. "The road is gone," he pronounced, staring down at the plain.

She saw immediately that he was right. What lay between them and the mountains was an unbroken stretch of grass rippling in the cool breeze.

"What are those dark spots?" she asked. Scattered in a disorderly fashion across the plain were small, dark circles.

Quinn shook his head. "I don't know."

She shaded her eyes and stared again at the mountains. "I don't see any way through them."

"There will be a way," he said confidently as he dismounted. "We'll give the horses a rest here."

They sat side by side at the very edge of the cliff. Quinn slipped an arm around her and drew her close, then planted a kiss on her brow. He said nothing, and neither did she. The moment was a strange combination of giddy happiness and utter tranquillity. Even Jasmine no longer doubted that their valley lay beyond those mountains, while Quinn was confident that a way through would be shown to them.

But what lies beyond the end of the dream? she wondered. *It won't be enough just to find the valley there. We must know why it was taken from our people, so that it can never happen again. And what will we do if there* are *demons—and they're waiting for us?*

"We'll know what to do," Quinn said in that annoyingly confident tone.

For one brief second Jasmine thought that she'd only imagined his voice because she knew that was how he would respond if she'd actually spoken aloud. Then suddenly she knew that she hadn't just imagined his response; he'd actually spoken. A chill slid along her spine as she turned to him.

"What did you say?" she asked. Perhaps he'd said something else and she'd misunderstood.

"I said that we'll know what to do. There will be answers for us when we find the valley. And if the demons are there, we'll know how to deal with them, too."

"Quinn!" she cried, drawing a puzzled look from him as he turned to face her. "How did you know what I was thinking?"

His frown deepened. "I don't know what you're thinking. I only know what you just said."

"And what was that?" she asked, chilled all the way through now.

He repeated the questions she'd been asking herself. "I don't understand. What's wrong?"

"I didn't ask those questions. I was only thinking them."

"You were? But I heard you."

"You were reading my mind!" she cried accusingly, moving away from him and getting to her feet.

He got up slowly, obviously still confused. "If I was, it wasn't intentional. Are you sure you didn't speak?"

"Yes, I'm sure." But she no longer was, if only because it was safer to believe that she'd been mistaken.

He shrugged and gave her a crooked smile. "Then maybe I was just guessing."

They rode down the winding trail to the plain. The journey took much longer than they'd expected because the narrow road wound around and around, avoiding the steepest part of the descent. The sun was low in the western sky behind them by the time they came to the end.

Seen from this perspective, the mountains were even more awesome, rising starkly at the far edge of the undulating waves of tall grass. They looked unnatural, she thought—out of place with the rest of the landscape. In the waning light they had become even darker, but the tops of the highest peaks still glistened with reflected light, once again tinged with color from the sun.

"We'll camp right here," Quinn said. "Since there are no more hills to climb, I think we can cross the plain in one day."

Jasmine realized that distances had become impossible to determine. Up there the mountains had seemed very far away, but now they appeared to be much closer, perhaps because they now completely dominated the horizon.

She also realized that she could no longer see any of the strange dark spots she'd seen from above, and she reminded Quinn about them.

"We can ride out there a bit and see if we can find any of them," he suggested.

They left the packhorses behind and rode onto the plain. The grasses were more than three feet high and filled the air with a pleasantly sweet aroma that reminded Jasmine of the alfalfa her family had grown in fields near her first home. The scent triggered a flood of memories, vague but poignant, of that brief period of happiness: a laughing child being hoisted onto her father's broad shoulders as they walked through the field, the wonderful scents in the big barn, a black pony that had been her birthday gift just weeks before the soldiers came.

Her gaze went to the mountains and her thoughts to what lay beyond them. Was it possible that she could regain that innocent, peaceful happiness—the days of sunlight and laughter?

Beside her, Quinn suddenly brought his horse to a halt and pointed. "Over there!"

She followed his pointing finger and saw a dark shape within the grass. Then, as they moved in that direction, she saw that it was a pile of dark stones. Quinn drew up beside it and dismounted, and she did the same. He stood there frowning at it, then turned to her.

"I think it might be a burial place." She gave him a puzzled look and he explained.

"If there is no time, or no implements to bury someone, this is a way of preventing wild animals from getting at the body. We did that a few times in battle."

Jasmine stared at it, thinking of the others she'd seen from the hilltop. If he was right, then many bodies had been buried in this manner.

Quinn approached the stone pile and began to remove them carefully. Jasmine hung back, uncertain that they should be doing such a thing and not really wanting to see if he was right.

He'd removed about a half dozen of the large rocks when he suddenly made a sound of surprise, then gestured to her. She edged forward cautiously, then gasped when she saw what lay within the remaining stones. She couldn't see all of it, but she could see enough to know that it was a human skull, nearly upside down, with two rows of yellowed teeth visible.

Quinn picked up the rocks he'd removed and replaced them. "They were our people, Jasmine," he said as he turned to her.

"How do you know that?" she asked, still annoyed at the tone of absolute certainty he tended to use when making these pronouncements.

"It fits with the story: the battle between the demons and our people and their retreat from the valley. Either the battle continued here on the plains, or the bodies here are those wounded who were carried from the valley and then died."

"They could be anyone," she insisted, even though his theory made terrible sense.

"Have you seen signs of anyone else living in this whole area?" he challenged. "We haven't passed any villages or farms or any of *these* before this."

"Well, maybe there was a battle here," she admitted, albeit reluctantly. "But that doesn't mean anything."

Quinn threw her an exasperated look. "You won't believe until you see a demon, will you—even though you've already seen them in your dreams?"

"I don't know that what I saw in the dream were demons—and neither do you. It was too dark."

"They exist—and they killed these people—our

ancestors. This whole plain is one big graveyard. I wonder how many actually got away. Not very many, I suppose. Most of them probably died in the valley—or in the mountains."

Jasmine shivered. The sun had now sunk behind the hills, and the mountains were growing steadily darker and more menacing. A cold wind blew across the plain, making the tall grass seem alive with movement. And as the wind bent the grasses, she could see more of the dark stone piles.

Then suddenly she thought she heard cries: faint sounds carried on the chill wind. She lifted her head and stared into the heavens that were still lit by the vanished sun. The sound had reminded her of seagulls, but there were no birds anywhere to be seen.

"Did you hear that?" she asked in a near-whisper.

"Hear what?"

"Nothing." She shook her head and started toward her mare. It must have been birds—not seagulls, of course, but some other bird that mimicked human cries.

They realized by noon the next day that the plain was much wider than they'd thought. Even though the horses were making good time on the flatland and, they were less than halfway to the mountains. Quinn remarked that they'd have to camp on the plain one night. He didn't sound particularly concerned, but Jasmine suspected that he didn't much like the idea. Neither did she, though the mountains didn't seem any less threatening.

Throughout the day, they regularly passed other stone piles. Quinn insisted on stopping at several of them to confirm that there were bodies beneath them as well. The cairns varied greatly in size, and in one of the larger piles Quinn found three skulls, including that of a very young child.

"Stop this!" she demanded when he held up the tiny skull for her to see.

He replaced the skull, then rebuilt the stone heap. She had remained seated on her mare, and Quinn came over to her. "Don't you care that these are our people?" he asked.

"Of course I care—even if they aren't our people. That's why I want you to stop."

"I wanted to see if there were any that didn't look human," he replied in a maddeningly even tone. "If there was a battle out here, then some of the demons must have been killed as well."

"I'm tired of hearing about battles and demons, Quinn."

He raised a hand to trace his fingers slowly along her jawline. "I'm sorry. I won't stop at any more."

He drew her face down for a quick kiss that, at least for a moment, banished all her anger and unpleasant thoughts. Then he swung into his saddle and they rode on. His kiss lingered on her lips and she stared at the mountains that were growing steadily closer. Tomorrow they would be there, trying to find a pass that would take them into the valley of their dreams.

The next morning dawned cool and damp as a thick fog filled the plain. When she opened her eyes, Jasmine was surprised to discover that she'd slept at all—and that she hadn't dreamed. Even Quinn had seemed uneasy and had slept close to her with his rifle beside him and his knife under the pillow he'd made of a blanket. Now he was crouched a few feet away, trying without success to rebuild the fire that had been put out by the dampness. The fog was so thick that she could just barely make out the shapes of their horses, tethered on long lines only a short distance away.

She got up, wrapping the blanket around her as she walked over to him. He looked up with an apologetic smile. "I can't get the fire going. Everything is too damp."

They ate a cold breakfast of hard biscuits and some dried fruit as they waited for the fog to burn off. The sun was a pale, ghostly disk above the mountains, which were invisible now except for the tallest snowcapped peaks that gleamed like beacon fires.

Quinn was impatient. He wanted to reach the mountains by nightfall, or before that if possible. Given the fact that they'd misjudged the distance across the plains before, he was eager to be off as early as possible in case it took longer than he anticipated. They left as soon as the fog had thinned out enough to allow them at least minimum visibility.

They had been traveling for less than half an hour when the fog once again became so thick that Jasmine could barely see beyond her mare's nose. Quinn was riding slightly ahead, with the packhorses trailing behind Jasmine. She called out to him that they should stop and wait until they could see better, but he didn't respond—and a few seconds later, he had vanished into the swirling mists.

Jasmine kept going, trusting that her mare could see better than she could and would follow Quinn's stallion. Then suddenly she saw a dark shape off to her right side.

"Quinn!" she called out, irritated. "We have to stop until we can see again."

But there was no response, and then the figure she'd seen vanished into the mists. At this point, Jasmine was more angry than frightened. Even if he had no intention of following her suggestion, he could at least respond.

Then she saw him again—this time off to her left. But before she could call out, a second figure on horseback appeared. She began to hear muffled cries: screams of men in pain and the high-pitched whinnies of frightened horses!

Jasmine was so shocked that for a moment she did nothing at all. Then she reined in her mare and screamed for Quinn. But the sounds of battle—for there was no doubt that was what it was—were now so loud that her voice was merely one among many.

The mists shifted, thinning out and then closing in again—and in those moments when it became almost clear, she saw a shifting panoply of men on horses and others on foot, fighting with swords. The sounds of death were all around her. She turned her mare in a circle, seeking a way out, but everywhere she looked she could see dark shapes.

Then her mare and the packhorses began to panic. The well-trained pack animals had been set loose after their first few days on the road, since they followed along without need of being tied. Now, however, they bolted, and within seconds were gone in the fog. Jasmine could do nothing about them, since it took all her strength to keep her mare from bolting as well.

Suddenly one of the riders passed quite close to her, and for one brief instant she caught a glimpse of a pale face and long blond hair the same shade as her own. Then another figure followed, calling out to the first man. He could have been a brother to the first rider, the resemblance was so striking. Both men had seemed to look straight at her, but neither one gave any sign that they had seen her before they vanished again.

The answer to this madness had been lying there in her mind, but now it burst forth. She was seeing the battle that had resulted in the stone burial mounds—a battle that must have happened at least two hundred years ago!

She wanted desperately to scream again for Quinn, but she forced herself to remain silent, fearful of drawing any attention to herself. So she simply sat there, struggling with the mare, and nearly sliding off as the animal reared in fright.

The fog had become thick again, but as Jasmine fought to keep her seat and quiet the mare, she saw something else: another figure, this time on foot. It was just ahead of her and was probably the reason her mare had reared up.

The scream that welled up in her came out as little more than a gurgle. What she saw before her was not a man. The creature stared directly at her and bared its hideous fangs, then lunged at her.

"Begone, demon! I command you in the name of the gods!"

The words came out without her knowledge, and her fingers clutched the pendant, drawing it from beneath her shirt. Then there was a burst of brilliant golden light—and the demon was gone.

Jasmine sat there trembling, her fingers still clutching the pendant. It was warm and it glowed with a soft golden light that died away even as she stared at it. And after a moment, she realized that the only sounds she could hear were her own rapid breathing, the thudding of her heart, and her mare's anxious whickering. She turned slowly in the saddle, peering into the fog. It was thinning out again, so much this time that she could see the sun.

"Jasmine!"

The voice was distant and muffled, but it was definitely Quinn. She called out to him.

"Stay where you are and keep calling," he ordered. "I'll find you."

It seemed to be forever to her, but it was in fact no more than a few moments before she saw him emerge from the mist ahead of her. He brought his horse to a halt, then leapt from the saddle and ran to her, pulling her down and into his arms.

"The battle," she said, trembling even in the

solid comfort of his arms. "I saw one of them—a demon."

Quinn stroked her hair and kissed the top of her head. "I know. I saw it, too."

"How?" she asked, tilting her head back to look up at him. "It happened two hundred years ago."

He didn't answer, but instead drew her head against his shoulder. "I thought I'd lost you. I heard you say we should stop, but when I did, I couldn't find you. I never want to let you out of my sight again."

She pressed herself against him, feeling the rapid beating of his heart, and feeling the tremors that shook him as well. She understood instinctively that his fear stemmed not only from what he'd seen, but also from the belief that he had lost her. And she understood this because the same thought had been within her. Her fears began to fade, replaced by the wonderful feeling of being cherished—and loved.

They held each other for a long time, saying nothing because nothing needed to be said. Then finally they both looked around. The sun had burned its way through the fog, which now lingered in only a few places. The plain was empty, and the tall grasses showed no sign of having been disturbed. Only a short distance from where they stood was another of the stone burial mounds. The world had righted itself again. Time had flowed back to the present.

Quinn asked her what she'd seen, and she described the two men. He said that he'd seen one man with long blond hair the same shade as hers and several much bigger men with dark hair. But they had seen more, and each of them knew that.

Jasmine told him about the creature that had tried to attack her. The words came reluctantly. "It wasn't human, but it walked upright. It looked like

177

a wolf, but it wasn't." And then she told him what she'd done.

Quinn nodded. "I saw two of them. They came at me and I said just what you said. Then there was that burst of light—and they were gone."

"But you don't have a pendant," she protested, frowning. "I thought it was my pendant that drove them away."

He shook his head. "It must have been the words."

"But if that worked for us, then why didn't it work for them?" she asked, referring to their ancestors.

"I don't know." Quinn stared off at the mountains, now revealed by the bright sun. "Perhaps the gods chose to protect us—or maybe it was just because we weren't of that era. Maybe they didn't really see us, after all."

"I know it saw me," she stated firmly, not wanting to recapture the memory of staring into its red eyes, but doing so anyway. "It saw me—but my own ancestors didn't."

Quinn's fingers traced the line of her jaw and the curve of her neck. He bent to kiss her softly. "All that matters is that we're safe—and together."

"For now," she reminded him, unable to let go of that image. It seemed to her now that those terrible red eyes had held a threat even as the creature vanished.

Quinn made no response as he turned and pointed back across the plain in the direction from which they'd come. "We'd better go get the pack-horses."

Jasmine had forgotten all about them, but she saw them now, grazing a considerable distance away. They mounted their own horses and rode to them. All three shied away as they approached, though they'd never done that before. It took them some time, chasing them both on horseback and then on foot as they spoke soothingly to them, attempting to get them under control. It was only then, as she was leading one packhorse back to where Quinn waited with the other two horses, that she saw the damage done to its pack.

"Quinn, look at this!" She gestured to a long gash in the thick quilt that held some of their belongings.

Quinn examined it. "It looks like it was done by a sword."

And so it did. She could think of no other explanation. *It's a reminder*, she thought—proof that it happened. It would have been all too easy, in the bright sunlight that now flooded the plain, to believe that the fog itself had created an illusion.

They rode across the plain all day, with the sun at their backs and the great mountains filling their vision. The mountains now seemed almost close enough to touch, and yet it seemed to Jasmine that they still had as much plain to cross as they'd had when they started out. But Quinn said that he'd seen this type of illusion before when he'd crossed a large desert in his homeland. That reassured her somewhat, since she'd begun to fear that they might be the victims of yet another magic trick.

I will never completely trust my eyes again, she thought. *He accepts this magic because he's always believed in it—but I still don't. I've seen it, and I don't believe it.*

Then, late in the afternoon, she knew they were indeed drawing closer to the mountains because she could see details that hadn't been visible before. It had seemed before that the mountains simply rose like gigantic cliffs directly from the grassy plain—but now she could see that was not the case. Instead there was a space between filled with huge boulders, almost as though pieces of the mountains had fallen to the plain. Still, the sense persisted within her that this was an unnatural place.

Quinn saw it, too. "That should be a good place for us to camp tonight. There might even be a spring." They were low on water again.

The sun was sinking below the hills at their back when they reached the first of the rocky outcroppings. Jasmine had to lean as far back as possible in her saddle now to see the peaks, and when she did, she actually felt a wave of dizziness as she gazed upon those heights. Even the sky was lost to view.

Quinn suddenly brought his horse to a halt. "Listen! Do you hear that?"

For a moment she heard nothing but the wind as it rushed down at them from the mountains. Then she heard something else: the musical sound of water trickling over rocks.

They found the spring a short time later. It wasn't large, but it flowed steadily down over the rocks from a narrow crevasse above. And there was even a small pool, formed by giant boulders. Quinn pronounced it a perfect place to set up camp, though Jasmine was far less willing to trust the protection of the surrounding rocks than he was.

"Where will we go tomorrow?" she asked later, as they sat at the campfire. Her voice echoed strangely off the surrounding stress. For the first time in their long journey, the way ahead wasn't clear.

"We'll start looking for a trail of some kind that will lead us to a pass through the mountains."

That sounded nearly impossible to her, but she didn't say so. Quinn was determined, and he'd come a very long way to reach these mountains. If she didn't yet completely share his optimism that a way would be found, she at least wanted to believe it.

For three days they rode along the base of the mountains, looking for signs of a trail or even for the pass itself. And for three nights they lay close to each other, with Jasmine, at least, fearing what sleep might bring. But there were no dreams—and no intruders in the night. It began to seem to her that the mountains themselves were watching them, even laughing at their puny attempts to conquer them.

Quinn's patience and determination were daunting, and kept her own frustrations in check. His sharp eyes picked up one sign after another, and when none of them proved to be what they were seeking, he simply shrugged and went on. At some point she realized that these traits must stem from the many years he'd spent working long hours in the quarries and living frugally as he'd saved his money to pursue his dream.

He's a remarkable man, she thought, wondering if she might be only now coming to appreciate him. In a way, he was like the mountains themselves: solid and enduring. She watched him scale rocks that she herself would never have attempted, then stand at the pinnacle and turn slowly to study their surroundings. His hair was longer now, and he shaved only when his beard began to bother him, and the profile he presented was as rugged as the rocks upon which he stood.

On the fourth day, when Quinn once again climbed up to get a better view, she expected him to come down again, shrug in that familiar way, then tell her they should move on. But this time he remained motionless for a long time, staring fixedly at one spot off to his right. Then he climbed down quickly, his rugged features alight with triumph.

"I saw burial mounds," he proclaimed. "Several of them. They're not far."

They rode partway, then were forced to lead the animals as the terrain became ever more treacherous. But an hour later they were standing before five mounds, each of them large enough to hold numerous bodies.

"They came this way," Quinn stated excitedly. "This must be where they buried those who died coming through the mountains."

"But where is the path?" she asked, seeing nothing.

"It must be around here somewhere. We'll leave the horses here for now and start looking. I think they buried them here because there are a lot of small rocks. But they wouldn't have strayed far from the path."

The trail was almost invisible. In fact, Jasmine didn't see it at all—but fortunately Quinn did. They went back for the horses, then set out. The trail was obvious in most places, but nearly invisible in others, causing many delays as they tried to find it again. But as dusk arrived, they had left behind the rocky outcroppings and were in the mountains themselves.

A brilliant full moon washed the land with silver, deadening all color and leaving deep shadows beneath overhanging rocks. A chill wind whistled through the narrow gaps where the trail wound ever upward. Jasmine stood with Quinn on a rocky ledge above the trail and stared out at the plain they'd left behind—the place where she'd finally come to believe in magic.

Quinn curved an arm around her shoulders and drew her close. He was making a pretense of being at ease, but she knew he was worried. The closer they came to the valley, the greater the likelihood that the demons would try to stop them.

Despite the evidence presented to her by her

own eyes, Jasmine was still reluctant to accept that creatures from a nightmare could actually inhabit the real world. And she was even less inclined to believe they could actually defeat such supernatural beings, despite her having seemed to have banished one.

But above all, she wanted to know how their people had been driven from the valley. Why had their magic failed them? Her and Quinn's very lives might well depend on that knowledge, and yet they had no way of gaining it.

The night passed peacefully—for Jasmine, at least. When she awoke with the sun, Quinn was already awake and looked as though he'd slept little, if at all. But his eyes lit with pleasure when he saw that she was awake. She thought that it was probably because he was eager to move on, but soon found that she was wrong when he came over to lie down beside her.

He propped himself up on one elbow and bent to kiss her, softly and carefully, as though she were too fragile to bear the force of his passion. That desire, which he always kept reined in, indeed did feel like a great weight, a powerful presence, upon them. In fact, as the days passed, she found herself in the grip of old fears, even as her body melted at his touch.

"I worried that you might be lost in your dreams forever," he said, his face scant inches from hers.

"I didn't dream—not at all."

"You must have. You were talking in your sleep."

She was surprised. "What did I say?"

"I don't know. I couldn't hear you well enough to make out the words, and I didn't want to disturb you by coming closer."

He stared at her, and she felt as though his gaze were burning through to her very soul. It was a feeling she'd had often in the past few days, when she would turn and find him watching her. There was something different about it now, something disturbing.

Quinn kissed her lips again, then began to trail kisses down over her neck. His hands slid beneath the blanket, then molded themselves to her curves. That familiar yearning welled up in her, but so did a fear of unleashing that dark passion within him.

Her nipples grew taut, pushing against the light fabric of her shirt. Quinn pushed the blanket away impatiently and brushed them with his tongue, driving her to new heights of sensation. He lay half on top of her, one leg thrust between hers, his hardness pressing almost painfully against her.

She made a sound that was half moan and half cry, eagerness mixing explosively with fear. He lifted his head and stared at her, and she saw sudden confusion in his eyes. Then abruptly he moved away from her.

"Quinn?" She gasped, confused.

He didn't respond for a moment, then reached out to take her hand. He was trembling, but when he looked at her again, the confusion was gone and she saw only gentleness.

"The valley," he said, his voice deep and harsh. "We must wait."

Why? she asked silently, the question never quite forcing its way out. He spoke with that same absolute certainty that she'd heard before, a certainty that made her wonder—not for the first time—if he knew things he wasn't telling her.

They ate a quick breakfast and were once again on the trail, with very few words spoken between them. A terrible dread began to gnaw at Jasmine. It seemed that the closer they came to the valley, the more Quinn was once again becoming a stranger to her.

* * *

Quinn was also becoming a stranger to himself. For the first time in his long journey, doubts were nagging at him. Something had changed, and he didn't need to look hard to know when it had begun. It had begun back there on the foggy plain, when time had turned itself inside out and shown them a battle that had happened centuries ago.

He'd listened carefully to Jasmine's description of her encounter with the demon, then admitted that he'd seen them, too. But it had been a lie she'd fortunately accepted.

As they rode along the winding trail, moving ever higher and farther into the mountains, Quinn closed his eyes and relived that moment. The two demons had appeared out of nowhere. He'd just been calling out to Jasmine, knowing that his voice was being muffled by the fog, but desperate to find her.

They hadn't tried to attack him. Instead they'd simply appeared, only a few yards away. There were shreds of what he feared must be human flesh hanging from their terrible talons, and he thought he'd seen strands of long blond hair. He'd already seen one blond warrior, and he could only pray that the hair belonged to one of them, and not to Jasmine.

Quinn could recapture the moment, but it was difficult for him to summon up again the feeling he'd had. Fear for Jasmine, certainly—but something else, something that kept him from drawing his knife or grabbing the rifle that was strapped to his saddle.

For what seemed like a very long moment, he'd stared into those two pairs of red eyes and felt that he was staring into a darkness so vast and so powerful that it threatened to swallow him whole. Then they'd simply disappeared, but not before one of them had given him a horrible grin.

It was the grin he recalled now: an acknowledgment of something. But what was it? He hadn't known then, and he didn't know now.

Jasmine had said many times that there were questions that needed to be answered, that their very lives could depend on those answers. Until that moment when he was face-to-face with the demons, Quinn hadn't been troubled by the mysteries that had followed him here. But now he felt himself at the mercy of forces he couldn't understand.

Something dark was growing within him—and he suspected that Jasmine had sensed it. He'd felt it ever since the encounter with the demons, but never more strongly than when he'd just held her.

He'd been a long time without a woman, and his need was great, but until now he'd held his desire in check, understanding that he needed to be gentle with her. Not only was she a virgin, but he knew that she'd never let anyone get emotionally close to her before. There were many barriers that had to come down slowly if they were to come down at all.

Then, too, almost from the beginning—from the first time he'd felt desire for her—he'd had a strong belief that they should wait until they reached the valley.

But this morning that darkness within him had very nearly overwhelmed his careful control. The hunger he'd felt for her had an ugly side to it: a desire not merely to possess her, but to conquer her.

Still, that darkness wasn't a complete stranger to him. He'd felt it many times on the battlefields, when he'd known only after the fact about his exploits. And he'd seen the fear in the eyes of other seasoned veterans as they'd recounted them to him. "That boy's got blood lust," one of them had once said, believing that Quinn was out of earshot. It had happened too when he'd hunted down and then killed the men who'd raped his sisters—and it had nearly happened that time when he'd found the drunken farmers about to attack Jasmine.

His behavior on those occasions hadn't troubled him too much, though, because killing was what soldiers did—and because his sister's attackers deserved to die as well. There was even a certain pride in knowing that he was very good at it.

Besides, he'd always been able to tell himself that he wasn't evil or a criminal, though he had no compunction about breaking laws that were unjust. He thought of himself as being basically a good man, and knew that others thought that as well.

Now he wondered if that dark side of him had somehow been unleashed by his encounter with the demons. That made sense, since they were the ancient enemies of his people. But what was even more terrifying he knew that what he'd felt in that moment hadn't been hatred.

Throughout the day, they traveled deeper into the mountains. At times the trail was so narrow and the surrounding peaks so high that they could see no more than the narrowest strip of sky. On one side, sheer rock walls rose to unimaginable heights, while on the other side, the land dropped away to dizzying depths.

By late afternoon, such sunlight as had managed to penetrate into the narrow crevasses was gone and an early dusk had descended. An eerie half-light made the trail visible, so they kept going. Even though they'd been climbing steadily, Jasmine didn't have to look up to see that they had much farther to go. Quinn was still hoping to find a pass that would take them through the mountains more quickly, but that seemed increasingly unlikely.

They stopped to eat, being forced now to remain on the trail itself. The strange half-light persisted, and Quinn wanted to go on. There would be a nearly full moon that would provide as much light as they had now. Jasmine agreed because she wanted to get through this strange place to the valley. Her eagerness to reach the valley had grown in direct proportion to her fears about Quinn.

He'd been nearly silent all day, but it seemed to her to be a brooding sort of silence now. She told herself that it was only because they were so close to their goal and he was beginning to ponder what they'd do when they got there—but she didn't quite believe her own rationale.

The weird light gradually gave way to bright moonlight as they rode slowly along a particularly narrow stretch of the trail—so narrow that her boots actually brushed against the sheer rock walls that were now on both sides.

She'd been lost in her thoughts about Quinn, who rode a short distance ahead of her, and so she never knew what made her suddenly look up at the cliff to her left. But just as she did, a dark shape separated itself from the top—aiming directly at Quinn.

Chapter Nine

She screamed.

He reined in his horse sharply and whirled around just as the creature struck.

Jasmine's mare reared and she slid off its back, landing in a heap on the path behind the frightened horse. It blocked her view of Quinn as it continued to rear and dance around. She managed to slip past its flailing hooves only to be confronted with Quinn's equally terrified horse. Beyond it, Quinn and the creature were moving shadows and nothing more.

Flattening herself once more against the rock wall, Jasmine maneuvered around the second horse. Quinn and the creature were locked together, rolling on the path. And now Jasmine saw to her horror that there was an opening in the high wall on one side of the path. What lay beyond it she couldn't tell, but if it was another precipitous drop . . .

"Begone, demon! I command you in the name

of the gods!" She shouted the words—and this time they were intentional. She could feel her pendant growing warm and she pulled it out, holding it up in front of her.

In the moonlight it was difficult to see them clearly, but she thought she saw the demon hesitate and turn toward her. Then, as she drew closer, she saw those red eyes staring directly at her for one brief instant. Pure hatred broke over her, shaking her to her very core.

But Quinn was able to use that moment's hesitation to gain the upper hand. She saw his arm come up and saw the flash of a knife. Then the demon turned its attention back to him, and for a moment that seemed to stretch to eternity, Quinn's arm remained motionless.

Jasmine moved closer still, until she could smell the foul odor emanating from the creature. "Begone!" she cried again, holding out the pendant and praying for that blinding light that had banished the other monster.

But it didn't happen. Suddenly Quinn's arm swung in a wide arc and the knife was buried deep in the creature's chest. It thrashed wildly, but made no sound. Jasmine turned her back, glad that it was dying but unable to watch. Her mare was nowhere to be seen, but Quinn's horse had stopped just a short distance away. She ran to it and grabbed Quinn's bow, although she feared she might not be strong enough to use it.

And when she turned to face them again, the sight that met her eyes was nearly as horrifying as the one she'd turned away from. Quinn stood over the creature, partially blocking her view. The knife in his hand was dripping blood onto the ground— blood that looked nearly black in the moonlight.

She started toward Quinn, then stopped as he suddenly backed away from the still creature. And then she saw why. From its unmoving body rose a fine, gray mist, and as she watched, openmouthed in horrified amazement, the creature simply vanished, as though all its substance had been turned into a smoke that quickly dissipated into the night.

Even when it was gone, Quinn didn't move. His back was to her and his hand still clutched the knife. Afraid to move, Jasmine called out his name—and after a moment he turned to her. He stared at the knife as though he'd forgotten it was there, and then threw it to the ground before coming to her.

She was still clutching the bow when Quinn reached her, and he pried it from her hands, then set it aside and drew her into his arms. She recoiled as the stench of the creature assailed her nostrils. Quinn let her go and stared at her.

Jasmine forced herself to stare back, even though she felt at that moment that she was staring into eyes as cold and deadly as those of the demon.

"Quinn?" she said softly, half-fearing that the man who stood before her wasn't him.

He blinked rapidly several times, then ran a hand through his hair. Then he turned back to the spot where the demon had lain.

She waited, her heart pounding against her rib cage, glad that he'd turned away so she wouldn't have to see his eyes. But when he turned slowly to face her again, what she saw propelled her into his arms.

He held her close, murmuring soothing words, and she hugged him, knowing that he was Quinn again.

"Did you see what happened after I killed it?" he asked, his voice barely above a whisper.

She nodded.

"It didn't die," he said. "It just vanished."

"Maybe the pendant just took longer to work," she suggested, desperately seeking an answer that made sense, even though nothing made sense now.

Quinn kissed her softly, his lips featherlight against hers. It was the kind of kiss she needed—to remind her of the good and gentle man she knew him to be.

"If you—or your pendant—hadn't slowed it down, I might be dead," he said, his tone betraying his reluctance to admit such a thing. "You distracted it just long enough for me to gain the upper hand. But I think it vanished on its own."

"After it was already dead?"

He shook his head. "It wasn't dead, even though it should have been. I struck its heart—if it has one—but it was still staring at me when it started to turn to smoke."

Jasmine felt a shudder go through him and she hugged him even tighter. It did nothing at all for her peace of mind to know that he must be as frightened as she was. But this time she didn't question the wisdom of continuing their journey. They had to find the valley. She accepted that now, as Quinn always had.

Neither of them wanted to travel farther tonight, however, even though the moon was still bright. They camped where they were, taking turns staying awake in case the demon should return.

Quinn fell asleep quickly and she sat there, a blanket wrapped around her shoulders, and reflected upon their brush with death. It had surprised her that Quinn was unhurt. There was blood on his hand and on his sleeve as well, but it wasn't his. She hadn't seen the creature all that well, but she had seen yellow fangs and long, sharp talons. It was a miracle that Quinn had escaped unscathed.

Then she wondered why he hadn't sensed the presence of the demon, when she clearly had. It surely couldn't have been a coincidence that she'd looked up at just that moment. Was it possible that she had some form of protection that he lacked?

She drew out her pendant once again. The diamond winked at her in the moonlight, while the onyx was nearly invisible. People of the light, and people of the darkness. Two distinct races, once enemies.

Her thoughts seemed to be reaching out toward something important as she stared at the pendant, but whatever it was eluded her, like words that seemed to come to the very tip of her tongue, but refused to be spoken.

In the bright, clear light of the next day, it was almost impossible for Jasmine to believe that the attack had occurred. She opened her eyes to find that she'd slept with her head on Quinn's lap as he leaned against the rock wall beside the path. And only when she saw the spots of blood on his sleeve did she know that it hadn't been a dream.

Quinn stroked her hair, then bent to kiss her when she lifted her face. She could still smell the foul odor of the demon on him, and he apparently did, too.

"There's not enough water for bathing," he announced as they both stood up and stretched. "I wish we could find another spring."

What they found, only a few hours later, was more than a spring. The trail continued to climb higher, though it became somewhat wider, and both of them heard the sound at the same time: a low roar that grew steadily louder as they rode on.

"It's a waterfall," Quinn told her happily.

And then they rounded yet another sharp curve—and there it was. Water dappled by sunlight rushed down from a high ledge. And below them, off a side trail, lay a mist-enshrouded pool.

It was a spectacularly beautiful sight, and it was also the first time that Jasmine allowed herself to enjoy this wild place. As the waterfall struck rocks in its path, it sent up a fine spray that sparkled in the sun like a million tiny diamonds. The breeze carried to them the scent of damp earth and the dark firs that surrounded the waterfall and the pool at its base.

The path down to the pool was treacherous, so they dismounted and led their horses down, and then Quinn returned for the packhorses. Jasmine saw that the pool was in fact only a way station for the waterfall, which then plunged many hundreds of feet farther down the mountainside until it was lost in the thick forest.

By the time he returned with the packhorses, Jasmine was already damp from head to toe from the spray and wondering if the pool was shallow enough for her to bathe in. Even getting into it would be a problem, since it lay at the bottom of a natural rock bowl.

There were several very small, shallow pools that provided water for the horses, and after Quinn had let them drink their fill, he sat down and pulled off his boots, then stripped off his shirt as well.

"It doesn't look too deep, but it's hard to judge from here. I'll go in first."

Jasmine averted her gaze as he reached for his belt buckle, and he chuckled softly. "After all this time, would the sight of my naked body upset you?" he asked teasingly.

"No," she said quickly, but without looking at him.

"I already saw you," he said.

"You did?" She turned toward him just in time to see him leap toward the pool.

He vanished beneath the water for a few seconds, leaving her with a brief image of a hard, hair-roughened body. Then his head bobbed to the surface.

"It's deep. I'm treading water. Jump in and I'll catch you."

Jasmine started to shake her head, then stopped. She was being foolish. She wanted a bath, and this might be her only chance for some time. Besides, the pool looked so inviting.

"Is it cold?" she asked, temporizing.

"Not too cold—and I saw you that time when you were bathing in the lake. It wasn't intentional."

He gave her that crooked grin that could make him seem so harmless and boyish—not an easy feat for a man like him, and she'd often wondered if he'd perfected it for that reason. Quinn, she thought, was hardly above such things.

She told herself that her need to bathe outweighed any lingering modesty, and began to remove her clothes. Quinn's head disappeared, then resurfaced on the far side of the pool. It took him only a few powerful strokes to return to the spot just beneath the ledge.

He raised his head to stare at her. With his black hair hanging wet around his face and his dark beard, he looked more like a cold killer than like the gentle man she loved. Jasmine shrank back from the edge, more from fear of him than from a fear of leaping into the water.

"Jump!" he urged. "I won't let you drown."

She hesitated. Her nakedness made her feel powerful and exposed all at the same time. She started forward, then stopped and began to lift the chain that held the pendant.

"Don't take it off," he called.

Hearing the urgency in his voice, she let the pendant fall once again between her breasts. It seemed that Quinn had more faith in its magic than she did.

She took a few more steps—to the very edge of the rock—then jumped. The cool water slipped over her—and then Quinn's arms were around her, pulling her to the surface. She coughed and spluttered and tried to brush the wet hair from her eyes. When she opened them, Quinn was grinning at her.

"I guess I forgot to tell you to hold your breath," he said as he thumped her on the back.

She clung to him, terrified of going under again. But she wasn't so frightened that she failed to notice his hard, naked body pressing against hers.

"Time for a swimming lesson," he announced, loosening his hold on her.

"No!" She gasped, grabbing hold of his arms.

But he persisted, and to her amazement she was swimming in no time, the movements seeming as natural as walking. Still, Quinn stayed close to her, murmuring words of encouragement.

Jasmine luxuriated in the freedom of moving about the small pool on her own, her earlier fears forgotten completely. Then Quinn showed her how to float on her back and she drifted, staring up at the waterfall thundering down around them and the great mountains standing as silent sentinels beneath the blue sky. It was a moment to cherish, a time to remember.

They stayed in the pool for nearly an hour. Once the novelty of swimming and floating began to wear off, Jasmine found herself becoming all too aware of Quinn's naked body close to hers, and their movements became a sort of intimate dance designed to keep them apart in the small space. Floating on her back and unable to see where he was, she would brush against him and hurriedly push off—but not before she felt the imprint of his body.

Once, when she reached the far side of the pool and turned to swim back, she collided with him, and they both sank briefly beneath the surface in a tangle of arms and legs. Quinn wrapped his arms around her and drew them back up again, and they both hesitated, unwilling to separate but unwilling to move beyond the moment, either.

"Soon," he whispered as his hands slid down her body and his mouth covered hers briefly before he let her go.

She felt ripe and heavy with wanting, and she could think of no better time or place for them to take that final step. But somewhere along the way, she'd come to accept Quinn's decision that they should wait until they reached the valley. It simply felt right to her, even though her hunger was surely as great as his.

"Time to be on our way," Quinn announced, though what she saw in his eyes suggested otherwise.

Jasmine looked around. "How are we going to get out?" she asked uneasily. On all sides of the pool the rocks were too high and there were no footholds.

Quinn laughed. "I'd never have guessed that you'd leap into something without considering how to get out."

"Quinn!" She looked around wildly, then saw their only route out. "Oh, no!"

"Oh, yes. We'll just climb through the waterfall."

And before she could protest that there must surely be another way, he was swimming into the spray. She hesitated, then followed.

They climbed carefully because the rocks were wet and slippery. Quinn insisted that she go first, so that he could catch her if she began to slip. Blinded by the rushing water, Jasmine was frightened at first, but soon discovered that there were plenty of footholds.

Quinn followed her, enjoying the view even though he ached with desire. He'd come very close to forgetting about his promise to wait until they reached the valley, and he knew that she wouldn't have resisted. But something made him hold back, no matter how difficult it was.

The darkness he'd felt within him was gone, but in its place was an even greater sense of urgency to reach the valley before it could come again.

Ahead of him, Jasmine stepped onto a dry ledge, then moved over to make room for him. They both stood there for a moment, staring up at a distant peak where snow glistened in the sun. He took her hand and felt all her strength and vulnerability and offered a silent thanks to whatever force had brought them to this place. His long years of working toward this goal marched through his mind. They were close now; he was sure of it.

Quinn reined in his horse and stared at the steep ascent ahead of them. The trail disappeared from view at the top, apparently curving around the mountain. They'd been following the trail for four days now, and it seemed to him that they were no closer to getting through the mountains than they had been when they started. Behind him, Jasmine voiced the same thought.

"This has to be the way through," he said. "Why else would it exist?"

They dismounted and led the animals up the nearly perpendicular trail. All the way up, Quinn let himself hope that they would see the valley below them, but when they reached the top and saw nothing other than more mountains, it was Jasmine who expressed her frustration.

"We're going nowhere," she complained. "I keep expecting to see the plains again at any moment."

Quinn said nothing. The same thought had occurred to him. He had a good sense of direction under normal circumstances, but that sense had long since failed him. Now he could tell what direction they were going only by watching the sun—

and that told him they were mostly going in circles through the mountains.

"No wonder they so rarely left the valley," she said morosely as she stared at the endless rock face before them. "Maybe the demons haven't bothered us again because they know we're just going in circles."

Quinn didn't answer. He was grateful for the fact that there'd been no further attacks, but he was also bothered by it. If they were getting closer to the valley, why hadn't the demons tried to prevent them from reaching it?

"If they could make the road disappear, they could make us wander around forever," she said disgustedly.

"I told you, that wasn't the demons." He wrapped an arm around her shoulders. "We're going to get there. It's just taking longer than I'd thought."

The trail curved in a long, downward path, then started to ascend once more, though more gradually this time. Or so it seemed at first. But when they came around a blind curve, yet another nearly vertical climb lay ahead of them.

"We should probably make camp here," Quinn told her. The horses were tired and it was already late in the day. He turned to Jasmine to find her staring up at the steep trail.

She shook her head, surprising him. "No, we should go up there now," she said, so softly that he could barely hear her.

He stared at her, frowning. "Are you sure?"

Suddenly, she blinked and lowered her head to look at him. "What did you say?"

"I said are you sure that you want to go on?"

"I thought you said we would camp here." She frowned.

"I did, but you said you wanted to go on."

"No, I didn't."

"Yes, you did."

She frowned and he saw her fingers go to the pendant. "Maybe I did. I felt strange there for a moment."

"We're going up there. I suppose it would be better to camp on higher ground."

She merely nodded, still seeming distracted as she continued to clutch the pendant. Quinn dismounted and she did too, and they began to lead the horses up the trail. Every time he glanced her way, he saw that she was still clutching the pendant in her free hand.

Quinn reached the top ahead of her and stared in disbelief. It couldn't be! After all this, they'd come to the end of the trail—and not to the valley.

The trail ended at a cliff that plunged hundreds of feet into a narrow, rock-strewn crevasse. By the time Jasmine joined him, he had satisfied himself that there was no other trail anywhere—noplace for them to go but back.

He expected her to voice his own frustrations, but instead, she merely came to a halt beside him, still clutching her amulet. It seemed she barely noticed that the trail had disappeared. His frustration drained away, replaced by a certainty that something was wrong with her.

The pendant was warm and pulsing in her hand as Jasmine came to a halt beside Quinn. She felt strange. Her vision was blurring at the edges as she looked around. She heard Quinn say her name, but she ignored him as the blurring got even worse.

Then suddenly her gaze became focused again—on the thick, dark forest opposite the cliff. The trees were very old and thick clumps of blackberry bushes grew beneath them. She heard Quinn call out to her again, but she was already wading into the prickly bushes, only barely aware of the thorns that scratched her arms and legs.

"Jasmine!" Quinn caught up with her and grabbed her arm. "What are you doing?"

"It's here somewhere," she said, though she didn't know what she meant.

"What's here?" He stared around them in bewilderment. There was nothing but forest.

"The cave," she replied, then heard the echo of her own voice and shuddered. What on earth had made her say that? What cave?

"A cave? I don't see . . ."

She started forward again, pulling away from Quinn, who trailed along after her in confusion. And then they both came to a sudden stop.

Before them lay stone steps carved out of the dark rock—and at the bottom, barely visible in the preternatural gloom, was the mouth of a cave.

"Let's get the horses," Quinn said. "And we'll need to make some torches."

"We won't need torches. There's light."

Quinn cupped his hands around her shoulders and shook her. "Jasmine! What's happened to you?"

"I . . . I don't know," she said, frowning. "It feels like I was dreaming."

"You just said that the cave is lit. Do you remember that?"

She shook her head. She couldn't really remember anything very clearly after they'd stopped at the bottom of the hill back there. She vaguely recalled reaching the cliff, and that was all.

"Come with me to get the horses," he said gently. "Then we'll have a look at the cave."

Jasmine followed him back to the end of the trail. Quinn was holding her hand tightly, as though he feared that she would take off or perhaps disappear. She felt the fog in her mind lifting slowly, giving her back to herself.

"What happened to me?" she asked plaintively when they reached the horses.

Quinn touched her face gently. "I don't know, but you might have found the way to the valley."

Only now, looking around her, did she realize that the trail had ended here on this cliff. She turned to look back the way they had just come and saw nothing but thick woods. Quinn turned, too.

"There must have been a path there once, but the bushes grew over it."

"I don't want to go into a cave," she said, shuddering. She'd never been in one, but she didn't care at all for the idea of being under the ground.

"I'll go in first," he said. "You can wait until I have a look around."

They led the horses through the woods and down the wide rock steps. Quinn stepped into the mouth of the cave, and suddenly, quite without intending to do so, Jasmine was running toward him.

"No! Wait, Quinn. You can't go without me!"

He stopped and turned. "I won't go far."

She shook her head, certain somehow that they had to go together. Cool, musty air rushed out at them as they stepped through the entrance into darkness.

"I'll have to make a torch," Quinn said, starting to turn back.

"No, wait!" Jasmine took his arm.

And then, as their eyes began to adjust to the darkness, they could both see a faint light. Even as they stared at it, it seemed to grow brighter, until a pale golden light filled the narrow space.

"What is it?" she asked, trying to see where the light was coming from. It seemed to have no source at all, and yet the floor and the walls and even the roof were lit.

"Magic," Quinn pronounced. "This is the way. I'm going to get the horses."

A few moments later, they were leading the horses through the wide part near the entrance and then into a space so narrow that they had to walk single-file. The eerie light continued as they made their way slowly down a slope, going deeper and deeper into the mountain.

Ahead of them it was always dark, but they never reached that darkness because the light seemed to be moving with them. Several times they came to places where other passageways branched off, but always the light showed them the way.

Jasmine knew she should be terrified. If the light failed them, they would never find their way out. And yet she knew somehow that it wouldn't fail them. She also noticed that in spite of the chill in the air, her pendant was warm again and pulsing faintly.

Quinn was in the lead, and so he was the first one to feel the change in temperature. "I think we're coming to the end," he said excitedly, his voice echoing off the stone walls.

A few moments later the light began to fail. She was about to cry out when Quinn's voice cut her off. "I can see light!"

The passageway widened and she brought her horse up beside his. There ahead of them was light—natural this time. Fresh, pine-scented air rushed in at them. Jasmine felt her heart beating rapidly. Surely they had found the valley!

And so they had. When they emerged from the mouth of the cave, it lay far below them: a long stretch of woods and fields and a shimmering lake, nestled at the base of the tallest mountains.

"It's so big!" she said in a whisper. "I thought it would be smaller."

"Look!" Quinn said excitedly, pointing off to the right. "Do you see them?"

She looked where he indicated. Small dots of white were moving slowly around a huge meadow.

"The horses," he said, his voice as soft as hers had been.

Jasmine felt tears running down her cheeks, and when she looked up at Quinn, she saw that he, too, was crying. They walked to the very edge of the cliff and stood there, arms around each other.

"Home," he said in a choked voice.

She nodded, unable to speak. *Home.* Now, finally, she understood the true meaning of that word. The dream had come true.

The trail was much the same as before: a winding, narrow path that seemed to be constantly turning upon itself. The valley was still visible as they began their descent, but within a short time it was lost to view amid a thick forest of ancient trees.

Each time the trail seemed to be turning away from the valley, Jasmine grew anxious, fearing that they had been tricked: given a view of a place they would never reach. But later it would still be there, even if it was no more than a tantalizing glimpse through a break in the trees as they traveled.

She had stopped worrying about what would happen when they reached the valley. It made no sense to question a dream when it became reality. Instead she began to feel Quinn's certainty that they would know what to do. After all, it had already proven to be true. They'd reached what had seemed to be the end of the trail, but something had guided her to the cave, then lighted their way through it.

The path turned away from the valley once more, and this time continued in that direction for some distance. Jasmine was about to express her concern to Quinn, when he turned in his saddle.

"Don't worry. We're still descending, and that's all that matters."

He turned around again to guide his horse over a particularly steep and rocky place, and Jasmine, following behind, stared at his broad back. Was he reading her mind? Or was it only that they were both thinking the same things?

She guided her mare carefully down the rock-strewn path as she thought about the other times when he'd seemed to reach into her thoughts. Perhaps this always happened when two people became very close. She couldn't know because it had never happened to her before. She'd always thought that she'd been close to her mother, but now she wondered. Her mother had kept the existence of the pendant from her, and she'd often seemed lost in a place Jasmine couldn't reach.

Had her mother dreamed of the valley as Quinn had, but kept that dream to herself? What else might she have known that she'd never told Jasmine? And what else might her grandmother have told her that she'd forgotten? A child's memory probably wasn't very precise. It was possible that Gramman had told her more, but she'd remembered only part of it.

The trail, while still steep, now began to curve back toward the valley, and Jasmine let her mind slip back to those days at the farm before the soldiers had come. There'd been long winter evenings when they'd all sat before the fire, her mother knitting or doing some chore and her father working on a piece of farm equipment while Gramman spun her tales.

Something about centuries of peace finally ending, Jasmine thought, snatching desperately at a memory that hovered just out of reach. Something about old hatreds. She could almost hear her grandmother's soft voice, but nothing more than a few words remained in her memory.

Then she was abruptly jolted out of those memories by something that felt almost like a slap against her entire body. The pendant nestled between her breasts felt like a hot coal. She blinked in disbelief. Quinn was gone!

Panic welled up in her. The trail ahead was straight for some distance, but there was no sign of Quinn or his horse, even though he'd been riding just ahead of her. She swiveled around and saw that the packhorses were still behind her; then she began to shout his name.

The ancient forest seemed to swallow her cries, and it gave nothing back. She reined in her mare and looked around frantically. Could he have just disappeared like the road? And when had it happened? She had no idea how long she might have been woolgathering.

She kicked the mare into a brisk trot, still shouting his name. The straight stretch ended in a wide bend, and through the forest she could see the trail for some distance beyond. There was no sign of Quinn.

She slowed the mare and tried to think; then she dismounted and tied the packhorses to a tree. Whatever she was going to do, she didn't need the additional burden of them to deal with.

Where could he be? She recalled his description of how she'd disappeared that time when the road had vanished. But he'd brought her back. He'd also been certain that that wasn't the work of demons. She was equally certain that this was.

She decided to go back—back to the area where she'd last seen him, before she'd let herself get lost in her memories. But as she rode back up the trail, she wondered how he could possibly have disappeared without her noticing.

When she reached the spot where she'd suddenly become aware of his absence, she stopped—and for the first time she saw the hoofprints. The ground here was soft and the prints were plain, but there was no way to tell how many different prints there were. Still, if he'd turned off the trail for any reason, she might be able to find a diverging trail of prints.

She called to him again, but there was no response. After waiting for some sign, she gave up and began once more to retrace her tracks, leaning over to watch for any sign that he might have left the path.

Anxious moments passed as she rode along slowly. Then she saw through the trees the steep, rock-strewn part of the trail. She was quite certain that he'd been ahead of her for some time after that, so she stopped. Whatever had happened had happened in this area. She shouted again, but to no avail. Then she dismounted and began to lead the horse as she studied the ground. Many hoofprints were visible, but they still told her nothing.

Tears of frustration and fear and anger began to fill her eyes, so it was a miracle that she saw one print among many. She wiped her eyes and stared at it.

It was about two feet off the path, and she knew something was wrong even before she figured out what it was. The print was at the base of a blackberry bush—but the bush itself was intact. She circled around it, frowning. It seemed to her that if any of the horses had strayed there, the bush should have been broken. Furthermore, the print indicated that the horse had gone forward, through the thick cluster of bushes, and yet not one twig was bent, and there were no more prints.

Jasmine peered into the forest. The shadows were deep in there—too deep, it seemed to her, even though the tall trees kept out much of the light. A chill slithered through her. The pendant felt warm again. And she knew that whatever had happened to Quinn had happened here.

She tethered the mare beside the trail and set off into the woods, trying to keep her eyes on the ground while also scanning the woods. Within a few moments she realized that the chill she'd felt wasn't just from fear. The atmosphere itself was cold in here—far too cold for such a warm, sunny day.

She walked on, calling Quinn's name every few steps. But the only sounds she heard were her own footsteps as twigs snapped beneath her feet. The silence was as unnerving as the chilled air. And her pendant was now very warm—and pulsing again.

Deeper and deeper into the forest she went, ignoring the cold and her fears, her mind focused on Quinn.

As she walked along, she realized that the depth of the cold seemed to vary somewhat. A few steps in one direction or another and the air felt no cooler than was natural this deep in the forest. The cold air was like an invisible stream running through the woods—or a path.

Jasmine stopped. That was what it was: a path! She couldn't see it, but she was sure it was there. The knowledge settled into her with the absolute certainty that Quinn had exhibited so many times. He had trusted his instincts, so she must, too.

She wove her way through the trees, staying within the narrow band of cold air. And then suddenly she saw a flash of rusty brown ahead: Quinn's horse. Once more calling his name, she ran toward the mount. She was still some distance away when she saw it clearly enough to know that Quinn wasn't in the saddle, and she ran faster, her mind conjuring up an image of him lying wounded or dead.

But he wasn't there. The horse was tethered to a tree, waiting patiently, as though its master had just gone for a moment. And she saw that Quinn's longbow was still strapped to the saddle.

She studied the land around her. Just ahead, it dropped off into a small gully, where a narrow ribbon of water ran along the base of a steep, rocky wall. She could see no footprints near the horse, but the ground was firm here and covered with pine needles. She walked over to the edge of the bank—and saw footprints in the soft earth where he had half-walked and half-slid down the bank.

Jasmine hesitated. Where could he have gone? Had he climbed the wall on the far side of the little stream? She shivered. It seemed even colder here than it had behind her. His footprints led down to the stream, and then vanished. That meant he had either walked in the stream itself or he'd crossed it and climbed the rocks.

She made her way carefully down the bank. His footprints stopped right at the edge. She could see the bottom of the shallow stream, but any prints there would have been quickly washed away. She stared at the rock wall, then stepped into the stream and began to climb.

It was difficult going, but not as treacherous as the climb from the waterfall had been, since the rocks were dry. But the air was now so cold that her fingers became clumsy and her teeth were chattering.

She pulled herself up onto a ledge and saw that she'd climbed nearly halfway. The narrow ledge ran off to her right, out of sight around a bend in the mountainside. She saw no indication that he'd passed this way, but she started to walk along the ledge anyway, once again drawn by a certainty she couldn't explain.

The blast of cold, fetid air that struck her when she rounded the bend very nearly made her lose her footing on the narrow ledge. She swayed, then righted herself, closing her eyes briefly as she stared down at the hundred-foot drop. Then she turned toward the source of the chill.

It must be a cave, she thought, although the opening was so narrow that she didn't see how Quinn could have fit through it. She approached it cautiously but with determination. Quinn was in there.

When she reached it, she saw that it was somewhat wider than she'd thought, but he would certainly have been forced to go through sideways. She shouted his name, then listened. Nothing. But she could feel his presence. She stepped through the opening.

Blackness engulfed her, and a foul odor she recognized assaulted her nostrils, nearly making her retch. She knew that stench. It was that of the demons. Her hand went involuntarily to the pendant that still lay warm against her chest. She drew it out, then gasped as it began to glow, at first faintly and then much more brightly. She held it before her like a torch and advanced into the cave.

Unlike the other cave, there was no light, and her pendant pierced the blackness for only a few yards. The cold made her shiver and the foul odor kept her gagging, but she still moved deeper into the cave.

"Quinn!" she shouted, even as she wondered if making her presence known was a wise thing to do now.

She'd become so accustomed to her calls going unanswered that she almost missed the sound. It was low and more of a grunt than a word. She hurried on through the narrow passageway. And then, just as she was about to call again, she saw him.

He half-sat and half-lay against the wall, his head slumped forward on his chest. For one horrifying moment, she was sure that he must be dead, but then she saw his head bobbing slightly as his chest heaved.

She ran to him and grasped his limp hand as she

studied him, seeking evidence of injuries. But he seemed only to be asleep. She touched his face, then bent to kiss him. His head jerked up and the hand she still held twitched—and then his eyes opened.

"Quinn?" she whispered softly, seeking recognition in his eyes but finding nothing. "Quinn, it's Jasmine."

He studied her for a few seconds, then closed his eyes again. She shook him, lightly at first and then more vigorously. "Quinn! Wake up!"

Once again he roused himself and stared at her without recognition. Then suddenly his hand shot out and grasped her pendant. But before she could make a move to stop him, his whole body jerked convulsively and his hand fell away. This time, however, his eyes remained open and focused on her.

They stared at each other for a long moment, and then the clouds in his eyes dissipated and he whispered her name. When he put up his hand again, she thought at first he was going to grab the pendant, but instead his fingers traced shaky lines across her face, as though only by touching her could he believe she was real.

"Quinn," she said softly, "what happened to you?"

Chapter Ten

Her voice had begun to pierce the fog in Quinn's brain, though he was having trouble with the words themselves. His body still ached from the jolt he'd received when he touched her pendant. In his confusion, he wasn't sure why he'd reached for it. All he could remember was that it was a light in the darkness: both the darkness around him and the darkness inside.

He hauled himself up into a sitting position, but was unwilling as yet to attempt to get to his feet. Was he injured? He didn't think so. There was no particular source of his pain—just an aching tiredness, a feeling that he'd come as close as he ever had to sheer exhaustion. That, and the lingering ache from the pain that had shot through him when he touched the pendant.

He tried to focus on her as she knelt beside him, holding his hand. Her face was lit by the glow from the pendant. He could see the worry that knitted her brows and made her face taut, and he could also see the fear in her eyes. She was still asking questions, and he was still trying to answer them himself before he spoke.

His gaze shifted to the darkness around them. The glow from the pendant told him he was in a cave, but it didn't look like the cave they'd traveled through earlier: yesterday, he thought, but he wasn't sure. The passageway was narrower here, and the air was much colder—and now he noticed that there was a bad smell that seemed familiar.

He cast about in his battered brain for the memory of that awful odor; then he remembered the demon's attack on the trail. He narrowed his eyes, trying to see into the darkness beyond the glow. Had the demons returned?

"Demons?" he croaked, barely recognizing his own voice as he interrupted her.

She looked around in alarm, then shook her head. "I haven't seen any—but that smell . . ." Her voice trailed off as she continued to stare at him.

"Did they attack you?" she asked.

He shook his head. "I . . . don't know. Can we get out of here?" The cold was making his teeth chatter and the smell threatened to make him ill. But her hand that still held his was warm, and although she, too, had noticed the smell, it didn't seem to be bothering her. He thought that was strange, but there were too many other strange things for him to focus long on that.

"Yes," she said, then frowned. "But there's a narrow ledge and then a rock wall to climb down. Don't you remember them?"

He didn't answer her as he struggled to his feet. She tried to assist him, but her strength was inadequate to the task. He was probably twice her weight.

He was standing—but just barely—and he had to brace himself against the wall. She slipped his other arm over her shoulder and they made their slow way along the narrow passage.

"So warm," he said, and she turned to him with a frown.

"You aren't warm, Quinn. You're ice cold."

"You." His voice was still little more than a croak.

"I'm not warm, either. It's cold in here."

He was too busy trying to walk to argue with her. Then he saw daylight up ahead and began to push himself harder, eager to flee the darkness.

They emerged from the mouth of the cave, which was in fact only a narrow cleft in the rock. He had to turn sideways to get through, and a vague memory of having done this before came to him. But it seemed a very long time ago.

Then he saw the ledge she'd mentioned—and the hundred-foot drop beyond it. He leaned against the wall on the other side, then slid down until he was sitting. "Have to rest," he told her as she knelt beside him.

She sat down, too, and he was grateful that she'd stopped asking questions.

Jasmine continued to hold on to his hand, fearful that he might disappear again if she let go. She'd stopped asking questions because it was clear that she wasn't going to get any answers now. Whether he knew what had happened and didn't want to tell her, or whether he truly didn't know, she couldn't begin to guess.

She was still concerned about injuries, but even out here in the light, she couldn't see any. Her hand went unconsciously to the pendant, and she thought about the way Quinn's whole body had shaken when he'd touched it. It was warm and he was cold, but that didn't seem to explain it.

And she couldn't explain the coldness, either. His skin felt as cold as the winter ice that was cut up and stored in a cave at the manor for summer use. She hadn't thought a person could get that cold.

There was no doubt in her mind that his condition was the work of demons. That telltale smell still clung to him, though it was far less noticeable out here in the open.

Twice now, the demons had attacked him—but not her. Was it because they knew they'd have to subdue him before they could get to her—or was there another reason? She touched the pendant again and saw, out of the corner of her eye, that he was staring at it, too. The heat was gone from it now. It had become nothing more than a piece of jewelry. She slipped it back beneath her shirt.

"The valley," he said, breaking a long silence. "We did find it, didn't we?"

"Yes." She turned to him and saw the relief in his eyes. "Are you ready to talk about what happened?"

"I don't know what happened," he replied. "You tell me."

So she did. He didn't interrupt her, and when she'd finished, he still said nothing. "I don't understand how you could have just disappeared, Quinn. I was daydreaming, but still . . ."

He stood up, still moving carefully. "We have to get away from here before dark."

The shadows were growing deeper even as they sat, but it seemed to Jasmine that it was no darker than it had been when she'd come up here.

"Quinn, you can't possibly climb down there—and if you fall . . ."

He peered down over the edge. "Is this where you climbed up?"

"No, it was over there—past that bend. But there's not much better."

Without waiting for her, he began to walk slowly along the ledge, still reaching out every few seconds to brace himself against the wall. She followed along, terrified that he would become dizzy and collapse. But he made it. His horse was still where she'd left it, and she saw his eyes traveling the path he would have to take to reach it.

"You can't," she said again. But she knew that he was going to try.

She started to go ahead of him, but he put out a hand to stop her. "Wait until I'm down."

Only after he had swung himself out over the ledge did she realize why he'd told her to stay up here. He was worried that he might fall and carry her with him.

The next half hour was the longest of Jasmine's life. She had to stuff her fist into her mouth as he made his way down, slipping twice but somehow regaining his handhold or foothold. And then, finally, he was standing in the middle of the little stream, swaying a bit, she thought, though it was hard to tell from such a distance.

She began her own descent, finding it far more difficult than the climb up had been. When she half-turned to see how much progress she'd made, he shouted up to her not to look down. And then his hands were around her ankles, her legs, and finally her waist as she reached the bottom at last.

They stood there in the middle of the stream, with the water lapping around their boots, and held each other tightly. Jasmine looked back up at the cliff. How had she managed to climb up there? She couldn't believe she'd even attempted it, let alone succeeded.

Quinn kept one arm around her as they left the stream. Then he untied his horse and led it down to drink. One of his more endearing qualities was his great concern for the animals. He always tended to them even before he met his own needs, and she'd seen him cut back on his own share of the water several times to be certain that they could have enough.

When the animal had drunk its fill, Quinn untied the leather bottle from the saddle and filled it, then drank deeply himself. Jasmine thought that he seemed to be recovering—but what was he recovering from? Now that she knew he was safe and well, she became irritated with him, suspecting that he was withholding information because he didn't want to frighten her.

"Let's go," he said, leading the horse to her. "We can both ride him back if the way isn't too steep."

She made no move to mount the animal. Instead she folded her arms in a gesture of obstinate determination. "I want to know what happened to you, Quinn."

He very nearly smiled. It was no more than a hint of a grin, but it warmed her to see it. "I'll tell you as soon as I remember."

They led the horse up the steep slope. Then Quinn mounted and pulled her up in front of him. "Which direction are we going?" he asked.

"Oh!" Jasmine looked around them. "I don't know. I just followed that cold draft I told you about. But it's gone."

She thought about it, aware of his impatience. "I think I went more or less straight from here."

He chuckled and urged the horse forward, then bent to kiss her ear. "You were very brave, you know."

"I wasn't brave," she protested. "I was desperate."

"Even so, what you did took courage—especially climbing that cliff."

She leaned back against him, overwhelmed with happiness at the strong, hard feel of him. But she still wanted to know what had happened. And she also decided that she would never again let herself wander off into her memories.

By the time they reached the trail and then found the packhorses, it was nearly dark. Quinn started toward them to feed and water them, but Jasmine told him to rest and let her take care of it. By the time she had given them their grain and some water, she saw that he had fallen asleep, leaning against a tree.

She made herself a meal of fruit and some nuts they had gathered, then got out a blanket and tucked it around him. The unnatural coldness was gone, but the night air was cool. She drew a blanket around her shoulders and sat down near him.

She was exhausted, but felt certain that she wouldn't be able to sleep this night because she feared that the demons would return. Quinn stirred uneasily and muttered something she couldn't hear, so she moved closer to him. Without waking, he wrapped an arm around her and she laid her head against his chest.

Jasmine's eyes flew open and she immediately felt the heat from the pendant. She stared into the darkness, holding her breath and listening for any sound. The woods were silent, but she knew *they* were out there. She could feel their frustration and their rage. And then Quinn began to stir.

Twigs snapped—first in one direction, and then in another, until the sounds were all around her. The horses began to whicker and stamp their feet. Quinn started to mutter again. Then his legs shifted and he tried to get to his feet.

Jasmine grabbed his arm and pulled him back down again. "No, Quinn! They're out there!"

He struggled for a moment, whether with her or with himself she couldn't tell. And then he sank down again and drew her against him. She heard more twigs snap, but farther away—and then all was silence.

*   *   *

Quinn stood in the middle of the trail, at the bottom of the steep, rocky slope where she said she'd last recalled knowing he was with her. Then he began to walk along slowly, his head turned toward the woods. She showed him the hoofprint that had first alerted her to the direction he'd taken. When they'd reached the trail again last evening, it had been at a point farther on.

She looked at him questioningly and he shook his head. "I still don't remember anything about leaving the trail—or what happened after that."

"I think we should tie the horses together," she suggested as they walked back to where they'd left the animals.

"That's a good idea," he agreed, dropping an arm across her shoulders.

He'd been like this ever since he awakened this morning: holding her hand, putting an arm around her. Quinn was often affectionate, but Jasmine thought that his behavior now was different—that he was clinging to her, incredible as that seemed.

It made her uneasy to think that he could be dependent upon her, when the reverse had been true throughout their journey. Quinn seemed so strong to her, so very sure of himself. She'd been the one afflicted with doubts and fears, and yet it seemed to her now that she was gaining courage even as he might be losing his.

"They came last night," she said. She hadn't told him about the demons' visit, but she must tell him now. She still harbored the suspicion that he was withholding information from her, and she was determined not to be guilty of the same thing.

"They did?"

She described what had happened, including his attempt to get up. "I think they're trying to lure you away, Quinn. And you must be right about the pendant protecting me."

He said nothing, then maintained his silence as they mounted their horses and set off on the trail. It continued to curve back toward the valley, but the forest was too thick to afford them any glimpses such as they'd had before.

Quinn's silence masked turbulent thoughts. After the fifth time in as many minutes that he'd turned in the saddle to be sure she was still there, he resolutely faced forward. But his hand kept slipping to the rope that tied their horses together.

He didn't know which frightened him more: whatever it was that had happened to him, or the fact that he couldn't remember any of it.

And then there was the question of Jasmine. She seemed to grow more sure of herself by the moment. He could still hear the echoes of her calm voice, telling him about the demons' visit last night. And there'd been her climb up that cliff to find him. Clearly either he'd underestimated her or something was changing.

Quinn had never questioned his own courage—nor had he ever felt compelled, as men often did, to prove it. A willingness to face whatever needed to be faced had always been a part of him, something he wasn't even conscious of as he made his way through life. But now he feared that he was losing that courage.

Jasmine had said several times that there were so many questions that needed answering, while he had simply accepted that the answers would be there when they were needed. But he was wrong. No matter how hard he tried to recall what had happened to him, he couldn't get beyond that sense of looking into a bottomless black pit—a pit that seemed to be calling out to him.

He thought about her statement that the demons were trying to lure him away. It had the unmistakable ring of truth, though he couldn't say why.

And that was the question that tormented him. If they wanted him dead—which they surely did—then why hadn't they killed him when they had the opportunity? He guessed that as long as he was with her, the pendant must be protecting them both—though now that he thought of it, even that was questionable. He had been with her when it happened.

But leaving aside that question for the moment, why hadn't they killed him once they'd gotten him away from her? There were no marks on him, so it was obvious that he hadn't fought them.

He thought back to that other attack. The demon hadn't really fought him then, either, after landing on him and knocking him from his horse. In fact, he'd thought at the time that it had seemed much weaker than he'd expected. Could that have been because she was nearby? Certainly she'd distracted it, giving him the chance to stab it.

They want something from me, he thought. But what was it? How could he fight them if he didn't know what their goal was? As a former soldier, he knew that understanding the enemy was at least half the battle—but he was now forced to operate in a situation where he knew nothing.

Furthermore, he no longer believed that their problems would cease when they reached the valley.

The day wore on as they followed the trail, which became increasingly twisted, turning upon itself time after time and ascending for some distance before going once more into a downward spiral. Once, they left the horses on the path and climbed a nearby hill, hoping to find the valley again. But when they reached the top, they saw only another, higher hill.

By late afternoon, darkness settled over the forest, and a strong, cold wind began to blow, swaying the tops of the ancient trees. They could see very little of the sky because they were deep within the forest, but when they looked up they glimpsed dark clouds. A moment later they heard a low rumble of thunder.

Quinn set up a shelter, and they prepared to wait out the storm. It descended on them within moments. Jasmine's ears rang from the great claps of thunder, and the bright flashes of lightning left her momentarily blinded. Quinn remarked that it was the most ferocious storm he'd ever witnessed.

The cold wind found its way through the trees to their shelter and ripped away the oiled cloth that was protecting them. The horses, tethered nearby, shivered and whinnied with fear. Quinn got up.

"I'm going to try to calm them," he told her. "Stay here. It's still fairly dry." He'd strung up their shelter beneath a thick cluster of broad-leafed trees.

She watched as he walked the fifty feet or so to another thick clump of trees where he'd left the animals, touched as always by his concern for them. She could barely see him in the unnatural darkness, and then suddenly he stood out briefly in stark relief as the lightning flashed once more. The very ground shook with the thunder that followed.

Protect him! They will take him!

Jasmine gasped and stared wildly around her, seeking the source of the low but very distinct voice that had spoken. No one was there, and yet she was certain that the voice had been real.

Hurry! it urged in the same tone.

She scrambled to her feet. In the dim light she could see Quinn among the horses, who were now moving about even more restlessly. Even as she ran toward him, one of the animals reared up and tore loose its tether—then headed straight at her.

Jasmine had only a moment to see the wild fear in its eyes before she flung herself out of its path and crashed headfirst into a tree. The horse stampeded past her with scant inches to spare.

Get up! the voice ordered. *They are taking him!*

She got to her feet, ignoring the dizziness that came over her. She could just barely see Quinn now, in the midst of the remaining horses. Then there was a flash of lightning—and she saw that he was not alone!

She half-ran and half-stumbled toward him, then plunged into the midst of the frightened horses. Her mare reared up, and she was nearly struck down by flailing hooves—but it was not the animals that held her attention.

There were two demons, standing on either side of Quinn, their hideous talons gripping his arms. Another flash of lightning cast their horrible faces and their misshapen bodies into stark relief, burning the images into her brain.

But however terrible they were, what sent chills down her spine was Quinn. He stood there calmly, showing nothing more than a slight frown, as though he were mildly puzzled.

"Quinn!" she shouted over the thunder that followed the flash.

His frown deepened and he started to move toward her, then stopped as the demons tightened their grip on him.

"Let him go!" she screamed. "I command you!"

"He belongs to us."

Both demons' mouths were drawn into a horrifying parody of a grin as they stared at her, and she couldn't tell which of them had spoken, but there was no mistaking that the hissing voice belonged to one of them. Jasmine drew out her pen-

223

dant, only then realizing that it hadn't grown warm this time.

"It won't work now," one demon hissed.

She saw Quinn's knife in its scabbard, dangling from his belt. Without considering the wisdom of what she was about to do, she lunged at him and grabbed the knife. Quinn didn't move.

She raised the knife and lunged one demon, who had no time to move before the blade struck. It began to vaporize immediately, filling her lungs with a smoke even more noxious than its body odor. Coughing, she whirled to see the other demon turning itself into smoke as well. Quinn began to cough.

He stared from her face to the bloody knife and back again, still wearing that puzzled frown. "Quinn!" she said, moving closer to him. But his eyes were glazed and she knew that he didn't see her. Still, he didn't resist as she led him back to their former shelter, then left him there while she minded up the horses.

Fortunately, two of the horses were still tethered, and of the three that had broken loose, two hadn't strayed far. She gathered them up and tied them again, deciding not to take the risk of going after the missing packhorse.

The storm had moved on, leaving only a fine mist in its wake. Light began to return to the forest. Jasmine sat down next to the silent Quinn and took his hand. Her pendant began to glow warmly against her wet shirt and chilled skin.

The storm, she thought. Perhaps that was why the pendant didn't work. But she'd still managed to subdue the demons. So even without its protection, she had some power over them.

He belongs to us. The demon's words echoed in her mind. What could then mean?

And what about that other voice—the one that had alerted her to the demons' presence? She didn't even know if it had been male or female. All she knew was that it had been real and it had spoken to her in her own language.

"Horses," Quinn said suddenly.

She turned to him. His gaze was focused now, though he still wore that frown of uncertainty that was so at odds with his strong, rugged face.

"They're safe—but one of the packhorses got away."

He said nothing for a long time, though his hand moved to enclose hers. Then, in a hollow tone that frightened her, he said, "It happened again, didn't it—the demons came?"

"Yes," she replied, wrapping her arms around him tightly. "They said you belonged to them."

He lapsed into silence again for a time, then asked her what had happened. But he seemed uninterested in her reply, as though his mind were elsewhere. Thinking that perhaps he remembered some of it this time, she was about to ask him when he abruptly set her aside and got to his feet.

"Maybe they're right," he said slowly, his face turned away from her.

"Quinn!" she cried, getting to her feet and moving to him. But when she tried to take him in her arms, he moved away.

"There must be a reason why they keep coming after *me*," he said, still turned away from her.

"Of course there is! My pendant protects me—protects us both when we're together."

"But you just told me that the pendant wasn't working this time," he pointed out.

She said nothing and he went on. "So they could have gotten you, too—but it was *me* they wanted."

"What are you saying, Quinn?" She could barely get the words out through her suddenly constricted throat.

"I don't know. But that voice warned you that I

was in danger. It didn't warn me, which would have made a lot more sense."

"Quinn, you're being ridiculous. The demons are our enemy."

"Maybe it's not that simple," he said, finally turning to face her. "Maybe the stories I heard weren't really the truth."

Jasmine stared at him. Her grandmother's words came back to her: ancient enemies and old hatreds. Their people had been enemies long ago. She shook her aching head.

"Quinn, you're not one of them—and you don't belong to them, either. You have to believe that."

She saw him slowly relax, and then he drew her into his arms. But she could not rid herself of the thought that though she had told him what he wanted to believe—what she wanted to believe as well—it might not be the truth.

The sun returned, and because they still had a few hours of daylight remaining, they continued on their journey. The missing packhorse was found easily enough, as Quinn had predicted.

The trail was now almost level, though it still wound around the mountains. Though neither of them would speak the words aloud, they both began to believe that their journey would never end.

Jasmine was tormented by her thoughts. She might have convinced Quinn that he didn't belong to the demons, but she was less certain than she'd sounded. "Dartuli" meant "people of the dark," and where she'd believed that referred only to his coloring and his hair, she now wondered if it could have a wholly different meaning.

She'd seen that darkness within him, even though she'd also seen his essential goodness. Was there now a war going on within him—a battle for his very soul?

In the last light of the day, they saw ahead of them the end of the forest, and even before they rode out into the meadow, Jasmine knew that they had finally reached their destination.

The valley stretched before them in the shadows of the great mountains. The broad, flower-filled meadow gave way to forest, and beyond that, to more open land. The valley wasn't flat, but rather consisted of low, rolling hills that stretched as far as they could see in the waning light.

A small herd of deer emerged from the forest and headed toward a stream at the far edge of the meadow. Their passage startled a flock of pheasants that rose into the air with shrill squawks of protest. Beyond the first of the hills, a small portion of the lake was visible, and a flock of geese was settling down for the night.

Jasmine rode up beside Quinn and reached out to take his hand as they both stared at the land of their ancestors—the land of their dreams. It was all they had dreamed of and more. But as she gazed upon it, Jasmine knew that whatever she'd expected to feel at this moment, it wasn't the sense of foreboding that filled her now. And when Quinn's eyes met hers, she knew he shared those feelings.

"My grandfather once said to me, after I'd told him that I was going to find this place someday, that I should beware of my dreams," he said as he stared at the beautiful, peaceful scene. "I think now that he was trying to warn me."

Jasmine lifted her gaze to the mountaintops, where the last rays of the sun had turned the snow-caps to a delicate orange-pink shade. "We had to follow the dream, Quinn. We had no choice. I didn't know that as early as you did—but I know it now." From the first moment she'd laid eyes on him in that dark, dirty alley, all this had been fore-ordained.

The breeze picked up her words and carried

them out over the meadow, where the flowers seemed to nod in agreement.

Jasmine opened her eyes to the soft half-light of the coming dawn. Once more, the mountaintops were brushed with color from the sun she couldn't yet see. In the utter stillness, she could hear faint bird cries. The flowers were bent from the weight of dewdrops. A pheasant cried out sharply not far away.

They had spread their blankets on the gentle slope where the woods ended and the meadow began—at the very entrance to the valley. Quinn had set the horses free, and she could see them all now, some distance away, grazing placidly.

Quinn lay beside her, his long body against hers and one arm curved about her waist, brushing the soft undersides of her breasts. She moved slightly and his grip tightened. The movement sent a rush of warmth through her, making her even more aware of his closeness.

She lay there quietly for a long time as the rising sun moved down over the peaks to the west, then burst into view across the valley. The meadow sparkled as a million tiny dewdrops caught the sunlight and held it. In the distance, the horses raised their heads in curiosity as the deer once more headed toward the water.

But even as she feasted her eyes on this scene, Jasmine was thinking: about Quinn and about their peoples' history. Would they find the answers they needed here—perhaps in the village they had yet to find? But how could there be answers for them there? Even if there were records, neither of them could read their shared language.

Perhaps there would be other clues—or perhaps the voice that had alerted her to Quinn's danger would come again.

She shivered. Were there ghosts in this valley,

as well as demons? Only a short time ago she would have considered such thoughts to be a sign of madness, and even now, gazing upon this inexpressibly beautiful scene, she found it nearly impossible to believe such things.

The sun rose higher, its light now flooding the valley. Beside her, Quinn began to stir.

Chapter Eleven

Quinn's beard tickled her pleasantly as his mouth covered hers and his tongue joined hers in a sensuous dance. Every fiber of her being cried out in expectation. She was glad that they'd waited until they reached the valley before taking this final step into intimacy. Quinn had already become such a part of her that it would be only a small step, not a plunge into the unknown.

He held her close, his big hands gliding down her back as his lips and tongue brushed soft strokes along her jaw and down her neck to the throbbing pulse point at its base. She could feel the full force of his hunger for her, but instead of frightening her, it drove her own passion to still greater heights.

Then he lifted his head and stared down at her. His dark beard gave him a sinister appearance, but that was offset by the black curls that had strayed across his brow. Jasmine smiled at him, ready to declare her love for him—but the words remained locked in her throat.

He sat up abruptly and moved away from her. She sat up, too, her heart pounding, certain that he must have seen something. Were they to be denied even these few moments?

But there was nothing to be seen. The only change in the peaceful tableau was that the horses were now headed toward the stream and the deer were disappearing into the forest.

"Quinn, what is it?"

"Nothing," he replied in a clipped tone that sent a chill through her and drove out the last traces of that warm, heavy desire.

"I want to get an early start. We have a lot of exploring to do."

If Jasmine had been more experienced, she would surely have questioned this abrupt change in him. But she knew next to nothing about men, and so assumed that his interest in exploring the valley was far greater than his desire to make love to her. And her belief seemed to be confirmed when he bent to kiss her again.

"We have time. But first I want to see the valley."

They walked hand in hand through the meadow, carrying fresh clothing with them. Then they bathed in the stream, which was too cold for more than a quick wash. Quinn seemed preoccupied, but she took that to mean he was eager to be off on their expedition. And she was moved when he ran his fingers lightly over her cheeks and announced that he'd better shave before he scraped her skin raw.

They devoured the last of their food supplies for breakfast, and Quinn said that from the evidence he'd seen thus far, they would have plenty of game to sustain them.

"If we're lucky," he went on, "we'll find orchards and maybe even some vegetable gardens gone wild. There are probably cows as well, but I'm not sure how they'll take to being milked."

As he talked, Jasmine let go of the last of her uncertainties over his strange behavior. It all sounded like a wonderful game—a chance to regain the childhood that she'd been denied.

Quinn collected the horses, which were frisky and as eager to be off as they were, after their taste of freedom and sweet grasses. Already the sun had burned away most of the dew and warmed the cool air. Jasmine had chosen for her first day in the valley a fine white cotton dress she'd bought back in Halaban, with loose, full sleeves and a bodice that had been embroidered with bright flowers. The effect was diminished somewhat by her heavy riding boots, and the dress had to be bunched up in her lap as she rode, but Quinn had smiled for the first time that morning when she put it on.

They rode across the meadow and into the forest, which climbed a hill. Quinn commented on the mass of blueberry bushes that bore fruit that was just beginning to ripen. When they reached a small, sunny clearing, they found bushes heavy with the sweet purple-blue fruit and stopped to eat their fill.

There were blackberry bushes as well, though the fruit was still tiny and green and hard. Jasmine thought Quinn was right: they would never go hungry in this bountiful valley.

When they reached the top of the hill a short time later, the lake lay below them, dazzling in the bright sunlight. It was larger than she'd expected, oval in shape, but there was a portion she couldn't see from here. The forest grew down to its banks on all sides. A flock of ducks appeared, paddling slowly as they trolled for food in a marshy area where tall grasses grew.

She was watching the ducks when Quinn made a sound, and she turned to see a magnificent white horse slowly emerge from the forest, its handsome head swiveling about as it approached the lake.

Moments later a dark foal appeared, its shiny black coat contrasting sharply with the glistening white of its mother.

"I thought they were all white," she said in a low voice, not wanting to frighten the animals.

Quinn shook his head. "They're all black when they're born. Then they turn gray, and finally white. It takes several years, I think." He glanced at her briefly, but it was obvious that his attention was focused on the horses.

"How do you know that?"

"The tales I heard. My grandparents talked a lot about them."

She thought about his love of horses. "I wonder if your family once raised them."

He nodded. "I've thought about that myself. It's possible."

The mare nudged the foal toward the water, even though the little horse obviously had a different type of refreshment in mind. Her whickers and the foal's protest carried to them across the water, but finally the foal edged into the shallows and began to drink. They waited until both had returned to the forest before continuing their journey.

Atop the hill on the far side of the lake, a very different sight greeted them, once more bringing them to a stop. There, spread out below them across a flat, open space, was a village—or what had once been a village.

The homes were just as they'd been in her dreams: rough stone cottages that had once been covered with thatched roofs. Excited by this discovery, Jasmine stared at them for a long time before she realized that something was wrong.

"It isn't like it was in my dream," she told him with a frown.

"What do you mean? It looks the same to me—

except for the condition of the cottages and the overgrown gardens."

"No. It's arranged differently. The cottages were in circles that curved around a marketplace and a park with trees and stone benches."

"That's not what I remember," he said, shaking his head, then urging his horse down the hillside toward the village.

Jasmine followed more slowly. She knew her memory was correct. They'd never discussed their dreams in great detail, but she'd assumed they were identical. The fact that that appeared not to be the case filled her with an uneasiness she hadn't felt since they'd first set out to explore the valley.

She tried to remember the one time when they'd both dreamed about the valley—and each other. Had they visited the village then? She wasn't sure. Most of what she recalled of that dream was making love with him. The rest was a blur.

Jasmine's uneasiness grew as they left the horses to graze in a field and began to walk through the tumbledown village. She even felt a slight chill, though the sun was warm. Since she'd come to associate that chill with the demons, she glanced into every shadow. She wondered if they could be inside one of the houses, but she realized that her pendant was still cool against her skin, and decided that she was wrong.

Perhaps the chill came from the sadness she felt at seeing this place, which must once have been full of life, with its well-tended gardens and brightly painted shutters and doors she remembered from her dream.

If Quinn shared her sadness, it certainly wasn't evident. He moved through the ruins of the village in long strides, peering in through empty windows and kicking piles of rubble in the small front yards. His enthusiasm was childlike, and she remembered how only a short time ago, she'd shared his buoyancy. She tried for a time to mimic it, hoping that pretense would make it real.

The interiors of the cottages were covered with many layers of rubble, topped in some cases by weeds and flowers that had sprouted after the thatched roofs had fallen in. Quinn announced his intention to excavate them after they had seen the whole valley.

"If they were driven out, they must have left most of their things behind," he told her as he stopped in the doorway of one of the larger houses.

But Jasmine had barely heard him. She was staring at the door that hung from one rusty hinge. The wood was badly warped and weathered to a soft gray, but here and there she could see flecks of black paint. And when she looked at the one remaining shutter, she saw traces of black there as well.

She recalled the dream and frowned. She was sure that all the cottages had had doors and shutters painted in bright colors: reds and greens and yellows. She walked to the next house in the row and once again saw faint traces of black paint. And as they made their way up the street to the central marketplace, she saw it again and again. If there was any trace of paint at all, it was always black.

They reached the market square, which was completely empty. It was paved with huge stones, just as she remembered from the dream, but where were the stone benches and the flowering trees? The only greenery in the whole square were weeds that had taken root in the cracks between the stones.

She studied the scene in mounting confusion. While it was true that the delicate flowering trees might have long since died, that couldn't explain the absence of the benches. Stone didn't die or crumble away. Furthermore, she realized that there weren't even any spaces where trees might once have stood. The entire square was paved.

"Quinn," she said, her voice firm, "this isn't the village I saw in my dream."

He had walked to the middle of the square, and now he turned to her. "Of course it is. Don't you remember this square—and the building over there that must have been an indoor market?"

"I remember a square—but it wasn't this one." She went on to describe her dream. "There's no place that the trees could have been planted, and the benches should still be here. There was grass, too—and flowers."

Quinn's dark brows knitted in thought. Then he swept an arm around them. "This is what I remember—right down to the shutters on that building over there."

"What color were they?" she asked.

He frowned in thought. "Black, as I recall."

"And what about the doors and shutters on the houses?"

"They were black, too—or some dark color."

"The ones I saw were all bright colors." She drew in a deep breath. "Quinn, we saw two different places. That's the only explanation."

Instead of answering her, he started off up a street that led away from the market and up a slight hill. She followed, feeling guilty about casting a pall over his joy of exploration. But when she reached him at the top of the hill, she saw him gazing around with a thoughtful look. From this vantage point, the entire village was visible, as it hadn't been before.

"There must be another village," he said. "If everyone had lived here, it would be much bigger."

"How can you be so sure?" she asked, although she was relieved to hear his explanation.

"I'm not," he admitted. "But it seems to me that there must have been more people than this. Remember how many cairns there were?"

"I wonder why we saw two different villages," she mused, vaguely disturbed by the thought.

"It might be because at one time our people lived separately. Don't forget: We were enemies once. The houses might well go back to that time."

"So you're saying that I saw my people's village and you saw yours."

He nodded, and they walked back down the hill, then continued their exploration of the village. Jasmine found familiar herbs growing in what had once been gardens behind many of the houses. Quinn went into one of the houses where the roof, almost unbelievably, hadn't completely collapsed.

He came out with several pieces of broken crockery. There were tears in his eyes as he told her that the designs were almost identical to those on an old jug that had been revered by his family as having been one of the few things brought with them from the valley.

They moved toward the outskirts of the village, where the houses were more widely separated and evidence of much larger gardens could be seen amid the weeds. Jasmine stood in the center of one former garden and breathed deeply of the mingled scents. One scent in particular caught her attention, and she finally tracked it down to a white-flowered shrub just as Quinn appeared.

"I don't know what this is," she told him, "but it's wonderful."

Quinn bent down and picked one of the delicate white flowers, then handed it to her with a smile that was lit with both amusement and love.

"A jasmine for Jasmine," he pronounced solemnly.

"This is jasmine?" she asked in delight. "Are you sure?"

He nodded. "I told you that my grandmother grew it."

She put the flower into the vee of her embroidered bodice, where it rested over the pendant. It pleased her to think that she'd been named for such a lovely flower. Her mother had told her once that it was an old family name, but she knew nothing of its origin.

They started back to where they'd left the horses, each of them lost in private thoughts. Then Quinn spoke in a musing tone.

"You know, it seems kind of strange that our ancestors would have had time to bring seeds and crockery with them when they were driven from the valley. People fleeing for their lives aren't likely to take anything but the clothes on their backs."

Jasmine frowned. He was right. She'd never given it any thought before. "What do you think it means?" she asked.

"I don't know. Maybe nothing. Or maybe the stories that were handed down changed over the years—as you once suggested."

"But the valley is real—and so are those graves we saw," she added, thinking about the stone mounds on the plain.

"And the demons," he said, adding the one thing she didn't want to talk about on this day.

"Ancient enemies. Old hatreds," she murmured, quoting her grandmother.

"What do you mean?"

She explained how she'd recalled her grandmother saying that. "It was just before I realized that you had disappeared."

"You don't remember anything else?"

She shook her head. "I was so young, Quinn. And my mother refused to talk about it."

They rode out of the village and into open fields that had undoubtedly once been farmland. Amid the tall weeds, Jasmine could see various grains like the ones grown in the fields of the manor: wheat, barley, and sweet-smelling alfalfa. Cornstalks were scattered here and there as well, though they weren't as tall as those she was accustomed to.

And then, after a short ride through a small woods on a path that was almost completely overgrown, they came again to open fields. They both reined in their horses. Scattered across the field were the white horses.

Jasmine knew little about horses, but she knew enough to understand that these were different. They were larger than most horses—nearly as big as the draft horses used on farms. But unlike those heavy, muscular animals, these were almost delicate in appearance, despite their size.

She also saw that Quinn was right about their color. The herd included dark foals, some adult-size animals that were a sort of muddy gray—and the magnificent whites. She laughed in delight as several yearlings gamboled about their elders, leaping high into the air and even dancing on their hind legs.

Quinn dismounted, then handed her his reins. "I want to see if I can get close to them. You wait here, because I don't know how wild they are."

She watched as he began to approach the herd cautiously. Several of the animals closest to them had already spotted them and were watching them warily. Jasmine held her breath, certain that they would bolt at any moment. But Quinn moved closer and she could hear him speaking to them, though the words were lost to the breeze.

Then, as he came closer still, the animals began to move, drawing closer together. A few of them whickered, and the playful yearlings moved into the protection of the herd. Quinn kept walking, and Jasmine began to fear that they might panic and stampede in his direction. Every pair of eyes was on him.

He paused about fifty feet from the milling herd,

and once again she heard his voice, though not his words. Then a magnificent white stallion, the largest of them all, reared up and whinnied. Jasmine cried out in fear as she saw those flashing hooves.

But the stallion settled down again and then came slowly toward Quinn. Quinn held out his hand, and after prancing around him in a circle while Jasmine held her breath in paralyzed fear, the stallion bent its beautiful head to him and Quinn stroked it.

She released her breath in relief and wonder as he then walked right into the midst of the herd, crouching down to pet a dark foal that clung to its mother's side. By the time he left them, they had all returned to their grazing, including the watchful master of the herd.

Quinn's rugged face was aglow with pleasure as he came back to her, then turned to stare at the stallion that had followed him partway. His own stallion snorted with displeasure, and Quinn put a hand on its muzzle as the white stallion issued its own challenge.

"I'm going to ride him," Quinn said as he swung back into the saddle.

Jasmine gave him a doubtful look. "Just because he didn't attack you doesn't mean he'll let you ride him."

"He will," Quinn said confidently. "We just need time to get to know each other better first."

"What were you saying to them?" she asked curiously.

He shrugged. "I just told them that I was back and that they belong to me. The words didn't matter. I just wanted them to hear my voice and get used to my smell."

"They're so beautiful," she said, turning in the saddle as he was doing to catch one last glimpse of them.

"They'll be even more beautiful when they've been properly groomed."

His words made her vaguely uneasy. She knew that she hadn't yet faced their future, but it was clear that Quinn intended to stay here. During their exploration of the village, he'd commented on what it would take to make one of the larger houses habitable again. But how could they live here alone all their lives? Even if he returned at some point to Estavia and brought back his family, it would still be difficult.

She'd never before considered the importance of having other people around her because she'd never been so isolated. Not that she'd cared for anyone except for her mother, but she understood now how important it was to have human contact.

People are like deer and horses, she thought. *We need to live in herds, even if we don't always get along very well. There must be others like us—but how could we ever find them?*

She felt terribly sad, thinking about the lives that might have been lived in this wonderful place, but had probably been lived instead as hers and Quinn's had been.

Still, she thought, we found our way here, and others could, too. She turned to Quinn.

"Do you think there could be others like us who might find their way back here?"

"I don't know—but I hope so." He paused for a moment. "You know, I wasn't the first in my family to dream of returning here one day. I'm just the first to do it. And it makes me think that maybe the time is right. Look how I found you."

"You're saying that you think it wasn't just a co-incidence?"

"It could have been, but it could also mean that the gods have decided that the time is right for our return."

Jasmine was surprised at his mention of the

gods. He'd never spoken of them before. She herself had never believed in them because her mother didn't, though she had vague memories of her grandmother worshiping them.

The Borneash, among whom she'd lived, weren't religious people, although they nominally worshiped one god. But the priests were generally called upon only to perform marriages or officiate at funerals.

"Do you believe in the gods, then?" she asked him.

He gave her a surprised look. "Of course. How could I *not* believe in them, when we've seen their opposites?"

That brought Jasmine up short. He was right, of course. If there were demons, then there must be gods. She'd just never thought about it because her mother had dismissed it all as being nonsense.

"But how do you know that it was the gods who brought us back here—and not the demons?"

Quinn didn't answer her right away, and when she turned to him, she saw a troubled look on his face.

"It wasn't the demons," he replied after a moment—but she thought he sounded less than certain.

They rode on, following a road that was just barely visible in places. They were able to follow it only because it ran straight down the center of the valley. That it had been deserted long ago was made obvious by the fact that in some places, fairly tall trees now grew in it. The valley was slowly wiping out every trace of human habitation.

After passing through a thick wood, they came again to a broad, open field. Some distance ahead of them, they could see something blocking the road. As they drew closer, Jasmine saw that there were two tall stone mounds on either side of the old road, similar to the burial mounds they'd seen on the plain.

Then, when they were almost upon it, she realized that there were more of the stone pillars stretching across the field in both directions. The space between the two pillars that lined the road was choked with weeds, but beneath those weeds were what appeared to be rotting pieces of wood.

"It's a fence," she said as they stared down at it.

Quinn nodded as he looked out across the field in both directions. "And it looks as though it ran across the whole valley."

Quinn dismounted and began to examine the pillar nearest him. It had a strangely shaped top, as if something had once rested there—or was meant to. He reached down into the weeds next to it and picked up a large, perfectly spherical rock. Jasmine got off her mare, and when Quinn held the rock up, she saw that there were symbols carved into it.

He set it down atop the pillar, and it immediately became obvious that it belonged there. At the other side of the road they found another stone with identical carvings.

Quinn raised his head to stare at the mountains that guarded the valley. "We're about at the midpoint of the valley. I wonder if this was the dividing line between the Latawi and the Dartuli. If we find the village you dreamed about, we'll know that's it."

"I wonder what the symbols mean," she said as she stared at the sphere.

"They could be the symbols for our people," he suggested.

Ancient enemies. Old hatreds. The words came back to her again, refusing to be put from her mind no matter how hard she tried. If Quinn was right, this fence had likely been built at a time when his people and hers had been enemies.

Quinn began to drag the rotted logs out of the roadway. Jasmine watched him as he threw them into the field. It seemed strange that they'd been left there, since the Dartuli and the Latawi had lived together peaceably for centuries before they were driven from the valley.

She said nothing to Quinn about this, but she was thinking about how little they knew—and whether they could trust what they did know.

They found her ancestors' village just after the sun had disappeared from the valley. The mountains cast long shadows over the rings of houses and the circular marketplace and park at its center. Jasmine felt a wave of sadness greater than anything she'd felt before. How she would have liked to have seen this place when it was filled with life—with her people.

The village was nestled at the very base of one of the tallest peaks and was surrounded by low hills, except for one side, where a lake shimmered in the waning light. It was a small lake, perhaps more properly a pond, but the setting was lovely, with tall, graceful willows dipping into its waters. The stream that fed it vanished into the wooded hills opposite where they stood.

Quinn gave her a crooked grin as he urged his horse down the hill. "I like your home better. Let's have a look."

They rode into the village, which, except for its rather strange layout, proved to be much like the home of the Dartuli at the other end of the valley. Empty windows stared back at them from cottages and houses of varying sizes. Overgrown gardens covered the rear spaces, and Jasmine saw more herbs and several other jasmine bushes as well. On several rotting doors and fallen shutters, she saw faint traces of paint that had once been the bright shades from her dream.

When they finally reached the circular marketplace with the small park at its very center, they discovered that the paving stones had been cut and laid in a pattern that focused all attention on the park. From the hilltop, that hadn't been evident because of the weeds that were thriving in the cracks.

They left the horses to graze on the weeds and walked into the former park, which was now a dense woods choked with berry bushes and other tall weeds. In fact, they very nearly stumbled over the first of the stone benches before they saw it.

Jasmine looked up at the trees, recalling her dream of trees with drooping branches and lovely pale flowers. They weren't blooming now, but she had no problem determining which ones they were, both because they were the biggest trees there and because their lower branches still hung down in graceful arcs.

She turned to ask Quinn if he'd ever seen such trees, but he was gone. So successful had she been at setting the demons from her mind that she didn't panic. Instead she began to make her way through the dense undergrowth, calling his name. But when there was no response, her chest suddenly constricted with fear.

She called out again as she pushed her way through the brush, knowing that he must have come this way because she could see the trampled grass and broken branches.

She heaved a sigh of relief when she emerged into a small clearing and saw him. He was standing with his back to her as he stared at something she couldn't see. Then, as she drew closer, she saw, even in the dim light, the unmistakable gleam of gold.

She stopped beside Quinn and stared at it. Gold and diamonds.

The object was a golden sphere, perhaps two

feet in diameter, circled with a band of diamonds set into an intricately worked gold band. It was mounted on a stone pedestal whose base was carved with symbols of some sort. The whole object, including the base, was nearly as tall as she was.

When Jasmine could tear her eyes away from the gold sphere, she bent to examine the carvings in the stone pedestal. They were all the same, and she thought it was one of the symbols they'd seen on the fence post in the center of the valley.

"Quinn, I think this is the same symbol that—" She stopped as she saw his face. It was impossible to guess what his expression meant, but it was clear to her that he was in the grip of powerful emotions.

Tentatively, she reached out to touch his arm. "Quinn? What is it?"

A tremor ran through him, and he blinked a few times, then gave her a puzzled look, almost as though he didn't recognize her. Before she could repeat her question, he turned on his heel and walked away. She had the sense that what he really wanted to do was run, so she hurried after him.

When she caught up to him, he was already back in the marketplace. She approached him cautiously. "Quinn, what happened back there?"

This time when he turned to her, she knew that he recognized her. But his face had a haunted look, and there were beads of perspiration on his bronzed skin.

"Do you know what that is?" he asked. "Did you see it in your dreams?"

"No, of course not. If I had, I would have told you." Her tone was defensive—a reaction to the harshness in his voice. "I have no idea what it is."

He looked away from her for a moment, and she sensed that he was trying to regain control of himself. When he turned back, his expression had softened.

"I'm sorry, Jasmine. I . . . don't know what came over me."

The plaintive note in his words banished her anger quickly. "What do *you* think it is?" she asked, since it had obviously affected him strongly—unless, of course, this was all some demon trick.

He shook his head. "I don't know." Then he stared at her intently. "Didn't you feel anything?"

"No, but I wasn't there as long as you were. What did you feel?"

"I want you to go back there before I tell you. I'll wait here."

Jasmine hesitated. "I'm not sure that's wise. What if the demons come?"

"They won't. It isn't fully dark yet."

That was true enough, but the shadows were lengthening. "All right," she said, then turned to walk back into the woods. It was obvious that he wasn't going to tell her anything.

The last of the day's light reflected off the sphere and its circle of diamonds. She approached it, then reached out a hand to touch it.

The sphere began to glow as though lit from within. The diamonds sparkled with an unnatural brightness. And it felt warm to her touch. She drew her hands away, then put them back again. The warmth was soothing, generating a strange heat that seemed to flow through her whole body.

She took her hands away again, and the glow immediately began to fade, until it looked as it had when she'd first approached it. She put them back again and the glow and warmth returned.

Not until she forced herself to leave the woods did it occur to her to be frightened. Even then, what she felt was awe more than fear. As she emerged once more into the marketplace, her body still registered that wondrous warmth, as though she were glowing like the sphere.

She told Quinn what had happened as he peered at her intently. "Was that what happened to you?"

He shook his head, but said nothing.

"Well, what did happen?"

"I didn't feel anything when I touched it. When I first saw it, I was just surprised and thought how beautiful it was. But the longer I stood there, the more I felt that I shouldn't be there—that it didn't *want* me there." He ran a hand through his hair as he stared back into the woods.

"I know it didn't want me there. I don't like this place. Let's get out of here. We can camp over on the other side of the pond."

Jasmine started to protest, then stopped. In any event, he was already headed toward the horses. How could he not like this place, when he'd said earlier that it was prettier than the other village?

Then, as she mounted her mare, she remembered the chill she'd felt when they'd first entered the other village. It hadn't lasted, though—or perhaps she'd simply gotten caught up in their explorations and hadn't noticed it.

This must be the village of my people, she thought, *while the other one belonged to the Dartuli. But why should he be uncomfortable here? Are the demons somehow responsible?*

It was dark by the time they reached the far side of the pond, where the small stream that fed it emerged from the woods at the base of the mountain. And long before they stopped, they both heard the distant sound of a waterfall.

Quinn was silent as he built a fire, then skinned the rabbits he'd caught earlier for their dinner. Jasmine left him to tend to that and went down to the pond.

The pond was shallow, at least along its edges, and she stripped off her dusty dress and the heavy riding boots and waded naked into the warm water. A curved sliver of moon was rising above the mountain, and a cool wind blew down from the heights. When she entered the pond, her mind was still on Quinn's strange behavior, but as she walked slowly out into the deeper water, those thoughts faded away and a wonderful peace stole over her.

Without really intending to do so, she found herself swimming toward the center of the pond. The water was cooler there, but still quite pleasant after a warm day. She swam some more, utterly at peace and with no thoughts at all in her mind, then rolled over onto her back and began to float.

You must save him, the voice whispered. *They want him and they have a claim on him.*

It was the same voice that had spoken to her before. Jasmine was so startled that she stopped floating, then was briefly submerged before she began to swim. She broke the surface and looked around. The surface of the pond was like a giant mirror—utterly still except for the small ripples she was creating.

"But how can I save him?" she cried. "I don't know what to do."

Treading water, she waited impatiently for a response, but got none. Then she saw movement in the water between her and the campfire. Something dark. At first she thought it was a demon and she called out to Quinn. But then his voice floated over the water to her and she realized he was swimming out to her.

"Don't panic! I'm coming."

She started to call out that she wasn't in any danger, then decided instead to prove it by swimming toward him. She was surprised to see how far out into the pond she'd gone, but she felt no fear of the water.

"Are you all right?" he asked, reaching out to draw her against him.

She nodded. "I just didn't realize how far I'd gone."

He let her go—too quickly, she thought—and they swam together back to shore, where Quinn turned his back on her as they both got dressed.

Later, after they'd eaten their dinner, she tried to decide if she should tell him about the voice and its warning. Whatever or whoever it was, it clearly had his best interests at heart and wanted to help him. But she thought about his silence and his withdrawal from her and decided to keep it to herself for the moment. It seemed to her that Quinn had quite enough on his mind. Besides, what good would it do to repeat the voice's message when she had absolutely no idea what it was talking about?

Quinn built up the fire for the night, then spread his blankets out and fell asleep without even saying good night to her. The wonderful sense of peace she'd felt out in the pond eluded her now. Instead she felt a dark chill moving through her as she thought about the voice's warning.

She got up and walked down to the pond again, not to swim this time—though the notion was tempting—but to think. There was surely something she should be doing, but what was it? What could she do to save Quinn? The thought that he might be taken from her because she couldn't figure out a way to save him terrified her.

She stared out across the pond to the village, which was barely visible in the pale moonlight. Her mind went back to her dream. Everything in it had come true. Even the waterfall, which she hadn't yet seen, but which she could hear right now. The dream had become reality except for one thing.

Frowning, she turned back to the campfire and

Quinn's blanket-covered form. There was one thing in the dream—the dream they'd shared—that hadn't yet happened. And it hadn't happened because Quinn had stopped it from happening.

Chapter Twelve

The waterfall was high, but not as powerful as the one they'd encountered earlier in their journey. Instead of roaring down the side of the mountain, it almost meandered, finding its way over rocks and across ledges with a musical sound that delighted Jasmine. And no matter how far back she tipped her head, she couldn't see its top. It seemed to originate in the very heavens themselves. Instead of a pool at the base, it drained into a small, pretty stream that fed the pond.

Jasmine looked around at the forest that surrounded the stream and the base of the waterfall. She was certain that this place had been part of her dream: a place of imcomparable beauty and utter peace.

She slanted a glance at Quinn. He'd wanted to leave as soon as they awoke this morning, but she had insisted upon seeing the waterfall. And now, as he looked up at the mountain, she could sense in him an impatience, though he'd come with her willingly enough.

If she were going to attempt to talk to him about what was on her mind, this should be a good time and place. But she found herself unable to begin. She knew him so well—better than she'd ever known anyone—and yet she was now discovering that there were still subjects that were difficult to broach.

Quinn put an arm across her shoulders, surprising her, since it was the first time he'd touched her in some time. "Are you ready to leave now?" he asked, his tone indicating that he certainly was.

She nodded and they started back along the bank of the stream to the pond where they'd made camp. She was angry with herself for her failure to ask him the question that was on her mind, but she rationalized that this was probably not a good time, since he was so eager to be away from here.

They rode through the silent village, then up the road. Jasmine stopped for a moment at the top of the hill to gaze down upon the ancient home of her people, but Quinn kept going without a single glance.

Several hours later, when they came to the old fence that stretched across the valley, Quinn suggested that they follow the fence line and then ride the rest of the way along the base of the mountain.

"That way we can do some more exploring," he told her. "Besides, it'll be cooler over there."

The day had become surprisingly warm—the balmiest yet on their journey—and since they were riding much of the time through open fields, Jasmine welcomed the thought of traveling through the cooler woods near the stream that flowed the length of the valley on that side.

They set off across the field, riding alongside the ancient fence, which was now only a series of tall stone pillars, many of which were nearly hidden by tall grasses.

The fence continued to trouble her for reasons

she couldn't understand. It must have been built
at a time when his people and hers were at war,
but that was very ancient history indeed. Nevertheless, it troubled her, and she was glad when
they reached the woods at the base of the mountain, where the fence ended.

She would have welcomed the opportunity to
stop and cool herself in the shallow stream, but
Quinn seemed determined to keep going. For once
he seemed not to consider that the horses might
want a drink after the long, hot ride.

What is happening to him—to us? she asked herself. *How can it be that we've found our dream and
yet we seem to be growing farther and farther apart?*
She wanted to say something or do something that
would bring them together again, and yet she
feared taking any action that might drive them
even farther apart.

She'd lived such a solitary life before Quinn had
appeared and changed everything that she had
very little understanding of human nature—and
especially of the nature of men. But she knew
enough about this particular man to know that he
had changed since that time when he'd vanished
and she'd found him in the cave.

They rode for perhaps another hour on the
mossy bank of the little stream before he finally
suggested that they stop to rest. It was a lovely
spot, deeply shaded by trees and an overhanging
bulge in the mountain. As she dismounted, she
caught the scent of jasmine and saw a number of
the pretty plants growing in the rich soil near the
stream.

She sat down on the moss-cushioned bank and
pulled off her boots, then dangled her feet into the
stream with a happy sigh. A faint, cool breeze
spilled down the mountainside. Quinn led the
horses down to drink, then tethered them in the
woods nearby.

He filled his leather flask from the stream and offered it to her. She drank deeply of the cool water, then lay back against the fragrant moss. A moment later Quinn sat down beside her.

It was strange, she thought, how some silences could seem comfortable, while others filled up with tension. Silence was silence, after all. But right now there were too many unspoken words between them, pushing at that silence as though it were a sack about to burst.

"Talk to me, Quinn," she said before she could stop herself.

"About what?" he asked without turning. She knew she wasn't imagining the wariness in his voice.

"About what we're going to do," she said, though what she really wanted to hear was how he felt about her and about the valley.

"When we get back to the village, I want to start fixing up one of the houses, so we have a place to live. Since I don't have the proper tools, it will take some time. And we need to be thinking about food, too. There are probably lots of things growing wild in the gardens behind the houses."

She said nothing. He was right, of course, that they had to think of such things, but it wasn't what she wanted to hear.

"What about the demons? Don't you think they'll be back?"

He shrugged. "We haven't seen them since we reached the valley."

"But Quinn, they can't be afraid to come into the valley—not if the stories you were told are true. And anyway, if you want to fix up a house, why not one back there?" She gestured toward her people's village. "I thought that some of them looked to be in better shape than the ones we saw first."

Now it was his turn to be silent. She let it go on

for a few minutes, then made a sound of exasperation.

"Quinn, you've changed. You're not the same man you were before you disappeared and ended up in that cave."

He gave her a quick, unreadable look. "Oh? And how have I changed?"

"I can't explain it—but you have." She took a deep breath, then forced the words out. "You said that you wanted to wait for us to make love until we reached the valley. Well, we're here—but you . . ." She faltered as she felt her skin begin to flush warmly.

He started to reach out to take her hand, then stopped and got up instead. Without another word, he walked away. She continued to lie there for a moment, then got up and followed him along the bank of the stream. When she caught up to him, she grabbed his arm none too gently.

"Don't you dare just walk away from me like that! You're in trouble, Quinn, and I can't help you if you won't let me."

He stopped walking and turned to her. "What do you mean, I'm in trouble?"

"You are. It's the demons. They want you. I don't know why—but they do. And I won't let them have you!"

His pale eyes searched her face. "Why do you think they want me—and not you as well?"

"I don't know. And I don't know why that voice speaks to me, either."

"What voice?"

She told him. "I don't know if it's a man or a woman—but I believe what it's saying. You're in danger."

"And you're going to save me," he said with a trace of sarcasm.

"How can I? I don't know what to do."

"Then I think you should stop listening to your

'voice' and let me take care of myself."

She folded her arms in a stubborn gesture. "You're not doing a very good job of it so far."

"I'm still here. We're both still here."

She glared at him. "You're being a *man*, Quinn—and I don't like that."

His eyes lit with amusement, and then he laughed outright. "In case you haven't noticed, I *am* a man. I have been for a long time—since long before you met me."

"That isn't what I meant," she stated, not about to be humored. "What I meant was that you're behaving more like other men—and not like the one I know."

"I see," he said, his eyes still glittering with amusement. "And you no doubt have much experience with men."

"Not the kind of experience you're talking about," she replied, lifting her chin defiantly. "But I know what they're like—and you were different. Now you're more like them."

To her surprise, tears sprang to her eyes. She was so frustrated. None of this had come out the way she'd wanted it to. She hadn't found the right words.

"Don't cry," he said softly as he drew a thumb across her cheeks to catch the tears.

"I'm crying because I'm angry," she said, turning her face away. "I don't like what's happening to us. I thought we loved each other."

"I *do* love you," he said in that same soft voice. "I just want you to be patient for a time."

"Why?"

"Because there are things I don't understand yet—and I don't want to . . . hurt you."

"It hurts me more when you won't talk about it, Quinn."

He turned his back on her for a moment, and she thought he was going to walk away again. But then he faced her once more, and she could see in his eyes that he'd reached some sort of decision. She could only hope that he'd decided to be honest with her, because she had no weapons left.

"I think that the stories I've been told might not have been entirely true," he said slowly. "Maybe things are more . . . complicated."

"In what way?" she asked when he lapsed into silence.

"That's what I don't know. It's just a feeling— and that's why I didn't want to talk about it yet."

"You think that the demons may have some sort of claim on you—just like they said," she stated. The words didn't come easily, but she knew they'd been there all along, refusing to be acknowledged.

"They might have," he admitted. "They've had three chances to kill me, but they haven't done it. I think they want me for some other purpose."

She saw the anguish in his eyes. "There's more, isn't there?"

He stared at her in silence for a moment, then nodded. "There's something in me sometimes. I felt it on the battlefield and I felt it the other times I've killed." His voice dropped to a whisper. "It's like I can't stop."

Jasmine felt a chill so deep that she seemed to have turned to ice inside. But somehow she kept her voice calm.

"You're wrong, Quinn. I know of one time when you were able to stop—when those men attacked me in the stable."

But even as she spoke, she was seeing those bloody bodies on the slope above their campsite. She forced the image away.

"I wanted to kill them."

"But you didn't. That's what's important."

"That was before the demons came."

"What does this have to do with *us*, Quinn? You wouldn't kill me."

He shook his head quickly. "No, I'd never do that, but I'm afraid that I could hurt you."

He took a deep, shaky breath, and Jasmine knew that she was seeing a side of Quinn that he'd never intended for anyone to see. He had been so strong, so very sure of himself, and now . . .

"When I touch you, I don't just want to make love to you. I want to dominate you . . . to conquer you."

She swallowed hard and tried not to shiver. "As though I were really your enemy."

"Yes."

He took her hand in his. "We have to wait—to let this play out. We'll find the answers somehow."

She stared down at their clasped hands. "What I don't understand is why I don't feel that way about you. I'm not afraid of you, Quinn—in spite of what you said."

With her free hand, she touched his cheek. "You're the only good thing that's ever happened to me, Quinn. That's why I was so afraid to trust you at first."

"Maybe you'd be safer if you didn't trust me now."

"But I do." She paused, frowning, then spoke slowly. "I think that's what the voice was telling me. Because I love you and trust you, I can protect you from the demons."

"It isn't supposed to be that way. I'm the one who's supposed to be protecting you."

"But you have. You've saved my life more than once. Now maybe it's my turn to save yours."

"I don't like that. It isn't natural."

"Quinn," she said exasperatedly, "we left everything that's natural and normal days ago. Besides, if it's true that our people had magic, then we aren't natural anyway.

"Don't you see?" she asked, warming to the subject. "If our people had magic, then they never lived as other people live. Men don't need to protect women who have magic to protect themselves. They'd be equals."

Quinn looked doubtful—and more than a little dismayed. She had to restrain a smile. Ever since she'd begun to talk about it, she'd felt a change coming over her.

"There's great power in magic, Quinn," she said enthusiastically. But then she sobered quickly. "Still, something went wrong. Otherwise we'd have grown up in this valley."

But Quinn had obviously been brooding about her earlier words. She saw many reactions flicker across his rugged features before she saw the one she loved best: a smile.

"So now you've decided that you're a witch—is that it?"

"No, that's not it," she replied, smiling herself. Quinn's grin was irresistible—especially now, since she'd seen so few of them. Besides, she sensed that he needed to regain his old self after his astonishing admission of his fears.

"Witches are evil—and I'm not evil." But the moment the words left her mouth, she wanted desperately to take them back.

"*You* aren't evil—but *I* might be."

"No, you aren't!" She began to pace around, clenching her fists determinedly. "And we're going to get to the truth here somehow."

Quinn watched her, more than a little dismayed. She apparently didn't see it—but he surely did. She had changed as well. In fact, she was changing now, before his very eyes. The frightened, withdrawn, and uncertain woman he'd rescued had vanished. From the beginning he'd sensed a strength in her—but he hadn't anticipated this. Furthermore, he wasn't at all certain that he liked the change.

She's getting stronger and more sure of herself while I'm getting weaker and more confused, he thought miserably. He'd never depended on anyone before, let alone a woman.

He regretted having told her of his fears. He should have kept them to himself until he could work things out. He was deeply chagrined. Here he was, a man who'd known many women, while she'd known no men at all—and yet *he* was the one who was afraid to touch her.

He continued to watch her as she stood there, staring defiantly at the mountains, as though she would challenge them and anything else. He thought she was the most beautiful woman he'd ever seen, but he could feel the beginnings of that darkness swirling around in him, threatening his better feelings.

"We'd better go," he told her. "If we don't go now, we won't reach the village before dark."

The night was sultry. Not even the cool breeze that flowed down from the mountains could quite dispel the heat of the day. Jasmine walked naked into the lake.

They had returned to the village of his people. The main body of the lake was on the far side of the hill north of the village, but a small, shallow portion of it curved around the edge of the hill to touch the village itself; it was there that she stood.

Quinn was not far away, on the shore. He'd caught some fish and was busy cleaning them— keeping himself occupied, she thought, keeping himself away from her. He'd turned his back when she announced that she was going to bathe in the lake, but as she walked into the water, she felt his eyes upon her.

She waded deeper, until the water climbed up her thighs and then midway up her hips. The temperature was perfect here in the shallows: cool enough to feel invigorating, but warm enough to be inviting. She turned back briefly and saw Quinn still bent to his task, a dark silhouette against the campfire.

After his earlier outpouring, he'd retreated into silence again. She knew he regretted telling her of his fears, but she was very glad that he had. The only question in her mind now was whether those fears were justified.

She smiled to herself, although her pleasure was tinged with guilt. She'd been so busy being concerned about the changes in Quinn that she'd failed completely to see that she too was changing. In view of Quinn's reaction, though, she should probably have kept quiet.

She couldn't even say exactly when the change in herself had begun, but she thought it might well have started when she climbed up that cliff after his disappearance. At the time, though, she'd been too preoccupied with her dangerous mission to wonder where the courage had come from to undertake it in the first place.

Power, she thought, as an almost sensual thrill ran through her. *It's in me now. I may not understand it yet, or know exactly how to use it—but I know it's there. Quinn may not like it much, but it will save us both.*

She crouched down in the water until it reached all the way up to her neck. Then she held her breath and submerged completely. When she stood up again, she began to lather herself with scented soap she'd bought in Halaban.

As her soap-slicked hands glided over her body, Jasmine left off her thoughts of Quinn and the demons, and drifted instead into very different thoughts about him.

She felt heavy and ripe—hungry for his touch. Her nipples grew taut and ached to be pressed against his hard, hair-roughened chest. The need rose in great waves from her female core, spreading through her until every inch of her cried out for him. She raised her face to the star-sprinkled heavens, then closed her eyes and imagined him there with her, his big, uncompromisingly male body as hungry as hers.

The warm breeze flowed over her, cooler now as her body heated at the thought of his hands, his lips, and she imagined them caressing her like that: soft and gentle, yet unyieldingly male.

On the shore, Quinn finished cleaning the fish and set them aside. The water, lapping gently at its pebble-strewn border, tempted him. He got up and began to strip off his clothes, keeping his eyes carefully averted from the lake with a great effort of will. He wanted her—more than ever—but his uneasiness was now magnified by the change he'd seen in her.

He walked into the water, his head down, determined to go only out far enough to wash off the day's dirt and sweat and the smell of fish that clung to his hands. But his determination failed him before he'd gone more than a few yards.

She stood near the middle of the cove, a pale figure against the darker water. He glanced away quickly, but not before her image had burned itself into his brain. Resolutely he began to scrub himself, wanting to be out of there and dressed and cooking the fish before she left the water. But the image remained, taunting him—and he looked again.

She was washing herself with slow, unbearably erotic movements, made all the more sensual because he knew how innocent she was. The warm breeze that blew over him had touched her, and he imagined that it carried her scent.

The ache inside him was a living thing with its own will, but for the moment his will was greater.

He turned his back on her and finished bathing quickly, then hurried back to shore.

Jasmine finished bathing as well, and turned to see Quinn emerging from the water, then disappearing into the darkness at the edge of the woods, where they'd left their belongings. She felt a moment's embarrassment, knowing that he must have been watching her, and recalling how he'd seemed on several occasions to reach into her thoughts.

But the shame departed quickly, eclipsed by a knowledge of the power that was in her now and the certainty that they belonged together. Truly together, she thought—not circling around each other warily as they had been.

She made her way slowly toward the shore as Quinn reappeared and moved toward the campfire. She was in no hurry. She wanted to savor this moment—to feel her hunger reaching out to touch his.

The breeze had all but dried her by the time she stepped out of the water. Quinn had his back to her now, poking at the fire. Her fresh clothes lay nearby where she'd put them before going into the water. She reached for them—and stopped, her eyes on him.

Her gaze drew him as surely as if she'd spoken. He turned his head to her, then got up from his crouch. They faced each other across ten feet of space that seemed to vibrate with tension. He wore light, loose trousers and was naked from the waist up. She wore nothing at all.

One moment filled up and then spilled into the next. She walked toward him across the soft grass. Behind him the fire hissed and crackled and a log shifted. Somewhere in the distance, a night bird cried out. The breeze toyed with the fire, sending a brief shower of sparks into the darkness.

The final few feet were the longest, filled with anticipation and then, at the last moment, a tiny quiver of fear that was lost the moment his arms came around her.

He held her for a long time—an eternity, it seemed. She thought that perhaps he would reject her, but when he lowered his head with a deep groan, she knew she had won. And she knew, too, that whatever darkness lay in him, was gone for the moment.

His mouth covered hers as his hands molded her soft curves to his hard planes. She felt the tremors in him and knew instinctively that he was trying to control himself, to keep in check the hunger that was coursing through him. She wanted to cry out and beg him to unleash that need because hers matched it, but she discovered that there was a powerful sensuality in that restraint.

He lowered her to the soft grass, then hurriedly stripped off his trousers and impatiently tossed them aside. The quick movements made her think that he had unloosed his passion, but when he lay down beside her, his kiss was soft and unhurried, at odds with the demanding hardness that pressed against her thigh.

"I love you," he said simply, though his eyes seemed to be begging for understanding, as though she might doubt his words.

"And I love you, Quinn," she said, holding his face between her hands. "I'm not afraid of you."

His mouth curved into a smile. "But perhaps I should be afraid of you."

The words were spoken in jest, but she could feel the truth hiding behind them. She slid her hands down across his neck, then felt his curly chest hair beneath her fingertips. "No," she replied softly but firmly. "There's no fear here tonight—for either of us."

They laid claim to each other slowly, inch by

inch, bodies arching and trembling. With lips and tongues and fingers they discovered each other, both taking their time even though the need was threatening to devour them. They'd waited so long that each seemed to need this time of exploration to accept that the time of wanting and denying that need were over.

Jasmine's sense of self began to melt away even as her knowledge of her own body increased. Quinn gave that sense back to her with kisses and caresses that touched her everywhere. So completely had he become part of her that when at last he slid into her, there was no fear, no sense of being invaded. Instead he was filling a space that had been empty until now—empty and waiting.

Her body moved with his as though they'd performed this erotic dance many times before. Waves of passion engulfed her, driving her against him, driving him deeper into her. She gasped from the sheer sensation of it all and he immediately slowed, his eyes searching hers with concern.

"Am I hurting you?"

His words and the concern for her behind them sent her love for him to an even deeper and still more wonderful place. She shook her head, unable to trust her voice.

Still, he moved more slowly now, letting sensation pile on sensation until they reached their former plateau—and then soared higher still into an explosion that rocked them both, then reverberated through their bodies, clinging to the moment as long as possible.

She made a small sound of protest when he left her. He chuckled and drew her against him. "Men have this curse on them," he said in a husky voice as he pressed his mouth to her hair. "No matter how much we want it to last, it never does. But it's different for women."

And so it was. He held her and caressed her and

stroked her—and her world exploded once more, and she saw that this different kind of pleasure could be his, too, as he watched her tremble and then quake beneath his touch.

Jasmine fitted herself to him, wrapping an arm around his waist as they lay in the soft, cool grass. Her body throbbed, even now, with remembrance and anticipation. Her head was pillowed against his chest and she felt their heartbeats merge. She smiled to herself at his remark about the frailties of men and wondered how long it would be before they could make love again. She'd never expected to feel such things, and now that she did she wanted to make up for the emptiness of a lifetime.

"You're not sorry, are you?" she asked, knowing that he wasn't, but unable to resist teasing him a bit about his reluctance.

He chuckled and the sound rumbled through his chest and into her ear as she rested against him. "*I'm* the one who should be asking that question."

"Well, are you?" She raised herself up until she was staring down at him.

He kissed her softly. "No, I'm not sorry."

She knew he spoke the truth, but she also knew that by morning he was likely to be worrying again. She stared out at the placid lake that was reflecting the crescent moon. It was a scene of inexpressible beauty and peace: everything they'd both dreamed that the valley would be. But it felt fragile—so very fragile.

They got up and bathed again in the cool waters of the lake, then cooked the fish and ate it with blueberries she'd gathered earlier. She'd also found some herbs for tea, and they shared a mug while they also shared one of the blankets as the night wind blew down from the shadowy mountains.

Later they made love again, lingering this time as lips and fingers found all the secret places and drew forth shivers of pleasure. It felt to Jasmine like the first time—and the thousandth. Already they knew each other's bodies well, but there were still unexplored territories and unexpected delights. Her inhibitions floated away on a tide of ecstasy, and Quinn discovered new and wondrous depths to an act that had heretofore satisfied only a physical need.

They slept as one, curved together in a tangle of spent passion, while the moon rose higher over the valley. In the distance, night birds called out and then fell silent. Across the lake, five deer came down to the water to drink, lifted their heads quizzically, and then melted into the forest again.

In the dark woods behind them, shadows moved and twigs snapped. There were angry hisses of frustration, and then the shadows were gone.

"Look!" Jasmine grinned, cradling the half-dozen eggs in her skirt.

"Where did you find them?" Quinn paused after he'd dumped some of the debris from the house.

"In the garden next door. If we can just build a fence, we can catch the chickens and have eggs every day."

She smiled at her find, thinking of the time when one or two eggs were so precious—when she'd stolen them at great risk for her mother and herself.

"First the house—then a fence," Quinn said. "Come see the furniture I found buried under the rubble."

There was a table that could easily be repaired and two unbroken chairs, plus several more that might be salvageable. They examined their treasure with delight. They were simple, but beautifully made.

"I think I'll start searching the other houses," Jasmine told him. "Maybe we can even find a bed."

Quinn chuckled. "Now *there's* something important."

She left him to his work, promising to be careful in the ruined houses. The two next door yielded nothing except for a few pieces of pottery and a small table. She walked out to the street and studied the other houses nearby, trying to guess which ones might contain usable items. No house they'd seen had an intact roof, but in some cases at least part of the roof remained, and those buildings seemed most likely to contain undamaged goods.

The treasures began to pile up as Jasmine searched the houses. She found pots and pans and cooking utensils and water jugs, as well as a few more items of furniture, including a large corner cupboard she couldn't move by herself.

Then, buried beneath the partially collapsed roof, she saw a bed. It was impossible to know what condition it was in, and of course the straw mattress would have to be restuffed, but she was delighted anyway. She was about to go get Quinn when she saw something she'd overlooked before: two large wooden trunks back in a dark corner.

The hinges were rusty, but she was finally able to get the first one open, and she gasped in surprise when she saw clothing inside. She reached out to touch it, then hesitated. She'd been so preoccupied with seeking items for their house that she'd given little thought to the lives that had been lived here. But now, as she stood there looking at the neatly folded garments in the trunk, she felt a terrible sadness.

These people had lived good lives, content in their lovely valley. And then they'd been driven out—or rather, the lucky ones had been driven out. Many had probably died here, though she had yet to uncover any skeletons.

Jasmine shivered, then grew angry at this sudden reminder of the past—and what it might mean for their future. Quinn seemed very much himself again, and so it had been easy for her to believe that the demons had given up and retreated to whatever terrible place they called home.

But she knew, as she stood there in the ruins of the house, that it wasn't over yet. She knew it as certainly as if that voice had spoken to her again.

Throwing off those thoughts, she took out the clothing and was pleased to see that it all appeared to be in excellent condition. There were heavy sweaters and men's trousers and warm woolen dresses. It was possible that the men's clothing might fit Quinn, but the women's things were far too big for her.

She turned to the other trunk, but the hinge wouldn't budge. As she tugged at it, she could hear things rattling and bumping around inside. She pushed at it and found it very heavy. Then it struck her that this might be the most valuable find of all—at least from Quinn's point of view.

She went back to the house he was working on and persuaded him to come with her. When they reached the house, she showed him the two trunks. He glanced at the clothing and said that he didn't need anything. He was obviously eager to get back to his work.

"I couldn't get the other one open," she said. "But I think you should try."

He gave her an amused look, as though finding her sudden obsession with clothing too typically female, but he obligingly began to work on the hinge. Then, when he heard the sounds from inside, he set to work with a vengeance.

Just as she'd expected, his eyes lit with pleasure when he finally got it open and the contents were revealed to be exactly what she'd thought. He took out the tools one by one, examining them as though they were the most valuable treasure in the world. She smiled smugly.

"You knew all along what was in here," he said with the grin of a boy with a whole set of new toys.

"I guessed," she corrected him. "And I think I found a bed as well."

He lifted her off her feet and swung her around. "We're going to be happy here, girl. We'll have a real house of our own in no time."

Days passed—and then a week. Thanks to the tools, Quinn's work went faster. Jasmine spent her days salvaging more items for their house and trying to befriend several shy cows so they could be persuaded to give milk.

She began to roam farther from Quinn, satisfied that the demons had—for now, at least—withdrawn from the valley. One day she found two kittens, newly weaned and wandering about a meadow in search of mice. They were shy but curious. So she came back the next day with pieces of fish for them, and when she returned to their soon-to-be home, they followed her.

Quinn picked them up, one in each big hand, and pronounced them an excellent addition to their household. Several nests of mice had long ago made the place into a home of their own.

Jasmine had by now explored all the houses in the village, except for several at the edge that were all but destroyed. Storms had apparently felled some tall trees that had turned them into little more than rubble.

She walked around the perimeter of the ruined houses, trying to see if there was a safe way to get inside. What she discovered instead was a path leading off into the woods at the base of a mountain.

She felt a certain disquiet the moment she spotted it, though it took her a few seconds to realize why she felt that way. Unlike the streets in the village and the road that ran the length of the valley, the path wasn't overgrown with weeds.

Her uneasiness grew and she was about to turn away, but curiosity got the better of her and she ventured onto the trail. She'd gone only a short distance into the woods when her pendant began to grow warm and throb faintly against her skin.

She stopped. The woods were dark—but not that dark, because the day was clear and bright and the sun was still high in the sky. She was certain now that the demons could not withstand daylight. It had been daylight when they'd lured Quinn to that cave, but they must have cast their spell from there. Besides, she knew she wasn't subject to their spells.

Later it would surprise her that she'd been so unafraid, but what she felt now was only curiosity—and so she continued along the path.

The first part of the path was level, but then it began to climb the mountain in a series of sharp angles. Obsessed now with knowing where it went, she gave no thought to her isolation. The pendant had become so warm that she pulled it out from beneath her shirt. It throbbed wildly in her hand.

And then, when she reached yet another sharp turn, the blast of cold, fetid air struck her. She stopped, experiencing her first pangs of fear. But she walked on slowly, now holding the pendant out before her.

What she found at the end of the path was the high, wide mouth of a cave. The foul, cold air surrounded her as she stopped beneath the stone arch and peered into the darkness beyond. As she stood there uncertainly, the pendant began to glow until its brightness reached into the cavern.

Inside, the room was huge and almost perfectly circular. On the far side from where she stood was a stone altar, and she could see the remains of candles. The source of the chill lay beyond that, in a darkness that resisted the pendant's glow.

Jasmine walked across the stone floor, her boots tapping out her progress in the eerie silence. She reached the altar, then pulled herself up onto it and stared down into the blackness.

The pendant was ablaze now, its light nearly blinding her—but even so, it penetrated only a short distance into the abyss that lay beyond the altar. The cold and the foul air rushed at her like a living thing.

She staggered back from the abyss, climbed down from the altar, and ran back through the cavern to daylight, where she collapsed against a tree and rubbed herself, waiting for the cold to go away as she gulped great quantities of fresh, pine-scented air.

I've found their home, she thought. It was the only explanation. The cold and the overwhelming odor were proof that this was where the demons lived. It was even stronger than from where she'd reserved Quinn.

She stared for a moment at the mouth of the cave, then turned in the opposite direction, where a rocky ledge jutted out from the mountain. There below her lay the village, all of it plainly visible. From down there, the mouth of the cave would also be visible, if one knew where to look.

Her gaze went from the valley to the cave and back again as she thought about that great room with its altar—and the path she'd just climbed.

"They worshiped the demons," she said, speaking the words aloud to herself. "The Dartuli worshiped the demons."

The implications of that sent her running from the place, back down into the valley. But when she reached Quinn at last and he proudly showed her the newly repaired and rethatched roof, she kept her discovery to herself.

Chapter Thirteen

"No!" Jasmine awoke to the echo of her own scream.

Quinn woke up even faster, and she saw the flash of the knife in his hand as he leaped from bed, his head swiveling around the room.

"I was dreaming," she said, the words forced out from between chattering teeth. She was so cold, and she imagined that she could still smell the foul odor from the abyss behind the altar.

"Are you sure?" Quinn asked, still crouched with the knife held out in front of him.

"Yes." She turned away, already feeling guilty. She hadn't told him about her discovery of the demon cave because he'd seemed to have put the demons from his mind. But his lightning-quick response to her scream indicated otherwise.

He set the knife on the floor and sat down beside her, on the edge of their new bed. "What were you dreaming about?"

"The demons," she said, even though none had

actually appeared in the dream. She'd climbed up onto that altar again and peered down into the abyss—but in the dream, someone or something had pushed her and she had begun to fall through the freezing darkness.

"I'm sorry I frightened you," she said softly, reaching out to take his hand.

He enfolded it briefly in his, then drew her into his arms. "You're so cold," he said, reaching for a blanket, then slipping back into the bed and drawing it over them both.

She merely nodded. She hadn't realized just how cold she was until she felt his warmth surround her.

He held her and stroked her and whispered soft words of love into her ear, and gradually the chill went away—but thoughts of the awful cave remained. She wondered if she should tell him about it. What if he discovered it on his own?

She decided that that was unlikely. His days were well occupied with work on their house, which they'd moved into just the past day, and the construction of a fence to hold their growing flock of chickens.

It's better if he doesn't know, she thought. *If I tell him about it, he'll want to go there.* She knew Quinn. He'd ignore any danger to himself, or even treat it as a sort of challenge—to prove to himself that the demons had no hold on him.

"They haven't gone away, have they?" he asked in a tone that was more a statement than a question.

"I don't know," she replied, though of course she did. They were still out there, down in their pit in the mountain, waiting for something.

He drew her closer and his caresses became more intimate, moving slowly from comfort to eroticism. The demons faded from her mind and she surrendered herself to the passion that he had awakened in her. Her body, which had been so cold only moments ago, now glowed with a voluptuous warmth.

Quinn threw off the covers and began to make a trail of kisses down the length of her until her legs parted for that most intimate of kisses. She gloried in the sensations that rippled through her—in the newfound power of her own body, and in its aching vulnerability.

And she had learned to please him as well—to tease him with her lips and tongue until he could stand it no more—even though it was obvious that he wanted to very much. They were both finding that perfect balance between pleasure and the unbearable pain of trying to hover at the very edge of ecstasy.

When she knew that he had reached his limit, she took him into herself and rode him to the ultimate pleasure, glorying in the feel of his body beneath hers, writhing and heaving with passion.

He drew her face down and kissed her as the aftershocks rippled through them both. "Ah, love, I can't get enough of you. At this rate I'll be an old man before my time."

She smiled. "Then perhaps you shouldn't have taught me so well."

"I didn't teach you," he replied, his voice muffled as he buried his mouth in the cleft between her breasts. "You came to me knowing exactly how to please me."

She thought he might be right. From the very beginning she'd felt as though he were no more than an extension of herself—a newly discovered part of her own body whose terrain was both strange and familiar.

She slid down beside him and fitted herself to him and they both fell asleep murmuring their love, the demons all but forgotten.

* * *

They had been in the valley for a month. High summer was upon them, with sultry days and warm nights made bearable by the cool breezes that spilled down from the mountains. Quinn continued to work on the house and built a fence for the chickens that now provided them with a regular supply of eggs. When he finished that, he started work on a pasture fence that would hold the cows Jasmine had finally persuaded to give milk.

He also made good on his promise to ride the white stallion, but not until he had completely won the animal's trust. And he was soon to begin work on the old stable, hoping to be able to house the animals there for the winter. He was determined to pamper them as they had been long ago by his people, and to increase the small herd.

He was happier than he'd ever been, and as time passed with no visits from the demons, he began to relegate them to his past as much as the long years spent working in the quarry.

The only strange thing that happened during this time was something he didn't mention to Jasmine because he dismissed it quickly each time it happened. He would be working on the pasture fence or riding the stallion or working at the old stable, and would find himself staring at a particular spot on the mountain at the edge of the village. There was a ledge and a rocky outcropping above it that cast a shadow even at midday so that it seemed as though it might be the mouth of a cave.

Several times he thought about trying to climb up there, but there was always work to be done and he would soon forget about it.

Jasmine's days were spent trying to make some order out of long-abandoned gardens: the one behind their house and several more as well. She pulled weeds until she thought her back would break, gathered from gardens and fields all the herbs she wanted, and tried, within the limitation of their supplies here, to make the old stone house a true home for them.

When the afternoons became too warm for work, they would strip off their clothes and swim in the lake. She became a very strong swimmer, and they often raced across the width of the lake. Quinn almost always won, of course, because of his superior size, but from time to time she'd win by cheating. She would dive underwater, and, grabbing his ankles and pulling him down, she'd race off again before he could surface.

In the long summer evenings, they walked through the fields or sat by the lake, content for the most part with silence. But when they did talk on these occasions, the conversation invariably turned to the things they didn't have and couldn't yet make here in the valley.

"We should make a trip to Halaban before winter comes," Quinn said one evening.

"Yes, I've been thinking about that," she admitted. She already had a lengthy list in her mind of items they needed.

"Are you afraid to leave?" he asked after a brief silence.

"I . . . don't know," she admitted. The thought did make her uneasy, though she wasn't sure exactly why. Maybe it was just that they'd come so very far to get here and already faced so many dangers.

"The valley waited all this time for us," Quinn said. "It will still be here when we return."

But neither of them spoke their true fears: that if they left the valley, the demons would be waiting.

*   *   *

A week after the issue was first raised, they set out on a warm morning that threatened to become very hot once the sun had burned through the haze.

Jasmine had awakened at dawn with a strong sense of foreboding, and when Quinn stirred beside her, she wanted to tell him that they shouldn't leave. But he awoke eager to be off, talking about the things he would buy and how much easier it would be for them. So she forgot about her fear and thought instead about scented soaps and fabric and all the other items she wanted to bring back.

Quinn had rounded up the packhorses several days ago, since they'd been running free all summer. Considering what they planned to buy, he said they would have to purchase several more in Halaban. He certainly wasn't going to press the white horses into such service. Nor would he ride the stallion to Halaban, because he feared that it would attract too much unwelcome attention.

As they rode through the fields, Jasmine stared up at the cave and silently ordered the demons to stay put. The cave had remained her secret, though once, she'd seen Quinn pause in his work and stare in that direction. She'd held her breath until he returned to his work. From down in the valley the mouth of the cave could easily be mistaken for a shadow, and he apparently thought that was what it was.

When they reached the base of the mountain and the woods, they stopped and turned to stare at the valley. Already it was shimmering in a heat haze that hung over the fields and forests, giving it the appearance of fading away.

Once more Jasmine felt a sharp stab of fear, but when Quinn started onto the forest trail, she followed.

The skittish packhorses, who'd apparently long

since forgotten their true purpose, kept them both well occupied as they rode up the trail toward the cave. Quinn said that they would settle down after a few miles, and she hoped he was right, or their trip would be made even longer.

They reached the magical cave at midday, coming upon it without warning because they were unfamiliar with the approach from the valley. Quinn suggested that they rest for a time and eat their noon meal.

They tethered the horses and walked off into the nearby woods, only to discover that there was a spot not far away where the valley was visible below them. So they sat on the rocky ledge and enjoyed the view as they ate. The angle was such that they could even see the village from here, though not their own house.

When they had finished eating, Quinn slid an arm around her and drew her close. "You've made me a happy man," he said softly, brushing his lips against her cheek. "When I met you I thought I'd found nothing more than a partner to help me on my journey."

She smiled. "And I thought I'd been rescued by a madman."

He chuckled as he gazed down at the valley. "It's going to take a lifetime of work to bring the valley back, but it will be worth it. By the time our children are grown, it should be the way it once was."

"Our children?" she echoed uneasily.

He slanted her an amused glance. "I'm surprised there isn't one on the way already."

She was, too—now that she thought about it. But her monthly had come and gone.

Quinn had apparently detected her uneasiness. "Does the thought of having children bother you?"

"Yes," she answered honestly. "We'd be so alone, Quinn—no midwife, no one to help me."

"I'll be there," he said, hugging her. "I helped deliver a baby once."

"You did?" She'd never heard of such a thing. Men had a tendency to disappear at such times.

He nodded. "It was during one of the wars. Some people were fleeing a village that was under siege, and among them was a young woman who was about to give birth. The enemy had followed them and killed the lot—except for her. She'd played dead until they left. My men and I found her, and someone had to help her. So I did."

"Did they both live?"

Quinn nodded. "I managed to get them both to safety in another village." He grinned. "She named the baby after me."

She smiled. It seemed that this man would never cease to amaze her. Fortune had certainly smiled upon her when Quinn had entered her life.

With one last, lingering look at the valley, they got up and returned to the cave. Quinn's thoughts were of the children they would have, she was sure. Perhaps it wouldn't be such a bad idea, after all. She'd sworn never to bring children into such a terrible world—but that was before she'd met Quinn. Things were different now.

They stood with the horses at the entrance to the cave. Jasmine's pendant was glowing, but the light reached only a short distance into the dark. Quinn took her hand and they started in, leading the horses. Jasmine was thinking how they were now at the total mercy of the magic within this cave, and she almost stopped as fear spread itself along her spine with icy fingers.

Why am I afraid? she asked herself. *The light showed us the way before and it will do so again.* But in that first moment when they entered the darkness, she was terrified.

Then the golden light spread before them, lighting the way into the narrow passage. She relaxed with an audible sigh, and Quinn turned to her with a smile.

"After all this time, you still don't trust the magic, do you?"

She shook her head, finding it ironic that he trusted the magic more than she did, when he was the one being pursued by demons. Of course, that might be exactly why he trusted the gods who'd created this light. He needed to trust them to combat the dark force of the demons.

But why don't I trust them? she wondered. *They have protected me and helped me to protect him.* And surely they'd been responsible for the change in her, and for that wonderful warmth she'd felt after she'd touched the golden sphere, which she assumed to be an object of worship.

But she *didn't* trust them—and the feeling persisted as they followed the light deeper into the cave. And then, almost as though they'd been spoken aloud, more words from her grandmother came back to her.

The gods bear us no ill will, but they have their own ways and we must accept that.

Accept what? she asked silently. *Accept that their way might not be our way?* She didn't like that thought much and wished that the memory had not chosen this time to return and torment her.

By now, she guessed, they were near the midway point in the cave—the place where she recalled several other passageways branching off. It was also a very narrow tunnel, and they could no longer walk side by side. Quinn took the lead, followed by his horse and the packhorses, and she brought up the rear with her mare.

At first, when the light seemed to get brighter, Jasmine looked down at her pendant, thinking that it was responsible. By the time she raised her eyes again, the cave was filled with blinding light.

She could barely see the horse directly in front of her, and Quinn was completely invisible.

Frightened, she called out to him. But her voice seemed so tiny and so muffled—and there was no response from Quinn.

By now the light had completely blinded her. She called out to Quinn again, and at the same time put out her hand to touch the wall. She was terrified that they would both lose their way. But then the light dimmed somewhat—at least enough for her to see the outline of a passageway and be directed there. She took a few steps in that direction and the light seemed to be slowly returning to normal. Once more she called out to Quinn.

But his name had barely left her lips before she stepped off into thin air! And then she was falling, falling, blinded by the light.

Quinn saw that they were nearing the very center of the cave, where there were other passageways. But the light had guided them through this before, and he trusted it would do so again. He kept his eyes on the darkness at the edge of the light, thinking that he should probably have insisted that Jasmine stay directly behind him instead of putting the packhorses between them. But the animals were still somewhat restless, and he didn't want any trouble with them in here.

He thought that she'd seemed strangely uneasy about coming into the cave and wondered why. After all this time and all they'd seen, didn't she trust the gods and their magic? He supposed that it was just part of her nature not to trust easily, and counted himself very lucky that she trusted *him*.

With his thoughts on Jasmine and his eyes on the darkness beyond the glowing light, Quinn was slow to realize that the light was growing brighter around him, though not in front of him. He didn't recall that having happened before, but he assumed that it was because the way here was more difficult. Indeed, he was now able to see the entrances to the other passages just ahead of him. But the light that went before him, guiding his way, indicated clearly which direction to take, and he followed it.

A moment later two things happened simultaneously. He was plunged into darkness—and he heard Jasmine crying out to him. Her voice seemed to be coming from a great distance, though in his panic he prayed that it was only some strange effect from the cave.

He whirled around and saw a glow behind him that faded into blackness even as he turned. "Jasmine!" he screamed, but the only sounds he heard were the echoes of his own voice. He pushed past his startled horse, trying to get back to her.

And then he too was falling through a black void where cold, foul air was rushing up at him. And as he fell, he knew that she'd been right: the gods were not to be trusted.

After the fall through the blinding light, Jasmine found herself in a semidarkness that was lit by a single point of light that gradually resolved itself into a candle. She stared at it, trying desperately to understand what had happened to her.

She dragged her gaze away from the candle and saw that she was in a small bedroom. As her eyes adjusted to the low level of light, she could see furnishings similar to those they'd found in the valley: ornately carved dark wood, though in this case it all gleamed dully from careful tending. On the narrow bed was a gaily colored quilt, and in a stone jug beside the bed was a bouquet of flowers and fragrant herbs. Loosely woven curtains in a bright pattern fluttered at the open window.

Then she became aware of sounds beyond the

walls of the room. She could hear low voices—
women's voices—but she could not make out the
words. The rhythms and patterns of their speech
told her that it was her own language, the shared
language of the Latawi and Dartuli.

And beneath all the soft murmurings she heard
the low, anguished cry of a woman in unbearable
pain. Her moans rose and fell, and it seemed to
Jasmine that the other voices were trying to comfort her.

"Quinn," she called softly as it all came back to
her: the cave, the light, the long fall to *where*?
Where was she—and where was Quinn?

She sat down on the edge of the bed, shivering,
even though the breeze that blew in through the
window was a warm, soft caress. The gods had
tricked them somehow. She should have trusted
her instincts; they had told her that they shouldn't
go into the cave again.

She clenched her fists helplessly. Whatever else
the gods had done to her, they'd separated her
from Quinn. And what had they done with him?
Had they allowed the demons to take him? Would
they do such a thing?

Beyond the room, the soothing murmurs and
the low, anguished moans continued. Despite her
fears for her own situation, she became curious
about what was going on out there. She hadn't
heard any male voices, so she made the decision
that it would be safe for her to go out there. She
needed to know what had been done with her, and
given the fact that they all seemed to be preoccupied with the woman who was moaning, she
doubted they would try to give her any trouble.

She pushed open the door and found herself in
a narrow hallway that was lit only by the light spill-
ing in from the room at its end. The voices were
louder now, and she could make out some words:
meaningless, soothing words, the kind of things

Saranne Dawson

people said when someone had died. Was that what had happened? Had the woman who was crying lost her husband or perhaps a child?

No sooner did she think that than she heard the cry of a baby—a very young baby, to judge from the sound. Could the woman have just given birth? That could explain the presence of the others, but why was she crying when the baby was obviously alive?

She edged forward cautiously, wondering if the sobs were the result of a deformed child. She'd seen that happen several times, generally when the child arrived early to a mother who was too malnourished to have given it life in the first place. But on the occasions when she'd known that to happen, the midwife had taken the baby away quickly and smothered it.

She reached the end of the hallway and stopped. There were six women in the room, including the one who lay crying on a pile of blankets on the floor. The first thing Jasmine noticed was that they were all tall with pale hair and very fair complexions: Latawi. Her own people. And the next thing she saw was that the baby, which had been put into a basket, was dark haired and darker skinned.

In fact the infant, clearly newborn, had more hair than she'd ever seen on such a young child. It was still wet, but already beginning to curl a bit, reminding her immediately of Quinn.

She moved closer to the basket, which had been set off in a corner, away from the group of women. It seemed quite healthy, and it clearly wasn't deformed. So why were they ignoring it? And why was its mother wailing as though it were dead?

"You should not have run away like that," a voice said behind her. "Your sister needs you now, Jasmine."

The words startled her, but the use of her name

snapped her head around to face the speaker, a very tall woman of late middle years.

"I don't know what's come over you this past month, niece," the woman continued in a low, accusing tone. "But you know how much Tulla and Grayvar wanted this baby after they lost the other one. Stop thinking about yourself and help your sister. I must go and give Grayvar the sad news."

Jasmine was too astonished to say anything, but it seemed that this woman wasn't expecting her to reply. She simply grabbed Jasmine—none too gently—by the arm and propelled her over to the woman on the floor. The other women parted to make way for her.

"Oh, Jasmine," the woman cried, reaching out to her. "How could this happen—again?" She sobbed. "And now they tell me that I can't have any more babies, that it would be too dangerous for me."

Despite her confusion, Jasmine's heart went out to this stranger. Because she herself had decided long ago that she would never have babies—or a husband, either, for that matter—she found it difficult to understand why other women who lived as she had lived could possibly want them. But that was before she'd met Quinn.

So, with her thoughts once more on Quinn, she gathered the suffering woman into her arms and held her and wondered who on earth she was and who the woman thought *she* was. Not to mention why this woman was so upset over the baby, which had now begun to cry again.

"Tell them to take it away!" the stranger in her arms pleaded. "Why haven't they taken it away?"

Jasmine turned to the other women, and one of them spoke up. "Mirra is taking it now." And through the small crowd, Jasmine could see someone lift the basket and disappear out the door.

Is she going to kill it? Jasmine thought with horror. *What could possibly be wrong with it?*

"Tulla, dear, you must rest now," said a kindly woman. "Jasmine, help her drink this so she can get some sleep."

The woman handed Jasmine a mug of something hot that she immediately recognized as being one of the herbal teas she herself had once made. It had a powerfully soothing effect and induced sleep.

She held the mug to the lips of the woman named Tulla, and she fell asleep even before she'd finished it. The brew had been much stronger than she'd ever made. She could tell that from the dark color.

Another woman helped her make Tulla comfortable, and then she and the others left. Jasmine stared down at Tulla's sleeping form, knowing she would not awaken for many hours. Her thoughts turned once more to the baby.

She left the house and saw, the moment she stepped through the doorway, that she was indeed in the village of her people. But it was the village of her dreams—not the place she'd actually seen. Lights glowed behind windows framed with painted shutters, and the mixed scents of flowers that bloomed in front yards filled the night.

In front of the house next door she saw a small crowd, which included the woman who'd scolded her and claimed to be her aunt. She was trying to comfort a tall, blond man while several other men stood about with the awkwardness that she'd seen men often show in emotional situations.

No one was paying any attention to her, so she hurried away along the curved street in the opposite direction, wondering where the other woman had taken the baby.

The streets of the village formed concentric circles around the marketplace and park, but there were also four streets that ran in a straight line from the center to the outer edge, one of which then became the road that ran the length of the valley. The others ended in the surrounding pastures.

Jasmine could see the one straight road up ahead when she heard the sound of horses' hooves. A moment later, two figures on horseback passed by on the intersecting street. One was male, but the other was the woman who'd left with the baby—and she was still carrying the small basket, which had somehow been strapped to the saddle.

She tried to orient herself. They hadn't spent much time in her people's village, and the circular streets were confusing, but she knew that there'd been some ruins at one end of a straight road that must have once been a stable. So she turned in the direction from which the riders had come, determined now to see what was going to happen to the baby.

There were lights on in only a few houses as she ran along the street, and fortunately she passed no one. She hadn't really had a plan when she'd set out, but now she knew that she was going to try to save the baby.

The stable loomed ahead of her at the edge of the village, except that it was whole and well tended—not the ruins she recalled. She paused for only a moment to think about the implications of all she'd seen, then ran into the stable and saddled the first horse she came to.

She saw no one at all as she rode through the village, following the same road she'd seen the people with the baby take. By now she was nearly certain that this was the street that led to the road through the valley. Moments later, when she reached the end of the houses, she saw that she was right. The road stretched before her. In the moonlight she could see all the way to the top of the hill, where she'd first seen the ruins of this village.

She urged the horse to go faster now that she was out of the village, while at the same time she kept an eye out for another road or path that they might have taken. She didn't recall any, but considering the present condition of the road she was now on, it could have been obliterated long ago.

Then, as she reached the crest of the hill, her attention was drawn to the mountainside off to her right. A fire burned brightly about a third of the way up the steep incline. She drew up the reins and squinted, trying to see it more clearly. It didn't appear to be a wildfire because it didn't spread. It must be a beacon of some sort, she thought with a frown.

It couldn't be the people she'd seen with the baby. There hadn't been enough time for them to get up there and light a fire. Thoughts of some terrible ceremony crept into her mind, and she wondered if that might be where they were going.

"No!" she said aloud. These were her people, and they wouldn't be engaged in evil practices. Besides, she'd seen no other road that could have taken them in that direction.

She kicked the horse into action and flew along the road, determined to find them and the baby. When she emerged a short time later from a stretch of woods, she saw them up ahead. She slowed her horse, deciding not to make her presence known until she had a better idea of where they were going. The moon was bright, and in order to remain undetected, she stayed far enough behind them that she could just barely see them.

As she followed them Jasmine began to try to make some sense out of what had happened to her. She felt a resurgent anger at the perfidy of the gods. Clearly they'd not only separated her from Quinn, but they'd also sent her back in time. Or could this be nothing more than a particularly vivid dream? Would she awaken in Quinn's arms?

She wanted to believe that, but she couldn't.

I'm really here, she thought with a shudder. *And perhaps Quinn is as well. But why?* Was it no more than some frivolous whim of all-powerful gods—not unlike those of her former mistress, who cared nothing for the inconvenience or suffering of her servants?

Or was there a purpose to this—and if there was, did that mean that she could hope to be returned to the present, and to Quinn?

She rode on through the night, following the couple but keeping her distance. And as the miles passed, she began to rethink her earlier fear that they intended to kill the baby. If that had been their plan, why would they be going such a distance in the dead of night? But she hadn't forgotten about that beacon-fire, either, and she still couldn't begin to guess its purpose.

Hours passed, and Jasmine began to understand why they weren't riding fast. They obviously had a long distance to travel. Could they be going all the way to the other village: the home of the Dartuli?

She thought about the people she'd seen thus far. They were all clearly Latawi—including the tall blond man she assumed to be the baby's father. But the child was just as clearly Dartuli.

Jasmine found herself thinking about things of which she had no knowledge. According to the stories Quinn had told her, their two races had lived together, and she'd assumed that also meant that they'd intermarried as well.

Now she was getting into thoughts that were murky at best. She remembered years ago a scandal at the manor house. A servant girl had given birth to a child that was very dark and didn't look at all like her or like other Borneash. Jasmine's mother had told her that the father was a gypsy—

one of a band that had passed through town from time to time: dark-skinned and dark-haired people.

But how did that help her to understand the situation here, where two Latawi had apparently had a child who was Dartuli? She thought some more. If there had been intermarriage between the races at some point in the past . . . She didn't know.

She was following the couple with the baby through open fields again. She could just barely see them in the distance. And it seemed that they had stopped. Jasmine looked about and saw where they were.

Her quarry had halted at the stone pillars midway through the valley—the fence. And now that she'd identified it, she could make it out in the fields on both sides of the road. Like everything else it was intact, including the round markers that sat atop the pillars. And instead of rotting timbers lying in the weeds, the gate was there, blocking the roadway.

The woman stayed on her horse, but the man dismounted. Then he went over and struggled with the basket for a moment before picking it up and walking toward the gate. Jasmine watched in shock as he pushed the basket through the slats and left it there on the roadway.

The man returned to his horse, and the two of them began to ride back in her direction. She had no time to consider what they were doing; she needed to find a place to hide. The woods were too far away, so she urged the horse off into the field. It was hard to be sure in the moonlight, but she thought there was a small rise out there that might provide a hiding place.

She found the horse and rode around it, then centered down a small, steep slope. When she had dismounted and sneaked a look around the end of the hillock, she could see the two riders plainly.

They apparently hadn't noticed her, since they rode on without turning in her direction.

Jasmine waited until she was sure they would be out of sight, then got on her horse and headed back to the road, turning in the direction of the fence. When she reached it, she dismounted and tied the horse to one of the slats, then knelt beside the basket.

The baby was bundled up and sleeping. At first she'd feared that it might be dead, but when she gently touched its face, it stirred slightly. Still, it wouldn't live long if someone didn't come and get it. She stared at the empty road beyond the gate and thought about that beacon fire. Was that its purpose—to summon someone from the Dartuli village? But why? Why was the woman Tulla so unhappy, and why had she given up her baby?

She was still staring at the road beyond the fence. It was visible for some distance before it rose to the top of a hill. She had all but decided to take the baby with her when she saw a pair of riders appear.

They were coming fast, and their speed frightened her. She untied her horse and climbed into the saddle, then rode about a hundred feet away from the gate and stopped. The baby lay, safe, its basket resting against the fence.

They rode to within twenty feet of the pillars, then stopped. She couldn't see them clearly, but she knew that it was also a man and a woman. The man dismounted, then stood staring in her direction. Then he and the woman conferred and he walked swiftly toward the fence—and the basket containing the baby. He picked it up, then turned in her direction again, and this time she could see what she'd already guessed: he was Dartuli.

He turned his back on her and carried the basket over to the woman, who lifted the baby and examined it. She then returned it to the basket that the man had strapped in front of her saddle. They wheeled their horses around and vanished back the way they had come.

Jasmine turned her own mount back to the village of the Latawi. Nothing made sense. It was obvious to her that she'd been sent back to a time before the Latawi and the Dartuli had made peace—but how could a Latawi couple have given birth to a Dartuli child? And how could her people have been so cruel that they would take a baby from its mother and give it to strangers: strangers who were their enemy?

All the houses were dark by the time Jasmine reached the village. She returned the horse to the stable, then retraced her earlier route to the house. In the dark the homes all looked alike, which worried her until she finally recalled that the group of people she'd seen outside the neighboring house had been standing beneath one of those trees with the sweeping branches. She remembered it because it was still blooming, as the one had been in her dream.

She walked along the deserted street, looking for the tree. After she had made a full circle without finding it, she tried the next street—and there it was. But the houses there were all dark, too.

Hoping that the door wasn't locked, she went up to it and pulled on the handle, then sighed with happiness when it opened. But her relief was short-lived. The pallet upon which the woman Tulla had been sleeping was empty.

Jasmine gnawed at her lip nervously. She knew that she was in the right house, but she also knew that Tulla couldn't have awakened this quickly after that heavy dose of herbal tea. Jasmine crept quietly to the hallway, barely able to see anything in the darkness.

There she heard the unmistakable sound of

someone snoring. She walked into the hallway and quickly determined that the sound was coming from behind a closed door on her right—just opposite the open door of the room she'd been in.

She recalled the tall blond man who must be Tulla's husband. He must have carried her to their bed.

Weary from her long ride and her confused thoughts, Jasmine went into the other bedroom and fell onto the bed. She was too tired to think any more about her predicament or about the strange behavior of these people who were her ancestors.

She awoke to confusion and the scent of sun-warmed herbs. The smell reminded her of her little garden back at the manor, and she felt a brief but intense longing for that much simpler—if grueling—time. But that lasted only until Quinn's image swam into her waking brain and she remembered it all: the cave, the blinding light, the long fall—and her present situation.

She got out of bed and pulled back the curtains. Beyond the window, a large garden bloomed in a profusion of colors and shapes. She stood there, admiring its neatness as she inhaled the aromas. She'd done her best with her own little garden, but when her mother had become too ill to do her share, Jasmine had been unable to keep it up properly.

She caught movement at the very edge of her vision and moved to one side of the window. The woman, Tulla, was sitting on a small wooden bench at the edge of the garden. Kneeling beside her with his arms around her slumped shoulders was the tall blond man. Grayvar, she remembered now. That was the name given him by the woman who'd said Jasmine was her niece.

She stood there watching the couple, feeling

ashamed at observing them but unable to tear her gaze away. He continued to hold her and to stroke her long hair that was almost identical in color to his own. His back was to her, but she could see Tulla—and the tears streaking her cheeks.

Finally Jasmine turned away, caught in a terrible wave of longing for Quinn. Where was he? Could he be in this time? It struck her then that if he was, he would be in the village of his own people—at the far end of the valley beyond the gate.

She was greatly tempted to steal a horse again and ride there, but she stopped herself. First of all, it might not be that easy now in daylight, and second, she needed to understand what was going on before she undertook to find Quinn. It would do no good at all for her to ride through that gate and be captured or even killed by the Dartuli.

Her dress smelled strongly of horse, so she stripped it off, then washed up as best she could, using the pitcher and bowl in the room. A small cupboard yielded a supply of dresses and, rather to her surprise, some trousers and shirts as well, so she selected a sunny yellow dress and slipped her feet into the worn but comfortable shoes she'd had on the night before. And then she went out to meet these strangers who were her relatives.

When she walked through the kitchen door into the garden, the man Grayvar saw her first. He stood up, and Jasmine had a sudden, very clear image of another blond man, not quite so tall and perhaps a little younger. Her brother Timoran. She swallowed hard. She hadn't thought of him in years—or rather, when she had thought of him, the image had been badly blurred.

"Here's Jasmine now," Grayvar said gently to Tulla, his hand curved around the point of her shoulder.

"I'm sorry I overslept," Jasmine said as she approached them. It seemed like the correct thing to say. "I thought Tulla would sleep longer."

"She woke up just a short time ago," Grayvar said with a worried look at his wife.

Tulla raised her tearstained face to Jasmine and reached out to take her hands. "Oh, Jasmine, you were so right. It's so cruel. He was our child—and they took him away."

Grayvar bent to her and kissed her cheek. "It *is* cruel, love, but he couldn't have had a life here. You must think of what's best for him."

Then he straightened up and laid a hand briefly on Jasmine's shoulder. "I'll be in the orchard if you should need me." He kissed his wife again and was gone.

Tulla moved over to make room for Jasmine on the bench. "Gray's right," she said. "But that doesn't make the pain any less."

"No, it doesn't," Jasmine agreed, taking her hand again. She felt very sorry for Tulla, but she also realized that this might be a good opportunity to learn some more about the situation here. "I don't understand such cruelty," she said indignantly.

"It's like Mamman always said." Tulla sighed. "Remember? When we were little—before the trouble really started again? She said that it would happen sooner or later, that the Latawi and the Dartuli would never live in peace for long, and the gods would become angry with all of us."

"Yes, I remember," Jasmine said, though of course she didn't. She was now beginning to understand what had happened. She hadn't gone as far back in time as she'd originally thought. In fact, she now worried that she might be in that most dangerous of all times: just before the two tribes had been driven from the valley. But who had driven them out: the gods or the demons? Tulla had said nothing at all about demons.

"Gray says that the Elders will let us have the next baby they send over," Tulla said. "I'm happy about that, but it won't be the same. Did you see him?"

"Yes. He was very beautiful, with lots of curly hair."

Tulla lapsed into silence again, and Jasmine suggested that she fix them something to eat. When Tulla didn't protest, she got up and went into the kitchen. No sooner did she step through the doorway than the woman who was her aunt appeared, carrying a basket.

"I've brought you some fresh bread," she said, handing the basket to Jasmine. "How is Tulla?"

"How would you expect her to be?" Jasmine replied sharply. She didn't like this woman, even though it was kind of her to bring food.

The woman's bright blue eyes flashed at her. "She'd be accepting it much better if it weren't for all your talk about how we misjudge the Dartuli and how unfair it is."

"I'm sorry if the truth disturbs you," Jasmine said icily.

"You were always a dreamer, Jasmine. It's time you learn to live in the world as it is. You'd do well to watch your tongue, because you're disturbing a lot of people with your ridiculous talk."

Then she set down the basket and went out to Tulla, leaving Jasmine to wonder just what "ridiculous" things she'd been saying.

Chapter Fourteen

Engulfed in the cold darkness, Quinn fell and fell until it seemed there would be no end. His thoughts were divided between fear of what lay below him and fear for Jasmine. He'd shouted her name into the black void until his voice was hoarse, but there was no answer. Then he cursed the gods and the demons both, since he had no way of knowing which was responsible.

Suddenly it ended. There was no jolt, no sudden breaking of bones against the bottom of the pit. He was simply *there*—wherever *there* was. And he wasn't alone.

His hand went immediately to the knife at his belt, and he felt considerable relief to know that it was still there. But even as he touched the hilt, he could see that those around him were paying him no attention at all. He was only part of a crowd. Those in front of him had their backs to him.

There was something troubling about this particular crowd—quite apart from the fact that he had no idea how he'd gotten there. And then he realized what it was. Except for the male members of his own family, Quinn had never been among other men as big as he was. In fact, one man in front of him was even taller. Already disoriented, Quinn now became further confused by this state of affairs.

He looked up and saw that he was in a cave again—but not the same one. This one had a high, vaulted ceiling and seemed enormous. Torches fixed in iron holders along the walls illuminated the place, casting flickering light over the people around him.

He studied them carefully, even as he wondered why they were all so silent. Then it struck him with the force of a blow these were his people: the Dartuli.

I'm dreaming, he thought with relief. *We must have fallen asleep after our meal. When I wake up, Jasmine will be there beside me.*

But that comforting thought lasted for no more than a few seconds. Too clearly, he remembered the events that had brought him here.

He was dragged out of his frightening thoughts as a low chant began, then grew in volume until it filled the cavern. Men's and women's voices rose and fell in words Quinn didn't understand, though perhaps it was because of the way they echoed off the stone walls.

He had a sudden urge to push his way through the crowd and get out. But his years of soldiering had taught him a few things, and one of them was to avoid calling attention to himself in a situation in which he didn't have all the facts. He stayed where he was, listening and waiting.

Since everyone around him was facing in the same direction, he tried to see what those in front must be seeing. Under normal circumstances, that posed no problem to someone of Quinn's great height, but now he was forced to move sideways a bit to see between two of the men in front of him.

At the far end of the cave was an altar of some kind: a raised stone bench that ran the entire width of the cave. It was completely empty except for some big candles that were struggling to stay lit, as though they were being whipped by wind. In the firelight it seemed to him that there was an opening behind and below the altar, though he couldn't be sure it wasn't just a trick of the light.

As the chanting continued, he began to think about edging back and trying to leave. A sideways glance told him that he was near the rear of the cave, and there must be an exit somewhere. But before he could put action to thought, the chanting rose abruptly to a crescendo—and then stopped.

Dark smoke roiled up from behind the altar, billowing to the high ceiling. The silence around him became tense and watchful. Quinn didn't like it. He could feel a coldness growing within him. Whatever was going on here, he didn't want any part of it, even if these *were* his people.

The smoke continued to pour out of the opening behind the altar, but it wasn't as thick as before—except for one part near the center that seemed to be particularly agitated. And then he saw the face.

The sound that escaped from Quinn's lips was only one of many indrawn breaths around him. The apparition hung suspended in the smoke, but it was strikingly clear. And as he stared at it, he was shocked to feel something in him reaching out, wanting to be drawn into that red, burning gaze.

The ghostly face was recognizably human, for all its dark harshness. It might even have been called handsome in a cruel sort of way. As he watched, unable to tear his eyes away, it began to expand until it was many times normal size.

When he heard the voice, Quinn realized that it

was the face speaking, even though its slightly sneering lips didn't move. Instead it seemed to be speaking directly into his mind.

The time is soon upon us, my children. You must prepare yourselves for the final battle—as our enemies are even now preparing themselves. This valley was my gift to you—and it will be yours again!

The face was already fading by the time the final words insinuated themselves into Quinn's mind, and within seconds it was lost in a cloud of black smoke. Then even the smoke was gone, though traces of its acrid odor tickled Quinn's nostrils.

The crowd began to depart. Stunned by what he'd witnessed, Quinn nevertheless tried to pay attention to the conversations around him. Some people were clearly elated, while others seemed sober and thoughtful. He was moving with them and still busy trying to figure out what was happening when a large hand clamped itself onto his shoulder.

"Time to get ready for battle, eh, Quinn? We've waited long enough to hear those words from the Great One."

Quinn turned to stare at the man, keeping his expression carefully neutral. It was the man who'd stood in front of him, and he was several inches taller even than Quinn. And as Quinn looked at him, he saw a resemblance to himself.

We could be brothers, Quinn thought with dismay. The man looked more like him than his own true siblings did.

"Have you nothing to say, brother?" the man asked as they left the cave. "It's a good thing that we've been putting the horses through their paces—but now we have to work even harder."

The horses. He must be referring to the white stallions. "They're ready," he said, since it seemed he'd better say something.

"Well, you'd know better than I would." The man

thumped him on the back. "The Latawi are no match for us even without them. But with them, we'll rid the valley of the People of the Light in no time."

Quinn understood, finally, where he was. He'd been sent back to the time when his people and Jasmine's had been driven from the valley. And he knew as well that the old stories had been wrong. But he still couldn't figure out exactly what would happen.

"Still brooding over your foolishness?" the man asked teasingly. "Don't worry about it. I might have let her live myself if she was as beautiful as you say. But I wouldn't have let her go without a bit of sport."

He leaned closer to Quinn and his voice dropped to a whisper. "To tell the truth, I wouldn't mind keeping a couple of the Latawi women around— but our own women would never permit it. You should have taken advantage of the last opportunity you're likely to have to bed one of them." The man chuckled.

"On the other hand, such things have been known to happen during a battle. I think the Great One would forgive us if we had a bit of sport with them before we finish them off."

Quinn wasn't shocked at such talk. He'd been a soldier and he'd heard it before. But it had begun to dawn on him that if *he* was here, then Jasmine might well be here, too.

"How soon will it begin?" he asked.

The other man shrugged. "My guess is that the Great One is waiting for Zhensas. But maybe it'll be sooner."

Zhensas. Quinn hadn't heard that term in a long time, but he knew what it was: the festival celebrated at the first full moon of autumn. If time hadn't been lost or gained during his journey back here, that was only a month away.

They were out of the cave now, moving slowly in the crowd. Quinn saw that there was a wide ledge beyond the cave's mouth that afforded a view of the village below and a full moon above.

Suddenly he realized exactly where he was. He'd stood down in the village several times staring up at this place, sensing something, but he'd believed that what was this cave's entrance was merely a trick of shadows.

Fortunately his companion had struck up a conversation with several other men and Quinn was left to his thoughts. The man must believe that Quinn was his brother, unless the term had been used more loosely. He didn't like the coincidence of his bearing the same name here, but that didn't bother him half as much as the fact that he was obviously in charge of the horses for a war he didn't believe in, in a time he didn't understand.

This could be my own ancestor, he thought. *I am living in the body of one of my forebears.*

The crowd poured down the mountainside on a winding path, and Quinn was swept along. He stayed close to his "brother" because he had no idea where to go when they reached the village.

His thoughts turned again to Jasmine. Was she going through this, too: trying to survive as a stranger among her own people? And why had this happened to them? It no longer seemed relevant who was responsible.

He recalled Jasmine's having said several times that they were unlikely ever to find the answer to their questions about why their people had been driven from the valley. It occurred to him that this might be the way the gods or the demons were answering those questions. But it was an answer he could have lived comfortably without knowing, he thought grimly, especially if it meant that they were going to be caught up in the final battle.

He wondered about the demons, too. Were they

nothing more than henchmen to the "Great One" back there? Quinn suppressed a shudder at the thought of that compelling face. A part of him was filled with loathing—but another part remained powerfully drawn to the face and its silent message.

They reached the end of the path and Quinn saw that they were at a corner of the village he hadn't paid any attention to because the houses there were in ruins. They weren't now, however. This was the village of his dreams.

As he passed by the first houses, still following his "brother," Quinn recalled that Jasmine had mentioned being out here. He wondered why she hadn't mentioned the path up the mountainside, then decided that it had probably become so overgrown that it was no longer visible.

Or maybe she didn't want you to know about it, whispered a voice inside his head—not the voice of the Great One, but something that seemed to come from within him. *Maybe she knew what was up there and didn't want you to know.*

Quinn felt a sudden flash of hot anger at her. He didn't like her belief that she had to protect him. She was a woman and a Latawi. He didn't need her protection.

"Let's get some horses and ride down to the fence," his brother suggested, breaking into Quinn's increasingly dark thoughts. "It's a fine night for a ride—and maybe time to test their magic again, eh?"

They brought the animals to a halt about two hundred feet from the fence. Quinn's gaze traveled the width of the valley, where the fence was now plainly visible in the bright moonlight.

"No one around," his brother said with obvious disappointment. "Did you hear what happened the other night?"

Quinn shook his head.

"Targa and Viola came down here to pick up a baby and found a woman here. He figures it must have been the mother and she didn't want to give it up. The Latawi are weak that way. If they knew that we kill more than we send to them, they'd be in a fine rage."

Quinn tried to sort out just what the man was talking about. He was liking this man less and less. In fact, if his people were killing babies, he wanted nothing to do with *any* of them. But why would they do it, and why would anyone come here to pick up a baby?

"Look! We're going to have some sport after all."

Quinn looked where he pointed and saw two riders approaching the fence, riding through the field. Their pale hair and even paler skin were given a ghostly cast by the moonlight. There was no doubt that they were Latawi.

Quinn shifted uneasily in his saddle. The cold rage was growing within him even as he told himself that these were Jasmine's people, perhaps even her own ancestors.

His brother rode closer to the fence and Quinn followed, having no idea what was about to happen. He could see no weapons of any kind on the Latawi, though his brother carried a long knife much like his own.

Suddenly green fire arced from his brother's fingertips as he raised his hand. On the far side of the fence, the two Latawi turned their horses sharply, and the fire struck the ground near them, then vanished. A moment later, golden fire flashed through the night toward him.

Quinn had no time to think, but his horse leaped out of the way easily, then reared up and snorted. And in the next moment the lines of fire shot over the fence from both sides. Quinn didn't even realize what he was doing when his hand left the reins and curved into the air, sending out a streak of glowing green that struck one of the Latawi and sent him tumbling backward off his horse.

"You're getting better—or else luckier." His brother grinned before loosing another burst that came close to the remaining rider.

The battle went on for another few minutes. The rider Quinn had toppled wasn't dead, and he had soon remounted his horse to fight again. Quinn was reacting instinctively, once more the soldier—though with very different weapons. The golden fire never struck Quinn, although once it came close enough that he felt a strange prickling sensation.

His brother wasn't so lucky. One struck him directly. He groaned and was jolted in his saddle, but he kept his seat. Quinn wasn't sure just what the object of all this was. Could the magic beams kill? It seemed that they couldn't. But when he saw the man he'd first struck toppled once more from his saddle, this time by Quinn's brother, he guessed that the object was to strike until one side or the other was too weak to continue. The man who'd been struck twice could just barely stagger to his feet this time, and his companion had to help him back into his saddle.

Then it was over. The two Latawi rode off into the night, headed back to their village. Quinn's brother whooped with laughter and raised his fist in victory and called his erstwhile opponents all the names that soldiers have always called the enemy.

He grinned at Quinn. "Just as well they gave up. Orders or no, I'd have fought to the death—their death, that is."

"Save your strength for the real battle," Quinn said as they turned their horses back toward the village. He guessed that the orders had come from those who were worried that hotheaded men like this one would waste their lives in mere play. He'd known men who were ready to do such things. They had been the sort who had often challenged him to prove their manhood.

He turned to take one last look at the fence, and a chill ran through him as he thought about those arcs of green and gold fire. In the heat of the moment, he hadn't had time to consider the fact that he'd used magic. Now he was overcome with awe as he thought how easily it had come to him.

He was tempted to rationalize it away, to believe that it came not from him, but rather from the man whose identity he'd assumed. But his instincts told him otherwise. Confronted with magic by his opponents, he'd found it within himself.

Furthermore, he now understood that darkness inside him because he now understood the Dartuli. "People of the Dark" didn't refer just to their hair and skin coloring. The Dartuli worshiped the dark god, the Great One.

His thoughts turned to Jasmine, who might well be in the valley herself, in the village of the Latawi. And if she *was* there, then she'd undoubtedly learned by now just what his people were.

His earlier burst of anger with her was gone, replaced by a haunting fear that nothing could ever be the same for them again—even if they could escape the coming battle.

Jasmine heard the news the next morning in the marketplace, where she'd gone with her aunt, whose name she'd learned was Esma. Her opinion of the woman was not improved by discovering that she shared the name of Jasmine's beloved grandmother.

The story was all over the village. Two young men, known to be risk-takers, had gone to the fence last night and engaged in battle with two Dartuli. They claimed to have killed or at least crippled one of the hated Dartuli, but since one of *them* was laid up as well, most people assumed that the battle had been, at best, a draw.

By listening carefully, Jasmine learned that such battles had been occurring with increasing frequency, despite the ban imposed by the Elders. And she further gleaned from bits of overheard conversation and from the look in people's eyes that the Latawi belived the Dartuli to be superior fighters who would almost certainly destroy them if it came to a full-scale battle.

What she didn't know, and seemed to have no way of learning, was how this state of affairs had come about. Tulla had suggested that they were mere pawns of the gods, and that the immortals had been the ones to end the years of peace between the two tribes. But Jasmine was unwilling to accept that explanation. She no longer denied the power of the gods; after all, they'd sent her back here. But what about free will? Had the gods taken control of both races?

To her mind, it was one thing for the gods to have snatched her away from her own time—but quite another for them to change the hearts and minds of a whole group of people.

All the talk in the marketplace about the Dartuli quite naturally turned her own thoughts to Quinn. Was he here, too—and if he was, was he safe?

She'd heard enough by now to know that the Dartuli worshiped someone they called the "Great One," who lived in a pit deep in the mountains. And she knew exactly where that pit was. Had Quinn been there—and what might it have done to him?

She wasn't yet certain about the role of the demons, but she assumed that they were the henchmen of this Great One. She shuddered as she thought about how Quinn had been unable to resist them without her help, and what that implied

about his ability to resist their master, the Great
One.

"There will be a battle soon—a real battle," Esma
said as they walked back from the marketplace.

"How do you know that?" Jasmine asked in
alarm.

"I can sense it," the woman said emphatically.
"The accursed Dartuli will never be satisfied until
they have the whole valley. They've always been
that way: too pushy, too arrogant. You know that
as well as I do. You've heard the stories."

No, I haven't, Jasmine answered silently, wishing that there were a way she could elicit more
information without giving away her own igno-
rance.

"I can't imagine why you've suddenly taken it
into your head that they're not all bad," Esma went
on, shaking her own head.

"But we lived in peace with them once," Jasmine
blurted out, knowing that she was taking a great
risk. At this point, she couldn't trust any of the stories she and Quinn had been told.

Esma made a disgusted sound. "If you want to
call that peace, you can—but I don't. Even then
the Dartuli were always wanting to run everything,
and we know they continued to worship the Great
One in secret, though they denied it, of course."

"But there were marriages," Jasmine said, thinking about Tulla's baby and prepared to say that it
was just something she'd heard if Esma denied it.

"Of course there were—many of them. I never
said that they weren't capable of great charm when
it suited their purpose. That's part of their evil, Jasmine. But what they can't charm, they conquer."

Jasmine's throat constricted painfully as she
thought about the ability to charm she'd seen in
Quinn so many times—and about his statement

that he didn't want only to make love to her—he wanted to *conquer* her.

She was very glad when they reached Tulla's cottage and Esma departed. She knew it was essential that she learn as much as she could, but it seemed that the more she learned, the more she feared for Quinn and herself.

The days passed quickly for Jasmine, who was kept busy maintaining the household as Tulla recovered her strength. She'd learned early on that the prime responsibility for the large herb garden was hers, and so she worked hard there, too. Tulla, it turned out, was a weaver of considerable talent, while Grayvar owned a large orchard, the ruins of which Jasmine could recall having seen the one time she'd visited her home village.

She grew very fond of both Tulla and Gray, who were obviously deeply in love. It was clear to her that not only was Tulla the sister of the Jasmine whose body she'd borrowed, but she was also her closest friend. And Gray treated her like a sister as well.

From comments and the reactions of others toward her, Jasmine came to form an opinion of the other Jasmine. She was apparently something of a loner or a budding spinster. The pretty little mirror in Tulla's room that had been a gift from Grayvar showed her that she was herself still, and observations of other women told her that she was certainly among the most attractive women in the village. But she also knew that she was well past the age when most women married.

That she had suitors was made plain to her on several occasions, after which Tulla would sigh and wonder aloud why she hadn't chosen one of them. Gray made no comment, but the amused look Jasmine saw in his eyes suggested that this was a long-running joke.

The certainty that a battle with the Dartuli was imminent lay heavily on everyone. When Jasmine repeated to Gray the statements she'd overheard in the marketplace about the Dartuli's superior strength, he nodded soberly.

"They were always warriors, but we must trust in the gods to give us the weapons we need to protect ourselves."

One evening Jasmine went with Tulla and Gray to what she guessed must be a regular ritual, though she'd never before heard of it. She'd almost forgotten about the beautiful golden sphere in the woods and gardens that formed the center of the marketplace. Her trips to the village center up to that point had been solely for the purpose of buying supplies or selling her herbs.

The entire village seemed to be there, including children and the elderly. A tiny sliver of a moon hung in the heavens as the people gathered among the trees and flower beds, talking in hushed tones. Then, at some signal Jasmine didn't see, they began to sing. Male and female voices floated on the warm night air, rising and falling in lovely cadences that awakened vague memories in Jasmine. She thought her grandmother had once sung such songs.

The songs were filled with praise for the gods and declarations of submission to the gods' will. And well before they were finished, the golden sphere with its circlet of diamonds began to glow.

By the time the voices fell silent, the golden light had swelled to touch everyone present, and Jasmine felt again that wondrous sense of warmth and peace.

But then the light began to flicker, as though there were some disturbance within the sphere. Glancing around her, Jasmine saw people grow tense, and she felt the warmth fade away.

There were no words, either spoken aloud or inside her head. What happened instead was a sort of birth of knowledge. War would come soon. The forces of darkness were gathering strength. In the end, the evil would be defeated, but perhaps at a very great cost. The People of Light had to accept this cost.

And then the brilliance faded slowly, until they stood in darkness again. People began to disperse, but no one spoke. Walking between them, Gray put one arm across Tulla's shoulders and one across Jasmine's.

Jasmine knew what that cost would be: They would either die or be driven from the valley. She felt terribly sad for these people, but at the same time she wondered if the triumph in the end that the gods spoke of was the return of both Dartuli and Latawi to the valley. Perhaps in a future none of them would live to see: the future that was her present.

However, as they walked home, she began to worry anew about how she and Quinn could escape the coming war. She had to find him somehow, so they could make their plans. And she ignored the nagging little voice that whispered to her, telling her that maybe he didn't want to escape back to the present with her because the dark forces had already claimed him.

After several days of agonizing, Jasmine reached a decision. She had to find Quinn, and in order to do that she had to know more about the situation than she'd been able to discover thus far. She would have to reveal the truth to Tulla.

The worst that will happen, she thought, *is that Tulla will believe I've gone mad. But she's already worried about me in any event.* There'd been too many times when Jasmine had failed to respond appropriately or had given her blank stares when

questioned about something she had no knowledge of.

What finally gave her the courage to confess,
though, was that she'd come to realize just how
readily Tulla and the others accepted the magic of
the gods. Once she stopped judging Tulla's prob-
able reaction on the basis of her own to such a
story, she realized that Tulla might well accept it.

The day she chose was sultry and heavy with the
threat of thunderstorms later. By midafternoon,
both women had retreated to a small wooded
glade at the rear of the garden, where several
wooden benches had been set beneath the tall
trees.

Tulla expressed concern about the storms that
were certain to come. If they were too violent, they
could ruin the orchard crop, driving half-ripened
fruit from the branches. Jasmine commiserated
with her, and then the two women fell silent, and
she knew it was time to begin her confession.

"Tulla, there is something I must tell you. I hope
you'll believe me, because it's the truth."

Without waiting for a response, Jasmine hurried
on with her story, telling the girl everything but
trying to keep it as simple as possible. Tulla stared
at her and gasped a few times, but said nothing.
Jasmine could only hope that she believed her.

"I know this must be difficult for you, but I had
to tell you because I need your help. I must find
Quinn."

"But where is my sister?" Tulla asked with a
catch in her voice.

Jasmine was caught unprepared. She'd wondered about that herself a few times, but she'd
foolishly forgotten that Tulla would naturally be
concerned for her real sister.

"I . . . don't know," she admitted. "Surely the
gods will restore her to you when I leave." At least
she hoped that would be the case.

"Yes." Tulla nodded. "I must believe that. But how can I help you? You can't possibly go to the village of the Dartuli. They will kill you as soon as they see you. And if he tries to come across the fence, the same will happen to him."

Despite the fact that her words were far from promising, Jasmine felt an overwhelming relief as she realized that Tulla believed her. And Tulla gave further evidence of that as she went on.

"Your behavior *has* been strange. Gray has remarked on it, too."

"There's just so much I don't know." Jasmine shrugged.

"But you're different in other ways," Tulla declared, then smiled. "Esma says that you act like a Dartuli sometimes—and that it's getting worse."

Jasmine wrinkled her nose. "I don't like Esma."

"My sister doesn't like her much, either. And neither do I, for that matter."

"Tell me what ended the peace between the Dartuli and the Latawi," Jasmine urged her. "Or were the stories we'd been told wrong?"

"No, they weren't wrong—as far as they went. There *was* peace, for many generations."

The story Tulla told her was one that didn't surprise Jasmine now that she better understood the differences between the two tribes. The Dartuli were indeed more aggressive and inclined toward impatience and arrogance, while the Latawi were a rather passive people, content to live as they'd always lived, distrustful of the Dartuli.

There'd always been, among both tribes, those who were not happy with the situation that existed between them. And Jasmine thought it probably wasn't helped at all by the fact that they had never really blended into one people. A child born to a Latawi mother and a Dartuli father—or the opposite—was always clearly one or the other.

Because both tribes traced their lineage through

the mothers, a couple who married between the races would always live in the village of the mother. This seemed to work reasonably well if the woman was Dartuli, but if she were Latawi, the presence of Dartuli males in the Latawi village was always a source of trouble because they were forever "stirring things up," as Tulla put it.

The end of peace had come slowly over the years. Among both tribes, the warmongers and bigots gained more and more adherents, feeding upon small incidents that only reinforced their beliefs that the two could not live as one.

Tulla said that war between them had come because their Great One, whom they continued to worship in secret while publicly disavowing him, had decreed that it was time for them to take the valley for themselves. And so, after many lives had been lost, they had withdrawn to their own ends of the valley and had rebuilt the ancient fence.

By agreement between them at the cessation of hostilities, all babies would be turned over to their own people, though the Latawi harbored strong suspicions that the Dartuli were killing some Latawi babies born among them.

Tulla sighed and choked off a sob. "If you are right, it will end badly for all of us, because we'll be driven from the valley."

Or killed, Jasmine thought, regretting that she'd told Tulla. She'd been so selfish, thinking only of herself and Quinn instead of realizing the effect her revelations would have on Tulla.

"I could be wrong," she ventured. "After all, we don't really know when everyone left the valley. That could be in the future—for you, that is," she added, thinking how confusing this all was.

Tulla sighed. "Well, if that is the will of the gods, then we must accept it."

I wouldn't, Jasmine thought, more than a little irritated at these people's submissiveness. She was

Latawi, just as they were, and she knew that she wouldn't have accepted such a terrible future without fighting against it.

On the other hand, she thought with sudden insight, I was prepared to accept living in slavery at the manor—until I was sent away and Quinn came along. Even after that, there'd been times when she wished she were back there, no matter how awful it was.

"Tulla," she said, "you must help me find a way to speak to Quinn. I know he's there."

"I'd help you if I could," Tulla assured her. "But I just don't see any way it can be done. Perhaps he'll find a way to come to you."

But Jasmine didn't want to depend on that. She had a growing fear that Quinn had been captured body and soul by the Great One.

That night Jasmine lay in her bed with a sense of hopelessness. Tulla had asked her to tell Grayvar her story, and she had, hoping against hope that he would have some suggestion to offer her. He accepted her tale as readily as his wife had, but he had nothing to offer except an echo of Tulla's certainty that she would be killed as soon as the Dartuli spotted her in their territory.

Desperately Jasmine had asked if there might not be some magic that could assist her. Gray and Tulla told her that the only magic either side possessed was that given to them to defend their land. There were old stories of other magic practiced long ago, but the gods, for whatever reason, had taken those abilities away.

Tulla suggested that she go to the onnara, the golden sphere that the gods had given them centuries ago. Perhaps, Tulla said, if she prayed for assistance there, the gods would help her.

So Jasmine went, hurrying through the dark streets and across the empty market square into

the sacred woods. The sphere had glowed softly
when she'd placed her hands on it, and she'd felt
that wonderful warmth—but nothing else had
happened.

Now, as she lay in her bed, she wondered why
she'd let herself believe they might help her. She'd
denied their existence and even now would fight
them if she could. She should probably consider
herself fortunate that they hadn't struck her dead.

She'd told Tulla and Gray about the voices that
had spoken to her, and asked if they were the gods.
But she was told that they were the voices of long-
dead Latawi, who were known to speak to the living from time to time. And they weren't speaking
now.

Jasmine faced a terrible decision. She could either stay here in the valley and hope to find a way
to get to Quinn before the battle began—or she
could leave the valley and take her chances in the
cave again, hoping that Quinn would do the same
thing and they would be returned to the present
time.

She fell asleep still wrestling with that decision—
and dreamed for the first time since she'd been
sent back.

She was riding along the fence that divided the
Dartuli and the Latawi: not the destroyed fence
she and Quinn had found, but the intact fence
she'd seen that night when she'd followed the couple with the baby. It was late in the day, and the
sun had already vanished behind the mountains,
casting a long, cool shadow over the day's heat.

She kicked the horse's flanks, urging him on to
the little stream and the woods at the base of the
mountain where she could escape for a time from
the sultry heat. And just as she reached it the animal stumbled, nearly unseating her. When it be-

gan to move again, it was heavily favoring its right foreleg.

Jasmine slid from the saddle and squatted down to examine the injured leg. When she turned over its hoof, she saw that a sharp stone had become wedged in there. She pried at it with her fingers, but the horse, obviously in pain, shied away from her, then refused to let her come near it.

She cast a nervous look back at the fence, which ended at the stream. She shouldn't have come here in the first place. Then why *had* she come? She felt confused, as though someone else was responsible—someone who'd done this many times before. Was it the other Jasmine—the woman whose body she'd borrowed? She thought that was the case, but she couldn't be sure.

Then suddenly a sound drew her attention to the far side of the stream, and she saw some pebbles tumbling down the steep bank. Her gaze traveled up the mountainside—and there was Quinn!

An overwhelming sense of relief swept over her, but when she opened her mouth to speak his name, nothing came out. Instead she stood there silently as he slowly descended to the stream. He was riding his magnificent white stallion.

But when he stopped on the far side of the little stream, she became confused. Was it Quinn? The man who sat there looked like Quinn, but the expression on his face suggested that he didn't recognize her. And he was dressed, not in his usual clothing, but completely in black.

Once again she tried to speak his name—and once again nothing came out. He advanced across the stream, his gaze going from her to the lame horse. And suddenly she knew she was in danger.

The portion of the stream on the Latawi side of the fence had a very steep bank, and so she'd ventured around the end of the fence and into Dartuli territory. She hadn't given it any thought—until now.

Her feet wanted to run even as her mind told her that this was Quinn and he would never harm her. The panic inside her grew until she felt as though she would burst from the pounding of her heart. In the meantime, the man who was Quinn and not Quinn crossed the stream and dismounted. He stared at her for another long and terrifying moment, then turned his attention to her horse. The animal stood some twenty feet away, its right foreleg bent to keep the weight off the injury.

"Your horse is lame," he said, breaking the tense silence. His voice didn't sound like Quinn's, though she couldn't have said what the difference was.

She merely nodded, still unable to speak.

He tugged once on the stallion's reins, then walked away from it. It stood there calmly watching Jasmine, who in turn watched the man as he began to walk slowly toward her horse, speaking to it in low words she couldn't understand.

To her amazement, the animal allowed him to approach, then didn't shy away as he picked up the injured hoof. He withdrew a knife from his belt and began to pry the stone from its hoof. Then, still without a word to her, he returned to his stallion and drew from a saddlebag a small pot of something that he spread into the injured hoof.

Finally he turned to her, his expression unreadable as he stared at her some more. There was a slightly puzzled look on his face, almost as though he were trying to place her face.

"Quinn," she said, surprised to find that this time she'd actually gotten his name out.

His look of confusion deepened as he nodded. And then he spoke her name slowly.

After another long moment during which neither of them moved, he abruptly swung back onto his stallion, then looked down at her.

"Don't come here again. Go back to where you belong."

And before she could say anything, he was thundering off along the fence, back toward the road.

"Quinn!" she shouted, knowing he couldn't hear her. "Quinn!"

Jasmine awoke to the echoes of her cry. The dream was still vivid in her mind, but she was as confused as before about whether the man had truly been Quinn.

There would be no more sleep for her as she tried to understand the dream and whether it might be telling her something important. But it wasn't until she heard Tulla and Gray stirring at dawn that she remembered a comment Esma had made not long after she arrived here: something about her defending the Dartuli.

It happened, she said to herself. *That dream actually happened—but to the other Jasmine. That's why she was defending the Dartuli.* The confusion in the dream had been because they weren't really her memories. And she was equally certain that the dream was important.

She waited until Gray had gone off to the orchards and she was alone with Tulla, sipping tea as they sat in the garden.

"I had a dream last night," she told Tulla, "but I think it wasn't really a dream. I think I was dreaming something that happened to your sister."

She went on to give Tulla the details of the dream, and Tulla nodded. "Yes, it did happen— exactly as you said. It was very strange. But she didn't learn his name and he didn't know hers. Jasmine told Esma about it, too, because she's always believed that the Dartuli aren't as evil as Esma and some of the others say. Esma didn't believe her, of course."

Tulla sighed. "This is all very confusing to me, but the gods sometimes work in ways we can't understand." Then she gave Jasmine a hopeful look.

"It could be that the gods have given you a way to find Quinn. Maybe Quinn was . . . is the man she met."

Jasmine had already reached that conclusion herself. She nodded. "If that's true, then perhaps he'll go back there as well. I must go there today."

Tulla put a hand on her arm. "It's so dangerous, Jasmine—especially now, with war so close."

"I know, but it's my only chance to find him."

Tulla's expression grew softer. "You really love him, don't you? How wonderful it would be to believe that this hatred between us could end someday."

It will, Jasmine thought—but only if I can get Quinn away from the dark forces.

Chapter Fifteen

Quinn managed, somehow, to fit himself into life in the Dartuli village without arousing any suspicion. Had he come at a different time that would undoubtedly have been much more difficult, but the Dartuli were preparing for war.

His days were spent working with the horses, training them in the lightning-quick maneuvers that allowed both horse and rider to escape the golden fire of their enemy. And when he wasn't training the horses, he was training himself—both to wield the green fire and to engage in hand-to-hand combat.

The latter, he discovered, was the reason the Dartuli would be victorious. The Latawi relied solely on their sorcery, while his people trained for closer combat. From conversations he overheard, he gathered that the Latawi were firmly convinced that their gods would save them, and that they therefore had no need to learn how to protect themselves without magic.

323

His own people didn't trust the Great One quite so much. The Great One was unpredictable and tended to favor those who didn't place all their faith in him.

The Dartuli regarded the Latawi with a contempt that Quinn found hard not to share. They were a weak and passive people, always humbling themselves before their gods and meekly accepting whatever those gods said. The Dartuli, on the other hand, tended to interpret the infrequent words of the Great One in whatever way they chose, although they would never disobey a direct order.

He learned that the numbers were roughly equal on both sides, but that if he so chose, the Great One could order his demons into battle on the side of the Dartuli. The Latawi had no such reinforcements.

Given the superiority of the Dartuli, Quinn wondered why they hadn't conquered the Latawi long before. At first he'd guessed that they wouldn't go to war without the Great One's approval, but then he discovered that there were among his people a sizable number who opposed war for any reason other than self-defense. The man whose body he'd borrowed was one of those.

Still, even those who opposed war now prepared for it, because the Great One had spoken.

There was one way in which Quinn's behavior cast some suspicion on him. Apparently the other Quinn had a healthy appetite both for strong drink and for women. When he limited his drinking and ignored the women who'd apparently shared his bed before, he was teased about it. But he told them that he was too busy now to fog his mind with strong drink or women, and they seemed to accept that.

At first Quinn was preoccupied with finding Jasmine and then getting them both out of the valley and back to their own time. Every opportunity he had, he would ride to the fence in the hope of finding her there, and then when he didn't, he would ride back and forth through the field, trying to come up with a way of reaching her.

He suggested to his brother and some other men that perhaps they should send scouts under cover of darkness into the enemy camp, in order to determine what preparations they might be making for the coming war. That, he thought, might allow him to seek out Jasmine. But his suggestion was greeted with the contempt his people had for the Latawi, and so came to nothing.

But as the days passed, a change had come over Quinn. In the midst of men who were eager for battle, he too felt a thirst for a life he'd left behind long ago. Only at night, alone in his bed, did his thoughts turn to Jasmine.

Quinn became two men. By day he was the warrior preparing for a great victory, and by night he was the man who'd known love in its deepest sense and wanted it again. But the memory of Jasmine and their love was fading into the past, which was in reality the future, both of which were beyond his reach.

The gods had spoken to the Latawi again. The enemy would attack on the eve of Zhensas, an ancient festival that began with the first full moon of the autumn season. Already the moon was swollen and would reach fullness within a few days.

Jasmine had ridden each day to the place from her dream: the small stream at the base of the mountain where the fence bisected the valley. But Quinn did not come.

Now she was making what she knew would be her last trip. She would leave the valley the next morning, to take her chances in the magical cave, hoping that the fickle gods would send her back to the present—and that somehow Quinn would be there as well. She wouldn't be part of the war.

Late summer heat lay heavily on the fields as she turned her horse and rode slowly along the fence, her head turned toward the forbidden land beyond. Her sadness lay even more weighting upon her than the oppressive heat. She hated leaving Tulla and Gray, and she feared that she might be abandoning Quinn as well. She'd spent the past few days trying to persuade Tulla and Gray to leave the valley with her, but to no avail. The gods had not directed them to leave, and so they would stay.

As for Quinn, she was more convinced than ever that he was lost to her forever, and was even now preparing to make war upon her people.

She reached the cool shade of the woods and the sparkling little stream and slid from the saddle, then let the horse drink its fill before slaking her own thirst and splashing water on her face and throat. Generally she did not linger here because there was always the chance that a Dartuli would come along. Although Tulla seemed certain that she would be able to defend herself if that happened, Jasmine herself was less inclined to trust in her magic.

But on this, her last trip here, she was reluctant to leave. So she let her horse graze in the tall grasses and sat down with a big, juicy apple from Gray's orchards.

Quinn urged his white stallion to still greater speeds as a sense of urgency came over him. He'd awakened this morning with the certainty that there was something he must do, but without the knowledge of what it was.

He'd tried to ignore it, as he was caught up in the final preparations for war. It occurred to him when he awoke that the feeling might have something to do with Jasmine, but as the day wore on, he began to doubt that.

If she were in the village of the Latawi, then she surely knew what her people knew: war was imminent. Knowing that, she would flee to the mountains—and to the magical cave. In all likelihood she'd already gone, because the trail out of the valley lay near the Dartuli village, and she would have to travel through the mountains themselves to reach it.

Quinn fully intended to go there himself—but not until the battle was won. He was a Dartuli and he'd been a warrior before; he would not turn tail and run from a battle. But he was confident that Jasmine would get herself to safety.

By noon, that certainty that there was something he must do had resolved itself into an obsession to go to the fence, and so he'd taken his stallion and was now within a few miles of the dividing line between the Dartuli and the Latawi, riding toward a place that would soon see the clash of both forces.

He reached the fence and began to ride alongside it, headed toward the stream and the mountain. And as he rode he suddenly felt that this strange compulsion had not come from the Great One. It was coming instead from the gods of the Latawi.

When that thought struck him, he reined in his horse sharply. Was this some sort of trick? Were the gods of the Latawi luring him to his death? There was a time when he'd trusted them, but no longer. He didn't truly trust the Great One, either, but his loyalties lay with his own people.

He started to turn the stallion back toward the road, then stopped again. It had been a long, hard ride, and he had with him water only for himself. The stallion's sleek flanks were sweating, and he knew he should give the animal a drink before they rode back to the village. He started toward the base of the mountain and the little stream that flowed there.

Jasmine had fallen into a sort of daze, sitting by the stream. When her horse whinnied suddenly, she turned around to see what was troubling it—and there saw a lone rider approaching her through the field.

He was still some distance away, and in the heat haze she couldn't make him out very well. But her heart seemed to know, because it swelled with love and hope.

"Quinn," she whispered. "Please let it be you."

He was riding a white horse, but she knew by now that the Dartuli always rode them. Gray had told her that the animals were specially trained to dance or leap away from the magic fire. She held her breath, knowing that it would either be Quinn—or certain death.

He reined in only a few yards away, and the animal pranced on its hind legs for a few seconds, preventing her from gaining a clear look at the rider. And then he settled the animal and leaped from the saddle.

"Quinn!" she said, his name barely more than a whisper.

But then she feared she was mistaken, as the man who looked like Quinn stopped and scowled at her.

"What are you doing here? Why aren't you on your way out of the valley?" he demanded harshly.

"Quinn," she said, searching his eyes in vain for some sign that he recognized her. "It's Jasmine. Don't you know me?"

He hesitated, still scowling, and then in the next moment he was pulling her roughly into his arms. Cold fear engulfed her. This wasn't the man she knew.

She struggled to free herself, but his hold only

tightened, until she could scarcely breathe. She started to say his name again, hoping it would break whatever spell he was under, but before her lips could form the word, his mouth had claimed hers.

She continued to struggle even as the chill of fear was replaced by the burning heat of passion. Her mind told her this wasn't Quinn, but her body knew otherwise.

He pushed her roughly into the tall grass and began to tear at her clothing. She struggled and tried again to speak his name, but with his weight upon her, it was all she could do to draw a breath.

There was no gentleness in him, only a wild, raw passion that terrified her even as it drew her into its searing heat. She couldn't think, she could barely breathe, but she could feel his mouth and hands on her, laying claim to her—*conquering* her.

That word hung in her mind, an echo of something he'd once said to her. This was what he'd feared: the darkness in him.

His weight left her briefly as he struggled with his trousers. She thought about running, but even if she could get away from him, it would solve nothing. She told herself that this was Quinn, the man she loved, and that he loved her as well. But then she knew that she could not allow this to happen because it would forever taint their love.

He stripped off his trousers and lunged at her. She rolled sideways, out from beneath him as he fell. Then she pulled herself into a half-sitting position. Their eyes met. For a second she saw only lust in his eyes, the fire of a predator—but she held his gaze.

"Stop this, Quinn! I *want* you to make love to me—but not like this."

As she spoke, he reached out to grasp her arm roughly, but just when it seemed that he would pull her back to him, he stopped. The lust wasn't gone from his gray eyes, but it seemed to her that some confusion was there as well.

"You told me once that you feared this . . . this desire to conquer me. Don't do it, Quinn. If you do, you will have destroyed everything we've shared."

He let her go and sank back into a sitting position, his head lowered. She could see his chest heaving, and she knew that it wasn't from the struggle with her, but rather from a battle with himself. And when he finally lifted his head, she knew which part of him had won.

His hand reached out to her, slowly this time. She leaned forward as far as she could, and their fingertips touched lightly.

"I love you, Quinn."

He stared at her for a moment, then withdrew his hand and ran his fingers through his black curls, his head once more lowered. And when he looked up, there were tears in his eyes. She started to get up, to go to him, but he put out a hand to stop her.

"No! Get out of here, Jasmine. Get out of the valley."

"Not unless you come with me."

"Damn you, woman! Do as I say!"

She flinched slightly from the anger in his voice, but she made no move to leave. "I won't let them have you."

"They *already* have me—don't you see that? And I can't protect you when war comes."

"You can protect me by leaving with me—now."

"I can't do that. I'm one of them—and I will fight with my people."

"Stop it, Quinn! This is their battle—not ours. And we can't change what will happen. Neither side will win. You know that."

Once more she saw confusion cloud his eyes.

"Quinn," she said softly, "have you forgotten that we don't belong here?"

He shook his head, but said nothing.

"Staying here to fight alongside your people won't change things," she went on. "We must leave."

He regarded her with a curious expression. "How do you know it won't change things?"

"Because we know what happened. We know that our people left the valley—and we've seen those graves on the plain."

"But maybe it can be changed."

She knew that she was right, but finding the words to explain that to him was difficult. "If you change the future—if the Dartuli win and stay in the valley, then where does that leave *you*?" *And us*, she added silently. "If the Dartuli stay in the valley, then you would have been born here—but you weren't."

He finally nodded, but Jasmine wasn't at all sure that he accepted her explanation. In truth she couldn't blame him. The whole situation was so complicated—certainly complicated beyond her ability to understand it, anyway.

"Quinn," she said, knowing she shouldn't ask this question, but unable to prevent herself, "why did you attack me like that?"

"I didn't attack you," he replied defensively.

"You did!"

"I wanted you. I still do."

"And I want you—but not that way. Not in anger."

He turned away from her and said nothing.

"I've heard about your Great One," she told him. "I know all about him, Quinn. The cave where your people worship him. Everything. He's responsible for this."

Abruptly, he turned back to her, his eyes glittering with anger. "You knew. You found that cave long ago, didn't you, but you didn't tell me about it."

She nodded. "I was trying to protect you."

He glared at her. "I don't need your protection!"

"Fine." She pulled together the clothing he'd all but torn from her and got to her feet. "If you don't need my protection, you don't need my love, either."

He grabbed his trousers and put them on. "I didn't say that."

"You can't have one without the other." She lifted her chin defiantly and met his angry scowl.

"The Latawi are weak and passive and do whatever their gods tell them to do."

"So what does that have to do with me?" she challenged. "The Dartuli are aggressive and arrogant. But the blood of both races is in us, Quinn—and we haven't lived among them."

She took a few steps toward her horse. "If you think I'm not worthy of you because I'm Latawi, then go find yourself a Dartuli woman and worship your Great One. You were a good man once, Quinn—it took me a long time to learn that, but I did. You were a man who would never have allowed that darkness to take over."

She walked past him and picked up the reins of her horse, unable to believe that it could end this way. But just as she was about to mount her horse, he called out to her.

"I don't want you to leave."

She turned, brushing away the tears that had sprung to her eyes. "You told me to go before—and now I am."

"Not like this," he said in a voice that came very close to pleading.

He walked slowly toward her, his steps measured, as though he wanted her to know that he wouldn't prevent her from leaving. She dropped her foot from the stirrup, but held on to the reins.

He stopped before her, and now she could see the unshed tears in his eyes as well. "I don't want any other woman—Dartuli or not. I want you."

And I think you wish you didn't, she thought sadly, but she dropped the reins. If there was any chance that she could rescue him . . .

He reached out to brush a stray lock of hair from her cheek, and his fingers traced a slow line down her throat to the pendant that nestled between her breasts. He seemed to hesitate before grasping it, and then he lifted it gently.

"If I were as evil as you think I am, I wouldn't be able to hold this."

She remembered the other time when he'd touched it and been jolted. "I never said you were evil, Quinn." Her voice was very husky.

"You still want me, don't you?"

"Yes."

He dropped the pendant back into place and pried the reins from her hand. "Then stay with me now—for a little while."

She wanted to try to extract a promise from him that if she did, he would leave the valley with her. But this was no time for making demands or for placing conditions on their love. She nodded. If this was all he would give, she would take it. She couldn't bear any less.

At first they were tentative as they reached out to each other. Their fiery words had created a barrier between them. Quinn was careful. Jasmine was wary. He wanted her to see only the man she believed him to be. She feared that man might disappear at any moment.

But before long they had remembered everything that had once bonded them so close. Soon they were naked in the tall grass and lost in each other. Quinn had never been more sensitive to her needs and desires, and Jasmine floated away from the angry words into a realm of pure sensation.

They lingered along each pathway to ecstasy, tracing its outline with kisses and intimate caresses and the words of love that had been hidden behind the anger. Their mutual passion was a living thing between them, urging them on even as they tried to stay it for a time.

But then they were helpless, unable to control the force that was created by them, but now owned them both, uniting their bodies and their souls.

The passion was spent, but the love lingered on, warming them as the shadows grew longer and the mountain sent a cool breeze down to them. Both were holding their thoughts at bay for as long as they could, living only in the moment.

"We must leave," Quinn said, uttering the words neither wanted to hear, but both knew must be spoken.

They gathered up their clothes and dressed in a silence that masked thoughts just beginning to form. Quinn helped her onto her horse, then drew her down for one last, lingering kiss.

"Leave tomorrow, as early as possible," he instructed her. "Follow the mountain on the far side of the valley, until you reach the trail that leads to the cave."

She nodded, then waited for him to say that he would meet her. He stared at her for a long time in silence, as though memorizing her every feature.

"We'll be together again. I promise you that."

And then he turned away abruptly and mounted his stallion. Within moments he was a distant blur of black and white, growing smaller and smaller until he was lost to sight.

Jasmine rode slowly back to the village, clutching his final words to her as protective armor against her fears. She refused to let herself think about what he'd meant, but the thought crept in anyway. He wasn't going to leave with her.

It was well after dark when she finally reached the village, and as soon as she did she felt a powerful sense of foreboding. There was too much activity: people were scurrying to and fro and lights were burning in all the houses.

When she reached Tulla and Grayvar's home, she found the same thing. Several large blankets had been laid in the middle of the living room, and the couple were piling various things into them.

"Jasmine!" Tulla said with obvious relief. "We've been so worried about you."

"What is happening?" she asked nervously.

It was Gray who answered. "The gods have told us we must leave the valley at dawn."

"What? You mean they're convinced everyone?" She had tried so hard to persuade them that she thought perhaps they'd convinced themselves that the gods had decreed it.

"Yes," both Tulla and Gray said simultaneously.

"I don't understand. Do you mean that the gods have given the valley to the Dartuli?"

"So it would seem," Gray said bitterly, while Tulla bit her lower lip and nodded.

"You shouldn't be surprised, Jasmine," Gray said without rancor. "You said that we would be driven from the valley."

"Yes, but . . ." She frowned, not knowing what to say.

"If you are right, the Dartuli will not win," Gray went on with a note of satisfaction in his voice, "because they, too, will be driven from the valley."

But Jasmine barely heard his last words because something else was claiming her full attention. Tulla held in her hand a small, ornately carved wooden box, and now she opened it.

Seeing her interest, Tulla smiled sadly. "This is

jewelry that has been passed down through my family for many generations."

She drew out a pendant on a gold chain. "The story is that this was made long ago, when the Dartuli and Latawi lived in peace together. I can't credit it myself, but it's supposed to have been made by a Dartuli to show that we are one people."

Jasmine found she couldn't breathe for a moment, and her fingers went unconsciously to her own pendant. She'd never shown it to Tulla because she'd nearly forgotten about its history. Now she drew her own out, and it was Tulla's turn to gasp.

"Where did you get that?" Tulla asked, staring from one to the other. They were identical.

Jasmine told her. "Could it be the same pendant?" she asked in a soft, wondering tone.

"I've never seen another like it," Tulla replied in the same manner.

Both women hugged each other and began to cry, leaving Gray to stand there with a puzzled frown. Tulla finally turned to him.

"Don't you see what that means, my love? It means that we will live—and one day we'll have children."

Jasmine smiled. "And someday the pendant will find its way to me and help me to come back here." And to protect Quinn as well, she added silently, but with a sharp pang of fear. It wasn't protecting him now.

Tulla was studying her closely. "You found your man, didn't you?"

"Yes, but I fear that he won't leave the valley."

"But he must leave, Jasmine. We will all leave."

"That's true," she admitted, but privately she wondered if they might not be placing too much faith in the idea of a future that could not be changed. It made her head spin to think about such questions.

"Doesn't he love you any longer?" Tulla asked with concern.

"Yes, he loves me—but his loyalties are badly torn just now. He told me to leave tomorrow, and said that I should follow the mountain on that side of the valley." She gestured. "I'm not sure why he said that. I can't see that it makes any difference."

"I can," Gray stated grimly. "Many of us have suspected that the Dartuli planned to engage in some sort of trickery. They must be planning to mount a sneak attack on the village by coming up the other side, and he wanted to be certain you wouldn't encounter them." He gave Jasmine a grim smile.

"His love for you may well save us. We had planned to travel on the other side of the valley, and if we had we would probably have met them."

Gray went on to explain that earlier today they had reached a decision to travel along the mountain on the other side of the valley. The slope was somewhat gentler there, and it would be easier for the elderly among them. "But of course they would expect us to travel that way if they know we are leaving."

"But how would they know that?" Jasmine frowned.

Gray shrugged. "They must realize we know that we're no match for them when it comes to warfare. Perhaps their god told them. Who knows? Besides, they believe us to be weak and cowardly, so it might very well just occur to them that we would decide to flee."

He left to tell the others of her conversation with Quinn, and Jasmine wondered what Quinn would think if he knew that he was saving the lives of his people's enemies.

Quinn returned to a dark and deserted village. He knew immediately where they had gone. The demons had once more called them to the cave of the Great One.

For the past three nights, the demons had been seen just after dark, dancing on the ledge in front of the cave, backlit by a flickering red light from within. But when the whole village had hurried up the path and into the cavern, the Great One had failed to appear, despite their pleading chants.

Quinn was told that this wasn't at all unusual. The demons and their master could not be wholly trusted. It was their nature to taunt even believers. But they were powerful allies in battle because they loved to kill.

Quinn rode the stallion to the stable, unsaddled and then fed it, taking his time even though he knew he should join the others. The long ride back had not healed the torment within him. A part of him wanted to meet her tomorrow morning and leave this battle to their ancestors alone. But the closer he came to the village—and the cave that overlooked it—the more he knew he had to stay.

He started through the village to the path that led up to the cave, walking slowly even though he felt an increased hunger to be there and to look again into the compelling face of the Great One. But it was Jasmine's face that filled his inner vision.

He reached the path—and stopped. The war raged within him. He saw her face, and then the visage of the Great One. Suddenly two demons appeared on the path ahead of him, beckoning, their mouths drawn back in an awful parody of a grin. The breeze flowing down the mountain carried with it the faint sound of chanting.

"Begone!" he commanded them. "I command you in the name of the gods!"

They hissed and shared their terrible grins— then vanished in wisps of smoke that blew away on the breeze. Quinn stood there, hearing the echoes of his heretical words. What right had he to use the name of the gods?

And yet it seemed that he must have the right, since they'd obeyed. He listened to the chanting as it rose to a crescendo, then abruptly died away. Inside the Great One had evidently appeared. Quinn turned abruptly and walked back to the village.

He was back at the stables, tending to the horses, when he heard the rest of the village return. Whatever had happened must have pleased them, because he could hear shouts and whoops of joy.

Taber, the man who called himself Quinn's brother, appeared in the entrance to the stable. "You weren't there," he said accusingly.

Quinn shrugged and resumed currying his stallion. "I have work here."

"You weren't here earlier. I came looking for you before we went to the cave."

Quinn set aside the currying comb and faced Taber squarely. It had already become apparent to him that the two brothers had never minced words, so Taber's belligerence didn't surprise him. "So?" he challenged.

Taber sneered. "It sounds like you're spoiling for a fight, little brother. Don't you remember what happened last time?"

Quinn didn't, of course, but he could guess. Taber was both taller and heavier than he was, and had the additional advantage of being a born brawler.

"Maybe you need to remind me," Quinn said in the soft voice he'd always used in such situations. It always threw his opponents off balance—and this time was no exception. Taber frowned slightly, and for one brief moment Quinn was sure that he was going to accuse him of being an impostor.

But then Taber suddenly leaped at him, and both men crashed heavily to the floor of the stable. It took Quinn only a few seconds to know how this fight would end. Taber was probably stronger than he was and his longer arms gave him a better reach, but he lacked the fighting skills that Quinn had learned: skills designed to compensate for a disadvantage of strength or height.

Quinn put those skills to use now, thinking that his old instructor would probably be happy to know that he'd found a use for them, after all. He'd joked that teaching Quinn such things was a waste of time.

It was over quickly. Taber lay on the floor, groaning and staring at Quinn with stunned disbelief. "Where did you learn to fight like that?" he asked as he slowly got to his feet.

"No place you'll ever see," Quinn said, turning his back on Taber in a deliberate gesture of contempt. He picked up the comb and resumed currying his stallion.

"Well, you'll have plenty of opportunity to use that on the Latawi—if they don't turn tail and run, that is," Taber said, now back to his former self.

"What did the Great One say?" Quinn asked.

"That all the Latawi must die—even if they try to flee."

Quinn thought about the battle he and Jasmine had witnessed on the plain. "Do you think they *will* run?" he asked, hiding his concern. If that happened, Jasmine could be caught in it even if she left the valley.

"They'll run, Taber said contemptuously. "But they won't get far. We'll catch them before they get out of the valley."

No, you won't, Quinn replied silently. *You won't catch them because they'll be on the other side of the valley*.

He'd told Jasmine which way to go based on his

knowledge of their own war plans, which included sending a small force along the mountains to surprise the Latawi with an attack from the rear. Jasmine hadn't said that her people intended to flee, but if they decided to do so—or if the gods ordered them to leave—then she would tell them which route to take.

The gut-wrenching pain of divided loyalties tore at him again. If the Latawi fled, then he was betraying his own people by having assured their escape. But he could not tell Taber what he knew without putting Jasmine herself at great risk.

"Why bother to chase them if they're leaving the valley?" he asked with a shrug. "We'll only lose lives—and for what? The valley will be ours in any event."

"Because they're Latawi—and because the Great One wants them dead."

Quinn gave Taber a glance, then started to refill the water troughs. Taber was a leader of the Dartuli forces and as blood thirsty a man as he'd ever known. Taber's friends were just as bad. But even as Quinn secretly despised them, he was now haunted by his own past behavior in battle.

"You never did have much of a taste for bloodshed," Taber said with a sneer. Then he grinned—an expression that Quinn thought was scarcely any different.

"But I'll give you this—no one is better at training the horses. Sometimes I think you prefer them to women."

Quinn managed a grin. "Maybe I do. They're a lot less trouble."

Taber laughed and thumped him on the back. "So they are, brother. I'm off to the tavern. We leave at dawn."

Quinn nodded. Taber had already told him that he was to be part of the force that would be traveling through the mountains to the Latawi village.

It would be nightfall before they reached it, since keeping to the mountains would slow them down considerably. Then they would attack at dawn, just as the Latawi force was setting off on the valley road. That was, if they hadn't already left the valley.

As Quinn continued with his chores, he suddenly began to think about the plain they'd passed through on their way here, and the ghostly battle they'd witnessed, and all those graves. And then he knew how this would all end: not here in the valley, but beyond it, on the plains.

The Latawi would leave the valley, probably under orders from the gods—and the Dartuli would follow them, obeying the edict of the Great One: all Latawi must die. But who would be victorious—and why wouldn't the winner then return to the valley? And what about the children and the elderly Dartuli, who would remain in the valley?

He smiled grimly, thinking about Jasmine's frustration over questions with no answers.

Chapter Sixteen

The sun rose late in the valley, but it sent its light before it: a pale, tentative glow that outlined the dark mountains and spilled down into the woods and fields and silvered the streams and ponds and lakes. And in that fragile light both the Dartuli and the Latawi were on the move.

The village of the Latawi was empty before dawn, except for the livestock. The exodus had begun. A long line of people of all ages rode across the fields and into the mountains that ran along the southern side of the valley.

In the Dartuli village, most of the inhabitants remained. Only about a quarter of the inhabitants—all of them men—left to make their way along the northern slopes to the Latawi village at the far end. They were the best fighters—the killers—and the attack from the rear was left to them. The rest of the men, together with the women, would make up the main force that expected to meet the Latawi resistance near the fence.

*   *   *

More than two thousand people made up the long line of Latawi who rode into the mountains, most of them with pack animals to carry the few belongings with which each family had chosen to escape.

Jasmine rode near the end of the long line, together with Tulla and Grayvar. She'd expected weeping on the part of the women and tears in the eyes of the men. But all she saw were solemn faces, set and determined, and she realized that while they certainly loved their home, the valley had become a place of great sadness to them. It was hardly the haven it had been to her and Quinn.

Also, their faith in the gods was absolute. They trusted them completely and assumed they would find a new home that was just as beautiful and fertile. She wondered sadly if that would be the case.

Perhaps it will be, she thought. After all, her own family had been happy enough until the soldiers had come—and that was far in the future.

The future. Her thoughts turned to her own future—or more precisely to her return to her own time. She had tossed and turned through the night, wondering if Quinn would meet her. If he planned to meet her somewhere in the mountains or on the trail that led to the cave, what would he do when he saw the entire Latawi population coming toward him?

After thinking this over, Jasmine had decided that she would stay in the rear of the group. That way Quinn could conceal himself until they had all passed, then join her. Tulla and Gray had agreed that this sounded like the best plan. Then, when she'd expressed her fear that if Quinn were spotted he might be killed, Gray had gone to have a quiet word with the Elders who would be in the lead. They had agreed that if a lone Dartuli appeared, he would not be harmed unless he attacked.

I have done all that I can do, she told herself in what had become a litany. *If Quinn chooses to stay and fight, there will be no one for him to battle.* Then he would surely follow her, and, the gods willing, they would both be returned to the present.

But Jasmine was still greatly troubled by what she didn't know. What about the ghostly battle they'd witnessed? Tulla and Gray seemed sure that, despite her tale, the Dartuli would never follow them out of the valley. What reason would they have to do so?

Could that spectral battle have occurred much earlier, before the period of peace that was now ending? She thought that very unlikely, but had to content herself with having warned them.

Then she thought of a question that *could* be answered and rode closer to Tulla and Gray. "Would the gods allow the Dartuli to follow us through the cave?" She was certain now that the cave's magic was controlled by the immortals.

"Yes," Gray answered. "The cave is the only way in and out of the valley, and from the beginning both the Latawi and the Dartuli have been granted the right of passage. But no one else can get through."

"But surely if the gods know that the Dartuli are bent on war, they will stop them." Jasmine persisted.

Tulla shook her head. "The gods have never favored one tribe over the other, Jasmine. The valley was given to us both. Even when the Dartuli began to worship the Great One, the gods did not turn their backs on them."

Jasmine said nothing, thinking privately that this certainly gave the Dartuli an advantage. They had both the gods *and* the Great One.

"But who is stronger: the gods or the Great

One?" Jasmine asked somewhat impatiently.

Reared by a mother who had turned her back on the gods, Jasmine had only vague memories of her grandmother's religion.

"Oh, the gods are much stronger," Tulla replied, her tone implying shock that Jasmine could question that.

"Then why does the Great One exist at all?"

"The gods must have their reasons," Tulla stated calmly.

"And they've held him at bay for long periods of time in the past," Gray pointed out.

Jasmine asked no further questions because it was clear that she would get no answers—or no answers that made sense to her. In a way she envied Tulla and Gray and the others their simple faith. If she'd grown up in the valley, she, too, might have felt what they felt. But as it stood, the gods were for her an unknown and unknowable quantity—and therefore terribly frustrating.

And yet she knew that she had to depend on their kindness to return to the present. Furthermore, she'd come to the grudging acceptance that only the gods could send Quinn back to her as well.

The Latawi rode on, winding their way through the woods at the base of the mountains, at the beginning of their long journey out of the valley toward an unknown destination.

"They're gone!" Taber's pronouncement held both contempt and anger, with a touch of triumph thrown in for good measure.

"They could be keeping the village dark to fool us," Quinn suggested, though he was certain that Taber was right.

The two of them lay prone at the edge of a steep cliff surrounded by the thick forest. The Latawi village rose many hundreds of feet below them in the valley. Their force had arrived just at dusk.

Quinn learned that Taber and a few others had scouted out this place months ago, breaking the compact that decreed that neither tribe should set foot on the other's territory.

"Why would they do that?" Taber said dismissively. "They'd never suspect a sneak attack."

Quinn silently agreed. The Latawi were an honorable people who made the mistake of believing that others were also honorable. In the other wars, long ago, such behavior would have been unthinkable. Those wars had been fought using rigid rules of combat, much as wars had once been fought elsewhere. But that time was past—both in the valley and in the world beyond. However, in this as in other ways, the Latawi held to the old rules, the ancient ways.

Quinn, who'd taken part in such sneak attacks himself in his career as a soldier, nevertheless envied the Latawi, even as a part of him understood Taber's contempt for them.

"What do we do now?" he asked Taber, who was their leader.

"We'll wait a while, and then go down there. If they're gone, then we ride through the night, back to the village."

He scowled. "What I don't understand is why we didn't run into them on the way here. It doesn't make sense that they would have taken a route that would bring them close to the cave of the Great One."

Throwing his previous caution to the wind, Quinn suggested that perhaps they didn't fear the Great One. "They have their gods, after all."

"Bah!" Taber spat contemptuously. "Even the Latawi know that the gods are fickle and can't be trusted to protect them." He was silent for a moment, then went on in what was, for him, a philosophical tone.

"Maybe you're right. Maybe they *don't* fear the

Great One. It makes sense. We don't fear him either. He can help us, but he can't hurt us.

"We should have considered that. There were those old stories about how the demons couldn't hurt a Latawi who didn't fear them. And obviously most of the Latawi didn't fear them, or we would have won long ago."

Quinn was only half paying attention to Taber's musings as he wondered where Jasmine was now. Riding alone, she would probably have reached the cave before nightfall—or at least the trail that led to it. But if she were traveling with the rest of them, she'd be slowed down.

His thoughts turned again to the battle on the plain. "Are we going to pursue them if they're already out of the valley?"

"Damn right we will. It's time to get rid of them once and for all. We can't be sure they won't try to come back again."

"But what if the gods won't let us through the cave?" Quinn asked, his thoughts still on Jasmine.

In the silence that followed, Quinn was certain that he'd committed a fatal error. Taber looked at him in disbelief.

"Are you daft, little brother? Of course we'll get through the cave. The gods would never stop us."

Quinn thought sadly that he probably was right.

As they rode down the mountainside toward the Latawi village, Quinn thought about the gods and the Dartuli. It seemed to him that perhaps the gods didn't belong just to the Latawi, after all—which explained why he'd succeeded in getting rid of the demons when he'd called upon them.

The village was completely empty. Some of the men wanted to ransack the houses for valuables, but Taber vetoed the idea.

"There'll be time enough for that later," he told them. "After we get rid of the Latawi." Then his lips curled in that familiar sneering smile.

"But there's one thing we *can* do before we leave."

"The sphere!" several men chorused eagerly.

"Right!" Taber said. "We'll get it and take it back with us."

Quinn hadn't exactly forgotten about the sphere, but it had fallen to the back of his mind. Now, as they rode toward the market square, he recalled his own reaction to it and wondered what would happen.

The answer to that question began to grow clear as they rode across the open market area, hooves clicking loudly on the carved stones. The group that Taber had hand picked to accompany him were all men much like him: bloodthirsty, hard-drinking men who were spoiling for a battle and openly contemptuous of their opponents. And yet, as they drew near the wooded park surrounding the golden sphere, Quinn could feel and even see an uneasiness coming over them.

Taber apparently felt it, too. "It's long past our turn to have the sphere," he told them. "We're just correcting our ancestors' mistake."

So the sphere must have once been rotated between the villages, Quinn thought. It seemed to be further proof of the gods' connection to the Dartuli as well as the Latawi.

They dismounted and tethered their horses to the trees at the edge of the woods, then followed the path that led to the sphere. Despite Taber's words, it was clear that at least some of the men were uncomfortable.

Finally they were standing at the edge of the clearing where the sphere sat on its pedestal, surrounded by flowers and shrubs. The globe itself was plainly visible in the moonlight.

"It isn't glowing," one of the men said in a hushed tone.

"We'll take it anyway," Taber replied as he started forward.

Then suddenly the orb began not just to glow, but to blind them with its light. Quinn shaded his eyes quickly and stepped back, as did the others—including Taber. But they could not shield themselves from the feeling that came over them: a powerful urge to run. It was far stronger than the feeling that Quinn had experienced when he'd discovered the sphere the first time.

And run they did—all the way back to their horses. Taber cursed, though his voice lacked its usual measure of acrimony.

"We'll get it later," he said as he swung onto his horse.

"Maybe it's telling us to let the Latawi go," one of the men suggested, his voice rather shaky.

"So what if it is?" Taber challenged. "When did we start listening to the gods?"

They rode out of the village and onto the road through the center of the valley. The farther they got from the sphere, the more they resumed their bragging and their disdainful remarks about the Latawi, reminding Quinn of little boys who'd had a narrow escape but didn't want to admit it.

Left to his thoughts, Quinn began to wonder not about the gods, but about the Great One. He was still uneasy when he pictured that compelling face, but he thought that he was beginning to understand the demon master's true nature.

The first of the escaping Latawi reached the magical cave at midnight. Thanks to the bright moonlight, they had continued to travel after dark, pausing only to rest the horses and to feed the hungry children.

Still at the end of the line, Jasmine kept scanning the woods on both sides, even though she knew that if Quinn were there, she wouldn't be able to see him in the shadows. The moon illuminated the trail itself, but failed to penetrate the forest.

Finally, when she knew that they were nearing the cave, she spoke to Tulla and Grayvar. "You go ahead. I'm going to stay here for a while to wait for Quinn."

"The Dartuli may not be far behind," Gray warned her.

"I know—but I have to wait."

Tulla reached over to take her hand and squeeze it before they rode on, but that was the only acknowledgment between them that they might be saying good-bye forever. The woman who would join them on the far side of the cave might well be Jasmine—but a different woman entirely.

She dismounted and sat down on a big rock beside the trail, now completely alone in the forest. And she was still alone when the moon set. Knowing that she could wait no longer without putting herself or the other Jasmine at risk, she mounted her horse and rode toward the cave. The anguish she felt was so overpowering that it left her very nearly paralyzed.

She told herself that she had no way of knowing what would happen in the cave. She might be returned to the present—or she might remain to witness again the final battle. The same could happen to Quinn. She was completely at the mercy of gods she didn't trust and couldn't understand.

When she reached the mouth of the cave, she dismounted slowly, then led her horse into a darkness that immediately changed into soft golden light.

Leading the horse, Jasmine moved warily through the cave, both dreading and anticipating the moment when the light would swell and she would fall back through time. She was terribly afraid of leaving this place without Quinn. What if she returned—but he stayed?

But she had no choice. If she had stayed any longer the Dartuli would surely come along and kill her. Not even Quinn could prevent that, though he might well lose his own life trying.

Tears blurred her vision as she thought about their last meeting. Quinn belonged to her—but he also belonged to the Dartuli and the Great One. If they somehow managed to escape this place and return to their own lives, she knew it would take her a long time to forget the man who had set upon her with lust-filled eyes.

But she reminded herself that his love for her had won out; she clung to that thought as the passage began to narrow and she knew she was approaching the point where the gods had sent her back in time.

Nothing changed. She reached the midpoint and passed through it without incident, except for a strange, tingling sort of sensation that she convinced herself was only her own fear. And then she saw, far ahead, the end of the cave. The magical light began to dim and she was walking toward the soft breeze of outdoors.

Quinn was riding in the lead beside Taber. They reached the cave just as dusk settled over the land. He didn't dare hang back to search for Jasmine because he couldn't afford the risk that Taber and the others might find her first.

Behind them stretched a long line of Dartuli: the entire population, save for the elderly and children. Nearly two thousand people were about to make their way through the cave of the gods. They had been commanded to destroy the Latawi, and so they would. Given what had happened with the sphere, Quinn had expected his people to reconsider the wisdom of going into the cave, but apparently they all believed, as Taber did, that the gods would not turn them back.

They entered the cave, and immediately the soft golden light showed them the way. Quinn grew increasingly nervous as they neared the midpoint where he and Jasmine had been torn from their own time. What if the gods had taken her back but left him here? Or what if he went back while she stayed?

Silently he began to pray to the gods that his fellow Dartuli had forsaken.

As she emerged from the cave, Jasmine was still hoping that perhaps she'd somehow been returned to the present. But when she saw the stone steps that led up from the cave, she knew that nothing had changed. The steps were plainly visible now, though they'd been nearly obscured by shrubs and weeds when she found the cave.

She climbed back onto her horse and began to ride as fast as she dared, trying to catch up to Tulla and the others. She didn't know what else to do except to follow them out onto the plain—and almost certainly into battle.

Every few minutes she turned to search the trail behind her, fearing that the Dartuli might be coming and she would be caught between the two opposing forces.

By midafternoon, when she still hadn't caught up to Tulla and the others, she reined in her horse and then led it down a slope to a stream. She was hungry, thirsty, tired, and frightened. It seemed to her that as fast as she'd been riding, she should have caught up to them now, especially since they were slowed down by pack animals and children demanding attention.

Her gaze traveled back along the trail, which she could see through the trees as it wound down the mountain. It was strange, too, that the Dartuli hadn't appeared, since the location of their village nullified the Latawi's head start, nor would a war party be burdened by children and baggage.

Weary and heartsick, Jasmine got back on her horse and returned to the trail. By the time the sun had dropped below the mountains, she still hadn't found the escaping Latawi, and her nervousness had grown to a cold, hard lump of fear. Something was definitely wrong.

She got her answer when she reached another high point in the trail, and saw, far below her and beyond another mountain, the plain. In the fading light the plain was alive with magical fire: both the green of the Dartuli and the gold of the Latawi. The battle she'd witnessed in the fog was already under way.

She stared in disbelief. How could the Latawi have gotten that far ahead of her—and how could the Dartuli have gotten past her? It made no sense.

Then she remembered the tingling sensation she'd had in the cave and frowned. Was it possible that the gods had slowed down time for her—kept her prisoner for a time? The Dartuli must have come through the cave as well, and the gods had only freed her when they deemed it the right time.

"Quinn!" she cried. Where was he? Had he returned to his own time—or was he down there, killing her people or being killed himself?

She started to urge her horse forward, knowing that she must go down into that hellish battle and try to find him. But a sudden lethargy overtook her and she slumped in the saddle, almost unable to move.

This is not your battle, Jasmine.

She was too tired to look around, but in any event she recognized the voice. It was the same one that had spoken to her before. "I have to find Quinn!" she cried, though the words came out as a mere whisper. And then she slid from the saddle and the blackness swallowed her.

Quinn stared in disbelief at the plain below them. How could this be? It had taken Jasmine and him days to travel from the plain to the cave—and yet here they were, only hours after leaving the cave— and there, below them, were the Latawi, setting up camp on the plain.

No one else remarked upon it, which Quinn found strange until he remembered that the Dartuli hadn't left the valley for a very long time. Probably the only ones who would remember how long it took were the Elders, and they were still back in the valley.

Something had happened—and most likely it had happened back in the cave. He'd grown increasingly nervous as they reached the midpoint, and then, for a time, had felt a strange tingling sensation. The others had felt it, too, though no one had any explanation to offer.

But none of them had felt what Quinn had felt, because in addition to that strange sensation, he'd felt an absolute certainty that Jasmine was near. He couldn't see her—but he'd felt her presence, and for one brief moment he'd actually smelled her scent: that soft, flowery fragrance that she emanated.

"Let's go!" Taber shouted triumphantly. "Those fools are waiting for us, right out on the plain."

Quinn wheeled his stallion around to follow Taber. All he could think of now was getting down there and finding Jasmine to keep her safe.

This is not your battle, Quinn.

The voice, soft but clear, spoke at his ear. Startled, Quinn looked around him, but no one was paying him any attention. They were all riding hard, eager to do battle.

He was about to follow them and dismiss the

voice as being his imagination, when he remembered Jasmine's description of the voice that had spoken to her. And suddenly he knew it must be the same voice. Taber and the others who'd ridden from the trail to this hilltop were now back upon the trail, and they were all riding away at full gallop. No one seemed to have noticed his absence, but Quinn moved his horse into a thicket and waited, not at all certain what to do.

He still feared that she might be down there, but he trusted the voice—as she had. When the voice had spoken to her, it had saved his life, and he could not believe that it would now speak to him and let her die.

As the sounds of the horses faded into the distance, Quinn knew that he had left these Dartuli in more ways than one. He had put his trust back where it belonged: in the gods.

When he was certain the Dartuli warriors were all gone, he rode back to the trail, his thoughts again on Jasmine. What if she were down there, about to be caught up in the battle? The voice had said it wasn't *his* battle, but it had told him nothing about her.

You must return to the cave, Quinn.

Once again the voice seemed to come from a place near his ear, and even though he knew he'd see no one, he still looked all around, even turning to check behind him.

"But what about Jasmine?" he asked aloud. "Where is she?"

The only answer he received was the soft sigh of a breeze through the trees. He didn't like it. The fragile trust he'd put in the gods was fading. He even wondered if the Great One could be behind this.

Then he turned the horse's head toward the cave and started back along the trail. But the hands that guided the animal seemed not to be his own, and

his mind was growing dazed. Even his eyes began
to play tricks upon him, because it seemed that the
trees were fading to a blur of dark trunks and
green leaves and needles—almost as though he
were racing at an impossible speed.

Quinn saw her horse first, above him on the trail
where it made a wide curve. His senses suddenly
grew sharp again and he urged his stallion to
greater speed, racing around the bend and up the
steep grade.

She lay in a crumpled heap beside the horse, as
though she might have fallen from the saddle.
Quinn was off of his horse even before the animal
could stop. Cold terror propelled him to her, yet
made him want to hang back until he saw the
slight rise and fall of her breathing.

"Jasmine!" he whispered, his voice low but ur-
gent. "Jasmine!" He held her to him and felt her
heart beating, and finally felt her begin to stir.

Quinn was calling her, but his voice seemed to
come from a very great distance. She tried to make
her lips form his name in response, but nothing
came. Something or someone held her, and she
began to struggle, believing that her captor was
trying to keep her away from him.

But her body knew what her mind had not yet
grasped: it was Quinn who held her. She opened
her eyes and smiled, then reached up to touch his
thick beard.

"We've found each other," she said with a sigh.

"Thanks to the gods," Quinn confirmed, bending
to kiss her softly.

"But we're still here—or there, I mean."

"Not for long, I think. We're to return to the
cave."

"How do you know that?" she asked, still shaking off the veil of sleep.

"The voice told me."

She wasn't so sleepy that she missed the note of triumph in his voice. "The voice spoke to *you*?"

He nodded. "It said to return to the cave. What happened to you? Why are you here?"

"I . . ." She struggled with her thoughts. "I can remember the voice telling me that this wasn't my battle. I was going down there—onto the plain—because I thought you were there. Then I must have fallen asleep."

Now she remembered what she'd seen and struggled to her feet. "Quinn, the battle . . ."

She stopped abruptly as she stared at the distant plain. It was nearly dark now, and it should have been invisible. But instead an unholy greenish gold light filled the space where she knew the plain had been.

Quinn stood up, too, and wrapped his arms around her as they both stared at the strange light. It filled the space beyond the next mountain.

"What do you think is happening?" she asked in a hushed tone.

"I don't know—but there is nothing we can do to change it."

"I think we may have already changed it, Quinn," she said.

"What do you mean?"

She told him about the Latawi changing their route out of the valley because of what he'd told her. "You saved the lives of the Latawi, Quinn—or some of them, in any event," she added as she looked again at the eerie scene in the distant valley.

"If they'd gone the way they planned to go, the Dartuli might well have killed them all."

"And then I would never have met you," Quinn said, kissing her.

"But you wouldn't have needed me, because you

358

would have grown up in the valley," she reminded him.

He smiled. "I think that I could become the madman you once thought I was if we talk about this much longer. It's time to go back to the cave."

It was full dark when they entered the cave, but the soft golden light reached out to them this time. Quinn had set the horses free and they walked into the cave hand in hand. Even when the passage began to narrow, they clung to each other, determined not to be separated this time.

Once more the light swelled up and blinded them, but Jasmine could feel Quinn's strong grip— and she continued to feel it as they fell through the darkness.

On the plain, the battle was over and darkness had settled onto the land. The magic fire was exhausted, as were those who had wielded it. The gods spoke to both the Latawi and the Dartuli in the voices of their ancestors, instructing them to bury their dead and giving them further orders as to where they were to go. The valley had been taken from them until such time as they could both return in peace and love.

As they set out on their separate journeys, only two people—and then three—among them knew that such a day would come. Tulla and Gray found Jasmine as they were helping to bury the dead in the stone mounds. Tulla gave her sister the pendant and said that it would one day be worn by another Jasmine, who would return to the valley with her Dartuli lover.

In the Dartuli village, the gods spoke in a different manner. The earth began to tremble, and as it grew worse even the mountains themselves appeared to be moving. The old people and the children packed hurriedly and followed the others out of the valley, leaving the valley to the demons, who danced among the houses while the Great One slumbered.

Hands still clasped tightly, Jasmine and Quinn traveled out of the darkness into the sunset. Ezra Bartegan was waving to them. This time the old man was actually trying to get up from his chair. They raised their hands in greeting, then lowered them and stared at each other in joyous wonder.

They were back! Quinn's thick beard was gone, and they were both dressed as they had been when they'd set out on their trip from the valley to Halaban. Behind them were the packhorses, waiting to bring back the goods they intended to purchase.

"Did it really happen?" she asked in a hushed tone.

Quinn nodded, then gave her his wonderful, mischievous grin. "Do you think we should thank the gods for making the trip shorter this time?"

Jasmine laughed as they waved once more at Ezra Bartegan, then rode on. By the time they reached Halaban, they had filled in the missing days and weeks of each other's lives. Then Quinn talked about the Great One, and told Jasmine what he'd concluded.

"I think when the Dartuli looked into the face of the Great One, what they were really seeing was evil of their own creation. It was a manifestation of the warped magic of the Dartuli—a reflection of their evil. And the demons had been summonded by Dartuli hatred. They are no match for those who love."

Jasmine considered that, then told him all that Tulla and Gray had said about the gods and the Great One. "I think you're right," she finished.

"There will be no demons and no Great One in the valley when we return," Quinn stated firmly. "I looked into his face and turned away. It's finished."

"Yes," Jasmine agreed, but she knew better. The Great One would still be there, buried deep in the mountain, waiting for a time when evil would summon him forth again. Their lives' work was to see that that would never happen, and she was prepared.

"Are you ready to return to the valley?" Quinn asked, his breath fanning softly against the swells of her breasts as he kissed the spot beneath the pendant.

"Yes," she murmured, running her hands along the hard, bristly expanse of his chest. They'd been in Halaban for four days, and both of them felt the valley calling to them.

"I think we have all we need," she added.

His lips moved lower, nibbling at the smooth flesh of her stomach before trailing lower still. "I already had all I need and want."

The slow dance of love moved into a quicker tempo, spinning them both into a dizzying frenzy of passion that joined them body and soul.

Quinn checked the packhorses. They'd been forced to buy two more, but both he and Jasmine were now convinced that they had all they needed to see them through their first winter in the valley. He turned to tease her about one last trip to the market, when his gaze was arrested by two people coming toward them. Beside him, Jasmine gasped.

The man was tall and blond and fair skinned, and the woman, who was nearly as tall as he was, had dark hair and bronzed skin. They stopped a short distance away, then smiled tentatively.

"Are you going to the valley?" they asked.

"Yes, my friend," Quinn replied. "And so shall you."

Futuristic Romance

Star-Crossed

Saranne Dawson

Bestselling Author Of *Crystal Enchantment*

Rowena is a master artisan, a weaver of enchanted tapestries that whisper of past glories. Yet not even magic can help her foresee that she will be sent to assassinate an enemy leader. Her duty is clear—until the seductive beauty falls under the spell of the man she must kill.

His reputation says that he is a warmongering barbarian. But Zachary MacTavesh prefers conquering damsels' hearts over pillaging fallen cities. One look at Rowena tells him to gird his loins and prepare for the battle of his life. And if he has his way, his stunningly passionate rival will reign victorious as the mistress of his heart.

_51982-8 $4.99 US/$5.99 CAN